*The qualities that make Jayne Ann Krentz
a bestselling author...
make her romances unique, irresistible
and just plain wonderful to read.*

"ANOTHER SIZZLING ROMANCE FROM THE PEN OF SUPERSTAR JAYNE ANN KRENTZ.... One of the great pleasures of reading Ms. Krentz is the marvelous symmetry between characters and plot.... This gratifying intricacy makes each and every Krentz book something to be savored over and over again."

—*Romantic Times* on *Gift of Gold*

"ROMANCE, MYSTERY, AND A DASH OF THE OCCULT FOR SPICE.... *Gift of Gold* proves again that Jayne Ann Krentz is a master."

—Ann H. Wassall, Hearst Cablevision

"JAYNE KRENTZ ALWAYS GIVES HER READERS MORE THAN ROMANCE. Suspense, mystery, fantasy and history are all woven into the meticulous fabric of characterization and plot that make her novels memorable."

—*Affaire de Coeur*

"A GREAT AUTHOR!"

—*West Coast Review of Books*

Also by Jayne Ann Krentz

Crystal Flame
A Coral Kiss
Midnight Jewels
Sweet Starfire
Gift of Gold

Published by
WARNER BOOKS

JAYNE ANN KRENTZ

Gift of Fire

A Time Warner Company

WARNER BOOKS EDITION

Cover design by Diane Luger
Cover photo by Alexa Gabarino

Warner Books, Inc.
1271 Avenue of the Americas
New York, N.Y. 10020

Visit our Web site at
www.warnerbooks.com

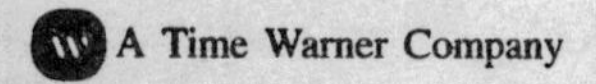
A Time Warner Company

Printed in the United States of America

First Printing: January, 1989

Reissued: July, 1993

15

Chapter One

"*THIS* entire plan," Verity Ames announced, "is a really stupid idea. When it came to giving out common sense, the good Lord obviously overlooked you two. Or maybe he just overlooked men in general."

She glared across the table at the two men who sat opposite her. One was her lover and one was her father. She loved them both but right now she could cheerfully have strangled them. That she could be so fond of a pair of chauvinistic, bullheaded rogues probably indicated a serious character flaw in her.

"Now, Red, just calm down. I've told you there's absolutely no reason to worry. It's gonna be a cakewalk. No sweat." Her father's teeth flashed from the depths of his bushy, graying red beard, and his aquamarine eyes sparkled with enthusiasm. Emerson Ames, part-time author and full-time adventurer, was a big man with a huge appetite for life in the dangerous lane.

Verity had gotten her flaming hair and curiously striking blue eyes from him. Emerson had raised her single-handedly after her mother's death, and he'd seen to it that his only child grew up with a thorough, if eclectic, education, and the ability to take care of herself. One of the things Emerson had not managed to instill in her, however, was his unquenchable desire to wander the far corners of the earth. Verity valued home and hearth.

"Don't try to reassure me, Dad. I've listened to the whole scheme and I still think it's stupid and risky. Samuel Lehigh got himself into this mess. Let him get himself out of it. There's no need for you and Jonas to get involved."

"Lehigh's in real trouble this time, Verity. He needs help. He needs someone he can trust," Jonas said. He extended one arm with unconscious grace and picked up the glass of vodka in front of him. That smooth, masculine grace was an intrinsic part of Jonas Quarrel, a manifestation of the quiet power within him. Verity imagined it was the kind of power one might have seen in a sixteenth-century Renaissance nobleman—a civilized savagery.

Although he had the grace and power of a Medici, Quarrel certainly did not dress like one. Tonight he wore his usual attire—blue denim work shirt, jeans, and scuffed boots. The leather belt around his waist was supple from years of wear. While he might not dress like a Renaissance aristocrat, Quarrel did possess the unique talents of a Medici or a Borgia. He was, in other words, equally capable of quoting poetry or wielding a dagger.

He was definitely overqualified for his present job, Verity thought wryly. Jonas Quarrel was one of the few dishwashers around with the right to put Ph.D. after his name. His field of expertise was Renaissance history; specifically, the weapons and strategies of that era.

He was not a handsome man, but men of power and grace

have never needed to depend on anything as superficial as masculine beauty. Whenever she looked into the depths of his eyes—eyes the color of Florentine gold coins, filled with intelligence and the shadows of ghosts—the last thing on Verity's mind was how Quarrel rated on a scale of one to ten. He could seduce her with a touch or a look. She was deeply, passionately in love with him.

And now he was getting ready to leave her.

"Lehigh wouldn't have asked for help if he didn't need it," Jonas continued reasonably in his rich, dark voice. "He made it clear on the phone that Emerson is the only one he can trust to handle the ransom payoff. Emerson has no choice. He has to go down to Mexico to deal with the kidnappers. Do you really want your father to go alone?"

Verity had realized hours ago that she had lost the battle, but she struggled on hopelessly. "The Mexican police can deal with the situation."

Emerson shook his head. "Come on, Red, I raised you smarter than that. The last thing Lehigh can afford is to have the cops brought in, even if he could trust 'em not to take the ransom and run. And let's face it, when you're dealing with the upholders of law and order in Mexico, you're playing with a stacked deck. No, old Sam knows this has to be handled privately."

"And there's absolutely no one old Sam can call on to handle the payoff besides you?" Verity asked suspiciously.

Emerson gave a huge shrug. "No one he can trust."

"That certainly says a lot about old Sam's lifestyle and choice of friends, doesn't it?" Verity muttered. "Imagine living to the ripe old age of eighty and not having another person on the face of the earth he can call on in an emergency."

"How do you think he got to the ripe old age of eighty?"

Emerson drawled. ''Not by trusting the wrong people, that's for damn sure.''

Verity gazed at Jonas for a long moment. He sipped his vodka quietly and looked back at her, his eyes steady and intent. She knew there was no point in arguing any further. She had been trying to talk them out of the venture since Lehigh's call on the restaurant phone yesterday morning.

It wasn't so difficult to accept her father's decision. Verity was accustomed to Emerson's restless, adventuring ways. But when she thought about Jonas going away, she could feel a knife twisting deep inside.

''What about your writing, Dad?'' she tried, knowing it was a futile attempt. ''You said you had a deadline for that first futuristic western. You'll miss it if you go chasing off to Mexico.''

''I can probably get an extension,'' Emerson replied easily. ''But if the editor doesn't want to give me one, he can shove it.''

Verity winced and turned to Jonas. ''You were just starting to make some real progress in learning how to cook. I had great hopes for your lentil stew. The customers love it.''

Jonas's mouth crooked slightly at one corner. ''When I get back you can finish giving me cooking lessons.''

Verity put both palms flat on the table. ''So,'' she said, accepting the inevitable with bad grace, ''when will you be leaving?''

Jonas studied her for a moment. ''Tomorrow morning. Early.''

Verity nodded. ''Well, good luck. Tell Sam Lehigh I said hello.'' She pushed herself to her feet abruptly. She was dazed at the implications of having lost this battle. If this was not the end, it was surely the beginning of the end.

Perhaps it would be better if Jonas made the break a clean one. Then again, maybe it would be infinitely harder. The thought of never seeing him again filled Verity with despair, but the idea of having him drift in and out of her life over the next fifty or sixty years was equally hard to accept. The vision of a lifetime filled with uncertain farewells and greetings almost overwhelmed her.

Dammit, I'm getting maudlin, Verity thought as she swept a couple of glasses off a nearby table. She walked through the empty restaurant and into the kitchen of the No Bull Cafe, angrily blinking back the tears that threatened to spill down her cheeks.

This wasn't like her, she never cried. She was irritated by her unusually emotional reaction. What was the matter with her? She had known that sooner or later it would come to this, that one day Jonas would succumb again to the restless spirit that had driven him for years before he had met her.

Verity had tried to prepare herself for this day, but now that it had arrived she realized she had done a poor job of protecting herself. She was shockingly vulnerable. She had surrendered far too completely during the past few months, given too much of herself to Jonas. He had taken everything she was able to give, and now he was casually walking out.

Granted, he would probably return. But she couldn't be sure it would be because of a bond of love. She wouldn't have even that much satisfaction. If and when Jonas came back, it would be because of the psychic bond they shared. He needed her for a unique reason. Lately Verity had begun to wonder how much longer he would need her even for that.

Jonas Quarrel was rapidly taming his strange talent for psychometry, which had once threatened to turn him into a killer or at the very least drive him insane. In Verity he had discovered a way to control his trips into a dimension where violent moments from the past were frozen forever in a mysterious time corridor.

Yes, she thought as she placed the glasses into the sink,

Jonas would drift back to her as long as he needed her help to understand his dark, powerful ability. But if he ever got to the point where he could control it by himself, he might take off and never return.

Or the end might be far more final, Verity reflected as she turned off the kitchen lights. Jonas might simply wander off on an adventure one day and get himself killed.

Either way, she could look forward to a lot of time alone.

Well, maybe not completely alone, she thought uneasily. She touched her stomach lightly. There was no need to panic. Lots of women skipped periods occasionally. Stress and anxiety could play strange tricks on a woman's body.

Verity picked up her favorite leather bomber jacket and opened the back door of the cafe. The February night was bitterly cold. There were patches of ice on the path that led from the cafe to the two cabins nestled in the trees a short distance away. She picked her way carefully toward the cozy little cottage she'd been sharing with Jonas since shortly after his arrival last fall.

It was going to be a long, cold winter.

A heavy silence descended on the two men left sitting at the table in the empty restaurant. Jonas listened to the door close behind Verity and wondered how long that hollow sound would haunt him. Then he reached for the nearly empty bottle of vodka.

"She'll be here when you get back," Emerson said. "Verity's not going anywhere. She'll be right here waiting for you."

"Christ. I didn't think she'd take it this hard," Jonas muttered. "I expected a few fireworks at first, but I thought she'd simmer down eventually and be reasonable. Dammit, you'd think we were leaving for a year instead of a few days."

Emerson eyed his companion thoughtfully. "If you want

out, just say the word. I should be able to handle this on my own."

"Don't be an ass. It would be pretty stupid for you to go up against three men alone when you've got backup help available. You know damn well it isn't going to be a simple matter of handing over the ransom the way you told Verity. They'll kill Lehigh if they can get away with it. Much simpler and neater for them that way."

"Yeah. I'm sure Lehigh considered that when he chose me to pick up the cash and deliver it."

"At least he managed to convince the kidnappers that you were the only guy on the planet who could be trusted to handle the exchange."

"Old Sam is one smart bastard. And he's right. If he asked anyone else to handle this, he'd probably be playing pinochle with the kidnappers until doomsday waiting for the payoff. I regret to say it, but most of his so-called friends, once they got their hands on the goodies, would forget all about the bonds of friendship."

"Pays to have one or two close friends in this world," Jonas observed.

"True. Speaking of which, I appreciate your offer to tag along, Jonas. But I don't want to be the cause of you and my daughter splitting up."

"Verity and I are not going to split up over a little thing like this," Jonas assured him quickly, his voice hard. "She'll come around. She's just mad because she's used to getting her own way. That's your fault, you know. You're the one who brought her up to be a world-class brat."

Emerson sighed. "I don't know, Jonas. I've never seen her quite the way she was tonight. At the end there, it was like she just sort of gave up. Not like Verity to give up on anything. I raised her to fight for what she wants."

A cold fist gripped Jonas's insides. The thought of Verity

giving up on their relationship hit him with stunning force. He hadn't considered that possibility. He was accustomed to the way she surrendered completely in bed, the way she fussed about his career, or lack thereof, the way she lectured him to reform his casual attitude toward work. He had been reveling in her attention for the past few months, he realized, taking for granted that she was in love with him.

Worse, he had complacently assumed that the psychic bond they shared was inviolate and unbreakable. It underlay everything else in their relationship, and it would always be there between them.

Jonas forced himself to relax. That bond was his high card. Verity couldn't deny it. It bound them together, a more certain glue than love, or sex, or business. *She couldn't deny it.*

But he had learned over the past few months that Verity had the strength and determination to do just about anything she set out to do.

Jonas knew that if she planned to write him off as a lost cause, he was in big trouble.

He finished his vodka. The glass made a sharp sound as he set it down on the table. He rose to his feet. "I'd better go back to the cabin and pack."

"You do that," Emerson said, his bushy brows arching. "I'll lock up the cafe. Don't forget to set the alarm. We've got to be out of here by five o'clock to catch that flight for Mexico City. It's a ninety-minute drive to the San Francisco airport."

"I'll see you at five." Jonas didn't look back as he strode out of the cafe. Getting up on time was not his main concern. Reassuring himself that Verity wasn't about to write him off was a much higher priority.

Jonas's list of priorities in life was short and simple. His relationship with Verity was at the top. She had originally ranked first because she had the talent to help him control the power that was buried inside him. But now there were other bonds that tied him to her. Passion, friendship, and love were all mixed up with the psychic link. Jonas didn't worry about separating out and analyzing the bonds that tied him to Verity, but he sensed that occasionally Verity's very feminine mind did tackle that issue.

Women had a talent for creating problems where, as far as a man was concerned, none existed.

Outside, Jonas took a deep breath of the night air. The little town of Sequence Springs was in the grip of winter. All of Northern California was experiencing an unusually cold season. There had been some snow in January, and Jonas suspected there would be more before February was out.

It would be warm in Mexico—but not as warm as Verity's bed.

He groaned at the thought of sleeping without his red-headed beauty for the next few days. Then he pulled up the collar of his new fleece-lined suede jacket. He liked the jacket, mostly because Verity had given it to him for Christmas. He hadn't owned a heavy jacket when he'd first arrived in Sequence Springs; he hadn't needed one before.

Most of the places he'd been drifting in and out of for the past few years while he'd been on the run had been in the South Pacific and Mexico. Places with warm, humid climates, balmy breezes, and a relaxed attitude. Places where people drank too much rum and tequila and didn't worry much about the past. Places that somehow drained a man of any desire to focus too intently on the future. Places where a man could hide, even from himself.

Jonas shoved his hands deep into his pockets and headed down the path to Verity's cabin. He could see lights glowing warmly from the windows. A few hundred yards away, on the edge of the lake, the impressive, neoclassical facade of the elegant Sequence Springs Spa Resort was lit with powerful floodlights. The building glowed in the distance, appearing almost otherworldly. Verity sometimes went to the spa in the evenings to soak in the hot pools. Jonas hoped she hadn't decided to go there tonight.

A shadow moved behind the window as he walked up the front steps and across the deck of the cabin. Jonas relaxed slightly. Verity was home, waiting for him. He opened the front door and went in, not certain what to expect.

Verity turned abruptly as he stepped into the rustic room and closed the door behind him. She was ready for bed, wearing a quilted robe over a long flannel nightgown, her wild red curls pinned up on her head, emphasizing her fine-boned face and huge, expressive eyes.

As always, Jonas felt a fierce, twisting rush of passion and an overriding need to protect his little firebrand. She needed him, he told himself, not for the first time. She could be amazingly stubborn, but in spite of that prickly exterior she was very sweet and vulnerable. She needed a man to look after her.

She was still a little too thin, Jonas decided, examining her critically. He had been trying to fatten her up this winter, but it was difficult. Verity worked too hard. The No Bull Cafe was hers, and she suffered all the anxieties and pressures of the small-business entrepreneur. Jonas had been her dishwasher, waiter, and handyperson since he had answered her ad last fall. Lately she had been teaching him how to cook the gourmet vegetarian food that was the cafe's specialty.

On the whole, he liked the work, and the fringe benefits were outstanding—he got to sleep with the boss. And he knew for a fact that no one else had ever slept with this particular boss. Verity had been a virgin until he had walked into her life.

"What are you drinking?" Jonas asked as he shrugged out of his jacket. He would try the calm, rational approach first.

"Chamomile tea." She clutched her mug in both hands. "Want some?"

"No, thanks."

"It's very soothing. Helps you sleep."

At least she wasn't yelling at him. Jonas risked a small grin, letting his gaze rove over her. "I've got a better remedy. Come to bed and I'll show you." He started unbuttoning his shirt. She said nothing, just stood there sipping her tea. He didn't like the hint of uncertainty he thought he saw in her eyes. The fingers of the cold fist that had assaulted him earlier returned to flex painfully on his insides.

"What time are you and Dad leaving in the morning?"

"Five. I'll get up around four-fifteen. All I have to do is throw a few things in my duffel bag. Won't be needing much. We won't be gone more than a few days." He tried to subtly emphasize the last words.

"I suppose one of the things you'll be tossing into your bag is that damn knife you carry?" she asked with a hint of renewed aggression.

"Honey, I've been traveling with that knife for so long I'd feel naked without it. Don't worry. It's just a precaution. I don't plan on using it."

"I don't believe you," she said quietly. "You and Dad aren't planning on just handling the ransom drop, are you? You're going to try to rescue Samuel Lehigh."

Jonas's mouth tightened. He slung the shirt over one shoulder and studied her for a moment. "It's just a ransom swap, Verity. No reason to think the guys holding Lehigh want anything except the cash. It's just a business deal."

"Sure."

Jonas shrugged impatiently. "Lehigh's a good friend of your father's. Do you really expect Emerson to do nothing?"

"Nope." Verity sipped her tea.

"And do you expect me to stay here while Emerson goes down to Mexico alone to handle the payoff?"

"Nope." Verity put her mug of tea on the counter. She turned away from him for a moment as she did so. When she turned back, she was smiling.

It wasn't her brilliant, melt-'em-in-their-shoes smile, Jonas thought, but at least it was a smile. It was a small, oddly gentle smile, filled with far too much wise, superior feminine understanding for his taste.

He'd caught traces of this particular smile on her soft mouth a couple of times during the past week, and it was beginning to make him uneasy. It was as if Verity knew something he didn't know.

He dropped his shirt across the back of a nearby chair and moved toward her. When he held out his arms, she walked into them and wrapped her arms around his waist. He buried his lips in her hair as she leaned her head against his bare chest.

"I'll be back as soon as I can, little tyrant," he vowed. Her sweet scent relaxed something inside him that had been wound too tightly for the past few hours. Everything was going to be all right, he told himself. Verity would be waiting when he returned. She was a home-loving woman. She would be here.

"You'd better get to bed early tonight," she said softly, ignoring his last comment. "You'll need the sleep."

"That's the best idea you've had all day." He picked her up and started down the short hall to the bedroom. Through the fabric of her nightgown and robe he could feel the sleek muscles of her thighs. His body stirred eagerly, the familiar, powerful hunger beginning to seize him.

By the time he got her into the bedroom and slipped off her robe, Verity's strange little smile had reached her eyes.

She climbed into bed and leaned back against the pillows, watching as he unzipped his jeans.

"You know something? This is beginning to have a familiar feel," Jonas said suddenly as he finished undressing and crawled into bed beside her. He was aroused and ready.

"What is?"

"Going to bed with you every night. It's getting to feel sort of comfortable and natural." He reached for her and felt the slight stiffening of her body.

"Maybe it feels a little too familiar," she suggested, not meeting his eyes. Her fingertips toyed with the curly hair on his chest.

Jonas tensed. "What the hell does that mean?"

Verity shrugged. "Nothing. I just thought you might be getting a little bored with life in Sequence Springs. This isn't exactly an exciting place."

He relaxed and began to nuzzle her throat. "It's exciting enough for me."

When she moved against him he trapped one of her legs between his own, chaining her gently so that he could lift off her flannel nightgown. As she lay there naked he ran one hand down the length of her body, luxuriating in the feel of her gentle curves. She was so soft and sweet and warm. He palmed her breast and felt the instant tautening of her nipple. When he heard her faint intake of breath, he groaned and bent his head to capture her mouth.

Her hand trailed down his hip to tease the inside of his thigh, then she took his hard manhood into her palm. She could drive him over the edge with just her touch. She knew exactly how to stroke him, sensed precisely how to cradle the throbbing fullness until he was on fire for her. When she squeezed gently, it was his turn to suck in his breath.

"Jesus, honey, that feels so good," he said huskily. "You've got the magic touch."

"Thanks to you," she murmured demurely. "Everything I know I've learned from you."

"Remember that," he retorted as a wave of possessiveness surged through him. "This wouldn't work with anybody else."

"Is that right? I thought all men were pretty much the same in the dark."

"A vicious myth. Totally untrue!" Deliberately he parted her legs with his hands, seeking the hot, damp core of her body. "Verity, I'm not joking. What you and I have is special and you know it. Why else would you have avoided getting involved with any other man until I came along?"

He sensed her smile in the darkness. "You've made it clear on many occasions that the only reason I was still single when you showed up was that no other man was willing to put up with my sharp tongue and my temper."

Jonas grinned. "Well, those were contributing factors, I'll admit. But the main reason you were still alone was that you were waiting for me. You didn't know it, but that's what it was. Fortunately for you, I didn't let the thorns get in my way when I decided to go after the rose."

"Jonas, your arrogance is showing."

"A man should take pride in his accomplishments. Taming a shrew is a hell of an achievement. Very few men around these days are even capable of it. It's a lost art."

"Is that right?"

"Uh-huh." He prowled slowly down her body, inhaling her intoxicating scent as he drew closer and closer to his goal. He settled himself between her thighs, lifting her legs over his shoulders. He parted her gently with his fingers and lowered his head.

"Jonas."

Her short, neat nails dug into his shoulders as he tasted

her rich, hot flavor. He could hear her small gasps of pleasure and gloried in the way she responded to him.

It always sent a primitive thrill through him to know that he could turn Verity from a prim, disapproving, aggressively independent little tyrant into a passionate, seductive sorceress who craved him and him alone. He would never get enough of this kind of reaction, Jonas thought as she shivered in his arms. Verity had a way of making him shatteringly aware of his manhood. He was addicted to the sensation.

Deliberately he deepened the intimate kiss, reveling in her earthy, feminine taste and scent. Verity's nails raked his skin. She would leave her mark on him tonight and he was determined to leave his on her.

It was all he could do to hold himself in check as he listened to her husky cries of delight. He sent his tongue on passionate forays until she was a shuddering, writhing bundle of femininity.

Then he could wait no longer. When he felt her body begin to tighten, he surged up along the length of her. She reached for him, pulling him close and wrapping her legs around his waist. He found her mouth and let her taste herself on his lips. The erotic kiss drove him wild.

"Hold me." His voice was hoarse with passion. "Hold on to me, Verity." His demand was very much like the one he made on her when he unleashed the psychic power that allowed him dangerous glimpses into the past. He needed her when the past came up around him, and he needed her when he was in the grip of his own raging desire.

"Yes, Jonas, oh yes."

He pushed slowly, heavily into her, needing to feel the silken walls of her soft passage close around him. As always he was aware of the slight resistance with which her body greeted him. She was small, and tight, and so warm. Then, under his insistent, filling pressure, the hot, moist sheath began to accommodate him. He buried himself deep inside until he lost himself in her clinging heat.

Together they lost themselves in the rippling, clashing currents of desire. When Jonas felt Verity convulse around him and heard the tiny, unmistakable cries that signaled her release, he gave himself over completely to the surging sea.

His own climax followed soon after hers. A hoarse shout of triumph and satisfaction shook him. Then he collapsed, his head on her breast. His chest was damp, as traces of his perspiration mixed with hers. He savored the last, fading tremors deep within her body. He was still inside her, and the effect was similar to an exquisitely gentle massage on the most sensitive part of his body.

He knew from previous experience that if he stayed where he was, he would get hard again. If he wanted any sleep tonight, he'd better stop now.

"I love you, Verity." The words were raw.

"I love you, too," she whispered.

He waited a long moment, enjoying the sweet, lingering aftermath of their lovemaking. Then he withdrew reluctantly and rolled to the side. He settled her within the curve of his arm and told himself that everything really was going to be all right now.

Jonas was on the edge of sleep, his mind relaxed and his soul at peace, when Verity spoke again.

"I think," she said quite clearly in the darkness, "that I need a vacation. Maybe I'll take one while you and Dad are in Mexico."

Jonas's peace vanished in an instant. Rage roared through him. It was the kind of fury that had its roots in a very primitive fear, a fear that had been nibbling at him for the past couple of weeks, a fear he had refused to acknowledge.

It was the fear that Verity might be growing dissatisfied with her live-in lover.

Chapter Two

"VACATION!" Jonas jackknifed upright in bed. "What the hell do you mean?"

Verity lay back on the pillows, staring thoughtfully up into the darkness. Jonas's violent reaction had startled her. "I think I need one. You've told me yourself that I'm working too hard," she pointed out reasonably. "Well, now is a perfect time to slow down for a while. It's the middle of winter. Business is slow. There's just a handful of tourists and a few people from the spa at the cafe in the evenings. Nobody's going to mind if I close up for a week. Hawaii would be perfect this time of year."

"You think nobody's going to mind if you take off by yourself for a week of sun and fun in the islands?" Jonas was outraged. He loomed over Verity, caging her face between his hands. "I've got news for you. I'll mind. A lot. If you think I'm going to let you go off by yourself to wiggle around in a bikini in front of a flock of beachboys for a week, you can think again."

Verity began to feel annoyed. "It's okay for you to fly off to Mexico for a week of sun and fun, but I don't have the same right, is that it?"

"Christ almighty." Jonas's voice was raw with exasperation. "You know damn well I'm not going to Mexico for fun and games. Don't you dare try to pretend it's a vacation."

"I could fly down with you. Maybe wait for you and Dad in Acapulco," she suggested, considering the possibilities.

"Not a chance. I don't want you anywhere near Mexico. How do you expect me to keep my mind on business if I'm wondering what you're up to in Acapulco? Forget it, Verity. You're going to stay right here, where I don't have to worry about you. If you're serious about a vacation, we'll take one when I get back. You can spend this week thinking about a place for us to go. Make the plans."

"How can I make plans for a trip when I don't know when you and Dad will return?"

"We'll probably be back within a week. How long can it take to arrange a ransom payoff? Ten days at the outside. Make the plans for two weeks from today. That should be safe enough. Or make them for next month. Hell, use some common sense." Jonas spoke with clenched teeth, clearly working hard to hang on to his temper.

Verity put her arms around his neck and felt the tension there and in the muscles of his broad shoulders. "You'll be very careful in Mexico, won't you?"

"I'm always careful. Verity, about this stupid idea of a vacation. I don't want you going anywhere until I get back. Do you hear me?"

"I hear you." She tugged gently at his neck, aware of his resistance. She tried a seductive smile. "I'm going to miss you, Jonas."

He hesitated a moment and then slowly relaxed, lowering himself alongside her. He gathered her into his arms. "I'm going to miss you, too, little tyrant. You behave yourself while I'm gone."

"Take care of yourself, Jonas. Take care of Dad, too. He's not as young as he once was."

"Your old man can still whip most guys half his age. Whatever Emerson is losing to the years, he's more than making up for with an increasingly devious mind." He bent down and brushed her lips with his. "But don't worry about him, honey. I'll keep an eye on him for you."

"Keep an eye on yourself, too. Good dishwashers are hard to find."

"Always nice to be appreciated. Just don't start interviewing any replacements for my job while I'm gone."

"Yes, Jonas." She slid her hands down to his firm, muscular buttocks and squeezed.

"You're insatiable." He kissed her breast, his tongue warm and damp.

"Lucky for me you always rise to the occasion."

"Luck has nothing to do with it." He slid one knee between her legs. "The hell with it," he muttered against her throat. "I can sleep on the plane."

Emerson glanced out the window of the Jeep and waved at his daughter standing in the doorway of the No Bull Cafe. Verity waved back and blew a kiss.

"Looks like you did a good job of sweet-talking her last night," Emerson remarked. "Verity seemed downright cheerful this morning. I expected a lot of last-minute lectures on the subject of brainless male machismo."

Jonas turned the Jeep onto the road leading out of Sequence Springs. It was still dark, and the sleepy little town slumbered peacefully beside the lake. "Things weren't so cheerful for a while there last night. You should have heard her, Emerson. She started talking about taking a vacation. A vacation all by herself. Can you beat that? Something about going to Hawaii while we're in Mexico. If she hadn't left claw marks in my leg the last time I tried it, I would have turned her over my knee and paddled some sense into her. She was planning to take off for the islands the minute my back was turned."

Emerson's lips twitched briefly. He studied the road ahead with a thoughtful expression. "You talk her out of it?"

"Damn right. Told her that if she really wanted to go on vacation, we'd go when I got back from Mexico. She can spend the next week planning the trip. It'll give her something constructive to do."

"I think she needs a vacation," Emerson remarked slowly. "There's something different about Verity lately. You noticed?"

Jonas was silent for a long moment. "I've noticed," he said finally. He would have given a great deal to know exactly what was going on in her feminine brain. More than once he'd caught her in a strange mood of self-absorption, as if she was looking inward and thinking about making some changes in her life.

The thought filled Jonas with a strong feeling of uneasiness, and an even stronger feeling of possessiveness. His hands tightened around the steering wheel. If Verity was thinking of changing lovers, she could damn well forget it. She had waited twenty-eight years for him—twenty-eight years for her first sexual experience. And she had taken to his lovemaking like a dolphin to water. Jonas didn't like the thought that she might be wondering now if she'd waited for the wrong man.

"You sure you talked her out of going off alone to Hawaii?" Emerson asked.

Jonas set his jaw, remembering belatedly that Verity had changed the subject last night, without giving him any promises. "She wouldn't dare. She knows there'd be hell to pay."

"Ah, the comforts of 'brainless male machismo.' No

wonder we men cultivate it so carefully. Gives us a nice, pleasant, totally false sense of security when we need it most.'' Emerson laughed wryly.

Jonas took a hand off the wheel long enough to touch the golden earring he carried in his pocket. The earring belonged to Verity. He had carried it with him since the night he'd found it in a dirty Mexican alley. ''Some of us get our sense of security from other things.'' The gentle vibrations from the gold soothed some of the uneasiness in his mind.

''Well, since there's not much we can do about my daughter, I guess maybe we ought to talk about the plans for springing Lehigh.''

''Plans?'' Jonas shot his companion a quick, amused glance. ''You mean you've actually got some?''

''Hey, I make a living at writing fiction, don't I? Of course I've got plans. Besides, you know damn well we can't just drop off the cash and expect to see Lehigh again in one piece. We'll have to go in and bring him out.''

''Let's have it, Emerson. What's involved?''

''You and your trusty knife are involved, among other things. Fortunately for us, my boy, you're a man of many talents.''

Four days later, Verity spent the morning at the office of the one and only travel agent in Sequence Springs. That evening, the crowd at the No Bull Cafe was so light she closed earlier than usual, and trekked up the path to the pool room of the Sequence Springs Spa Resort. A stack of travel brochures was tucked under her arm.

The European-style spa room was almost empty. Gleaming white and blue tile shone under the bright lights, and the spa pools bubbled invitingly. Verity undressed and slid naked into her favorite pool, a hot bath that smelled strongly of therapeutic minerals. Stacking the brochures on the tile rim beside her, she leaned back in the soothing water and began to study pictures of sun-kissed shores and tropical seas.

Earlier that evening she had made a promise to herself that she would not spend another night sitting at home waiting for the phone to ring. Jonas was not likely to call tonight. He certainly hadn't bothered to call during the past four days, and they had been the longest four days of Verity's life.

Furthermore, she was sick of reading and rereading the poem she had found pinned to her pillow the morning Jonas had left.

Wait for me, my lady, though the wind blows chill and cold,
wait while all is locked in winter's icy fist.
I will dream of you, my lady, hot dreams of fire and gold,
Dreams of gemlike passion too wondrous to resist.
And if you're on vacation when I return, my lady,
I swear I will be most extremely pissed.

Extremely pissed. Verity wrinkled her nose. If Jonas expected her to believe that little ditty was another of the Renaissance love poems he claimed to have loosely translated, he was wrong. And it certainly didn't make up for his failure to phone her.

"Verity! Just the person I'm looking for. I rang the cafe and the cabin but there was no answer. I figured you might be here."

Verity looked up from the enticing photo of a gleaming white resort on a private bay. "Hi, Laura. What's up?"

Laura Griswald grinned cheerfully. "I'm not positive, but I get the feeling that a job for Jonas may be available."

Verity set aside the brochure. "A job?"

"I knew that would get your attention." Laura shook her head, her shoulder-length brown hair shining. Everything about Laura sparkled with radiant good health. She and her husband, Rick, owned the Sequence Springs Spa Resort, and they were walking advertisements for the place. She crouched at the edge of the pool. ''A young couple—brother and sister, I gather—checked in early this evening. They mentioned they're looking for Jonas Quarrel. They came to Sequence Springs to find him.''

Verity straightened quickly. The last time someone had come looking for Jonas he had nearly been killed. ''They asked for Jonas by name?''

''That's right. Said they wanted to see him in a professional capacity. But they wouldn't come all this way to hire a dishwasher, so I figured they must mean in his professional *academic* capacity. I knew you'd be interested, even if Jonas isn't. You've been trying to get that man back into a respectable job since the day he started washing dishes for you.''

''I'll have you know that he did an article for a history journal that appeared two weeks ago,'' Verity announced proudly. ''You can have one, if you like. I ordered twenty copies.''

''Is that right?'' Laura appeared genuinely impressed. ''I remember you mentioned something about it. An article in his field? Something on Renaissance history?''

''That's right. A comparison of modern-day fencing techniques with the style used during the late Renaissance.'' No need to mention that Jonas had learned the differences in techniques the hard way. He had a nasty scar on one shoulder to prove it.

Verity had nagged, cajoled, and otherwise made a nuisance of herself before Jonas had finally surrendered and written the article. She hated to see a well-educated mind going to waste while its owner washed dishes, although it didn't seem to bother Jonas in the least.

When notice of the article's acceptance had arrived in the mail, she'd strongly suspected that she was much more elated than Jonas was. Then she'd remembered that as an instructor at Vincent College, he'd probably been published in far more prestigious journals. Still, she planned to have one of her twenty copies of the *Journal of Renaissance Studies* framed. She had made Jonas autograph the rest.

"Who are these people and what do they want with Jonas?" Verity asked.

"As I said, they're brother and sister. The name is Warwick. Doug and Elyssa. Doug's a stockbroker, twenty-nine or thirty, I'd say. Likable. Probably drives a BMW and wears designer underwear. Elyssa is a couple of years younger and she positively radiates sweetness and light. Always smiling. It's enough to make you nauseated. I have a hunch she's into this new metaphysical stuff."

"You mean she believes in channelers and crystals and that sort of thing?"

"That's the impression I got. Doug seems normal enough, though, and I got the impression he'll be paying the fee."

"I wonder what they want with Jonas."

Laura shrugged. "You said that before he took off to see the world a few years ago, Jonas had a reputation for authenticating antiques and museum artifacts. Maybe the Warwicks want his professional opinion on something they've purchased. Think Jonas would be interested?"

"I don't know, but I'm certainly interested. It's time that man put his education and, uh, experience to work." She had never attempted to explain to Laura or anyone else that Jonas's real talent was psychic in nature. "I have a nagging fear that he's going to waste his life the way Dad has." Verity shook her head in exasperation.

"I know. Reforming Jonas has become your chief hobby. Lucky for you he doesn't take offense." Laura chuckled, well aware of her friend's opinion about using one's education and abilities. "When will Jonas and your father be back from their business trip?"

"Any day now." Verity drummed her fingers on the edge of the pool and ignored the unspoken questions in Laura's eyes. She could hardly explain that Emerson and Jonas had gone off to Mexico to rescue an old, highly disreputable family friend who had gotten himself kidnapped. Such friends did not reflect well on the family. She had told Laura that Jonas was simply helping Emerson settle a private business matter.

"I'm not sure how long the Warwicks will wait around for him," Laura said dubiously.

"If the Warwicks have a legitimate job for Jonas, I don't want to put them off by telling them I don't know when he'll be back. If the deal looks good, I'll have to find a way to keep them here. Why don't you send them over at lunchtime tomorrow, Laura. Tell them I'm in charge of booking Jonas's business arrangements or something."

Laura tilted her head. "Are you in charge of booking Jonas's business arrangements?"

Verity brightened. "As a matter of fact, I just appointed myself his business manager. Don't look at me like that, Laura. Nobody else is stepping forward to handle the job, least of all Jonas. Looks like it's up to me." She frowned intently, thinking quickly. "You know, with a little publicity work, this sort of thing could turn into a very lucrative sideline for Jonas. I know I'll never persuade him to go back to the academic world, but he could still use his abilities as a consultant for people like the Warwicks. Hey, that's it!"

"What's it?"

"We'll call Jonas a consultant. An historical consultant. How does that sound?"

"I can see the wheels turning in your head." Laura stood

up. "Okay, I'll send 'em over tomorrow for lunch. I just hope Jonas doesn't have any objections when he gets home and finds out you've been booking 'consulting' assignments for him."

"I'll handle Jonas," Verity said with more assurance than she felt. "He'll just have to understand that I'm doing this for his own good. He's got far too fine a mind to be a dishwasher all his life. One day he'll thank me for this."

"If I were you, I'd think twice about forcing upward mobility on a perfectly good dishwasher-waiter-handyperson. It's hard to find reliable help these days. But far be it from me to spoil your fun."

"Fun?"

Laura grinned. "Don't play innocent with me. You and Jonas seem to understand each other perfectly. You give orders, lecture him on self-improvement, and generally bully him until he's had enough. Then he puts his foot down and carries you off to bed just like he did last week. Clement, the bartender, and everyone else had a good laugh after you two left. Your father howled."

Verity's cheeks turned bright pink. She remembered the incident clearly. "That was so embarrassing. I could have killed Jonas."

It had all started when she had begun to nag Jonas about doing another journal article. Having just received the twenty copies she had ordered of the *Journal of Renaissance Studies*, Verity had decided she was on a roll. Convinced that important doors were opening for Jonas, she had pushed her luck—and Jonas—one step too far.

Jonas had tolerated her enthusiastic lectures all afternoon and into the evening. It wasn't until late that night, when they were having a nightcap with Laura and Rick in the resort's cocktail lounge, that he had finally lost his patience.

He'd listened to one more tirade on the importance of

writing another article while he was still a hot literary property. Then he had taken Verity's glass of juice out of her hand, picked her up, and carried her all the way back to the cabin in that humiliating position. Then he'd made love to her until Verity had temporarily forgotten all about journal articles and self-improvement.

"It might have been embarrassing for you," Laura said, smiling, "but it certainly provided memorable entertainment for everyone in the lounge. Quite a show."

"Whose side are you on, anyway?" Verity glowered at her.

The amusement faded from Laura's eyes. "I'm on your side," she said with unexpected seriousness. "You know that, don't you? We're friends."

Verity smiled ruefully. "I know that."

"And speaking as your friend..."

Verity tilted her head. "Yeah, friend?"

"I'm not sure how to ask this, so I'll come right out with it. Is anything wrong, Verity?"

Verity stiffened. "Wrong?"

"You know. As in 'not quite right'? There's something a little different about you lately. As if you've got something on your mind. I just wondered if you've got problems. If so, you know you can tell sister Laura all about them."

Verity swept her hands back and forth just under the surface of the crystal-clear water. Small waves rippled out to the sides of the pool. "I know, Laura. And thanks. But nothing's wrong. Really. I've just been doing some thinking lately, that's all."

"Thinking about Jonas and the future?"

"Something like that."

"Well, it's about time. When are you going to marry the man, Verity?"

Verity's head came up with a snap. "I haven't been asked," she replied tartly.

"Since when does Verity Ames wait around for someone else, least of all a man, to make a major decision in her life?" Laura's mouth curved upward. "You don't fool me one bit. If you wanted to marry Jonas, you'd find a way to nag him into it."

"As you yourself have pointed out, Jonas can only be nagged so far," Verity retorted dryly.

"Maybe. But somehow I don't think he'd fight too hard if you tied him up and dragged him to the altar."

"Not exactly a romantic image."

"No smart woman lets romantic illusions get in the way once she's decided what she wants. And you're one smart woman, Verity. Ergo, I have to assume you haven't made up your mind about Jonas Quarrel. So we're back to my original question. What's wrong, pal?"

Verity thought about the pregnancy-test kit she had surreptitiously examined and then put back on the shelf at the local pharmacy that afternoon. Then she remembered how casually Jonas had left for Mexico, carrying only a few changes of underwear and a wicked-looking knife that he knew how to use quite well.

"Nothing's wrong, Laura. I've just been feeling a little depressed lately. I think I need a vacation." She took one hand out of the water and picked up a glossy brochure. Water dripped on the photograph of the beachfront hotel. "Hawaii sounds nice."

"A vacation, hm? You know something? I think that might be a good idea."

Doug and Elyssa Warwick walked into the No Bull Cafe at two o'clock the following day. Verity saw at once that Laura's brief descriptions had been right on target. Doug

Warwick was a good-looking young professional, with expensively trimmed sandy brown hair and a salon tan. His shirt was Ralph Lauren's version of outdoor wear, and his khaki slacks had pleats in them.

Verity was impressed with the pleats. She had tried to persuade Jonas to buy a pair of pleated trousers the last time they had gone to San Francisco. It had turned into one of those all-too-frequent occasions when Jonas had, as Laura bluntly put it, put his foot down. They had come home with a new pair of Levi's that hadn't even been prewashed for the fashionable broken-in look. Clothes were not one of Jonas's passions.

Elyssa Warwick was a surprise. Thanks to Laura's description, Verity had been prepared for the wide, luminous eyes and serene smile. What she hadn't expected were the undeniably attractive face, the lushly rounded figure, and the silvery blond hair worn in a sleek, shoulder-length bob.

Elyssa was dressed all in white—a white silk shirt that was open one button lower than necessary for fashion, a white wool trumpet skirt, and white ballet shoes.

The unrelieved white made a perfect backdrop for the glittering jewelry that adorned every limb, finger, and ear. Huge, sculpted pieces of metal hung from her ears; several rows of colorful necklaces swung over her full breasts; her bracelets were wide cuffs that extended almost to her elbows; bands of gold adorned with small bells circled her ankles. She tinkled and chimed whenever she moved.

"You must be Verity," Elyssa said warmly as she extended an elegantly shaped hand. Each graceful finger wore a ring, and her long nails were painted in a variety of glittering colors. "Laura Griswald told us all about you. She said we mustn't miss your cooking while we're here in Sequence Springs."

Verity escorted her guests to a table. "Please sit down.

I'll be able to talk to you in a few minutes. I just have to finish up some things in the kitchen. Did you want something to eat?"

Doug Warwick spied the gleaming copper espresso machine in the corner and smiled. "Maybe a cup of espresso, or a café au lait. We ate lunch in the spa dining room."

Verity nodded. She'd had an espresso machine installed two months earlier. Actually, Jonas had installed it. He'd had the huge, complex machine up and running within two hours of its arrival. He really was quite handy to have around.

Verity made two small cups of potent espresso and carried them to the Warwicks' table. Doug and Elyssa smiled gratefully. A few minutes later the last lunch customer left, and Verity made herself a cup of tea.

"I understand you're looking for Jonas," she said as she sat down at the Warwicks' table. "I'm afraid he's out of town at the moment. Business, you know. He's doing some consulting work for a client in Mexico."

Elyssa stirred her espresso and looked seriously impressed. "I imagine his work takes him all over the world."

Verity coughed slightly. "His sort of work is international in scope, naturally. He certainly has done a great deal of traveling. I'm expecting him back any day now, however. In his absence I handle certain business matters for him. May I inquire how you heard about him? For the past few years he's been working out of the country a great deal. He's only recently made Sequence Springs his business headquarters." She wondered if she was laying it on too heavily. If Jonas could hear her he would be looking around for something to clean his boots.

But if Doug and Elyssa were concerned by the fact that the "consultant" they wanted to hire had based his world-wide headquarters in a small-town vegetarian restaurant, they were too polite to show it.

"Jonas was recommended to us by a friend," Elyssa said. "A close acquaintance of mine who has the most extraordinary intuition. I explained to him the sort of expert we needed, and he asked around for us. Preston has a wide variety of contacts."

"Preston Yarwood," Doug Warwick put in dryly, "makes a hell of a good living running psychic self-development seminars in the Bay Area. Elyssa's been a faithful student for the past six months. He's into crap like channeling and metaphysical massage. He also drives a Porsche and wears hand-tailored suits. I suppose the guy must be doing something right."

"Now, Doug, this is no time to make fun of Preston," Elyssa scolded in a gentle, sisterly tone. "He's a very talented, highly intuitive man. A wonderful teacher. He's actually got precognitive abilities, although he's too modest to admit it."

"Bull," Doug said cheerfully. "He never loses an opportunity to remind people of his so-called visions."

"You can't deny that he found Mr. Quarrel for us."

Verity eyed the Warwicks closely. "Just how did this Preston locate Jonas?"

Elyssa's smile was radiant. "He contacted the editor of a small journal that specializes in Renaissance studies. You see, we need an expert in that particular era of history. The journal editor said he'd just published an article by a Mr. Quarrel, who was quite knowledgeable about the Renaissance and might be just the man we needed. He told Preston that Jonas Quarrel once had quite a reputation for being able to authenticate almost anything. Apparently Mr. Quarrel did an article on fencing techniques for the journal?"

Verity smiled complacently. "You've read it?"

"I'm afraid not, although I'd certainly like to," Elyssa said with great charm.

"I just happen to have an extra copy," Verity told her smoothly. "I'll let you have it. I'm sure you'll find it very interesting. It's a brilliant piece."

"I'm sure it is."

"What exactly did you want Jonas to authenticate?" Verity looked at Doug Warwick.

"A sixteenth-century villa," he replied promptly.

Verity stared at him. "A villa? In Italy?" Visions of a vacation in the Italian countryside danced through her head. This might be even better than a trip to Hawaii.

Doug gave her a level look over the rim of his tiny espresso cup. "I wish it were that simple. If Hazelhurst's Horror were in Italy, I wouldn't have the problem of trying to assure my buyers that it's genuine. But since it's located on an island up in the Pacific Northwest, things get complicated."

"Good grief," Verity exclaimed. "How did a sixteenth-century Renaissance villa get to an island in the Northwest?"

"It was taken apart in Italy before the turn of the century, shipped here to the States, and reconstructed by an eccentric relative of our late uncle, Eustis Hazelhurst. Our uncle Digby, who was just as nutty as his relative, inherited the place when Eustis died. Then, two years ago, our uncle died and I inherited the monstrosity."

"Doug put it up for sale immediately," Elyssa explained. "Who can afford the taxes and upkeep on a thing like Hazelhurst's Horror? It costs a fortune to maintain. A group of businessmen want to turn it into a resort. They're very interested in the place, but they want proof that the villa is authentic before they pay what Doug is asking. So, Doug has decided to hire someone with a respectable academic reputation to look the place over and write a report for the buyers.''

Doug set down his empty espresso cup. ''In all fairness, you should know at the outset, Verity, that my sister has ulterior motives. She wants Mr. Quarrel to do a little treasure hunting while he's checking out the villa.''

''Buried treasure?'' Verity was enthralled.

Doug shrugged expressively. ''Probably just a wild goose chase, but my uncle left enough evidence to whet the appetite. The treasure is supposedly buried somewhere in the villa.''

''And I definitely think we should look for it before we sell the place,'' Elyssa declared stoutly.

Verity frowned. ''If there was any treasure, wouldn't it have been discovered when the place was taken apart for shipping?''

It was Doug who answered. ''That was my first thought, too. But apparently the villa was not literally taken apart stone by stone. Huge chunks of it were left intact. The workmen simply built a protective crate around the big pieces and put them on the boat. A lot of furniture and some artwork were also shipped over, but almost all of that is gone now. Poor Uncle Digby had to sell it off in order to keep the place going.''

''Uncle Digby was convinced the treasure existed and that it was still somewhere in the villa. He spent years looking for it,'' Elyssa explained. ''It only makes sense to take a shot at it ourselves before we give up the place.''

Doug smiled indulgently as he glanced at his sister. ''If Mr. Quarrel is willing to take on both jobs at once, I'd like to hire him for a week.''

It was time to do business. Verity smiled in a professional way. She hoped she didn't look too eager. ''You do understand that Jonas's time is very valuable, and the sort of project you're describing, a stone-by-stone examination of the villa, would be quite expensive."

"Oh," said Elyssa, "we're prepared to pay his going rate, whatever that is for a full week. Perhaps longer if necessary. Do you think Mr. Quarrel might be interested in the job?"

"I think," Verity said thoughtfully, "that Mr. Quarrel would be very interested." Visions of an island vacation in a Renaissance villa swam in her mind. The Puget Sound was not the South Pacific, but sometimes you had to take what you could get. "I generally accompany him on consulting trips within the continental U.S.," she said delicately.

"We'd love to have you come along with him," Elyssa said quickly. "We'd pay all expenses, naturally."

"Naturally," Verity said smoothly, feeling very business-like. "Can I offer you another cup of espresso while we work out the details?"

By the time Verity had finished explaining the whole thing to Laura as they soaked in a spa pool that night, she was convinced that she had heretofore undiscovered talents as a business manager.

"This could open up a real career for Jonas," she told Laura enthusiastically. "It's perfect."

"The part about the treasure hunt sounds like a waste of time," Laura stated.

"So what? At the very least Doug will get a proper academic report detailing the age and design of the villa. That should take care of impressing his potential buyers. If Jonas locates a treasure along the way, that'll just be icing on the cake."

"Think Jonas is going to go for the idea of a treasure hunt?"

"Why not? It's just the type of thing that might really appeal to him."

"And you get a week's vacation out of it," Laura concluded with a nod. "You know, it's not such a bad idea at all. A little unusual, but it has possibilities. Maybe Jonas really will go for it."

Verity leaned her head back against the tile. "Jonas doesn't have much choice in the matter," she admitted. "I've already accepted the job on his behalf. The Warwicks left a five-hundred-dollar retainer fee with me."

Laura's eyes crinkled at the corners. "Be interesting to see what Jonas thinks about his new consulting business."

Verity wondered about that herself. She had been pondering the problem since the Warwicks had left. She was still mulling over the right approach for telling Jonas about his new consulting assignment as she hurried back along the dark path that led from the resort to her cabin.

The path was treacherous. Crusts of ice were already forming. Verity plunged her hands deep into the pockets of her down parka, hunching her shoulders against the chill.

The steps leading up to her deck were icy and she used the rail to steady herself. The porch light was out. She frowned, certain that she had left it on earlier. Perhaps the bulb had burned out. Replacing bulbs was one of those little things Jonas was good at doing.

Verity had her hand on the doorknob when she heard a faint scraping sound within the cabin. A rush of excitement surged through her. Jonas was home!

"Jonas? When did you get in?" She pushed open the door and started to reach for the light switch. "Why didn't you turn on the lights?"

A dark body exploded through the doorway, shoving Verity violently to one side. She staggered wildly backward, her shoes slipping and sliding across the ice patches.

The dark figure bounded down the steps at a dead run. Rage raced through Verity. She started after the intruder, only to have her feet slip out from under her as she went down the steps.

She felt her balance going, and felt a sharp pain in her right ankle. Suddenly all she could think about was protecting the child she might be carrying.

She must not fall!

She grabbed frantically for the railing, catching it just as her injured ankle collapsed beneath her. She was barely in time.

Her breath coming in short, steamy little gasps, she lowered herself slowly to the icy step and watched helplessly as the intruder vanished into the trees.

"Damn, damn, damn." She was shaking like a leaf.

After a moment, she picked herself up, realized she couldn't put any weight on her ankle, and limped painfully into the cabin to call Laura.

Her friend arrived a short time later, the Warwicks in tow.

"They happened to be at the front desk when you called," Laura explained as she fussed over Verity. "Rick was busy handling a crisis in the bar."

"We'd better get you to a doctor," Doug Warwick said, examining Verity's rapidly swelling ankle. "I'll carry you to the car."

Before Verity could think of a response, he had lifted her into his arms and was heading for the door.

It was most unfortunate for the sake of future business relations that when Doug carried her back into the cabin an hour later, he got a knife at his throat for his trouble.

"What the hell is going on here?" Jonas asked. His voice was a cold, dangerous snarl coming from the shadows.

Chapter Three

"JONAS! Put down that knife this instant! Honestly, I have never been so embarrassed in my life." Verity scrabbled for the switch on the wall behind Doug. "I'm terribly sorry about this, Doug."

Doug didn't move an inch. He stood perfectly still, holding Verity in his arms. He blinked when the light came on, revealing the man holding the knife. "I think there's a slight misunderstanding here," he croaked.

"I think maybe there is," Jonas agreed in an ominously soft voice.

"Jonas, stop it. This is ridiculous. You're humiliating me. And just look at you. You're a mess." Verity glared furiously at Jonas. He definitely was not in any condition to impress clients. The knife he was holding at Doug's throat was the worst of it, of course, but the rumpled, stained work shirt and jeans and the rough stubble of several days' growth of beard did not help matters. His golden eyes glittered like those of a predator. At least he appeared to be in good shape physically, she thought, feeling a rush of relief.

''What's going on here, Verity?'' Jonas flicked a brief, grim glance at her before returning his gaze to his victim.

''Stop behaving like a Neanderthal and I'll explain.''

''This had better be good.'' Jonas lowered the knife with obvious reluctance. ''Put my woman down before I have a change of heart about what to do with this knife,'' he added to the man cradling Verity.

''Her ankle,'' Doug managed tightly.

Jonas scanned Verity's legs and saw the elastic bandage around her right ankle. ''For Christ's sake, Verity, what happened to you?''

''I twisted my ankle outside on the deck. If you had asked a few civil questions instead of going for poor Doug's throat with that knife, you would have saved yourself having to apologize.''

''Who's apologizing?''

''You will soon enough,'' Verity vowed. She smiled warmly up at Doug, who still stood there, frozen. ''I'm so embarrassed about this. Just set me down over there on the couch, will you?''

''You're sure you're all right here with him?'' Doug asked as he put her down carefully. He eyed Jonas warily.

''Heavens, yes. I'll be fine.'' The expression on Doug's face alarmed her. She could see Jonas's fat consulting fee slipping rapidly away. ''I can't thank you enough for all your help this evening. I don't know what I would have done without you. I'm really sorry about this. . . .'' She waved a hand that casually included Jonas and his knife. ''Sometimes Jonas overreacts to situations. He's a little high-strung. Impetuous. Leaps to conclusions. You know how these academic types are. But I can assure you that he's quite good in his field of expertise.''

"I see." Doug's eyes were on the knife that Jonas had not yet bothered to put away. "I was assuming that his field of expertise was Renaissance history."

Verity desperately tried to salvage the situation before Doug convinced himself that Jonas's field of expertise was slitting throats. "I'm sure he'll suit your needs just fine. I can certainly guarantee there won't be any more awkward scenes like this. As his business manager, I'll see to it that he behaves himself."

"Maybe we'd better discuss this in the morning," Doug said, edging back toward the door. "Laura and Elyssa are out in the car. Wouldn't want to keep them waiting any longer. Pretty cold out there this evening. Nice to meet you, Mr. Quarrel. Hope you had a good, er, business trip. Understand you were out of the country for a while." Doug was nearly at the door. Like any good stockbroker, he kept talking right up until the last second. "Good night, Verity. Take care of that ankle." He pulled the door shut behind him.

A taut silence fell upon the small room.

"High-strung?" Jonas finally echoed blandly. "Impetuous?" He tossed the knife into the open duffel bag that lay at the foot of the sofa. His eyes gleamed as he walked forward and loomed over Verity.

"Well, I had to think of something to explain your cretinous behavior." Verity settled back into a corner of the sofa and met his challenging gaze without flinching. Then she chewed on her lower lip. "Jonas, are you all right?"

"I was until I got home in time to watch you being carried over the threshold by this year's cover boy for *Gentlemen's Quarterly*. Practicing for playing bride?"

"Don't be ridiculous," she retorted tartly. "Where's Dad?"

"In Rio with Lehigh. Emerson said he needed a vacation.

He decided that watching string bikinis and topless bathing suits parading up and down the beach was just the thing to relax a man of his years. I,'' Jonas added virtuously, ''felt obliged to rush straight home to the little woman I just knew would be waiting anxiously for my return.''

Verity ignored that last crack. ''Sam Lehigh's all right? The kidnappers turned him over without a fuss?''

''He's fine. The guys who had him were not the brightest bunch.'' Jonas ran a hand through his tousled hair. As the tension drained out of his body, his exhaustion became obvious. He stifled a yawn.

''And Dad?''

''He's fine too. Nobody who counted got hurt.''

''Nobody who counted! What about the kidnappers?'' Verity asked anxiously.

Jonas regarded her through narrowed eyes. ''I said nobody who counted got hurt. You, being the upright little citizen you are, will be pleased to know that the three who had Lehigh are now enjoying the hospitality of a Mexican jail.''

Verity brightened. ''You turned the whole thing over to the police after all? I'm so glad. I knew it would be better if you handled it that way.''

''We didn't exactly turn them over to the Mexican cops,'' Jonas said carefully. ''We just sort of left the three jerks at the scene of the crime. You know how it is down there. Whoever's hanging around when the police move in is generally considered guilty.''

''What, exactly, did you leave those three hanging around with?'' Verity demanded suspiciously.

''A warehouse full of drugs. It belonged to relatives, I gather. The three fools were holding Lehigh in the back of the place. After we got Lehigh out, we made sure the kidnappers weren't going anywhere for a while. Then Emerson made an anonymous call to the cops. It was a nice, prestigious arrest for the authorities. Headlines in all the papers, medals for everyone."

"I have the distinct impression that you're oversimplifying things enormously."

"I'm just trying to be concise so that we can get back to the main topic here," Jonas declared ominously. "When and why did the Sir Galahad in a yuppie suit show up?"

"His name is Warwick," Verity said testily. "Doug Warwick. He and his sister Elyssa are staying at the resort. After I sprained my ankle on the steps this evening, I called Laura. She came right over, and the Warwicks came with her. It was really very kind of them. I was a little frightened, you see."

Jonas dropped into a crouch beside the sofa. He touched the bandaged ankle with surprisingly gentle hands. "Frightened because of the fall?"

"No, because of what made me fall."

Jonas's head came up sharply.

"Someone was in the house when I got home from the spa tonight, Jonas. He came rushing out, knocking me to one side. I barely caught myself in time to keep from falling down the steps."

Jonas stared at her in amazement. "Holy shit! Are you serious?"

"Very."

"Someone got in here?" Jonas's hand tightened on Verity's knee as he glanced around the comfortably furnished room.

Verity followed his gaze. "Doesn't look like he took anything, does it? The stereo is still here, and so's the television. I must have interrupted him before he had a chance to do any damage. That reminds me—I'm supposed to phone the sheriff's office and let them know if anything's missing.'' She reached for the phone on the end table.

As she dialed, Jonas prowled around the room, opening the cupboards and checking the closets. Then he disappeared down the hall to the bedroom. When he returned, Verity had finished her brief report and was hanging up the phone.

''Dammit, I go away for less than five days and you get yourself into trouble,'' Jonas growled as he stalked into the kitchen.

''I did not get myself into trouble. I was the innocent victim of an intruder.'' Verity heard the clink of a bottle against glass. ''Make mine juice.'' A moment later Jonas reappeared with two glasses. One was filled with cranberry juice.

''Did you lock the door before you went over to the spa tonight?'' He sat down beside her and handed her the juice.

''No. I never lock it. You know that. We don't have any crime around here.''

''Well, we do now, don't we? Of all the crazy, idiotic excuses. How many times have I told you to lock that front door?''

''Now, Jonas . . .''

''And this business of walking alone over to the spa late at night has got to stop. From now on, either I go with you, or you stay home and find something else to do.''

''Now, Jonas . . .''

''I'd like to know where this Warwick character got the idea he could just pick you up and carry you around. What made him volunteer to play rescuer, anyway? Laura and Rick could have handled things just fine.''

''Jonas . . .''

''Jesus. A man comes home after a hard week on the road, and the first thing he sees is his woman being carried through the doorway in some other guy's arms. It's enough to make a person think seriously about bringing back chastity belts.''

Verity lost her patience. ''Jonas, you're beginning to sound like an irate husband. I think you've said enough. In case it has escaped your notice, I am the injured party here. Furthermore, I don't want to hear another nasty word about Doug Warwick. He's a very nice man, and, more important, he's a client of yours.''

''He's a *what*?''

Verity coughed delicately. ''I think it would be easier to explain everything tomorrow morning. You look worn out, and heaven knows I'm exhausted after all the excitement. My ankle hurts, and I just want to go to bed and get some sleep.''

''Oh no you don't. What is this about Warwick being a client?''

''It's a long story, Jonas. I'd really rather explain it in the morning.'' She smiled up at him tentatively. ''It's just a business matter. Jonas, I'm so glad you're home safe and sound. I was so worried about you.''

''Verity. . .''

''My ankle is throbbing, you know. I thought I'd broken it at first. That deck is quite treacherous when it's icy.''

''Dammit, Verity. . .''

''It's so good to have you home, Jonas,'' she said wistfully. She touched his shoulder, letting her hand trail down his arm. ''You look like you've been through the wringer.''

''I need a shower,'' he admitted, swallowing the rest of his brandy.

''Why don't you go take one?''

He rubbed his jaw. ''I also need a shave.''

''I'm not so sure about that. The beard is kind of sexy.'' She touched the side of his face.

He looked at her with a sudden, fierce desire. "I also need you."

Verity's smile was very gentle and inviting. "I don't see any reason why you shouldn't have everything you need tonight. Why don't you start with the shower?"

He stared at her mouth. "Why do I let you get away with murder? Eating vegetarian food all these months must have softened my brain." He leaned down to drop a hard, fierce kiss on her waiting lips. Then he headed for the bathroom.

Verity waited until she heard the water running in the shower before she rose cautiously from the sofa. She found she could make her way around the room fairly well using the fireplace poker as a cane. Humming softly, she locked the door and turned off the living-room lights, then hobbled down the hall to the bedroom.

When the bathroom door opened fifteen minutes later, Verity was lying in bed, propped up against the pillows. Her red hair was a fiery halo around her head, and the nightgown she wore was one she had purchased shortly after Jonas had become her lover. It was not designed for cold winter nights. It was a froth of black lace and satin, and it did interesting things for the soft curves of her breasts.

Jonas came into the bedroom wearing a towel around his waist and using another towel to dry his thick, dark hair. He stopped abruptly when he caught sight of her.

"Given the fact that you were once upon a time a prissy little spinster, you certainly have come a long way." Jonas slung both towels over a chair and walked to the bed. He stood looking down at her, his body fiercely aroused. "I missed you, sweetheart."

"I'm glad." Verity pushed back the covers, making a place for him beside her. "I missed you too, Jonas. I was so afraid that something would happen to you."

He got into bed and took her into his arms. "You were

the one who wound up getting hurt. Just goes to show you.'' He kissed her throat and slid a hand inside the black lace bodice of her nightgown.

When his warm, deliciously rough palm moved down over her belly, Verity thought again of what she might have been protecting earlier that evening when she had fought to keep herself from falling. Maybe it was time to share her suspicions with Jonas.

''Jonas?''

He kissed her reassuringly. ''Don't worry, I'll be very careful.''

For a split second she wondered if he had guessed the truth. ''Careful of what?''

''Your ankle.''

''Oh.''

''God, I want you tonight.'' He was stroking her with increasing urgency, seeking the magic places he had learned so well. ''Welcome me home, love. I need to know how much you missed me.''

Maybe this wasn't the time to tell him. Clearly, his mind was on only one thing. When he had satisfied the compelling physical need that now drove him he would be exhausted. He needed rest, she could see that. Besides, she wasn't yet certain about the baby. Verity put her arms around Jonas's neck and pulled him close.

''Welcome home, my love,'' she whispered as he lowered himself along her slender length. Then he gathered her into his fierce embrace, and Verity forgot all about the future as she lost herself in the fire of their mutual passion.

A long time later, as she drifted toward sleep, Verity heard Jonas mumble something into the crook of her neck.

''What?'' she asked sleepily.

''I said, did I really sound like an enraged husband earlier?''

"Irate, not enraged. It was just a figure of speech." She was suddenly wide awake.

"A figure of speech, huh?" Jonas yawned. "You know, I think that's exactly how I felt when you came through the door in Warwick's arms. Except that *irate* doesn't cover it. *Enraged* is a little closer to reality. I wanted to put that knife into his throat. Don't ever upset me like that again, Verity."

She heard the clear warning in his words and shivered. She remembered the coldness she had seen in his brilliant eyes when he'd held the knife to Warwick's throat. There were times when it paid to remember that the man who lay beside her wasn't just a dishwasher with a Ph.D. He could be very dangerous; as ruthless as any Renaissance lord who had ever fought to protect what he considered his own.

And this was the man she loved, the man who was the father of her child. If she was carrying one.

Verity touched her stomach again. It was a long time before she was able to sleep.

"So you see," Verity concluded over breakfast the next morning, "it's a wonderful opportunity for you, Jonas. Assuming you didn't blow the whole thing last night, of course. I've already put the Warwicks' retainer in a special bank account, and arranged to have the rest of your fee paid at the end of the assignment. They'll cover all expenses. Just think of what a perfect job this is! We get a paid vacation, and you'll get a real start on developing a consulting business."

Jonas spooned up the last of his cereal. He chewed and swallowed slowly, considering his options. Verity was looking decidedly determined this morning. There was a vivid gleam of expectation in her aquamarine eyes that warned him to tread warily. She obviously wanted him to accept the Warwicks' offer of a consulting job. Jonas, however, wasn't keen on the idea. He preferred to stay right here in Sequence Springs, spending the rest of the winter making love to Verity and learning to cook gourmet vegetarian food.

"A vacation in the San Juan Islands in the middle of winter is not exactly the same as a week in Hawaii," he pointed out.

"I know, but I think this opportunity is simply too good to pass up."

"Doing an analysis of the villa will be fairly straightforward, but you do realize that a four-hundred-year-old legend is not going to produce any real treasure, don't you? Talk about a wild goose chase . . ."

"That's what Laura said. But I say, if the Warwicks are willing to pay you to chase geese, why should you complain? The treasure hunt is a side issue, anyway. The main thing is the report on the villa."

Jonas tried to think of another argument. He had a hunch that anything he came up with would get shot down. The whole idea sounded like a complete waste of time, but he was, as usual, feeling indulgent after spending a night in bed with Verity. The woman was slowly but surely wrapping him around her little finger. It was not an unpleasant feeling, he decided.

"I'll tell you what," he said finally, deciding to be generous. "I'll talk to the Warwicks myself this morning."

"You'd better apologize about the knife first."

"Don't push your luck, Verity."

"I'm not pushing my luck. I'm pushing you. Honestly, if I didn't, I think you would be content to wash dishes the rest of your life."

"I don't see the problem. You need a dishwasher. You also need a keeper. In me you get both for the price of one."

She smiled the dazzling, full-of-promise smile that always made Jonas catch his breath.

"Such a deal," she murmured. She picked up the plates and bowls and reached for the poker to steady herself.

"I'll take care of the dishes. I'm a pro, remember?" Jonas said. He frowned in concern as she started to hop toward the kitchen, the dishes wobbling in her hands. "Sit down, honey."

"Don't worry about me. I've got this hobbling business down to a fine art. I think I'll soak my foot in one of the spa pools later today."

"Verity . . ."

She stopped to drop a kiss on his forehead. "Thanks for agreeing to take the job, Jonas. I just know it's going to be the beginning of a great future."

"I didn't say I'd take the job. I just agreed to talk to the Warwicks," he reminded her, knowing that he was fighting a useless battle.

"You'll like them," she assured him breezily as she resumed her awkward progress toward the kitchen. "Elyssa's a little odd, but Doug's nice and normal. He's . . . *Oops!*"

Jonas saw the stack of bowls sway like a highrise building in an earthquake. He watched in fascination as they slid slowly off the empty toast plate and started the short drop to the hardwood floor. Casually reaching out, he caught the bowls in one hand, and placed them carefully on the table.

Verity sighed. "How do you do it, Jonas?"

"Do what?"

"You're so coordinated. I don't think you even realize how smooth and controlled you are when you move. It's amazing."

He grinned lecherously. "Is that a roundabout way of telling me I'm good in bed?"

She sniffed disapprovingly. "Your male arrogance is showing."

"I could show you something even more male if you'll put down that plate."

"Some of us have work to do. And this is your lucky day. You are among the chosen. You're actually being offered paid employment in your field of expertise. When you finish your coffee I'll call the resort and make an appointment with the Warwicks." She disappeared into the kitchen.

Jonas settled down to linger over his coffee. He sat gazing out the window into the cold, frosty woods and listened to the pleasant clatter of dishes behind him in the warm kitchen.

It was good to be home, he thought. Good to have a passionate little redhead waiting for him. Good to share a bed and breakfast with her. Good to have his books crammed into her bookcases. Good to feel he had a place where he belonged. He liked the thought of spending the rest of his life like this. He wondered how Verity would respond to that idea.

She never said much about their future together, and lately that had begun to bother him. Women were supposed to instinctively seek a sense of permanence in a relationship. They were supposed to want rings, and vows, and all the other symbolic bonds that spelled marriage and commitment.

But Verity had never once brought up the subject of marriage. That seemed strange, now that he considered it. Jonas frowned.

Last night she had accused him of acting like an enraged, no, an *irate* husband. Jonas let the word *husband* trickle through his mind again. He wondered if Verity ever visualized herself as a wife.

Probably not, he told himself realistically. Emerson had given his daughter a highly unorthodox upbringing. His main goal as a father, he'd explained, had been to teach Verity how to take care of herself in a rough world. The result had been a smart, self-reliant, fiery-tempered young woman who had managed to do just fine without a man in her life—until Jonas had arrived on the scene.

Jonas didn't kid himself about how she had managed to remain single for so long. She had driven off every eligible male with a tongue that had been honed to a fine, sharp edge. She was as good with her tongue as he was with his knife, he reflected wryly. The lady didn't hesitate to use her mouth. Jonas grinned at the thought, finished his coffee, and rose to his feet.

Verity stuck her head around the kitchen door. "You might put on a tie," she suggested brightly.

"Wouldn't want the Warwicks to think I'm trying to impress them, now would we?"

"Jonas," she said firmly, "a tie would be appropriate. You're supposed to be a professional."

He walked over to her, bent his head, and kissed her roughly on the mouth. "Like I said, lady, don't press your luck."

Verity held her breath during the formal introductions but after a few minutes she relaxed. It was obvious that Jonas was going to behave himself. After Doug Warwick realized that Jonas was apparently far more civilized in the light of day, he put out a friendly hand, which Jonas accepted with casual ease. The four of them, Jonas and Verity, Doug and Elyssa, were seated in the resort's solarium. The glass walls provided an expansive view of Sequence Lake shimmering in the cold sunlight. Elyssa was dressed in white again, Verity noticed—white pants, white sweater, white shoes. Her jewelry sparkled in the sunlight.

"Sorry about the misunderstanding last night," Doug

said. Verity thought it was very generous of him. She smiled at him warmly.

"I appreciate your helping Verity last night," Jonas said somewhat grudgingly. Then he sprawled in a lounger and eyed his potential clients.

"How are you feeling today, Verity?" Elyssa examined the now famous ankle. "Can you put any weight on it yet?"

"A little. It's still sore, but it should be back to normal in a few days. Laura found this cane for me and it's been a great help." She waved a hardwood staff aloft. "It's left over from two years ago, when Rick threw his back out."

"I have a friend," Elyssa went on helpfully, "someone I met in one of Preston's seminars. He works with crystals. He could probably do something for you."

"I should warn you, my sister is really involved in this crap," Doug Warwick said in an aside to Jonas.

"Pay no attention to Doug," Elyssa retorted gently. "He's still very linear in his thinking. He doesn't understand that the paths to enlightenment don't always follow the straight, one-dimensional approach of most Western thought. He hasn't accepted a holistic approach to truth yet, but I have confidence that he will one day soon."

"Don't hold your breath," Doug muttered.

"I think some of the New Age ideas are very interesting," Verity declared. "After all, it's not as if they're really new. Some of these concepts have been around for thousands of years. There must be some truth to them."

"Con men have a long history, too," Jonas said blandly. "That doesn't mean there's any more truth in a modern-day con than there was five thousand years ago. That's all most of this New Age stuff is, a good con."

"Jonas!" Verity glowered at him, willing him to shut his mouth before he mortally offended one of their potential clients. "Don't pay any attention to him, Elyssa. He's just got a typical academic bias against nontraditional methods of learning.'' A heck of a bias for someone who happened to have psychic abilities himself, Verity thought wryly.

''I understand completely,'' Elyssa assured her, gazing at Jonas. She appeared to be infinitely indulgent of his petty carping. She turned back to Verity. ''Will you be able to accompany Jonas to our villa with that injured ankle?''

''Oh, definitely. I'm looking forward to it.'' Verity nodded briskly, trying to pump some enthusiasm into Jonas. He ignored her.

''I can give you a report on the villa easily enough,'' Jonas said. ''But I understand you also want me to chase some damned legend. I should warn you that from what Verity has told me, it sounds like a complete waste of time. Are you sure you want to pay my, uh, consulting fee to help you hunt for a treasure that probably doesn't exist?''

Doug chuckled. ''It must sound a little silly to you, but I assure you that Uncle Digby was on the trail of something in that villa. Elyssa wants to see if we can find it before we get rid of the place. Since you'll be going over the villa anyway, you might as well keep an eye out for treasure.''

''What makes you think your uncle Digby wasn't just loony tunes?''

''Jonas!'' Verity hissed. He was being downright rude.

Elyssa smiled serenely. ''It's all right, Verity. Doug and I have also wondered about Uncle Digby. He might very well have been completely insane. He was certainly an odd character. But he definitely believed there was a treasure buried in that old villa. He left a diary detailing his search for it. Unfortunately, he kept his notes in Latin. He also found a crystal at one point.''

''Crystal?'' Verity tilted her head inquiringly.

Doug nodded. ''I saw it myself about five years ago. Digby showed it to me shortly after he found it. He was sure it was a key of some kind. It's green, about two inches long. It's egg-shaped and very smooth, with tiny, odd-shaped little facets cut into the bottom. It disappeared a couple of years ago along with Uncle Digby. He either hid it somewhere or had it on him when he disappeared."

Jonas sat forward, finally, showing real interest. "He believed the crystal was genuine Renaissance work?"

"Oh yes," Elyssa said. Her bracelets jingled as she turned to Jonas. "He may have been senile there at the end, but at one time Digby Hazelhurst had quite a reputation in academic circles. Thirty years ago he was considered an expert on Renaissance history."

"Hazelhurst?" Jonas repeated. "Your uncle was Digby Hazelhurst?"

"Have you heard of him?"

"I remember running across some early papers he did on Renaissance scientific learning," Jonas said slowly. "They were gathering dust in an old library file at Vincent College. I found them by accident."

"I'm afraid that by the time he died, Uncle Digby's academic reputation had been shot to pieces," Doug said. "His work got more and more bizarre during the last twenty years, I'm told. His colleagues ignored him, he couldn't get teaching positions, and academic journals stopped publishing him entirely. He eventually retired to his island to spend the last years of his life searching for the treasure."

"You said your uncle died a couple of years ago?"

Doug nodded. "Lost at sea. The old man had no business sailing on the Sound alone at his age. But old Digby always was independent. He'd had a bad heart for years. The authorities concluded he probably had a heart attack and fell overboard. They never recovered the body, although the boat eventually washed ashore on a neighboring island."

"And you're left with the diary, the reconstructed villa, and a missing piece of crystal," Jonas concluded.

Elyssa laughed and her earrings tinkled. "Doug's right. We really do have to sell the villa, there's no way we can afford to keep it. But I can't bear not to try to find the treasure before we do. It should be fun, if nothing else. I'm inviting a few friends to help in the hunt."

Jonas narrowed his eyes. "What kind of friends?"

"Don't worry, they won't get in your way," she assured him hastily. "There's plenty of room. Digby's housekeeper, a Miss Frampton, is still at the villa. She'll see to all the cooking and cleaning for us."

"Jonas, it sounds like fun," Verity said brightly.

He arched his brows and gave her a wry glance. "When it comes to business," he said to the Warwicks, "I leave everything to my business manager. Looks like we'll be seeing you in Seattle in a day or two."

"Great." Doug took a small, leatherbound volume out of his pocket. "I might as well let you have a look at the diary." He paused. "I don't suppose you happen to know Latin?"

"It's been a while, but I can manage," Jonas said with an air of dignified modesty. "Italian humanist scholars made a big deal out of learning Latin. It was considered the only suitable language for recording really important work. Looks like Digby felt the same way."

"In this day and age, it makes for an excellent secret code," Doug observed. "No one reads Latin anymore. There are a few pages missing from the back of the diary. You can see where they've been torn out. I don't know what happened to them."

Elyssa leaned toward Jonas as he reached for the book. Her jeweled fingers flashed light. "Mr. Quarrel, I have a personal question. . . ."

"Jonas," he corrected absently, examining the small volume.

"Jonas, then." She smiled with obvious delight. "Forgive me for prying, but I'm dying of curiosity. Is it true that you have a talent for psychometry?"

Verity saw the anger flare in Jonas's eyes and was suddenly afraid that the whole deal was going to end right then and there. She could have kicked Elyssa.

"The editor of the journal that published your article mentioned that you once had a reputation for authenticating items for museums and collectors," Elyssa explained, apparently unaware of the narrow line she was walking. "From his description of your work, my friend Preston Yarwood speculated that you might have a psychic ability called psychometry. Is that true?"

"Pure bullshit," Jonas said with clenched teeth.

"Preston said that you might not even be aware of how and why you can identify objects from the past," Elyssa went on innocently. "He said the talent might be very elusive, something you just take for granted, and don't even understand yourself."

"Who's Preston Yarwood?" Jonas demanded grimly.

"Mr. Yarwood is a friend of hers, Jonas," Verity cut in. "He's the one who contacted the journal editor who published your piece on Renaissance fencing techniques. The editor recommended you for this assignment." She gave Jonas her most brilliant smile. "Funny how things work out, isn't it? If you hadn't published that piece, the Warwicks would never have learned about you, and we wouldn't be on our way to Washington."

Jonas tapped the Hazelhurst diary thoughtfully. "Funny isn't exactly the word for it."

Chapter Four

"*WHAT* an ugly pile of rock. No wonder Doug said it was called Hazelhurst's Horror." Verity's disappointment was obvious. She stood in the stern of the small launch Doug Warwick was piloting and studied the grim island fortress ahead.

Jonas grinned. "Well, it sure as hell doesn't approach the architectural genius of Bramante or Brunelleschi."

"What style is it, then?"

Jonas shrugged and surveyed the rugged structure dominating the cliff that rose from the cold waters of Puget Sound. It was a plain, solid-looking stone mass, two stories high. The rough, unattractive facade was studded with tiny windows and capped by a thick, bulky cornice that outlined the roof. "I'd say it's late fifteenth century, probably Milanese, judging by the overall style. The architect will most likely remain anonymous forever."

"And deservedly so," Verity retorted. "When the Warwicks talked about an Italian villa, I imagined something a little grander.'' The noise of the launch engine kept her complaints from being overheard by their host, who was busy guiding the boat into a small cove.

Jonas chuckled, amused by her dismay. ''Not everything built during the Renaissance was an architectural marvel. Just ask anyone who was born and raised in Rome, or Milan, or Florence. The most important criterion for a Renaissance house was that it be able to withstand an armed assault. This sucker looks like it was built to do the job.''

''I'll say.'' Verity shivered. ''It's going to be dark and gloomy inside.''

''Well, it won't be cheerful, that's for sure, but it may not be too dark. It's built around an enclosed courtyard. The rooms will all have much larger windows on the inside walls.''

''Just as long as it has indoor plumbing.''

''Don't worry. Doug assured me that his uncle installed modern plumbing and wiring in the south wing. That's the wing facing us. Hazelhurst didn't fancy roughing it out here on an isolated island.''

Verity noticed a cheerful note in his voice and smiled. ''You're really getting into this, aren't you? I can't believe it. I practically had to threaten you to take this job, and already you're enjoying yourself. Admit it.''

Jonas glanced at his duffel bag, which contained, among other things, Digby Hazelhurst's diary. ''Might turn out to be interesting after all.''

''I knew it,'' Verity said with satisfaction. ''Jonas, I have the feeling this is going to be the beginning of a wonderful consulting career.''

''We'll see.''

But Verity refused to be put off by his cautious attitude. She had seen him poring over Hazelhurst's diary for the past two days. He had spent every free minute with it before they had left Sequence Springs, and he'd kept his nose buried in it during the flight from San Francisco to Seattle. He had also gone through several texts on Renaissance architecture. Jonas might not admit it yet, Verity thought, but he was fascinated by the project ahead of him.

Doug Warwick had met them at the airport in Seattle. Laura had been right about him—he did own a BMW. They had driven north of the city to the ferry terminal that served the San Juan Islands. The ferry had taken them to one of the larger, more populated islands, and from there Doug had driven them to a marina where he kept a launch.

"The island Uncle Digby built his villa on is too small and isolated to be serviced by the ferry system," Warwick had explained as he'd helped his guests into the boat. "He came over to this island to do his shopping and pick up supplies."

"Does anyone else live on Hazelhurst's island?" Verity had asked as she hobbled carefully into the boat, using Jonas's arm for support. Her ankle was still sore.

"Just Maggie Frampton, Uncle Digby's housekeeper. I was sure she'd give her notice after my uncle died. His death really shook her up. I gather the two of them had a thing going. I can't imagine why she would want to stay all alone in that pile of stone, but she seems content. She's free to use the launch whenever she wants to shop or visit her sister in Portland."

The island was tiny, just an oversized piece of rock covered by a thick forest of pine and fir. The stark, gloomy atmosphere was embellished by the gray skies and chill, damp breeze. Jonas had been right when he'd warned her this wasn't going to be like Hawaii, Verity thought wryly.

The small cove below the villa had a floating dock. Verity steadied herself as Doug cut the engine. Jonas leaped lightly up onto the dock and grabbed the lines Doug tossed to him. Then he reached down to help Verity out of the boat.

"With any luck, your room will be ready. Maggie's a good-hearted soul, but she's sometimes a little disorganized. She's not used to having a houseful of strangers," Doug explained as he collected the luggage from the back of the launch. "Uncle Digby rarely entertained, mostly because he only wanted the company of other scholars—and toward the end they all shunned him."

The villa's entrance was set deep inside a massive arch. The huge wooden door swung open with a protesting squeak just as Doug reached it. Elyssa Warwick stood inside, covered from throat to toe in a flowing white dress that emphasized her voluptuous curves. Her smile of welcome was, as usual, serenely glowing. Verity wondered how anyone could radiate so much goodness and light without using an electrical outlet.

"You made it," Elyssa exclaimed, as if there had been some doubt. Her gaze settled on Jonas. "I was getting worried. Preston had a vision of the plane being late. Was it?"

"A few minutes," Verity admitted. "There was a slight delay on the runway."

"I knew it," Elyssa said triumphantly. "Preston is almost never wrong. His visions are so clear."

"I hate to break this to you, Elyssa," Jonas remarked, "but most planes run late these days. It doesn't take any psychic talent to predict that one particular flight might be delayed."

"You haven't met Preston yet. When you do you'll see that he's right nearly all the time." Elyssa did not seem the least bit disturbed by Jonas's disbelief. "Do come in. Everyone else is already here. Maggie's got your room ready."

Verity realized that she was beginning to have a few problems with Elyssa Warwick. There was something about the way the other woman watched Jonas that was starting to bother her. Verity had the distinct impression that Elyssa hadn't believed Jonas when he'd told her he had no psychic ability. In any event, there was no doubt that the woman found Jonas fascinating.

"This is Maggie Frampton." Elyssa turned to introduce a stout woman with a riot of frazzled gray curls, standing in the hall behind her. "We're all totally dependent on her. She's the only one who knows how to keep the electricity and plumbing working in this wing. Doug's buyers are going to have to spend a fortune bringing the villa up to date. Maggie, would you please show Verity and Jonas to their room upstairs?" Elyssa glanced at Jonas again. "When you've had a chance to freshen up, please join us downstairs. I want to introduce you to my friends before dinner."

Jonas nodded, eyeing the stone staircase in front of him. He picked up his duffel bag and Verity's small suitcase. Then he gave Maggie Frampton one of his easy grins. "Lead the way, Miss Frampton."

The older woman nodded once and turned toward the stairs. Maggie had a grandmotherly figure, Verity thought, the sort of shape people used to label "buxom." Her faded blue eyes held a shrewd, knowing expression. She was wearing a flower-spattered housedress that appeared to date from the 1950s, and a thin metal chain around her neck disappeared beneath the collar.

"Right this way." Maggie moved heavily up the wide staircase. "Got a nice room for you, it overlooks the garden. Course, that ain't no big deal. Every room in the whole damn place overlooks the garden. Digby always said those old Renaissance types couldn't trust anyone but family, and that's why they built their houses the way they did.

Lots of stone walls on the outside to keep the neighbors from breaking in, and plenty of room inside to enjoy the gardens and privacy. But I expect a few of 'em learned you can't always trust family, either."

Jonas smiled. "A few of them sure as hell did learn that, Maggie. Family can be treacherous."

Maggie paused, one hand on the stone banister. She cocked a brow as she glanced back over her plump shoulder. "Is it true what Little Miss Sunshine down there says? You some kinda weirdo psychic?"

"No, ma'am," Jonas said blandly. "I am definitely not some kinda weirdo psychic."

"Good. We got enough nuts in this place right now as it is, don't need another one running around. Taking orders from Little Miss Sunshine is bad enough. Don't know what Digby woulda thought of all this, just don't know."

"Little Miss Sunshine?" Verity repeated curiously.

"The Warwick girl. I call her Little Miss Sunshine 'cause she's always smiling and saying how the whole universe is workin' together just to make her life perfect. That kind of cheerfulness just ain't natural, if you ask me. Course, I don't hold much with this hocus-pocus malarkey or the kind of folks who get involved with it. Ain't nothing new about it anyway. We had the same type of kook around when I was a kid, but at least most of 'em had the decency to work in a circus or at the county fair."

"I'm with you, Maggie," Jonas said. "What did Digby Hazelhurst think about all this psychic stuff?"

Maggie resumed climbing the staircase. "Old Digby was just fine up until about two years before he died. Then he started turnin' a mite weird, I'll grant you that much. But the man was in his eighties. Had a right to be a bit touched, I say. Besides, it didn't affect us one way or the other."

"Us?" Verity asked quickly.

"Him and me," Maggie explained with a wistful chuckle. "Digby and me used to have some good times together. We spent more years than I want to count stuck here on this island with only each other for company, and we weren't neither one of us bored. I'll tell you, when it came to certain types of activity, that old man had the energy of a high school senior in the backseat of a car. Had us some rare old times down in the torture chamber. My, my, yes, we did." Maggie reached the top of the staircase and trudged down a dim corridor.

Verity shot a highly amused glance at Jonas, who leered back comically.

Maggie opened the heavy wooden door of a room halfway down the corridor, revealing a large suite with huge, arched windows. A wide, canopied bed occupied the center of the room. The cold stone walls were hung with a faded tapestry and a couple of grime-encrusted paintings. The stone floor was bare.

"This do for ya?" Maggie asked expectantly. " 'Fraid it's the best I've got to offer. Used to have a lot of nice furniture in most of the rooms in this wing, but Digby had to sell the stuff off to keep going. Bathroom's off to the right there. At least old Digby had the sense to put in plumbing when he inherited the villa. I wouldn't have stayed with him all those years if I'd had to use a chamber pot, I can tell you."

"This is fine," Verity said. The end of her cane rang loudly on the stone floor as she walked to one of the windows. She leaned out, expecting a view of lush gardens.

What she saw was a large courtyard overgrown with weeds. There was a fountain in the center, but no water poured from the jug held by the naked nymph carved on top of the circular monstrosity. Dead pine needles and dirt littered the empty pool.

"See you folks later. Holler if you need anything," Maggie said, closing the door behind her.

Verity turned from the window to watch Jonas prowl the room. "Everything okay?" she asked softly, although she was almost certain it was. She would know if any strong force in the room was affecting him.

"Yeah." Jonas paused beside the threadbare tapestry and studied it without touching it. It was just barely possible to make out a scene of Renaissance maidens cavorting in a leafy bower. "Everything's fine. The bed's new, incidentally."

Verity glanced at the big bed. "Just as well. I wasn't looking forward to sleeping in a four-hundred-year-old bed."

"The tapestry's sixteenth-century, though. Can you believe it? It's just been hanging here, decaying all these years." Jonas shook his head and wandered over to one of the ornately framed pictures. "Same with the paintings."

Verity caught her breath. "They're originals?"

He nodded. "This one is. It would be interesting to see what's under all that grime. I have a hunch that the artist was just as second-rate as the architect who designed the villa."

Verity leaned back against the wide window ledge, folded her arms, and eyed Jonas closely. "You're not going to have any trouble sleeping here?"

"No. I'm fine, Verity. Everything's under control. I can sense a few faint vibrations, but unless I deliberately open up to them, they won't bother me. What a relief."

"That's one of the reasons you took this job, isn't it?" Verity asked suddenly. "You wanted to see how much control you've really gained over the past few months."

Jonas glanced at her as he walked across the room to open his duffel bag. "I'm a lot stronger now, Verity. I'm in control. You don't know how good it feels. And I owe it all to you. Just being around you seems to have strengthened my power to keep from being swept into that time tunnel. I couldn't have slept inside a genuine Renaissance villa before I met you. The vibrations locked in the walls alone would have overwhelmed me. Christ, it feels good to be able to manage this damn talent of mine."

"You're determined not to admit to Little Miss Sunshine and her pals that you're a genuine grade-A psychic?"

"I am not a psychic," Jonas stated forcefully. "I have a talent for psychometry, but I'm not clairvoyant. I don't have visions. I don't see the future or predict disasters. The only thing I can do is pick up certain scenes from the past."

"Scenes of violence."

"A very limited talent," Jonas pointed out dryly. "I'm sure as hell no psychic. And I would appreciate it if you would refrain from implying otherwise to Elyssa and her friends."

Verity grinned. "I don't know, Jonas. There might be more money in this consulting business if we let people know that you have a genuine talent."

"Not a chance. Normal, rational people wouldn't believe in my abilities and they damn well wouldn't want to pay for my services. Only eccentric weirdos would be willing to pay the consulting fees of someone claiming to have a psychic talent. Doug Warwick hired me as a Renaissance scholar, not a New Age nut."

"And instead he's getting both," Verity murmured happily.

Jonas scowled. "There's nothing New Age about me or my talent."

"I know," Verity agreed readily. Her momentary amusement faded. "There are a lot of things about you that aren't even twentieth-century. Sometimes I think you would have done very well back in the Renaissance, Jonas."

He moved across the room with that peculiar, gliding

grace that came so naturally to him, and tipped up her chin with one hard finger. "You think so?"

"I know so."

"They had ways of handling troublesome females back then."

"Is that right?" She grinned. "You'll have to demonstrate sometime. Meanwhile, we'd better get dressed for dinner." She moved away from him. "I hope you packed that nice sweater I gave you for Christmas."

"You know it's packed. You put it in my bag yourself."

"So I did."

"Very wifely of you to remember my sweater," he observed softly.

Verity flinched and began to unpack busily. "Packing your sweater wasn't a wifely act. It was the act of a shrewd business manager who wants you properly dressed for the client."

"I see." He watched her closely for a long moment, then silently started to undress.

Elyssa and Doug were waiting for them downstairs in a grand salon that ran most of the length of the old villa's south wing. Most of the room was in shadow, the old furniture covered in sheets. Only a small section at the far end of the salon, near the deep fireplace, had been made reasonably comfortable. Several people were seated on the worn furniture, chatting quietly. A fire blazed on the old hearth.

"Come in, we've been waiting for you. I want you to meet everyone." Elyssa swept forward, her jewelry jangling and her long white skirt swirling. She took Jonas's arm and guided him toward the small group.

Verity made a face behind her lover's back and limped bravely forward on her own. A young, thin, bearded man wearing round, wire-rimmed glasses rose and came toward her. He had very dark, serious eyes.

"Hello," he said in a low voice as he took her arm. "I'm Oliver Crump. Let me give you a hand."

"Thank you." Verity beamed at him, aware that Jonas had glanced back just in time to catch her dazzling smile. His disapproving look encouraged her to turn up the smile a few more watts. He deserved it for letting himself be swept off by Elyssa. "Verity Ames. I'm Jonas's business manager."

"Oliver is a healer," Elyssa explained brightly. "Aren't you, Oliver?"

"I work a little with herbs and crystals, that's about all," Oliver Crump said quietly. His brows came together in a fierce line as he looked down at Verity's injured foot. "What did you do to your ankle?"

"Slipped on an icy deck."

"How many days ago?"

"A couple." She looked down. "The swelling has started to go down but it's still sore."

Crump helped her into a heavy wooden chair with a threadbare green velvet cushion. The thick arms and legs of the chair were ornately carved. Verity leaned back experimentally, wondering how old it was. Late nineteenth century, she guessed—certainly not Renaissance.

"Let me introduce the people with whom I share the paths to enlightenment," Elyssa said. She stood gripping Jonas's arm as she waved at the small circle of faces. "Oliver Crump, as I just mentioned, is a psychic healer. And that's Preston Yarwood over there by the liquor cabinet. Preston is the leader of our little group. He's a marvelous teacher, so inspirational. He's been interested in psychic studies for years, long before it became so popular. He studied with Ilhela Yonanda, you know."

"Is that right?" Verity said, wondering who Ilhela Yonanda was.

"How do you do?" Yarwood spoke from the dark corner near the fireplace, where he was pouring drinks. "Understand your plane was a little late." He sounded vaguely satisfied about that.

When Yarwood stepped forward to nod at Verity and shake Jonas's hand, the firelight gleamed on the scalp showing through his thinning hair. He appeared to be in his midforties, a short, dynamic-looking man with a rather florid face and a slight paunch. His gaze was intelligent and observant. He had the serene, blissful smile Verity was coming to think of as the New Age look.

Yarwood wore a tastefully expensive plum-colored sweater. His well-cut wool trousers had pleats, and Verity was willing to bet that his loafers were Italian. There was a heavy gold watch on his wrist, the face of which was solid black. Verity was impressed. Running psychic-development seminars was obviously lucrative, as Doug had remarked.

"What can I get you, Verity?" Yarwood asked politely.

"Fruit juice would be fine."

"I had a feeling you would drink juice," Preston murmured softly, as if another prediction had just been verified. "And you, Jonas?"

"Scotch if you've got it." Jonas took the seat next to Elyssa.

"And this," Elyssa went on smoothly, indicating another young man slouched in a corner of the sofa, "is Slade Spencer. Slade is a new member of our circle, although he's been studying various paths on his own for years, haven't you, Slade?"

"Yeah, that's me. Always on the road to enlightenment."

Slade Spencer concentrated for a moment on packing a fragrant-smelling pipe. His hands appeared to tremble slightly.

The small task accomplished, he stretched out his long, jean-covered legs. Slade seemed to be in his late twenties or early thirties, but Verity couldn't tell for sure.

He ignored Jonas and smiled slowly at Verity as he reached for a glass on the table beside him. Spencer's face had a pinched, ascetic look, and his eyes were feverishly bright beneath his dark brows. He was so thin that he appeared almost gaunt. There was a sense of nervous energy about the man, as if some part of him was always in motion or, Verity realized with sudden intuition, always struggling to maintain control.

"I admit I've been attracted to the concept of an altered state of consciousness for some time now," Slade said, enunciating carefully, as if he didn't quite trust his tongue not to trip him up. "I have this theory that most of us are living in a very unnatural state of consciousness, and that the normal, natural state for human beings is actually what's usually referred to as an altered state. I see the true natural state as a deeply sensual one. A state in which we use all our senses to learn the true meaning of pleasure and personal satisfaction. What do you think? Are you headed in the same direction, Verity?"

Verity blinked. She realized that Slade Spencer had been hitting the booze rather heavily for the past couple of hours. "Actually, I'm into cooking," she said. She glanced around the room and saw the blank expressions. "Vegetarian cooking," she added quickly, hoping that would buy her some credibility.

Oliver Crump, who had been staring into the fire, looked over at her with sudden interest. "We'll have to compare recipes," he said with a slight smile.

"Verity runs a gourmet vegetarian cafe in Sequence Springs," Elyssa said helpfully. "Positively wonderful food, so wholesome. I've tried to explain to Maggie that we would all prefer vegetarian food while we're here at the villa, but I'm afraid she's a little set in her ways. I'm not sure what we'll get for dinner."

"I believe that cooking," Slade Spencer intoned as he fixed Verity with a deep, meaningful gaze, "is the most sensual of all the creative arts. Its appeal is fundamental and basic, isn't it? It provides stimulation to the senses, and satisfies us in ways that are almost sexual. Don't you agree, Verity?"

"I hadn't thought of cooking as sexy," Verity began slowly. Before she could finish the comment there was a loud crack of glass against wood. Verity turned to see Jonas release his glass and give Spencer a cold look.

"If you want to screw a rutabaga, that's your choice, Spencer. But don't try anything kinky with Verity's vegetable stew or oatmeal muffins. Understood?"

There was a titter of nervous laughter from around the room. The warning had certainly not been subtle. Spencer just shrugged, sinking deeper into his chair and concentrating on his drink and his pipe.

Doug Warwick frowned and took control of the conversation. Ice tinkled in his glass as he looked at Jonas. "How do you plan to approach this job, Quarrel?"

Jonas took a sip of scotch. "The first step will be to go through each of the wings and verify age and authenticity. It's largely a matter of making sure I'm working with the original structure, and not being misled by sections added on at a later date. Digby's relative might have imported part of a villa and had the rest designed and built to match. It's not an uncommon practice."

Doug nodded. "I see. I hadn't thought of that."

Jonas picked up his glass. "Once I've given the place a thorough walk-through, I'll get down to details. Fifteenth- and sixteenth-century architects were fairly predictable. Even the uninspired ones were very fond of mathematical symmetry, for example." He then launched into an impressive discussion of Renaissance laws of perspective and how they had influenced architecture.

Everyone in the room nodded wisely. Verity hid a smile behind her glass. Jonas had not spent all those years on campus for nothing—he could shoot the academic bull with the best of them. From across the room he saw her smile, and laughter danced in his eyes.

The shared joke made her realize something important. Somewhere along the line they had become a couple. They were at the point where they could exchange silent laughter in a room full of people. She shared ties with Jonas that had nothing to do with their psychic connection.

The knowledge warmed her. She took another sip of fruit juice and mentally added another day to the monthly calendar in her mind. There was still no indication that she might only be irregular. This was beginning to look like the real thing. The realization made her feel strange. She was heading inexorably toward a major turning point in her life, one for which she had never prepared herself.

The evening meal was composed mainly of mashed potatoes and carrots. Maggie Frampton had done her best to accommodate the preferences of the Warwicks' guests, but it was obvious that she was not accustomed to cooking meatless meals.

"A good hamburger never hurt no one," she muttered as she cleared away the last of the dishes. "What do you folks do for protein?"

Verity found herself seated between Oliver Crump and Slade Spencer during dinner. Slade was rather boring. He was obviously quite drunk, and his conversation consisted of a long monologue on the innate sexuality of the spheres.

Oliver Crump was another matter. He said little, his eyes

introspective behind the round frames of his glasses. But when Verity drew him out with a discussion of cooking and medicinal herbs, he proved very knowledgeable.

On the opposite side of the long table Jonas was seated between Preston Yarwood and Elyssa. The two of them kept him occupied all evening. Every time Verity glanced over she was partially blinded by Elyssa's gleaming rings and exotic bracelets.

Elyssa did not announce her surprise entertainment for the evening until after dinner.

"Now, then," she said as she led the group back into the salon. "I hope you're all in the mood for a special treat. Preston has offered to guide us in a psychic-clarity session. We thought it would be a wonderful way to help Jonas begin his search for the treasure."

Doug groaned. "Sorry, Jonas. I didn't know they were going to pull this. Feel free to opt out."

"What the hell's a psychic-clarity session?" Jonas asked warily.

"A session in which we all try to unite our individual energies into a single force that is capable of lifting all of us onto a higher plane. Once we are on that higher level we can communicate far more clearly and intuitively. It's very effective for relaxing and opening up the mind. I'm sure you'll find it helpful."

"Sounds like bullshit to me," Jonas said politely.

Verity groaned and poked Jonas in the ribs with the handle of her cane. "This is business, Jonas," she muttered. "Behave yourself."

Jonas massaged his ribs and smiled dangerously at her for a second. "I'll tell you what. You folks go ahead with your session while I have a look around the villa."

"Oh, you really must join us, Jonas." Elyssa's eyes were beseeching. "The sessions are so stimulating. Sometimes

I'm able to contact Saranantha. I'm becoming a channeler for her, you know," she added modestly. "I've just started picking up on her recently, but I'm getting better at communicating with her."

Verity heard Slade Spencer snicker faintly, and she knew that Jonas was having a hard time keeping his mouth shut. It was time for another shot of diplomacy.

"I didn't know you were a channeler," Verity said quickly. "Who is Saranantha?"

It was Preston Yarwood who answered the question. He gazed fondly at Elyssa. "Saranantha appears to be a high-ranking temple priestess from a land called Utilan. From what we can tell so far, Utilan may have been a lost colony of Atlantis. Elyssa has only recently established contact, so we still have much to learn."

Doug waved Jonas toward the hall. "I don't blame you one bit for wanting out of this nonsense. Go have a look around. We'll play Elyssa's little parlor game here while you're out getting your bearings. Watch your step, and stay in the south wing until tomorrow. I think I mentioned that the other three wings were never wired for electricity. You start wandering around in there and you might never come back out." Doug laughed.

Jonas nodded and took Verity aside. "You stay with the group," he said in a low voice. "I want to check out a few things I read about in the diary, and I don't want any of these turkeys around when I do it."

Verity was startled. "Is this something that might take you into the time corridor? You can't risk that alone. You'll need me."

"Relax. I'm not stupid. I won't risk anything like that alone. I just want to look around."

"Be careful," she whispered anxiously.

He grinned. "You're the one who'd better be careful.

Getting elevated to a higher plane of consciousness sounds like dangerous business."

"I don't believe this," Verity muttered. "The only person in the whole group who's actually got some real psychic ability and he's not interested in participating in a genuine psychic-clarity session. Spoilsport."

"I played enough psychic games back in the lab of the Department of Paranormal Research at Vincent College," Jonas said grimly. "I don't like them." He dropped a small kiss on Verity's forehead. "Besides, what makes you think there's only one person with genuine psychic talent here?"

Verity's eyes widened. "You think one of the others in there has real talent?"

He ruffled her coppery curls with an affectionate hand. "I was talking about you, you little idiot. I don't make those trips into the time tunnel alone. Have fun. I'll see you later."

Verity stared after him for a long moment before she walked slowly back into the salon. It was strange, but she'd never thought of herself as having any psychic ability. As far as she was concerned, the talent belonged to Jonas. She just sort of helped him control it.

Chapter Five

JONAS walked through the halls of the old villa, flashlight in hand, savoring the freedom of control. Before he had found Verity he would never have been able to take the risk of immersing himself in this four-hundred-year-old mountain of stone. There would have been a threat lying in wait around every corner. Any Renaissance building of this size was all too likely to be imbued with vibrations of ancient bloodshed and murder. Jonas Quarrel was attuned to suggestions of violence, especially violence that took place during the Renaissance.

It would have been far too easy to accidentally step into a room where a man had died on the point of a stiletto, or to pick up a rusty scrap of metal that had once been part of a sword. Such a mistake could have sent him headlong into the psychic tunnel where violent vignettes from the past replayed themselves endlessly, and where the lethal emotional energy that had infused those deadly scenes sought a path to the future through Jonas.

Jonas studied the stone walls around him as he browsed through the dimly lit second floor of the south wing. Hazelhurst had obviously not wanted to spend much money wiring the place. Jonas didn't want to think about the quality of the limited electrical work that had been done.

He concentrated for a few minutes. The faint vibrations he picked up here and there were very subdued, just enough to assure him that the place was genuine. He pulled the diary from his pocket as he turned the corner into the east wing. There was no electricity in this section. He switched on the flashlight.

Most of the doors along the passageway were closed. From the amount of dust on the floor Jonas judged that Maggie Frampton had given up on this wing long ago. He doubted if the west and north wings were in any better shape.

Jonas moved through the dingy hall, turned another corner, and found himself in more darkness. Doug Warwick was right. A man could wander around in here for quite a while. According to Digby Hazelhurst's lousy Latin, the room where he had discovered the crystal was in this passage.

Jonas found the room without too much trouble. It was in the center of the north-wing corridor and had a series of arched windows framing the dark courtyard. When Jonas looked out across the overgrown garden he could see the light he had left on in the bedroom he was sharing with Verity.

He turned back to the small room and swung the flashlight around from wall to wall. The place was bare. No frayed tapestries or rotting furniture, just plain stone walls and floor.

Jonas flipped open the diary to the page detailing the

discovery of the crystal. His Latin was rusty, but he had been able to decipher most of Hazelhurst's scrawl.

> South wall. Third stone up from the floor, two over from the left-hand corner. Press firmly on the right portion of the stone. Watch out for the blade. I'm sure the poison tip has long since become ineffective, but the edge is still quite sharp. I was only saved when I first discovered the crystal because the mechanism that triggered the trap was rusted. The design of the trap is quite fascinating. I have since oiled it, of course. Pity not to restore it as far as possible.

"Thanks, Digby, old pal. Why in hell did you have to oil the sucker?"

Jonas hunkered down in front of the designated part of the wall and studied the stonework intently. Digby did not say which stone concealed the booby trap. The hidden blade could snap out from the wall or the floor—or from the ceiling. Jonas glanced up and dismissed that possibility. It was too unlikely.

He tried to envision the kind of trap he might have set had he been hiding a crystal four hundred years ago.

A man attempting to open a secret hiding place in the floor would be crouching as Jonas was. Jonas trailed his fingertips cautiously along the stone.

Something shimmered in his mind and reality started to bend and stretch into an endless tunnel. Jonas jerked his fingers away from the stone that had caused the sudden reaction.

He didn't dare step into the psychic corridor without Verity nearby—she was his anchor. But just the intimation of ancient violence was enough to warn him that the trap had been sprung once before—by someone who had not been as lucky as Digby Hazelhurst. A long time ago some benighted soul had died in this room while searching for the crystal.

Died clutching his balls in agony.

Jonas sucked in his breath and stood up quickly. He moved back, away from the part of the floor that was sending out the dangerous vibrations. He'd learned enough. The thought of the deadly blade springing from the floor and stabbing him between the legs was enough to make him even more careful. He got to his feet and prowled the room, looking for something he could use to trigger the trap. He then went back out into the hall and opened a few other doors in the corridor.

When Jonas stepped into the third room down he hit pay dirt. At some point during the past few years Maggie Frampton had obviously tried to keep this wing clean. A long-handled broom stood forlornly in one corner as evidence.

Jonas picked it up and returned to the room that had contained the crystal. He stretched the handle of the broom out in front of him cautiously, applying pressure to the stone indicated in the diary.

With an almost silent hiss a sinister blade shot from between two floor stones. If he had been crouching where he'd been earlier, he would now have been a candidate for a boys' chorus, Jonas realized. He wiped sweat from his forehead.

He waited a moment and then stepped cautiously around the quivering blade to examine the hollow stone behind it. The surface of the stone had slid back, revealing an empty interior. Jonas leaned down to probe the inside.

He knew instantly that the move was a mistake—a bad one.

A violent wave of emotion roared through him and the walls of the psychic corridor began to take shape. Jonas fought to keep himself from being sucked into the time tunnel. An overwhelming sense of foreboding nearly drowned him as he struggled to fight the inexorable pull of violence long past.

Death awaited him. Death awaited anyone who dared to use the crystal.

"Verity. *Verity!*"

Jonas did not know if he screamed the words aloud or silently in his mind. Sweat was pouring from him as he gathered every ounce of his willpower and yanked his hand back out of the hollow stone.

"Jonas?"

He felt her there with him. It wasn't possible, he told himself, dazed. She was downstairs in another part of the villa. She wasn't close enough to help him.

"Jonas? What's wrong?"

Verity was reaching for him. He couldn't see her, but he could feel her presence, an anchor in the storm. Jonas squeezed his eyes shut and rolled clear of the section of floor that contained the trap and the hollow stone.

Suddenly his vision cleared and everything returned to normal. The images of violent brutality and death disappeared as quickly as they'd appeared.

The blade slid back into the floor and the opening in the stone vanished without a trace.

Jonas lay on the floor breathing heavily. He stared at the corner of the room where death awaited the unwary. He knew then that the real danger surrounding the missing crystal was not the blade hidden between the stones. Whatever the crystal was, whatever function it performed, it was evil. The knowledge sent a savage shudder of excitement through him. He was on the trail of something very big.

For Jonas, the treasure hunt had just superseded the consulting work he was here to do. There were secrets hidden in this old villa. Important secrets. He had to discover them.

Jonas rose slowly to his feet. He picked up the flashlight and edged out of the room, keeping his eyes on the dangerous stone until he was safely out in the hall. Then he firmly closed the door.

It seemed to Jonas that he could hear laughter in his mind as he made his way back to the south wing of the villa. He thought at first that it was his imagination producing echoes of Digby Hazelhurst's amusement. Then he realized that the laughter was much older. About four hundred years old, to be exact.

Jonas is all right. Verity felt reality slide gently back into place. Her pulse was still racing, and she felt lightheaded. She wished Slade Spencer weren't holding her right hand so tightly. On the other side of her Doug Warwick had his fingers laced lightly between hers. She felt trapped.

She opened her eyes and glanced around at the intent faces of the the small circle of would-be psychics. Doug Warwick was staring over his sister's shoulder into the fire. He looked bored. Oliver Crump had his eyes closed. He seemed to be concentrating intently, as did Elyssa and Preston Yarwood. Elyssa had a dreamy expression on her face, as if she was seeing an inner vision. Preston was frowning.

Slade Spencer kept squeezing Verity's fingers spasmodically. He had put aside his pipe and an afterdinner drink in order to join the circle. Sensing Verity's glance, he opened one eye and winked solemnly, squeezing her fingers until she thought they might break.

Verity pulled her hand free from Slade's and released herself from Doug's loose grip. Doug glanced at her with an inquiring smile.

"Bored already?"

"I . . . I have to go to my room," Verity whispered uneasily.

"I don't blame you for wanting out of this," Doug murmured. "Go on, you're excused."

Slade nodded at her as she edged free of the circle. His eyes were hooded and heavy with alcohol. "Night, Verity. See you in the morning," he muttered. Crump, Elyssa, and Yarwood appeared not to notice Verity's departure. They obviously had their minds on higher matters.

Verity slipped out of the salon. She paused outside in the chilly hall, letting her breathing return to normal. The sense of danger was gone, but she wouldn't be able to relax until she saw Jonas and found out what had happened.

Every time before, she had been drawn into the psychic corridor with him only when they were physically close. The link between them didn't hold beyond a distance of a few feet. Yet, she could have sworn that for a moment she had experienced the familiar feeling of stepping into the time corridor with Jonas.

She hurried painfully up the stone staircase to the bedroom she and Jonas had been assigned. She flung open the door hoping to find him inside but the room was empty.

"Dammit, Jonas," she grumbled aloud, "where are you?"

He could be anywhere in the huge villa. It was useless to start prowling the halls for him. She would just have to wait until he returned. Verity wandered into the bathroom to start getting ready for bed. She had a long list of questions she planned to fire at Jonas when he finally showed up.

But it wasn't Jonas who was waiting for her when she emerged from the bathroom wearing her flannel nightgown.

"Slade!" Verity stopped abruptly. Spencer was sitting on the edge of the bed, and he looked drunker than ever.

"Don't worry, Verity," he said in a slurred voice. "Got

the message. I ditched that dumb psychic circle right after you did. Told everyone I was feeling a little sick. Which I was when I thought of Elyssa going into her channeling routine. Got up here as fast as I could. Any idea how long your friend Jonas will be gone? Maybe we oughta go to my room."

"What in the world do you think you're doing here? Are you out of your mind?" Verity grabbed her robe and belted it around her waist. She was furious, but she realized that Spencer was too far gone to notice. "You're drunk, Slade. Or maybe not just drunk—that pipe of yours smells a little funny. Get out of here now!"

He looked bewildered and a bit hurt. He blinked his hooded, sleepy eyes in an attempt to focus on her face. "But you want me here. You invited me up here," he whined.

"I did not invite you up here, and if you were sober, you'd know that. Now leave. Immediately."

"Are you just upset 'cause I've had a coupla drinks? Hey, no problem, honey. I'm ready, willing, and able. You'll see. Can't keep a good man down, you know." He grinned stupidly and started to unbutton his shirt. "Might be safer if we went to my room, though. Don't think I want Quarrel walkin' in on us, know what I mean?"

"Get out of here!" Verity demanded furiously.

Slade leered at her. "Hey, maybe we got no problem. Maybe Quarrel's hoppin' into the sack with Elyssa even as we speak. Is that the way it is? You two have an understanding? Elyssa's convinced the guy's some kinda psychic, you know. She likes to sleep with psychics. She and Yarwood get it on all the time. She even made it with me a time or two. She's one hot ticket waiting to get punched." Slade frowned. "Think she tried it with Crump but he wasn't interested. Crump's not interested in anything except his damn herbs and crystals."

Verity was getting angrier by the minute. Slade looked too drunk to be physically dangerous, but she wasn't having any luck in getting him to leave. He was right about one thing: the thought of Jonas walking in on this little scene was not a comforting one. The memory of him holding the knife at Doug Warwick's throat was still fresh. Verity decided to take action.

She walked firmly across the room and took hold of Slade's sleeve. She used all her strength to pull him to his feet.

"Out," she said crisply. "Right now."

Slade staggered and looped an arm around her shoulders to brace himself. He smiled broadly and leaned against her, trying to plant a wet kiss on her mouth.

Verity ducked and dragged him toward the door, her nose wrinkling at the overpowering odor of liquor on his breath.

"Want to go to my room, huh? Okay by me. We're on our way." Slade then lost his balance and started to collapse.

It was like having a huge, limp puppet fall on her. Verity's weak ankle gave way painfully and she crumpled to her knees, and Slade's loose-limbed body sprawled over her. He scrabbled uselessly to find his feet, and the two of them wound up in a heap on the floor just as the door swung open.

Jonas launched himself through the doorway without a word. He grabbed Slade, yanked him off Verity, and hurled the younger man up against the tapestry-covered wall.

Spencer hit the wall with an audible thud, and the breath rushed out of him. He groaned and slumped to the floor, almost unconscious.

Verity looked up at Jonas as he headed toward his victim. She recognized the glitter in his eye.

"Jonas, no! He's just drunk and acting stupid." She scrambled awkwardly to her feet, gasping at the pain in her ankle.

"Stupid is right," Jonas said in his softest, most dangerous voice. He hauled the groggy Spencer to his feet and drew back his fist.

"Hey, wait a second, man." Spencer came to his senses long enough to hold up a weak hand. "Didn't mean anything. Just havin' a little fun."

"Live and learn, Spencer. This is the kind of fun that can get you killed. You should have stuck to rutabagas. Verity is off limits."

"No, no, it's all just a misunderstanding," Slade protested desperately. "Thought she wanted it. Thought all the chicks into this psychic stuff liked it. Hell, Elyssa sleeps with everyone."

"You're right about one thing," Jonas said. "There's been a misunderstanding. Verity sleeps with no one but me." His fist cracked against Spencer's jaw. The man's head wobbled, and Jonas prepared to hit him again.

"Oh no, Jonas!" Verity wailed. She leaped forward to grab his arm. "Stop it. There's no need for violence. Stop it right now!"

Jonas shook her off, his golden eyes gleaming with fire. Verity staggered back against the tapestry, unable to find her balance with her weak ankle. She started to fall and automatically grabbed at the tapestry.

"Verity!" Jonas let go of Spencer and caught her. He planted a hand on the tapestry, bracing himself and Verity against the wall.

As soon as Jonas touched the tapestry Verity felt strange vibrations ricochet from his mind to hers.

"What the hell?" Jonas yanked Verity away from the wall. "Jesus, that's all I need right now."

Verity relaxed slightly as the disturbing vibrations disappeared. Jonas glanced at the tapestry and back down at the man sprawled at his feet.

"I ought to kill him."

Verity sighed and brushed her hair out of her eyes. "He's drunk, Jonas. And Lord knows what he's been smoking all evening. Just get him back to his room so he can sleep it off. There was no harm done."

"The guy tries to rape you, and you say there was no harm done?"

"He didn't try to rape me. I was escorting him out of the room when he lost his balance and fell on top of me."

Jonas's eyes were savage. He stared at her for a long moment. Then he reached down to grab one of Spencer's ankles. "I'll be back in a few minutes." He dragged Slade Spencer out of the room as if the man were a sack of garbage.

Verity heaved a tortured sigh and sank down on the edge of the bed. Absently she touched her ankle and groaned when pain shot through it.

What a mess. Jonas was furious, Spencer had turned into a damned nuisance, and there was something very dangerous on the other side of that tapestry. At the moment she didn't know which problem was the worst.

Probably Jonas.

It was not going to be easy to pacify him; she had seen the fury in his eyes. Verity could only pray that he was not doing more bodily harm to Slade at that very moment. She didn't relish the idea of a lawsuit.

Jonas strode back into the room just as Verity was wondering how broad her insurance coverage was.

"What did you do with him?" she demanded.

"I dumped him in the courtyard fountain." He started to unbutton his flannel shirt.

''You did what?''

''You heard me. Take a look.'' He nodded toward the windows as he stalked into the bathroom.

''Oh, for heaven's sake, Jonas, you didn't really leave him there, did you?'' But she knew Jonas well enough by now to guess the truth. Verity gingerly made her way to the window and looked down into the gloomy courtyard. There was just enough light seeping from the windows in the south wing to show a dark form sprawled in the empty fountain. ''Jonas, I think it's starting to rain.''

''So what?'' He turned on the water in the old-fashioned bathroom sink.

''What do you mean, so what? You've left Slade out there and it's near freezing. Now it's raining. He's liable to catch pneumonia.''

''I don't give a damn what happens to him. With any luck he'll drown.'' Jonas came out of the bathroom drying his hands on a towel. His shirt hung open, revealing the dark hair on his chest. His Florentine gold eyes still glittered with masculine outrage. ''I've about had it, Verity. This is the second time in the past week I've walked in and found some man climbing all over you.''

''Now, Jonas, you're overstating the case and you know it.'' Verity tried to adopt a soothing tone. There were times when it didn't pay to go toe-to-toe with Jonas Quarrel. She clutched the lapels of her robe more tightly around her. ''Be reasonable. The first time doesn't count. Doug Warwick was just trying to be helpful, there was absolutely nothing else involved. And this time it was just a drunken fool making a pass. I'm sure Slade will be terribly embarrassed in the morning.''

''Terribly embarrassed, huh? I'll tell you something. He ought to be goddamned grateful he's not going to wake up with a broken neck.'' Jonas tossed the towel aside and came toward her. ''How the hell did he get in here, anyway?''

Verity stepped back and felt the window ledge cut into her back. She lifted her chin defiantly. ''The door was unlocked.''

''Why was the damn door unlocked?'' He reached her and his hands closed around her shoulders. He hauled her against him.

''I left it open for you. I thought you'd be along any minute.''

''I'm getting sick and tired of telling you to lock doors, Verity.''

''I hardly expected anyone but you to walk in,'' Verity retorted indignantly. ''Honestly, Jonas. We're guests here. How was I to know there would be any trouble?''

His hands tightened on her shoulders. ''I swear, one of these days, lady, you're going to go too far.''

She touched his wrists, her eyes searching his. ''Jonas, forget Slade. What happened to you tonight?''

He eyed her thoughtfully. ''I touched something I shouldn't have. A floor stone.''

''I felt you reaching for me. I was so worried. That's why I came back to the room early.''

''Next time lock the door, Verity.'' His mouth closed roughly over hers. ''I can't take seeing another man put his hands on you,'' he said against her lips. ''I just can't handle it.''

Verity gasped, aware of the violent rage still burning beneath the hot desire that gripped Jonas. His tongue thrust into her mouth, warning of the more intimate kind of possession that would soon follow. He pulled her more tightly against his body, as if he half-expected her to try to slip away from him.

''Jonas,'' she managed, ''we need to talk.''

"You talk too much," he muttered thickly. "I've decided it's one of your biggest problems." He then picked her up and carried her to the bed. He tossed her down onto the quilt and began unfastening his jeans.

Verity sat up, pushing her hair out of her eyes. "I'm serious, Jonas. Something happened tonight, didn't it? Something unusual, even for you. I want to know what's going on."

"I'll tell you what's going on. Every time I turn around these days you're sliding out of my reach. Don't think I haven't noticed, I'm not blind. I've seen that strange look in your eyes lately. I've seen the way you stop right in the middle of something and just stand there, staring off into the distance. I've felt you thinking your secret, private thoughts, Verity—thoughts you don't share with me."

"For heaven's sake, Jonas . . ."

"Then I come home from Mexico and find you've been hurt, and some other guy is carrying you through your front door—*our* front door. I walk into this room tonight, our bedroom, and discover that some jerk has felt free to invite himself in."

"Jonas, you're being irrational about this."

"Something's going on all right, Verity. You're starting to wonder if you made the right decision when you let me into your life, aren't you? You're starting to have second thoughts about us. But I've got news for you, little tyrant. It's too late. You belong to me, and I'm going to see to it that you never forget it." He stepped out of his boots and jeans and sat down heavily on the bed.

Verity backed across the quilt away from him. He reached out and caught her hand, checking her retreat.

"*Jonas*. Let me go."

He ignored her small cry of outrage as he rolled over to pin her beneath him. His eyes blazed. "I'm not going to let you get away from me, Verity. Don't you understand? I can't let you get away from me.''

''Jonas, please, we have to talk.''

''I've already told you, you talk too much.'' He started to peel off her robe. ''You're always using your mouth to communicate when you should be using something else. Something that's a lot more honest. Something I can understand.''

Thoroughly annoyed, Verity started to struggle. ''Dammit, Jonas, this is no way to communicate. Let me up! I want to talk to you. I mean it. Pay attention when I speak to you.''

But Jonas paid no attention. He yanked the robe free and anchored her wrists above her head so that she lay there helpless and inviting. Then he reached down and grabbed the hem of her flannel nightgown, pulling it up above her waist.

In spite of her determination to control the situation, Verity felt the excitement flaring in her. This was Jonas, who could set her on fire with just a touch. This was the man she loved with all her heart.

But he had a disconcerting habit of resorting to sex when he lost his patience. The typical male approach to a problem, she thought resentfully. When the brain ceases to function, fall back on the brawn.

Verity lost her temper. She twisted violently and kicked out at him with her good foot. ''Let me go, you big oaf.''

''Lie still, you loud-mouthed shrew.'' When she responded by kicking him again, he pinned her legs down with one of his own. ''Now I'm really getting irritated.'' He used his weight to hold her still while he wrestled the nightgown up over her head.

''Do you think I care if you're irritated?'' Her eyes sparkled with anger and hungry excitement.

''You better care.'' Once he had her nightgown off, he

used his free hand to reach over the edge of the bed and grab his belt.

Verity's eyes widened in disbelief. "You wouldn't dare."

"I've had it with your weird behavior lately," Jonas told her as he quickly captured both her wrists and bound them with the leather. He looped the free end of the belt around one of the canopy posts and inserted it back through the loop that held her wrists. She was chained to the bed.

"Jonas, you're fired!" It was the only threat she still had left. Verity struggled uselessly against the binding leather.

"You can't fire me and you know it. You already tried it once, and it didn't work." He watched her as she lay glowering helplessly up at him. "Listen to me, Verity, and listen good. If you're thinking of ending things between us, you've got a surprise coming. You can't get rid of me that easily."

"I don't have to work at getting rid of you. You take off all by yourself when the mood grabs you. Five days in Mexico without a phone call, Jonas. Five whole days."

"Christ, are you still holding that against me?" He scowled. "I thought we had that settled. I thought you understood."

"All I understand is that you feel free to take off whenever you want to, and you don't even bother to call."

"I told you, I couldn't get to a phone. And don't start trying to blame me for your spaced-out attitude lately. It started before I went to Mexico."

"Can you blame me if I need to think things over?" she retorted furiously. "This is a damn strange relationship we have, Jonas Quarrel." She tugged meaningfully on the leather belt. "Any woman in her right mind would want to think very seriously about what she was getting herself into by agreeing to live with you."

"I knew it. You *have* been thinking about us, haven't you? Plotting and scheming, I'll bet."

"So what if I have? That's a perfectly normal reaction under the circumstances, I'd say."

"Thinking is never normal for you. I don't trust the way your mind works," he muttered.

"Tough. It's my mind."

"Yeah? Well, here's something for your brain to think about." He shoved his knee between her legs, forcing her open for his touch. Then he reached down and put his palm against the vulnerable softness he had exposed.

"Jonas, you bastard." But she could already feel herself dampening his hand.

"Tell me you don't want me. Go ahead and tell me you're ready to ditch me." He kept his warm palm where it was, pushing gently at her.

Verity arched her hips instinctively, and Jonas eased his thumb into her wet channel. He probed her deeply, teasing her until the small, delicate muscles clenched around his finger. Verity gasped. "One of these days, Jonas. So help me, one of these days I'm going to . . ."

"I love you, Verity."

"You've got a funny way of showing it." She struggled helplessly against the leather strap. She felt his warm breath on her nipple and he sucked it gently into his mouth. Her body was flooded with hot, shivering anticipation.

"With you a man has to express himself in unusual ways."

He moved slowly down her body, tasting every inch of her as he went. Verity could feel the steel-hard shaft of his manhood thrusting eagerly against her thigh.

"Jonas, you can be so damn infuriating."

"Tell me you love me." He teased the small nub of

sensation hidden in the fiery curls below her stomach. "Say it, Verity."

"You know damn well I love you." She wriggled deliciously and opened her thighs a little wider.

"Say it."

"I love you. Now quit fooling around with the bondage-and-discipline bit and make love to me."

"I thought you'd never ask." Jonas settled himself between her legs.

"Get rid of the belt," Verity ordered, her voice husky with desire.

"Why? I kind of like you this way. Very sexy. Lift your hips higher. That's it." He knelt between her legs, parted her softness with his fingers, and pushed himself slowly, inevitably into her. When she tensed, he deliberately pushed harder. "Yeah, baby, that's exactly right." He leaned forward, bracing himself on his arms.

Verity moaned and closed her eyes as he filled her with his throbbing manhood. Her body was flooded with wave after wave of heat.

"Now move that beautiful tail, sweetheart. Come on, show me just how much you really love me."

"There must be a law against this sort of thing." Verity inhaled sharply as he squeezed her round derriere. Her pulse thrummed.

"You and I make up our own laws in bed. Move it, honey," he ordered again. This time his voice was low and infinitely sexy. He used his hand to guide her buttocks in a small circle. She responded at once.

"Jonas."

"That's it, love. Yeah, that's what I want. Jesus, sweetheart. So hot and tight. You make me crazy. See if you can take me a little deeper now. You can do it. I want to go as far as I can. Wrap your legs around me. Such beautiful, soft legs. Come on, honey, I want you to know I'm there."

"Ah, Jonas, *Jonas*."

"Damn, you feel good, honey."

He was stretching her, filling her completely, easing himself in and out slowly as she moved her hips in an increasingly frantic rhythm. She could feel the fire twisting inside her, waiting to explode.

When it did, he was caught up in it with her. His hoarse shout of satisfaction mingled with her small cries as together they gave themselves to the flames.

It was typical of Jonas to make love to her so outrageously, Verity thought fleetingly; typical of him to resort to this approach when he wanted to make a point; typical of him to overwhelm her with passion when she wanted to have a serious discussion about their relationship.

It was also very typical of him to have performed the whole scene while making absolutely certain he never once jolted her injured ankle.

Slade Spencer opened his eyes when the cold rain hit his face. He hurt all over. That goddamned bastard had had no right to hit him like that, no right at all. Spencer couldn't help it if women liked him. If Quarrel wanted to punish someone, he ought to beat his little flirt of a girlfriend. Verity had been coming on to Spencer all evening, he knew the signs. But, as usual, Slade had gotten the blame.

Quarrel was just like all the others, and Spencer was getting damned tired of being treated like dirt. One of these days he was going to show them all.

Groaning, he heaved himself up over the side of the empty fountain pool. He felt sick to his stomach. He waited a moment, breathing heavily while his insides settled. He was shaking.

He needed a pill—two. Unfortunately, the ones the doctors at the clinic had given him didn't seem to be doing much good anymore. But then, what did those stupid doctors know? No one understood him, Spencer realized. No one really wanted to help him. Everyone was against him. He'd come to realize that years ago.

He'd take a couple of those prescription pills when he got back to his room, but then he'd take a couple of the tabs he'd bought from his dealer last month. Those suckers really worked. When he was on them, he felt good. They made him feel in command of himself. It was good to feel in control.

Spencer climbed slowly out of the pool and trudged toward the villa's dark entrance. The rain beat down on him, and he asked himself for what seemed the thousandth time why everything he tried to do in life turned to shit.

It was a rhetorical question. Slade knew why everything always went wrong for him. Everyone was out to get him. It was him against the world.

And he always lost.

Chapter Six

"I just want you to know that one of these days, I'll get even." Verity stirred languidly, turning on her side and propping herself up on one elbow. She picked up the leather belt Jonas had used to bind her and trailed the buckle through the wiry hair on his chest. "You'll never know when it's coming. But someday, somewhere, when you least expect it, *zap!* You're gonna get it."

Jonas flashed a wicked, laughing grin. "Really getting into the leather-and-bondage bit, huh?" He took hold of the belt and tugged it free of her grasp. He then dropped it over the edge of the bed and it clunked on the floor.

Verity managed a reasonably severe glare. "No, I am not getting into leather and bondage. I was forced into it. You're the one who likes kinky sex. I used to be such a nice girl before I met you."

He put a hand behind her head and pulled her close for a quick, hard kiss. "Damn, but I love corrupting you," he said with great satisfaction. "You take to it so naturally. Ouch! Dammit," he added as Verity slapped his bare thigh.

Verity's hand stung from the blow, but she decided it was worth it. She sat up and crossed her legs. "Okay, Jonas, enough with the distracting fun and games. As usual, sex has made you relaxed and indulgent, so now I expect a few answers."

"Relaxed and indulgent. Is that what sex does for me?"

"Sure. Haven't you ever noticed? You come on like a lion, so to speak, and pull out like a lamb."

"A lamb?" He looked disappointed.

"Lamb, kitten, poodle, whatever." Verity waved her hand to indicate a whole world of limp, cuddly things that included the present state of his manhood.

"If I weren't feeling so relaxed and indulgent, I'd argue that point with you."

"Later, maybe. Right now I want some answers."

Jonas turned his head on the pillow, enjoying the direct view he had of her triangle of soft hair. "How can I concentrate hard enough to answer questions when all I can see is your pretty little . . ."

Verity pulled a sheet over her legs. "Talk about a one-track mind."

"You never want me to have any fun," he complained, his eyes bright with laughter.

"You're right. All fun and no work makes Jonas a very poor boy. Back to business. What happened tonight when you went gallivanting through the corridors of Hazelhurst's Horror?"

"You have no respect for four-hundred-year-old architecture?"

"Not when it looks like this place. Quit stalling and tell me what happened." Verity's eyes grew serious. "I got a scare tonight, Jonas. I could feel you coming very close to something dangerous."

"I know. I could feel you there with me."

"But where were you?"

"Clear over in the north wing. Second floor."

"But that's a long way from where I was. You were much too far away for us to connect."

He sat up against the pillows, his golden eyes becoming as serious as hers. "The link was weak but you were with me. Both of us felt it. I think the connection between us is growing stronger, Verity."

Verity tugged the sheet more closely around her, covering her breasts. She glanced distractedly toward the window. "It's chilly in here, isn't it? It must cost a fortune just to keep this wing heated. No wonder the Warwicks want to unload this place as soon as possible."

"It scares you, doesn't it?" Jonas asked quietly. "Is that why you've been acting so distant lately? You've sensed the link between us getting stronger, and you're not sure you want that?"

"I haven't been acting distant," Verity said forcefully. "I've just been doing some thinking, that's all. Now tell me exactly what happened this evening."

Jonas folded his hands behind his head and regarded her for a long moment. "I found the place where the crystal was hidden. The hiding place was empty, which was no surprise. But the booby trap that had been left to guard it still worked just fine."

"Oh, my God. What kind of booby trap?"

"A stiletto sunk between two stones in the floor. Pressure on the hollow stone where the crystal had been triggered the spring mechanism that activated the blade. It was designed to strike the intruder in a very sensitive part of his anatomy.

Typical Renaissance mind at work behind the design—clever and brutal.''

''A spring mechanism? And it still functioned after all these years?''

''Luckily Hazelhurst's diary mentioned it. Apparently old Digby was so delighted with his discovery that he oiled the mechanism and got it working again.''

Verity groaned. ''What a nitwit Hazelhurst must have been.''

Jonas looked annoyed at her lack of understanding. ''He wasn't a fool. He was just a scholar who was really into his subject. I can see why he did it—I might have done the same thing. There's a certain thrill in making a four-hundred-year-old gadget work again.''

''Nonsense. The booby trap should have been destroyed once and for all,'' Verity said resolutely.

''Obviously you have the sort of mind that's incapable of appreciating the esoteric joys of true historical scholarship,'' Jonas said with grand condescension.

''Really? What sort of mind do I have?'' Verity retorted with an artificially sweetened smile.

''A feminine mind.''

''Like I said, Jonas. One of these days . . .''

''Promises, promises.''

''You'll see,'' Verity said benignly. ''You're going to regret everything. One of these days, I'll have you begging for mercy. Now tell me about that brief flash you had when you got too near the hidden stiletto. I caught some of it, just enough to get the feeling someone had died there. Was that what you saw?''

Jonas nodded, frowning. ''Yeah, but the impression I got was that it happened a long time ago. Maybe a couple of centuries or more. It wasn't anything recent.''

''There have probably been other treasure hunters going

through this heap over the years, trying to find the missing gold, or jewels, or whatever they think was hidden in here." Verity scowled. "You know, Jonas, I may have made a teensy mistake when I negotiated your fee for this job. I elected to take a flat rate, figuring there probably wasn't going to be any real treasure left after all this time. But what if we find something? It might have been smarter to negotiate for a percentage of the treasure in addition to the consulting fee for the authentication report."

Jonas chuckled at her concerned expression. "Ah, the stress and worry of higher management. Sure glad that all I have to do is the physical labor." He sat up abruptly and tossed aside the covers. "I'd like to know what happened to that crystal," he remarked, yanking on his jeans. He walked across the room to the tapestry hanging on the wall. "Hazelhurst makes it clear in his diary that he considered it the key to finding the treasure." He reached out and lightly touched the frayed, woven wall-hanging. Then he pushed against the tapestry, touching the wall underneath.

Verity felt the air around her shimmer slightly. She got out of bed and pulled on her robe. "Okay, master historical scholar. What's with that section of wall?"

"I'm not sure yet. Whatever it is, it's not enough by itself to trigger a trip into the psychic corridor. But there's something here. Let's take a look behind this tapestry." He lifted the old fabric carefully and peered at the wall. "You with me?"

"I'm here." She walked over to stand near him.

"All I'm getting are a few faint vibrations. I can keep them under control."

Verity nodded and sucked her lower lip between her front teeth. She could feel herself beginning to perspire again.

Jonas put his hand flat on the wall and moved it slowly along the stone surface.

"Watch out for booby traps," Verity muttered.

"I think we'll sense them before we spring them."

"Only if they've already been sprung by some other unfortunate treasure hunter," Verity pointed out. Jonas's psychic talent was linked to violence. If the traps had been used in a deadly manner at some point in the past, he would sense it. But if they had never been sprung, there would be no previous history of violence to alert him.

"All I'm getting is a vague feeling of danger—almost like a warning. It was the same way when I opened the stone where the crystal had been kept. It's strange, Verity. It's as if someone managed to plant mental warnings around his secrets, not just a few hidden stilettos."

His hand continued to glide over the stones. When he touched a chink in the mortar there was a distant dull thud that sounded like ancient machinery moving inside the wall. Verity shivered inside her robe.

"I think I'm onto something here," Jonas said softly.

Verity heard the controlled excitement in his voice. "You're enjoying this, aren't you?"

"I think I could get into treasure hunting. It'll never replace dishwashing as a satisfying career, but it might make a hell of an interesting hobby. What do you think?"

"I'm beginning to think I was nuts to have you take this job."

"But this is a hobby we can share together. Some people ski together; others play tennis. You and me, we'll be part-time treasure hunters."

Verity was considering the pros and cons of this when a large section of the wall creaked loudly, groaned, and then swung inward. A wave of musty air billowed out.

"Whew!" Jonas stepped back quickly.

"It smells awful in there." Verity peered into the dark passage that had been revealed. "Probably full of rats."

Jonas went back across the room and returned with the flashlight and his knife.

"What's that for?" Verity demanded, eyeing the knife.

"You never know. The door is so heavy I don't think it can close again unless it's pushed, but I'll prop this chair against it, just in case. Wouldn't want to get trapped inside this passage." He hauled a heavy chair to the opening in the wall and placed it firmly across the threshold. "All right. Stay behind me and don't touch anything."

"Don't tell me, let me guess," Verity said. "In spite of what common sense dictates, we're going to explore this secret passage, right?"

"We're after treasure, remember? This is the sort of place people bury treasure. At least, it's the sort of place they would have buried it four hundred years ago."

"Are you still getting some vibrations, Jonas?" Verity hurried over to where she had left her shoes. Jonas was already stepping into his boots and buttoning his shirt.

"All I'm getting are a lot of old echoes. Nothing specific, and nothing to worry about."

"If you say so." She followed him into the dark corridor. The passageway was narrow. The stone ceiling was just barely tall enough for her to stand upright. Jonas had to duck his head.

"Men were a little shorter four hundred years ago," he remarked.

The flashlight beam revealed an empty stone tunnel that seemed to follow the inside wall of the bedroom. At the point where the adjoining wall connected, the interior corridor turned to follow it.

"Do you suppose this passage connects the entire villa the way the main hall does?" Verity asked.

"Possible."

"Yuck. Look at the dust." Verity lifted the hem of her

nightgown and then gasped. "Jonas—look at the *footprints* in the dust! Someone's already been in here."

Jonas bent to examine one footprint. "There's a thick layer of dust inside it, so it's safe to say it's been a long time since someone walked through here."

"Maybe it was Digby Hazelhurst."

"Could have been. The prints are too mixed up to tell if there was more than one person in here. Digby probably made several trips down this passage once he discovered it. I'll bet he was excited." Jonas stood up and started down the corridor.

"It's cold in here. You should have brought your jacket, Jonas."

"Yes, dear." He glided on down the passageway.

Verity raised her eyes toward the dark ceiling of the stone tunnel and swallowed a retort.

"You know, I don't think I like this place, Jonas."

"Want to go back to the bedroom and wait for me?"

"No, I most certainly do not."

"Then stick close and stop complaining."

"I was not complaining. I was making an observation, and I do not want . . . Oops." Verity stopped and looked down.

"What's wrong?" Jonas swung around, playing the flashlight over her.

"I hit something with my foot."

"Let me see that. Looks like part of an old sword." Jonas picked up the dark, tarnished chunk of metal. It fit into his palm as if made for it.

"Wait!" Verity cried out as the stone corridor immediately began to give way to another kind of corridor, one that she knew existed only in her mind and Jonas's.

She was too late to stop the transition. Jonas was gripping the broken sword firmly, and the walls of the psychic time tunnel coalesced around them. She held her breath as reality shifted and a second reality was superimposed on the first. When she opened her eyes she was standing beside Jonas in an endless tunnel, staring at an apparition that hovered in midair in front of them.

The image was of a grim-faced, powerfully built man who appeared to be in his late forties or early fifties. He was seated at an intricately carved wooden desk littered with ancient tomes and writing instruments. The man was dressed in a wine-colored velvet doublet and hose, and he wore a waist-length fur-trimmed cloak. Several heavily embossed rings adorned the apparition's fingers, and the hilt of a jewel-encrusted sword was just visible under the fold of his cloak.

There was a small black case on the desk that appeared to have been carved out of some dark, shiny stone. It was open to reveal an egg-shaped chunk of green crystal.

The man and the desk were in a small, stone room. Behind him was a long, black, ornately carved chest. Its lid was raised, revealing a heap of gold coins and glittering jewels.

Verity stared at the figure frozen in time. The wraith stared back at her. "Something's wrong," she whispered tautly. "Something's different about this image. I've been in this psychic corridor with you several times now, Jonas, but I've never seen a phantom vision like this."

"Nothing's moving, that's what's wrong." Jonas took a few steps forward. "There's no action." The scene in front of them remained still, as if it had been rendered in marble.

"I don't like the green glow coming from the crystal." Verity took a wary step backward. "There's something really wrong here, Jonas. I'm sure of it. Why doesn't this image move like all the others? Why aren't we witnessing a scene of violence connected to that sword hilt you're holding? That's the way the time corridor always worked in the past.''

''I don't know what's going on, but I'm sure it's harmless, Verity. I've told you a hundred times the scenes in this corridor are just visions. They can't hurt you.''

''I'm not so sure about that.'' Her brows came together in a sudden scowl. ''Where are the ribbons? There should be ribbons.''

Always before when she had entered the psychic corridor with Jonas there had been an immediate rush of strange, writhing ribbons. They converged on Verity as if drawn by some invisible force. It was her ability to harness those dangerous tentacles of emotion that enabled Jonas to control his psychic abilities. Without her, he could be overwhelmed by the hungry ribbons of seething emotional energy that sought to escape through him to the real world.

''I don't know,'' Jonas said softly. He walked slowly toward the image of the man seated at the desk.

Verity stared at the figure in the scene. ''Jonas, I think his eyes are following you.''

''Just an optical illusion.''

''I'm not so sure. Jonas . . .''

''You're right about this vision being different in several ways, Verity. The scenes in the time corridor have always been scenes of violence connected to whatever object sends me in here. I'm still holding the sword hilt, but there's no action, no violence.''

''Do you think that piece of crystal on the desk is the one Digby Hazelhurst found a few years ago?'' Verity asked softly.

''It's possible. It fits the description.'' Jonas studied the frozen image for a few more minutes. Then he moved back to stand beside Verity. ''It's just not a normal corridor image.''

She shivered. "How can you say that anything in this corridor is normal?"

"It has its own rules and its own physical laws, you know that. You've been in here often enough with me. This vision doesn't fit the rules we've learned. We're not looking at a scene of violent action. Nothing is moving within the image, and there are none of those energy snakes that always pour out of the scene and try to lock onto me."

"It's as if whoever is sitting there has reversed the usual way things work in here," Verity agreed.

"Christ, I learn something new every time I step into this crazy place." Jonas shook his head in bemusement. "Wish I knew what the hell this all means."

"I think," Verity offered slowly, "that if that's the crystal Digby eventually found, there might be some truth to the legends of a treasure buried here in this villa. Look at the chest behind that man. It's heaping with gold and jewels. Maybe that guy in the cloak is the one who originally owned the treasure."

"I wonder if this piece of metal I'm holding was the hilt of that sword the man in the image is wearing. In the past, the object that took me into the corridor has always appeared in the vision. Something is very, very different here, honey."

Verity's intuition was prodding her. "I think we ought to get out of here, Jonas. I really do not like this whole set-up, not one bit. This psychic thing has always been pretty weird, but this is stranger than ever."

"Okay. I want to see where this passageway goes. Guess we'd better get going." He dropped the hilt of the sword.

It clattered on the stone floor of the real-time corridor, and the psychic corridor vanished. A cold draft made Verity tighten the sash of her robe again.

"You take the sword hilt," Jonas said. "It's got a strong

pull. If I pick it up again, we'll jump right back into the corridor."

Verity scooped it up. "Got it." She was about to comment on the dirt encrusting the ancient metal when the faint shaft of light that had been seeping into the passage from the bedroom dimmed. An ominous creaking sound from around the corner of the passage warned her too late of what was happening.

"Jonas, I think the door is closing!"

"Shit." Jonas raced passed her, his face grim behind the flashlight.

Verity limped after him, her heart pounding as the distant angle of light narrowed, then vanished completely. They rounded the corner of the passageway in time to see the heavy door slide into place with a very final thud.

Something clattered eerily in the darkness behind the closing door. It sounded like a handful of kindling being tossed against rock.

Or bones being dragged across stone.

Jonas raised the flashlight and Verity sucked in her breath at the sight of the skeleton. It lay just behind the massive door. The bones were bound together by the remnants of what had once been a natty pair of pleated trousers, an oxford cloth shirt, and a corduroy sport coat with suede patches on the elbows. A pair of gold-rimmed spectacles glittered in the dust near the skull. The sleeve of the jacket had gotten caught under the closing door and had jarred the bones, thus causing the unnerving rattle.

"Oh, my God, Jonas. It was there all the time! We didn't see it because the door was open."

Jonas ran the flashlight beam over the inside wall. There was no handle, knob, or other obvious means of reopening the stone gate. "We'll have to assume that whoever built this place didn't want to get accidentally trapped inside here himself. There's got to be a simple way out."

"Apparently our friend here didn't succeed in finding it," Verity said grimly.

Jonas looked down at the tangle of cloth and bones. Metal shone dully as the flashlight wandered over the remains of the body. Jonas knelt beside the bones and studied the blade that was projecting through the corduroy sport coat.

"I don't think our pal died of natural causes. And it doesn't look as if he starved to death in this corridor." He probed the pocket of the pleated trousers.

"What are you doing?" Verity demanded.

"I was just wondering who he is—or was. Ah, here we go." Jonas tugged a stiff, scratched leather wallet out of the trouser pocket. He flipped it open and studied the driver's license photo of the bald, smiling man wearing gold-rimmed glasses.

"Well?" Verity prompted. "I don't think I can stand any more suspense. Anyone we know?"

"It's Digby Hazelhurst."

"Good heavens! He's supposed to have disappeared while swimming or something."

"Sailing."

"That poor man. What an awful way to die! I think I've got a new definition of Hazelhurst's Horror. Imagine being trapped in this passageway . . ." Verity broke off as reality hit her. "Uh, Jonas, you do think you can find the mechanism that opens the door from the inside, don't you?"

"I'm good at manual labor, remember? Relax, boss. We'll get out. But I don't want to make the same mistake Hazelhurst made."

"What mistake? Oh, you mean that blade sticking out of him? You think it might have been another booby trap?"

"It's possible. The metal is old and heavy. Probably early

sixteenth century. Let's see if we can get a clue as to which direction it came from.'' He reached down and picked up the blade.

''Jonas, I'm not sure I'm ready for another one of these trips,'' Verity began hurriedly, but it was too late. The flat stone walls around her were already curving into the familiar vision of the endless time corridor.

''Verity?''

''Right here, Jonas.'' She turned at the sound of his voice. In the dimension existing inside the psychic corridor he was standing a short distance away. With an effort Verity could control both realities simultaneously. She could keep her awareness of the real, solid passageway, and at the same time concentrate on the psychic tunnel. It was a somewhat disorienting sensation, but she was getting better at maintaining the two realities.

''There. Straight ahead.'' Jonas took a step closer to her, indicating a misty vision materializing ahead of them in the psychic corridor. His expression was grim. ''It's pretty vague, isn't it? Probably because it's relatively recent in time.''

Verity followed his gaze, aware that the visions were sharper when he dealt with older events, especially those of the Renaissance. This was definitely a recent act of violence. ''Oh, no,'' she whispered helplessly as the short, violent drama unfolded in front of her.

There was nothing to be done and she knew it. It was like watching a film—a never-ending instant replay of the sudden demise of Digby Hazelhurst, gentleman scholar and lifelong treasure hunter.

The scene wavered indistinctly, as if it lacked sufficient power to project itself. In the weak vision, the man whose picture they'd seen in the wallet was clawing at the wall of the stone corridor. He had a look of breathless terror on his features. His fingernails raked along a line of mortar between two stones just as a dark, tarnished blade was plunged into his back. A hand was clutched around the hilt of the stiletto, and on one finger of the hand was a magnificent ruby ring.

Verity barely had time to notice the ring before curling tendrils of terrifying color and hideous light began to flow from the image. The ribbons writhed blindly for a moment, as if seeking a target. Then they headed straight for Jonas.

Then, as always, they seemed to sense Verity's presence.

She held her breath, as usual a little unnerved when the ribbons of mindless emotional energy began to swarm restlessly about her ankles. They didn't touch her skin, but they swirled violently around her. Jonas was left free to study the vision.

"You okay?" he asked softly.

"Yes."

"I think we've seen enough." Jonas released the old stiletto. It clattered to the floor.

The vision and the psychic corridor vanished instantly, leaving Verity and Jonas alone in the all-too-real tunnel.

Verity looked at Jonas. She could barely see his features. He had the flashlight trained on the part of the wall where Digby Hazelhurst had been scratching when the blade was plunged into him.

"Jonas, Digby didn't die because he accidentally triggered a hidden mechanism somewhere around here. There was a hand wrapped around the handle of that stiletto."

"I know, Verity. Now keep quiet for a few minutes," he added gently. "I have to concentrate."

Verity bit her lip and watched as Jonas trailed his sensitive fingers along the section of wall Hazelhurst had tried to reach as he died. A moment or two later something shifted deep within the stones.

"Here we go," Jonas said with soft satisfaction. "I've got it. Leave that sword hilt in here. It'll be safe. No one will see it and ask awkward questions. Leave the stiletto behind, too. I don't want to have to explain it to anybody yet."

Verity dropped the tarnished metal hilt on the stone floor as the heavy door swung open. "I don't mind admitting I'm somewhat relieved. Not that I doubted for a moment that you'd get us out of here, of course," she added with instinctive loyalty.

"Of course." Jonas patted the stone door affectionately. "I tell you, there is nothing as refreshing and interesting as the Renaissance mind."

"You ought to know," Verity said as she stepped out of the corridor into the safety of the bedroom. "You've got one yourself."

Chapter Seven

JONAS followed Verity out of the stone passageway feeling more relieved than he wanted to admit. Hazelhurst's dying clue revealing the location of the door mechanism had been very welcome, to say the least. Jonas knew he could have spent a long time trying to find it on his own.

As he stepped into the relative warmth of the bedroom he thought he could hear echoes again, echoes of ancient laughter. He started to close the stone door.

"What are you doing?" Verity asked.

"What does it look like I'm doing? You want to spend the night staring at old bones?"

"No, of course not, but what about poor Hazelhurst? We have to tell someone we found him."

"He's been in there for a couple of years," Jonas observed as the door groaned shut. "He'll keep awhile longer."

Verity's eyes widened in disbelief. "You're not going to tell anyone we found him?"

"Not just yet. If we report it now there'll be an investigation. Things will be disrupted around here for days, maybe weeks. Rumors of the treasure will leak out, and the place will be overrun with reporters, fake psychics, and God knows who else. We've only got a week, Verity. I want to spend it getting some answers. Something very important is hidden in that corridor."

"But someone killed Digby. He didn't die by accident—murder took place in that corridor."

"I know. But the murderer has been gone for over two years. Hell, he might even have died in that passageway himself, trying to find a way out. For all we know he's lying at the other end of the tunnel." Jonas stopped talking, hoping she hadn't noticed the rest. He should have known better. The woman had eyes like a hawk.

Verity wandered over to the window. "The hand that held that stiletto had a ring on it. A big ruby ring."

"I know. I saw it."

She glanced back at him over her shoulder. "It looked very old, Jonas. In fact, it looked like it could have been part of the jewelry collection in that treasure chest in the vision, or it could even have been one of the rings the man in the image was wearing."

"There was a certain resemblance," Jonas agreed carefully. He saw the expression in her eyes and walked over to put an arm around her shoulders. "Hey there," he said softly, giving her a slight shake. "Don't let your imagination run away with you."

"You know what I'm thinking?"

"Yep. You're wondering if the four-hundred-year-old man in the frozen vision managed to come alive long enough to kill old Hazelhurst. It's utterly and completely impossible."

"Jonas, you've said yourself that you learn something new every time you explore that psychic corridor. You don't know everything about how reality works in there. And you've admitted there was something very strange about that first vision. What if he figured out a way to survive in the time corridor, and he's been sitting there all these years protecting his treasure?"

Jonas felt a shudder run through her and he tightened his comforting grip around her shoulders. "Not a chance. Relax, honey. There are no ghosts in that corridor, just small scenes from the past. Postcards caught in time. That's all."

"The postcard of that man seated at the Renaissance writing desk didn't look like it had 'wish you were here' written on the back. I got the feeling that guy didn't want us around."

"That vision was different from anything we've seen before in the corridor, I'll grant you that. But that doesn't mean a lot at this point. You've got too much imagination for your own peace of mind, honey." He blew a fiery ringlet away from her temple and kissed her there. She smelled sweet and felt warm. He could feel himself getting hard, not an unusual reaction after a trip into the psychic corridor—not an unusual reaction around Verity at any time, for that matter.

"Someone killed Digby," she reminded him stubbornly.

"Yes. But it was a long time ago. You want my best guess?"

She nodded quickly.

"I think he had a companion helping him in the treasure hunt. Someone he trusted enough to take into that passageway. Maybe someone he even trusted with the crystal."

"And maybe that someone figured that as long as he

knew about the passageway and the crystal, he no longer needed Digby?"

"Makes sense."

"But where is that person now?" Verity persisted. She leaned her palms against the wide stone window ledge and gazed out into the rainy darkness.

"Who knows? There's no mention of Hazelhurst discovering the hidden corridor in his diary, which means he must have found it shortly before he was killed. Either he never got the opportunity to write it down or the information is in those missing pages. I haven't come across any reference to a companion either. Our best bet may be to talk to Maggie Frampton. She might know if Hazelhurst had involved anyone else in the treasure hunt."

"Good idea. And in the meantime . . ." Verity stopped, peering intently out the window. "Jonas, he's gone."

"Who's gone?" He followed her gaze down to the dark fountain. "You mean Spencer? Maybe the man had enough sense to come in out of the rain, after all."

"He could have come back here, Jonas. He had enough time to get back into this room and pull the chair out of the passage doorway. Maybe that's why the door closed on us."

Jonas considered that, his eyes darkening. "I locked the bedroom door. How could he have gotten in?"

"Who knows? There may be plenty of keys floating around. The locks on the doors here in the south wing appear to be relatively new."

Jonas gave her another small, affectionate shake. "I don't think it's very likely. He couldn't have known about the corridor, and he wouldn't have dared try to come back into this room knowing I'd be in here with you. Besides, the man was falling-down drunk; he was just about unconscious by the time I dumped him in that fountain."

"Well, he recovered sufficiently to get himself out of the pool," Verity pointed out.

Jonas studied the shadowed garden. "You're right, he did. I guess I didn't hit him hard enough."

"I just want you to know that if he sues, you're the one who's going to have to explain everything to the insurance investigator."

"Don't worry. I'll come up with something," Jonas said, not the least concerned. His mind was definitely on something else now. He put his arms around Verity's slender waist and drew her back against his thighs. His jeans were drawn taut across his burgeoning manhood. "In fact," he murmured into her ear, "something is already coming up."

"You can't possibly be thinking of . . . of sex when there's a body lying not more than fifteen feet away."

"Don't look so shocked. You're such a little prude, you know that? I keep telling you, that body's already been there for a couple of years. It won't bother us." He unzipped his jeans with one hand, keeping his other arm around her middle. His rigid shaft sprang free. Jonas eased Verity back again so that she could feel him through her quilted robe.

"Jonas, I'm shocked. I really think you should show a little more respect in a situation like this."

"Don't tell me you're not as excited as I am. Going into that psychic corridor always has this effect on both of us." He grabbed a fistful of robe and raised it up above her waist. His hands closed lovingly over the soft, firm flesh of her derriere. "Lean forward, honey," he whispered against her nape. "Brace your hands on the window ledge."

"Jonas, this is embarrassing. Someone might see us through the window."

"No one will see us. Everyone's in this wing. You'd have to be in another wing of the villa to see into this window." He remembered belatedly how he himself had been in another wing earlier that evening and had had a perfectly good view of this bedroom. He reached out and turned off the bedside light. "Better?"

"No."

"Come on, honey, stop arguing. You know you want this as much as I do. Damn, you feel good." He urged her to bend forward until she was forced to grip the window ledge. Her rounded buttocks tilted upward invitingly, exposing her warm, womanly channel to access from behind.

"Honestly, Jonas, there's a perfectly good bed right over there that we can use if you insist on this. I don't see why you have to . . . Wait a minute. What are you doing? I think this might come under the heading of kinky. If you think I'm going to let you . . . Oh, *Jonas*."

He gripped her thighs and held her firmly in position while he probed the silken sheath. He felt her tighten in reaction to his penetration and he pushed harder, sliding heavily into her damp heat. He groaned as the dewy folds closed around him, and moved one hand to the front of her thighs to find the sensitive bud hidden in the tight red curls. Verity shivered in his arms and her head tipped back. "You feel so wonderful, sweetheart. So good."

"Jonas." She sighed passionately. Her hair cascaded down her back. Her lips were parted and her eyes were closed.

She gave herself to him in hot, welcoming, passionate surrender, the way she always did. At least when he was making love to her, she was fully aware of him, Jonas thought. He lost himself in the pulsing ecstasy of the moment, aware on some level that somewhere along the line Verity Ames had become as necessary to him as breathing. He could not imagine life without her.

It had become very important that she feel the same way about him, he realized. He would use sex or anything else he could to keep that withdrawn, introspective look out of her eyes. He couldn't let her leave him, mentally or physically. He needed her.

Jonas had learned over the past few months that when he was with Verity, he was home.

Verity was up before Jonas the next morning. She awakened with an instant awareness of what needed to be done.

"We'll have to talk to Maggie Frampton," she reminded her sleepy-eyed lover as she urged him out of bed and into the shower. "If we get downstairs early enough, we might have a chance to interview her before any of the others show up for breakfast."

"The trouble with business managers is that they rarely consider the well-being of the troops. I didn't get much sleep last night."

"Who's fault is that?" she demanded without sympathy. "Hurry up and get dressed."

They found Maggie Frampton humming to herself in the kitchen. She was whipping up pancake batter and seemed startled to see them. She had on another faded print shirtwaist from her vast collection of housedresses, this one with small dots all over it. The chain around her neck disappeared beneath the prim white collar.

"Well, hello there. You two are up bright and early. Didn't think any of this crowd were what you'd call early risers. How about some coffee? Got some made over there on the counter. Old Digby always had to have his coffee first thing in the morning. Doctor told him he shouldn't drink the stuff, but Digby said he needed it to get his heart started. Help yourself."

"Thanks, Maggie." Verity poured two cups and handed one to Jonas.

"How's the big treasure hunt going?" Maggie asked as she lifted a stack of chipped crockery out of a cupboard.

"You know about that?" Jonas asked.

"I hear Little Miss Sunshine wants you to keep an eye out for it while you're writin' up the report on the villa. Talk about a waste of time and energy. Digby spent years going through this place and never found a dime."

Jonas cleared his throat. "As a matter of fact, we wanted to see if you could help us, Maggie. You must have been closer to Hazelhurst than anyone else. You lived here with him for several years, I take it?"

"This villa's been my home since I moved here twenty-three years ago come June." Maggie sighed wistfully. "I miss the old coot. Seemed like he was hornier than the devil himself most of the time, but I didn't mind. Him and me, we got along fine together. After he disappeared, my sister down in Portland kept tellin' me I should get off this island. But I can't bring myself to do it. This place is home—I can't just up and leave. Digby would have wanted me to stay on here, I know it. He used to say so."

"What exactly did he say, Maggie?" Verity asked gently. She sensed the unhappiness lying just beneath the surface in Maggie Frampton. It was obvious the woman still mourned Digby Hazelhurst.

Maggie rattled a pan and sniffed. She blinked rapidly a few times and then went on in a steadier voice. "Digby said this place was ours—his and mine. He'd have wanted me to keep an eye on it. The villa meant the world to him. He always said I was the only one who never laughed at him, the only one who understood. Claimed if anything ever happened to him, he'd see to it I got to stay here as long as I wanted. But after he disappeared, there wasn't no will. Digby never got around to writin' one up. Just like him to put it off until it was too late. In the end, the court and a bunch of lawyers gave it to Doug and Elyssa.''

''Doug and Elyssa will have to sell it,'' Verity pointed out gently. ''They can't afford to keep it. How did Digby expect you to be able to pay the taxes and keep the place running?''

''You'll laugh, but the truth was, Digby always said that when he found the treasure there'd be plenty of money to run this place in style. He had big plans to buy back all the furniture and paintings he had to sell off over the years. He wanted to restore the villa to the way it must have looked back in the sixteenth century. Oh, he had lots of fine plans, Digby did. And I was gonna help him with 'em. We was a team, him and me.''

''Too bad he never found the treasure he searched for all those years,'' Jonas commented, leaning back casually against the counter as he sipped coffee.

''I never did believe in that story about a treasure, though I'll have to admit findin' it would have been great,'' Maggie said. ''But I used to think that for Digby, most of the fun was in the looking, you know?''

Verity found her remark unexpectedly insightful. ''I can understand that,'' she said quietly. ''You and Digby were obviously very close.''

Maggie nodded. ''You bet your jeans we were close. He didn't have no one else. His academic friends abandoned him as the years went by, and as for family, well! You'd have thought he was an orphan.''

''What about Doug and Elyssa?'' Jonas asked sharply.

''You think they ever bothered to visit Digby much before he died? Not on your life. Oh, Doug did come out here once or twice a few years back, but that was about it. Little Miss Sunshine never showed any interest in the villa till after she and Doug inherited it. Now all she can talk about is finding the treasure. Fat chance,'' Maggie concluded in satisfaction. ''If Digby couldn't find it, she sure as heck won't be able to.'' She glanced quickly at Jonas. ''And neither will you. Not unless you're a lot smarter than Digby, which ain't very likely.''

Jonas nodded soberly. ''You're probably right. Digby was quite smart, even brilliant in some ways. I read some of his early investigations into the nature of Renaissance science. They were first-class. Hazelhurst was a scholar in the old-fashioned sense. I still remember how much I learned about the Renaissance mind from a piece he wrote on sixteenth-century anatomy studies. He understood those men, knew how they thought.''

A reminiscent gleam appeared in Maggie's eyes. ''Anatomy was one of Digby's favorite subjects, all right. Whenever I think about some of those nights the two of us spent studying it down in that torture chamber I just kinda melt inside.'' The gleam faded and was replaced by a hint of moisture. Maggie wiped the back of her hand across her eyes.

Verity choked on her coffee. When Jonas reached over to pound her between the shoulders, she saw the laughter in his gold eyes.

''Maggie, did Hazelhurst ever tell anyone besides Doug and Elyssa about the treasure? Did he ever ask anyone else to help him hunt for it?'' Jonas inquired.

Maggie opened the refrigerator and removed a tub of butter. ''Sure. A few. Not many, though. Couldn't trust most folks. And he damn sure didn't want no one but historians hearing about the treasure. Real insistent on that, he was. But every so often he'd think he was making real progress, and he'd get excited and invite some old pal from his teaching days to stay here for a while. He'd tell 'em about the legend and swear 'em to secrecy. Sometimes they'd get curious enough to help him look for a while. None of 'em ever stayed interested for too long. It always hurt Digby real bad that none of his pals from the university believed him."

"Did he try to get anyone else to believe him?" Jonas asked. "Someone from outside the academic world?"

Maggie shook her head. "Not really. He only told men he considered real scholars. Never invited nobody but scholars here, said they were the only ones who could appreciate it. Except for Doug, that is. He did tell Doug. Said his nephew was kin and deserved to know about the legend, even if he didn't have time to help him look for it."

"Those are the only people he might have told about the legend?" Jonas prodded. "A few friends from his teaching days and Doug?"

Maggie's forehead wrinkled for a moment in concentration. "Well, there was one other. A young hotshot grad student who showed up claiming he'd heard about the legend from a professor. The kid claimed he was getting a degree in history, with a specialization in Renaissance art. Said he was curious about the villa and the legend, and wondered if Digby would let him help look for the treasure. He said it would be the chance of a lifetime to work with a scholar of Digby's reputation and all that malarkey. Said if they found the treasure, he'd write up the find in a fancy journal, and Digby would get all the credit."

"Did Mr. Hazelhurst let him help with the search?" Verity asked.

"For a while. Digby was gettin' a bit past it by then, if you know what I mean." Maggie tapped her temple with a forefinger. "For a time I think he was just glad someone from the academic world was interested enough to help him search again. But he sent the kid packing soon enough. Said the kid was just a two-bit treasure hunter, not a real scholar, and it would be a cold day in hell before he ever got a Ph.D. after his name."

"Did anyone else ever get out here to the island?" Jonas asked.

"Over the years a couple of cheap treasure-hunter types contacted Digby saying they'd heard about the legend, but Digby never gave 'em the time of day. Never let 'em come to the island. Claimed he'd never turn this place over to a real treasure hunter because that type wouldn't have any understanding or appreciation of the history locked up here."

"What about you, Maggie?" Verity asked. "Did you ever help Digby look for the treasure? You must have known a lot about the progress he was making."

Maggie concentrated intently on her breakfast preparations. "Sure, I helped out when I could. Held the ladder for him when he went inch by inch over the ceiling, that sort of thing."

"Did you ever believe the treasure might exist?" Verity asked gently.

Maggie paused in her work and stood gazing out the window into the weedy courtyard. "I had a few hopes during those first years after I came to live here, but that was about it. I stayed on account of Digby, not because of the treasure. Lord, I miss that man."

Elyssa's indefatigably cheerful voice hailed them from the doorway, breaking into Maggie's reverie. "Good morning, everyone. Isn't it beautiful outside today? Positively gorgeous, the sort of day that makes you aware of all your senses. The kind of day one can use to really get in tune with the different levels of nature's reality."

Verity glanced out the window. "It's raining." A dull, steady gray mist was falling.

"That's what I mean," Elyssa said, sweeping over to the

counter to help herself to coffee. "A day to delight the senses. How did you two sleep last night?" Her gaze was on Jonas.

"Fine." Jonas poured himself more coffee.

"Did it seem strange to sleep in a genuine Renaissance villa?" Elyssa demanded, watching him closely. "Did you get any feeling of attunement with the past?"

"No." Jonas turned at a sound in the doorway. "Morning, Doug."

Doug Warwick walked into the kitchen. "Hi, everyone. Ready to go back to work today, Jonas?"

"Sure," said Jonas. He began to detail a stone-by-stone examination of the west wing, and Doug paid close attention to his description of how to differentiate original construction from later patches and additions.

Verity listened with proud satisfaction. She also found herself quite interested, even though she knew that Jonas was simply playing the role she had assigned him. The man knew his stuff, she thought.

"Mustn't forget the influence of Alberti's treatise on architecture," Jonas said gravely. "He wrote it in the fifteenth century. It was heavily influenced by the classical works of Vitruvius, of course. Alberti accepted a lot of the principles unquestioningly and passed them along to his contemporaries. But his work had an impact on all major Renaissance architecture. This villa isn't exactly a shining example, but it definitely reflects the Alberti influence."

"I see," said Doug, looking quite impressed.

"There was a lot of concern for harmonic proportions in architecture at the time this villa was built. That makes certain features very predictable, which in turn makes my job easier."

Preston Yarwood and Oliver Crump wandered into the kitchen just as Jonas launched into a fine monologue on the differences between the architecture of Milan and Florence in the sixteenth century.

"The great Florentine palazzos became models for the other city-states," Jonas continued as everyone nodded knowledgeably. "Everybody who was anybody wanted a big house just like the Palazzo Medici or the Palazzo Rucellai. You can see the influence even in this old pile."

Verity studied her lover discreetly as she sipped coffee. No doubt about it, it was getting hard to tell where the bull stopped and the scholar stepped in. Jonas was really getting into this, she thought.

But her own enthusiasm was rapidly waning. She remembered Digby Hazelhurst's body hidden in the stone passage and shuddered. At first, hunting for the treasure had seemed like a nice sideline to the consulting assignment. But now she was not so sure. The only positive aspect of the situation that she could see this morning was that Jonas was genuinely interested in the project—and anything that gave Jonas a long-range career interest was not to be discarded lightly.

Slade Spencer did not show up until midway through breakfast. When he did appear, he looked so terrible that no one said a word. He ate very little and retired to the salon before the meal was over.

Verity took his wretched silence as a hopeful sign. Perhaps he wasn't planning to sue, after all.

"I'm afraid our friend Slade really tied one on last night," Preston remarked. "Pity. The man can't hold his liquor, apparently. I'm not at all sure we should have invited him along, Elyssa."

Elyssa smiled gently. "He'll be fine."

Oliver Crump said nothing, but his eyes were narrowed as he watched Spencer leave the room.

Jonas, Preston Yarwood, and the Warwicks got up to

begin exploring the west wing as soon as Maggie cleared the dishes.

"Aren't you going to come with us?" Jonas asked in surprise when Verity announced she was going to read instead.

"I don't think so." She held up her cane. "I think I'd better stay off my ankle. It's not feeling so hot today."

Crump pushed his wire-rimmed glasses more firmly up on his nose and peered at her ankle. Then, without a word, he got up and left the room.

Elyssa shook her head at his departing figure. "He's not much of a conversationalist, I'm afraid."

"Well, then, let's be on our way," Doug said. He took charge of the small party and led them out of the room.

Verity wandered into the salon with a book she had brought along on the trip and found Slade Spencer standing near the liquor cabinet. From the doorway she watched him tap two tablets out of a bottle he carried in his shirt pocket. He popped the pills into his mouth and chased them down with a long gulp of whiskey.

He looked up as she came into the room, but his eyes didn't quite meet hers. His hands shook a little as he replaced the pill bottle in his shirt pocket.

"Sorry about last night," he said. "Guess I made a real ass of myself, huh?"

"Let's forget it, shall we?" Verity said quickly. "You'd just had a bit too much to drink, and Jonas is not the most understanding of men."

"Be glad to forget the whole damn night." Spencer rubbed his jaw. "Don't remember much about it anyway, except that Quarrel's got a mean right hook. But I gotta admit I deserved it. I completely misread the situation, and I apologize. If it's any consolation to you, I feel like shit this morning. Worst damn hangover I ever had in my life, and

I've had some humdingers. Too bad I didn't stay in the fountain. Drowning in the rain would have been more pleasant than waking up this morning.'' He flopped down in a tatty armchair and picked up a year-old magazine that was lying nearby.

Verity took a seat near the window, curling her good leg beneath her. Silence descended on the salon. She tried to concentrate on her book, but she found herself gazing out into the overgrown, weed-tangled garden. Her thoughts drifted to the secret within her body. One of these days she was going to have to face facts—she couldn't live in this self-imposed limbo forever. Her body would get tough any day now and force her to admit that it meant business.

But a part of her preferred not knowing the truth just yet.

Half an hour later Verity heard a sound in the doorway. She looked up and smiled at Oliver Crump, who was standing there with an armful of greenery. He was also carrying a pot of steaming water, a bucket, and some towels. He started toward Verity.

''Hello, Oliver. What have you got there?''

''I think I can make that ankle feel a lot better,'' he announced briskly, kneeling in front of her. ''Let me see it.''

Verity hesitated and then told herself that there was no harm in letting him look at her throbbing ankle. ''Are you going to make a poultice for it?''

Crump nodded, carefully removing her shoe and sock. His fingers were amazingly gentle.

''If you two will excuse me,'' Slade announced, ''I'm going to go hit Maggie up for another cup of coffee.'' He left the room.

Crump glanced over his shoulder. ''That man is not well,'' he observed softly. ''But I don't think he would accept help of any kind.''

Verity nodded. "I get the same feeling."

Oliver took a large lemon-colored shard of crystal out of his pocket and handed it to her. "Here. Hold this."

"Are you really into crystal therapy?" Verity asked, examining the shard with interest.

"Sometimes it helps. Sometimes it doesn't. Depends."

"I see." She didn't, but she felt obliged to say something. "I understand that a lot of people these days use crystals for various purposes. I don't know much about them myself."

"No one does," Oliver Crump said brusquely. "There are plenty like Elyssa who think they do, but the fact is, very few people have ever figured out how to use crystals and gemstones. Folks have been working with them for thousands of years though, because it's easy to sense that there's some power in them. The trick is figuring out how to use that power."

"Do different kinds of crystals have different powers?"

"Theoretically. But like I said, no one really knows too much about them. They have to be properly tuned, or programmed, as they say in the computer business. Sometimes I think I can almost sense how to align the forces inside a crystal, but other times..." He shrugged and dismissed the subject.

Oliver poured hot water over the green plants and crushed them in the folds of one towel. "This is a little makeshift, but it should do the trick." He began wrapping the compress around Verity's ankle. Then he glanced up at the crystal she was holding. "Why are you stroking it like that?" he asked abruptly.

Verity glanced down at the crystal in surprise and realized she was rubbing it with her index finger. "I don't know. Just fiddling around, I guess."

Oliver touched the crystal and frowned. He started to move his finger on it.

Verity frowned. Something wasn't right. "No, not like that." She concentrated for a moment, then slowly moved her hand to guide Oliver's finger. Immediately things felt sharper and clearer—more tuned. "That's it," she whispered. "Doesn't that feel better?"

"Yes. Much better." Oliver stroked the crystal for a long time under the guidance of her fingers. Then his eyes met hers.

"You are, you know," he announced calmly.

Verity flinched. "I am what?" she asked carefully.

"Pregnant." He stopped touching the crystal and deftly pinned the compress in place.

Verity's fingers closed violently around the crystal. "How do you know?" she demanded, her voice taut.

Crump shrugged and took the crystal from her hand. "Some things are obvious. You showed me the truth just now, when you touched the crystal. I could sense it." He put the translucent crystal into his pocket again. "How's the ankle feel?"

She looked down at her foot, realizing suddenly that her ankle was already feeling less painful. "Better. A lot better. Thank you, Oliver."

"Are you going to tell Quarrel soon?"

Disconcerted, Verity raised her eyes to meet Crump's serious, dark gaze. "I'll tell him soon. If it's true."

"It's true. And the sooner you tell Quarrel, the better. He needs to know."

"Why?"

"Because he needs to be reassured that he's got a secure place in your life. He's never had much in the way of security."

"Maybe he won't want to be a father," she said in a low, urgent tone. "Some men aren't cut out to be fathers."

"Quarrel isn't 'some men.' He's Quarrel. And he's permanently linked to you somehow. I don't understand it completely, but I can sense it. Tell him about the baby soon." Crump rose to his feet, gathered up his supplies, and walked out of the room without another word.

Verity stared after him for a long while.

As lunchtime approached, Verity decided that her ankle was feeling considerably better. She removed the compress, picked up her cane, and headed for the kitchen to give Maggie a hand with the meal. She wasn't accustomed to such a crowd.

Maggie was grateful for her assistance. After checking the pantry, Verity put together a creditable salad and some herbed cream-cheese sandwiches. When the treasure-hunting party returned, they were hungry.

"By the way," Jonas told Verity as he wolfed down his third sandwich. "You and I are going to borrow the launch and run over to that little town on the other island. The one we came through on the way here. I need to make some phone calls."

"Why?" she asked blankly.

"Research," he explained as if it were obvious. "Unfortunately, Digby never got around to installing a phone. Better pack a few things. We'll stay overnight and come back in the morning."

"Are you sure you don't want me to come with you?" Elyssa asked with a sympathetic glance at Verity. "Poor Verity really should keep off that ankle."

"Actually," replied Verity, "my ankle is feeling a great deal better." She was not about to offer her seat on the launch to Elyssa Warwick. Sunshine and enlightenment were becoming distinctly tiresome.

* * *

Preston Yarwood recognized that expression in Elyssa's eyes. He went into the salon after lunch, poured himself a drink, and thought about it. The dumb little bitch had the hots for Quarrel, that much was obvious.

Elyssa was ready to roll over for anything in pants, as long as the guy claimed to have psychic powers. Yarwood figured that he ought to know—she'd certainly rolled over fast enough for him. And there was no denying that she was a hot little number in bed. No one had ever gone down on him the way Elyssa did. When she screwed him she really put everything into it; she treated the whole thing as a spiritual experience. She was definitely the best lay Yarwood had ever had, and he'd gotten accustomed to that look of adoration in her eyes.

It was infuriating to see her panting after Jonas Quarrel now, but there wasn't much he could do about it just yet. Yarwood needed Quarrel for the moment, but they were natural enemies. When this was all over, Yarwood would show them all who the real psychic was.

Then it would be amusing to watch Elyssa beg him to screw her silly.

Chapter Eight

"ARE you going to tell me what this little jaunt is really about, or do I get to play twenty questions?" Verity stepped off the launch, using her cane to balance herself on the floating dock marina. She realized that her ankle wasn't nearly as sore as it had been that morning. "And where did you learn to drive a boat, anyway?"

"You don't drive a boat, Verity, you pilot it. And I don't remember where I learned. You work enough waterfront dives on enough islands and sooner or later you get the urge to learn how to get off the island alone, should the occasion arise. A simple safety precaution." Jonas finished making the lines fast and reached into the stern for his bulging duffel bag.

Verity wrinkled her nose. "Did you ever have to leave on the lam?"

"Not that I can recall," he retorted dryly. "I told you, learning to use a boat was just a safety precaution."

"Like learning to use a knife, I suppose?"

Jonas grimaced as he heaved the heavy duffel out of the launch. He didn't bother to respond to her last remark. "Hell, Verity, what have you got in here? 'Don't worry,' you said, 'there's no need to bring two bags, there's plenty of room in your duffel for my nightie and blow dryer.' Where did you come up with a ninety-pound blow dryer?"

"Quit complaining. It's not that heavy and you know it. Of course I had to leave a few of your things behind to make room for my stuff, but you won't miss them overnight."

"What things of mine did you leave behind?" He looked ominous as he strode up the dock beside her.

"Just one or two small items," she assured him cheerily. "Don't worry about it. Now about this little trip to civilization." She gazed at the sleepy town overlooking the tiny harbor. "Did we really have to come all this way just to use the phone?"

"You know there's no phone at Hazelhurst's Horror."

She shuddered. "I wish you wouldn't call it that."

"You're the one who said it was an appropriate label."

"Okay, okay, we'll argue over that later. Who are we going to call?"

"Caitlin Evanger." Jonas's mouth curved in satisfaction as Verity shot him a startled glance.

"Caitlin? Why on earth are we going to call her?" she demanded.

"I told you—research. Evanger is the one person I know who might have the answers to a few questions I've got. Besides, she owes us."

Verity looked at him. "How can she help us?"

"She's the one who inherited all the records left by the Department of Paranormal Research when the wise, far-sighted trustees of Vincent College finally came to their senses and closed down the lab. She claimed she was Elihu Wright's one and only heir, remember?"

"How could I forget?" Verity muttered.

Elihu Wright had been the wealthy eccentric who originally endowed the Department of Paranormal Research at Vincent College. It was in the department's lab that Jonas had developed his psychic powers to the point where they had almost turned him into a killer. He had fled the lab, running from the unknown potential of his talent. It wasn't until he had met Verity that he had begun to learn how to control his unique affinity with the past.

"There have never been very many places in the country where someone who thought he had psychic powers could get himself tested," Jonas continued. "Vincent College had one of the few legitimate labs on the West Coast. I want to know if any of that crowd back at the villa was ever tested, and if so, what the report was."

"Why do you want to investigate Yarwood, Elyssa, and the others? What have they got to do with this job?"

"I'm not sure yet. I just want to find out everything I can before I go any further. There's murder involved. Murder and treasure. That's a potent combination. I just want to check out a few things."

"That's assuming Caitlin can still find the old records."

"She had mine, didn't she?" Jonas's expression was grim.

Verity cleared her throat. "Well, yes, but she had a, uh, special reason to save yours."

"She sure as hell did." Jonas swung the duffel over his other shoulder. "As soon as we find a phone, we'll see if she had the sense to save any others. First, we'd better find a place to spend the night." He stopped at the top of the pier and scanned the picturesque Victorian buildings that lined the waterfront street. "Not a Hilton in sight."

Verity smiled happily. "Thank goodness. Let's try one of those quaint little bed-and-breakfast places I've been reading about. These island towns are famous for them."

"How do you know?"

"I brought along a handbook. It's in the duffel bag."

"A-ha!" Jonas set down the bulky bag and unzipped it. "I knew there was more than a nightgown and a blow dryer in here." He crouched beside the canvas bag and peered inside. The expression of shock on his face as he perused Verity's last-minute packing job turned thunderous. "Dammit to hell, Verity!"

"Now, Jonas . . ."

"You went crazy! What did you think we were going to do—set out on an expedition to the Arctic?"

"Jonas, be reasonable. This is winter, remember? It's cold, and it's liable to rain at any moment. I decided to be safe rather than sorry."

"So you brought along an umbrella, rain boots, a slicker, what appears to be a year's supply of makeup, two pairs of pantyhose, two changes of jeans, a couple of pairs of shoes, and a dress?" He looked up. "I know this is going to sound silly, but why did you bring the dress?"

She gazed down at the handful of shimmering green silk. She wouldn't be able to get into it much longer. Soon her body would be growing round and heavy. "I thought we might go out to dinner at a nice place," she mumbled. "I put in a tie for you."

Jonas started to say something about the tie that would have been scathing, but for some reason he changed his mind. Without a word he fished around inside the duffel bag until he found the guidebook. He zipped up the bag, slung it back over his shoulder, and handed the book to Verity.

"Here," he said gruffly. "Pick a place. Preferably something that isn't too far away. I didn't bring the pack llama."

Verity opened the guidebook, scanning the listings for bed-and-breakfast inns on the island. "How does the Harbor Watch Inn sound? 'Bedrooms are furnished with charming nineteenth-century antiques, including four-poster beds. Lobby has lots of rustic charm, with a comfortable stone fireplace and view of the harbor. Breakfast is ample, featuring eggs, scones, fresh juices, and plenty of good coffee.' "

"Well," said Jonas, his golden eyes gleaming in the cold sunlight, "I like the sound of the four-poster bed. As long as I have you, a four-poster, and my trusty belt, I can make do."

Verity felt herself turning pink. "Just remember that one of these days I'll be getting even for that little bondage number you pulled last night."

Jonas showed his teeth in a wicked smile. "All I ever get are promises," he taunted softly.

Verity shook back her mane of copper curls and stuffed the guidebook into her purse. "You'll see. Let's get going. The Harbor Watch Inn is only a couple of blocks from here, according to the guidebook."

The walk to the quaint Victorian inn turned out to be a little farther than Verity estimated, but Jonas kept his grumbling to a minimum. Verity refused to give him the satisfaction of complaining, but she was vastly relieved when they reached their destination. She was feeling a little guilty about having stuffed the duffel bag with her things.

It was cold, and there was a damp wind blowing. Verity decided that the island town probably looked bright and colorful during the warm summer months, but in the dead of winter everything appeared uniformly gray.

"You know, Jonas, you may have been right when you said this trip to the Northwest wasn't going to be quite the same as a jaunt to Hawaii."

"One of these days you'll start listening to me, little tyrant."

"I always listen to you." She batted her lashes outrageously.

Jonas chuckled. "Like hell."

"I just don't always pay attention. But that makes us even."

The Harbor Watch Inn was warm and cozy. It was run by a middle-aged couple who welcomed their new guests with a smile and a drop of sherry. Verity turned down the sherry, and Jonas drank her share as well as his own.

"Sure you don't want it?" he asked as he set down the tiny glass.

"No, thanks." She'd read somewhere that pregnant women weren't supposed to drink, and decided she'd verify that snippet of information when she finally went to a doctor.

They were shown to a room that overlooked the harbor. As soon as the door closed behind the manager's wife, Verity began eagerly to explore the small bedroom.

There was, as promised, a four-poster bed. A charming nineteenth-century ceramic pitcher and bowl sat on the old dresser, and sailing memorabilia adorned the walls.

"It's all so charming," Verity said in delight. "So quaint. So terribly cute."

"And it's all made in Taiwan." Jonas casually touched the pitcher on the dresser. "So much for that bit about the rooms being furnished with antiques. I wonder what other surprises are in store for us. Maybe they'll accidentally run out of scones at breakfast."

"Details. Don't be so negative." Verity unzipped the duffel bag and shook out her green silk dress. She carried it to the closet and was about to hang the garment inside when she glanced around and realized something was missing. "Jonas, there's no bathroom!" she exclaimed.

"Sure there is. Just down the hall."

"Down the hall!" Verity was horrified. "For the price we're paying?"

"The price of unbearable cuteness and quaintness, I'm afraid."

"Oh, damn. I should have realized. But that stupid guidebook didn't warn me."

"So what's the big deal? A little minor inconvenience, that's all."

"That's not all. I hate places where the bathroom is down the hall," Verity insisted stubbornly.

"Why?" Jonas was genuinely surprised by her vehemence.

Verity bit her lip, aware that she was overreacting. She didn't want to spoil the evening. Turning back to the closet to finish hanging her clothes, she tried to explain. "It goes back to my childhood, I suppose. When I was growing up, Dad and I lived in places like this a lot. Tahiti, Mexico, the Caribbean, you name it. They've all got places like this where the bathroom is down the hall."

"This is hardly in the same category as a flophouse on some backwater island," Jonas said reasonably.

"I know, I know. Those places were all cheap, dirty, and in a bad part of town. But I guess for me the bathroom-down-the-hall bit became symbolic of all those crummy joints. Dad never seemed to mind, but then, he wasn't the one who volunteered to clean the damn bathroom in exchange for a few bucks off the rent."

Jonas studied her face, fascinated. "Why in hell did you volunteer?"

"Because no one else would have cleaned it if I didn't, and I had to use it along with all the other drunks, whores, and assorted riffraff who lived in the place," she exploded.

"Hey, take it easy, honey." Jonas gathered her into his arms and gently stroked her hair. "If it bothers you that much, we can find another place."

Verity sniffed back tears, shocked by her emotional reaction. The smallest things seemed to get to her these days. "I'm sorry," she mumbled into Jonas's shirt. "This is stupid. I don't know what got into me. This is a lovely place—beautiful view, clean sheets." She surreptitiously wiped away a tear from her cheek. "The guidebook raved about it."

"Guidebooks have been known to give false information."

"But it is a nice place." Verity lifted her head and glanced around again. "Really it is. I was just a little thrown there for a minute when I realized where the bathroom was. I'm fine now. Pay no attention to me."

Jonas eyed her closely. She gave him a reassuring smile and blinked away the last of her tears. "Are you sure you'll be comfortable staying here tonight?"

"I'll think of it as a travel experience," she said wryly.

Jonas nodded. "If you're sure."

"I am."

"Nice bed," he remarked thoughtfully.

Verity beetled her brows at him. "Don't you dare look at it, or me, like that."

"What's happened to your sense of adventure, sweetheart?"

"This trip is turning out to be adventurous enough without having to put up with your kinky ways," she retorted loftily. "When are you going to call Caitlin?"

"Now is as good a time as any." He picked up the bedside phone.

"Let me talk to her first," Verity said quickly.

"Be my guest. I'm not exactly looking forward to the conversation. The woman still gives me the creeps."

"You're just biased. You never did like her very much."

Verity dug the number out of her well-worn address book, the same book that had countless entries crossed out under her father's name. She wondered fleetingly if the little book would be filling up with similar crossed-out entries under Jonas's name in the years ahead. Pushing aside the depressing thought, she dialed the number. She listened to the ringing on the other end and wondered if Caitlin or her companion, Tavi, would answer.

It had been over a month since she had last spoken to either of them. Jonas wasn't aware that Verity had called the Evanger house a few times since the events of last fall. He probably wouldn't have approved of it, but something within her had needed to make certain that the brilliant, moody artist had survived the emotional trauma.

The phone was picked up on the other end and a quiet, gentle voice answered.

"Tavi? It's Verity. How is everything?"

"Verity, I'm so glad you called. Everything is going well here. Caitlin is painting again. Isn't it wonderful?"

Verity smiled. "Is she pleased with what she's doing?"

"I think so. You know her, she demands so much of herself. But the gallery owner who handles her work in San Francisco is certainly happy enough. He says it's the best work she's ever done. Something about a new emotional maturity coupled with a brilliant sensitivity and awareness. Caitlin gets a kick out of that. You know her attitude toward art critics—she considers them all parasites."

"I know."

"But I think that deep down she's relieved that she didn't lose whatever it was that gave her work so much power. For a while she thought that if that terrible business from the past was settled once and for all, she would no longer feel so compelled to paint. But her desire seems to be as strong as ever. Here, let me call her."

A few moments later Caitlin picked up the phone. "Verity? I'm glad you called. How are you?"

"Hobbling around on a sprained ankle, but otherwise fine. I understand you're painting again?"

There was a pause, and Verity pictured the exotic woman with her scarred face and twisted leg. For a few seconds she wondered if all was not going as well as Tavi had implied. "Caitlin?" she prompted gently.

"I'm here. And it's true, I'm painting again. I was just thinking about how to tell you how grateful I am. I feel so different these days, Verity. I don't feel nearly as old as I did six months ago, yet in some ways I feel infinitely wiser. Isn't that a strange way to feel?"

Verity unconsciously touched her stomach. "No," she said. "I think I know exactly how you feel."

"You are still with Jonas?"

"Jonas?" Verity glanced at him; he was standing in front of the window, watching the harbor activity. "Yes, I'm still with him."

Jonas looked over his shoulder, scowling. She smiled blandly back at him.

"Good," said Caitlin. "The two of you need each other. You're so good for each other."

"Caitlin, I'm calling to ask a favor. Or rather, Jonas wants to ask a favor."

"Anything, Verity."

"Do you still have those old records from the Department of Paranormal Research?"

"They're filed in the basement. Why?"

"I'll let Jonas explain." Jonas walked toward her and Verity handed him the phone.

"I've got a list of names, Caitlin," he said without preamble. "I need to know if you've got any information on them in those old files."

"Just a second, let me get a pen and paper." There was a

small clatter on the other end of the line. "All right, Jonas. Give me the names."

"Elyssa Warwick, her brother Doug, Oliver Crump, Preston Yarwood, and Slade Spencer. I think the last one, Spencer, may have a drug problem."

"I'll see what Tavi and I can turn up. It'll take a while, though. How soon do you need the information?"

"As soon as possible." Jonas threw a wry glance at Verity. "Verity has chosen a new career path for me. I'm in the middle of my first consulting case." He read her the phone number off the phone.

"Where is that area code?" Caitlin asked curiously.

"The Northwest, near Seattle. The case is supposed to be part business and part vacation. We're on an island in the San Juans."

"At this time of year?"

"Yeah. Verity thought it would be a good substitute for Hawaii."

Caitlin chuckled softly. "Is she still of the same opinion?"

"You know Verity. She insists on looking on the bright side. She was doing a good job of it, too, until she found out the bathrooms in this bed-and-breakfast place are down the hall."

"Quaint. Probably reminds her of some of the dumps her father and she lived in when she was a kid."

Jonas raised his eyebrows. He held the phone away from his ear and just looked at it for a moment before saying slowly, "How did you know about the kinds of places she lived in as a kid?"

"Verity and I are friends," Caitlin said quietly. "We've talked. I hope one of these days you and I will be able to be friends, too, Jonas. In the meantime, I certainly owe you a few favors. I'll see if I can find any of these people in the old files."

"Thanks." The clipped word was grudgingly spoken, but it was meant. Jonas hung up the phone. He turned around to see Verity digging high heels and pantyhose out of the seemingly bottomless duffel bag.

"You've been keeping in touch with her," he said in a strangely neutral tone.

"We're friends."

"You've got a strange notion of friendship."

"If you think my friends are strange," Verity shot back, "you should meet my lover."

For an instant she thought he was going to lose his temper. But he shocked her by taking the remark seriously. "Do you really think I'm strange, Verity?" Jonas asked roughly. "Is that what's been bothering you lately? You've come to the conclusion that I'm some kind of freak?"

She wished she'd kept her mouth shut. "Don't be a total ass," she scolded. "Of course I don't think you're a freak. I think of you as the sexiest thing to come along since black lace underwear. Now stop talking nonsense and get dressed. It's almost dinnertime, and I've found a nifty place in the guidebook."

Jonas smiled slightly, but his eyes were still watchful. "Cute and quaint?"

"I believe it has a nautical theme," Verity remarked serenely.

"Why doesn't that surprise me?"

She handed him a strip of silk. "Here."

"What's this?"

"Very funny. You know perfectly well it's a tie."

"Is this a hint that I'm supposed to dress tonight?"

"It is." She collected her silk dress from the closet. "Wear something besides jeans with that tie."

"Right, boss."

* * *

An hour later, Verity confronted Jonas over her salad. This time the guidebook had not been misleading. The restaurant theme was painfully nautical. There were stuffed fish displayed on the walls, a display of ropes tied in intricate knots, and a variety of sailing apparatus strewn about in what Verity assumed was an artistic fashion. The menu featured fish cooked in every conceivable style. Fortunately there were also a few meatless pasta selections.

"Cute place, isn't it?" Verity spoke determinedly.

"Nobody else in the whole damn place is wearing a tie."

"So the locals don't dress for dinner. That's their problem. You look terrific." Which was the truth, Verity thought with a sudden pang. But then, Jonas always looked good to her—strong, lean, and hard, with that unconscious masculine grace that always fascinated her. His midnight-dark hair was still damp from the light mist that had been falling outside, and his eyes glinted softly in the dim restaurant light.

Jonas gave her an oddly speculative look. "You know something, you look pretty good yourself." He leaned forward and caught her hand.

> "*My mistress glows by candlelight.*
> *She leaves me breathless; I am undone.*
> *Her hair like fire, her eyes like gems,*
> *Then she smiles at me; She is my sun.*"

"Another four-hundred-year-old, loosely translated Renaissance love poem that you just made up on the spot?" Verity said lightly. But in truth, she was warmed to her soul.

"What can I say? You inspire me," he explained modestly.

Her love for him tugged at her heart, and she almost let herself get sidetracked. But this restaurant wasn't the place to tell him about the baby. She wanted privacy for that. She had no way of knowing how Jonas would react.

"First, let's talk about the case," Verity said briskly. She pulled her hand out from under his and picked up her salad fork.

Jonas studied her through narrowed eyes for a few seconds. Then he shrugged and picked up his own fork. He began poking through the salad to find the mushrooms. "Okay. First we'll talk about the case. Then what are we going to talk about?"

"Us."

His head came up abruptly, his eyes very golden in the shadows. "Us?" he repeated softly.

"Later," Verity said. She felt more nervous than she had anticipated.

"Verity . . ."

"Please," she begged softly.

Jonas started to argue, but something about her expression stopped him. "All right," he finally agreed. "Later."

Verity smiled gratefully. "Tell me, in your professional opinion, what exactly do you think is going on out there on that island?"

"My professional opinion is that the whole situation sucks."

"You academic types have such a way with words."

"It's a professional requirement. It's been a few years, but when called upon I can, as I've explained, still bullshit with the best of them. Have you noticed?"

"I've noticed," she said dryly. "You know something? You can sound awfully impressive when you try. When you gave that little dissertation at breakfast on the differences between Milanese and Florentine construction techniques, everyone was fascinated. Architecture wasn't even your specialty when you taught Renaissance history. How come you know so much about it?''

''Goes with the territory,'' he explained. ''When you're studying the various Renaissance war machines designed to knock down walls and buildings, you find yourself learning a little something about how the walls and buildings were constructed in the first place. And don't get any ideas about nagging me to write an article about Hazelhurst's Horror for some obscure little history journal. The report I'm doing for Doug is all I'm interested in turning out.''

''Now, Jonas, if you're going to establish a career as a historical consultant you'll need to have your name appear in print occasionally. It's good advertising. Speaking of Hazelhurst's Horror, let's get back to the case.''

''I love the way you call it 'the case.' Makes us sound like a couple of amateur detectives.''

''Well, maybe that's what we are. We've already found one body, haven't we? Poor Hazelhurst. What do you think happened to him?''

''My professional opinion is that he got a stiletto in the back,'' Jonas said, munching his salad.

''Not an uncommon fate during the Renaissance,'' Verity pointed out. ''Jonas, that ruby ring on the hand that stabbed Hazelhurst appeared in the first vision. I know I saw it, either in the chest or on the man's hand.''

''Maybe.''

''There's no maybe about it. I saw it.''

''There is no way the guy in the vision came alive and killed Hazelhurst,'' Jonas said forcefully. ''Forget it.''

''All right, if that's an impossibility, what does it leave us with?''

Jonas ate the last of his mushrooms. ''It leaves us,'' he stated slowly, ''with the possibility that Hazelhurst and somebody else found the treasure, or at least the ruby ring, and the guy with the stiletto didn't want to go halvesies."

Verity put down her fork and stared at Jonas. "Good grief, you're right. That's a perfectly plausible explanation. That ring alone is probably worth killing for, which means that two years ago Hazelhurst involved someone else in the treasure hunt. But Maggie said that he never had any luck getting his academic buddies to help."

"She also mentioned a guy who claimed he was a grad student in Renaissance history showing up a few months before Hazelhurst disappeared."

Verity nodded. "But she said Hazelhurst didn't work with him long. Claimed the man wasn't a real student, just a treasure hunter."

"It's possible the guy sneaked back into the villa after he was kicked out. If he was reasonably discreet, he could wander around a long time in that pile of rocks before anyone caught him."

"But maybe Hazelhurst did catch him. Maybe he ran into him in that hidden passage. And maybe one of them had found that ring along with a few others items, like the old stiletto."

"And maybe there was an argument. A fight." Jonas nodded thoughtfully. "It's possible."

"Which means that whoever was hanging around two and a half years ago has long since taken the treasure and vanished."

"Also possible. Probable, in fact."

"Which means we're wasting our time," Verity concluded with a sigh. "The treasure's gone."

"Not necessarily."

She looked at him in surprise. "What's that supposed to mean?"

Jonas shook his head. "I don't think the real treasure was found. Or if it was, I don't think the thief got away with it."

"Why not?"

Jonas looked at her, his eyes shadowed. "Because the treasure, whatever it is, will be very well guarded, Verity. No casual treasure hunter could have stolen it, not easily. Precautions were taken. I felt the echoes of them."

"Booby traps, you mean? But they might all have rusted by now, like the one that guarded the crystal."

"I'm not sure that all the traps are mechanical." Jonas became very busy buttering a chunk of sourdough bread.

"Jonas, for crying out loud, what are you trying to tell me?"

He hesitated, then said quietly, "I don't know. But I got a strong sense of warning, a feeling of real threat from the room where the crystal was found. I got an even heavier dose of it from that vision of the man seated at the desk. I've felt a lot of things in that psychic corridor, but what I felt this last time was different."

"Different how?"

"If I understood that part, I'd have this case solved." Jonas bit off a large piece of the chewy bread. "There's just this faint sense of impending action or violence. Like something's waiting to happen."

"I don't like the sound of this." Verity had been hungry, but she was rapidly losing her appetite. "Do you think we should drop the whole thing and go home?"

"Are you kidding? I wouldn't leave now if you paid me."

"Dammit, Jonas, you just said it was dangerous."

"I'll be careful." He grew thoughtful. "I could try exploring the passageway alone. You can stay behind in the bedroom. Apparently the link between us is strong enough now to permit some distance. I can get hold of you mentally if I need you."

"Now you listen to me, Jonas Quarrel. You are not going to go off merrily exploring that hidden passage on your own while I sit and wait in the bedroom. You take me with you, or you don't go at all."

"Now, Verity," he began soothingly.

"Don't even try to talk me out of it. You don't know what you're getting into. You don't know how strong the link between us would be in a real emergency if we were separated by a long distance. This whole consulting job was my idea, remember? I'm the one who got you the project, and the agreement was that I go along as part of the package. If you stay, I stay. And if you go into that secret passage again, I go with you."

"You are one stubborn woman, Verity Ames."

"It's part of my charm."

"I'll try to keep that in mind."

"Jonas," Verity said warningly, "don't get any ideas about sneaking off to explore that passage while I'm asleep. Try anything tricky and I'll never forgive you. I mean it."

"I hear you."

She wished she could read his mind. Unfortunately, the link between them did not include telepathy.

Chapter Nine

"IT will be interesting to see if Caitlin turns up any information on the Warwicks and their friends. Personally, I'm betting against it," Verity said later as they walked back to the inn.

The light mist was still falling, but Verity was dry. Jonas was holding the umbrella and he had most of it over her. They were walking through the small shopping district of the town. Everything was closed for the evening, but there were lights on in most of the store windows. A surprising variety of chic art galleries and sophisticated craft shops were scattered amid the standard small-town collection of old-fashioned hardware stores, insurance offices, and real estate firms.

"Worth a shot," Jonas said mildly.

"Maybe. What do you think of each of them, Jonas?"

"I think Doug Warwick is just a hardworking stockbroker who wants to sell that white elephant he inherited as quickly as possible. He's humoring his sister in the process by letting me do some treasure hunting."

"And Elyssa?"

"Elyssa is the fluff-headed enthusiastic type who gets carried away with every trendy fad that comes along—harmless. Preston Yarwood is a con man who's cashing in on the New Age craze. Oliver Crump is the earnest, well-meaning sort who just got sucked into the psychic stuff because he's genuinely interested in offbeat things. He probably means well."

"And Slade Spencer?"

"Spencer is the kind who will join anything that looks like it might offer free sex and drugs. In another time and place, he would have been a hippie or a beatnik."

Verity bit her lip. "Slade did mention that he and Elyssa had had a brief affair. At least he claims he slept with her once or twice. He also says she's now having an affair with Yarwood. Slade even says she tried to get it on with Oliver, but he declined. Smart man. Apparently Elyssa is into psychics."

"Or likes to get psychics into her. Sounds like you found out a lot about Little Miss Sunshine."

"Either that, or Spencer told me a pack of lies about her. Which is possible."

Jonas put an arm around Verity's shoulders. "I don't know. Personally, I'm inclined to believe it."

"That Elyssa likes sleeping with psychics?"

"Some women get the hots for race-car drivers, some like policemen. Some go for gurus. Elyssa goes for psychics."

"Can't imagine why," Verity said innocently.

"I'm crushed."

"You'll bear up nobly. You always do." Verity thought about what he'd said. "What it all comes down to is that you think there really is a treasure buried in that villa, and you want to go after it."

"This is going to sound crazy, but I feel like I've been challenged, Verity. It isn't just the damn treasure I'm after. I want to know how that frozen vision works. I want to know why it's different from anything else we've ever seen in the time corridor. I feel there's something really important about all this."

"Something more important than a treasure chest full of gold and jewels?"

"Yes." He hesitated, then admitted softly, "I won't be able to rest until I figure out what that vision and that hidden passageway are hiding."

Verity hugged her down parka more tightly around her. It was cold tonight. "I think we should be very careful, Jonas."

"I agree."

"And whatever happens, we stick together. Understood?"

"Speaking of sticking together," Jonas said smoothly, "what about that discussion you and I were going to have? The one about us?"

"Let's wait until we get back to the room. Oh, Jonas, look." Verity stopped in front of a shop window and stood gazing down at a pair of reddish orange earrings. The translucent stones were faceted, and reflected the display-case lighting. Fiery sparks danced in the core of the stones. Verity fell in love with them instantly. "Aren't they beautiful?"

Jonas peered into the case. "They're okay, I guess. Same color as your hair. You should get something to go with your eyes, not your hair."

"I like those red earrings," she insisted. "Maybe we could stop by this shop in the morning before we leave?"

"You're stalling, Verity. It's time for that discussion you

promised me.'' He took her arm and guided her firmly away from the shop window.

Perhaps she'd been a little hasty, Verity thought uneasily as they climbed the steps of the Harbor Watch Inn. Perhaps she should wait until she'd seen a doctor or at least used one of those home pregnancy-test kits. All she really had to go on was the calendar, and Oliver Crump's professional opinion—for what that was worth.

But Verity knew deep in her heart she couldn't put off telling Jonas any longer. She summoned her courage as she and Jonas walked through the quiet parlor and up the stairs to the second floor. Jonas unlocked the door, followed her inside, and watched her walk to the window.

''Well, Verity?''

She glanced over her shoulder and saw that he was unknotting his tie. His eyes were watchful.

''Jonas, I've been doing a lot of thinking lately.''

''I've noticed.'' He slung the tie aside and unbuttoned his shirt. His eyes were narrowed. ''In fact, I've about had it with your weird behavior lately. It's as if you're spending part of your time in another world or something. Or like you're making big plans that you won't tell me about. I'm warning you, Verity, I put up with a lot of your temperamental nonsense, but there are some things I won't tolerate. I've been very patient with you, but I've just about reached my limit. I'd like an explanation, and I don't want to be told it's my imagination.''

Verity moved restlessly to stare at a nautical print on the wall. The ship was foundering, men were overboard, and shark fins cut through the churning water. She knew exactly how they felt. She cleared her throat nervously.

''Sometimes things happen that aren't exactly planned,'' she began cautiously, her back toward him. ''Sometimes a person's timing isn't quite right. It's nobody's fault, it just happens."

"For Christ's sake, Verity, will you stop beating around the bush and just say what you have to say?"

"All right. How would you feel about becoming a father, Jonas?"

"*What?* Holy shit!"

There was a scrabbling sound, some thumping, and another muttered curse. Verity whirled around and saw Jonas staggering wildly, his arms flailing. His pants were tangled around his knees and he had lost his balance. He clutched wildly for the nearest bedpost, hopping around on one foot. The expression on his face was one of incredulous disbelief.

Verity watched in amazement as Jonas landed heavily on the edge of the bed and slid down to the floor.

She'd never seen him lose his balance before. All the effortless physical grace that characterized his movements had suddenly deserted him.

There was a solid thud as Jonas landed on his rear end, his ankles trapped inside his half-lowered pants. He sat looking up at her, his eyes filled with amazement.

"You want to run that question by me again?" he asked in a hoarse voice.

Something squeezed Verity's stomach tightly. "You heard me the first time. How do you feel about becoming a father?"

"I take it," Jonas said carefully as he kicked off his shoes and pants and climbed slowly to his feet, "that this is not a hypothetical question?"

Verity wrapped her arms around herself and shook her head. "I'm afraid not. I'm pregnant, Jonas."

"How long have you known?" He tossed aside the pants

and came toward her. His jaw was set and his eyes were unreadable.

Verity looked down at the floor. "I assume you're not thrilled. I didn't think you would be."

"I asked you how long you've known." He reached her and took her chin in his hand. He lifted her face so that she had to meet his blazing eyes.

"Not long. I had a suspicion before you left with Dad."

"And you kept it to yourself."

"I wasn't about to use the possibility of my being pregnant as a way to keep you from going off with Dad." Her eyes were alive with pride.

"Did it ever occur to you that I had a right to know?"

"I wasn't even sure about it myself until this morning," she said defensively.

"What happened this morning that convinced you?"

"I more or less had it confirmed," Verity explained, remembering the strange conversation she'd had with Oliver Crump. "Please don't yell at me, Jonas. I told you as soon as I was certain."

"Thanks. I appreciate that," he retorted grimly. He cradled her pale face between his hands. "Verity, you little idiot—you shouldn't have kept it to yourself this long. You should have told me the instant you suspected you might be pregnant. No wonder you've been more temperamental and emotional than usual. I should have guessed."

For some reason Verity grew furious at his words. "I have not been acting more temperamental or emotional than usual. I *never* act temperamental or emotional, so how could I be more so than usual? I always act in a perfectly reasonable, rational manner. I'll have you know I happen to possess plenty of common sense, unlike some people I could mention, and I resent the implication that I'm temperamental and emotional and strange!"

"Hush, honey." He laughed indulgently and pulled her tightly against him. "Take it easy." His arms went around her and his palms moved soothingly up and down her spine. "Just take it easy, sweetheart. Everything's going to be okay."

"You haven't said how you feel about being a father." Verity buried her face against his chest.

"Well, I haven't had too much time to think about it," he admitted lightly. "But I don't see that it's any big deal. I'm a fast learner. I can always ask Emerson for advice. Look at what a great job he did raising you."

"Oh, *Jonas*, this is serious!" Verity was torn between laughter and tears. In fact, all her emotions seemed suddenly to be too close to the surface. She clung to Jonas, her arms wrapped around his lean waist. "Are you sure you don't mind?"

"Did you think I would?" he whispered into her tousled curls. "Is that why you couldn't bring yourself to tell me earlier?"

"I wasn't sure how you would feel about it. I mean, it's a big responsibility."

"And you've always been a little worried about my attitude toward responsibility, haven't you?" he concluded with a hint of exasperation. "Jesus. No wonder you were so upset about my going off with your father to rescue Lehigh. You probably saw that as an example of how life was going to be from now on. Except that in the future you'd be left behind with a kid whenever I took off."

"I didn't know what to think."

He gave her a small shake. "I told you that was a one-shot deal, not a lifetime pattern. I'm different from your father. We have some overlapping interests and experience, but we're not the same. Come on, Verity. Don't you have any more faith in me than that?"

"I didn't know what to think. I hadn't planned to get pregnant. Hadn't even thought about it. We were taking precautions most of the time and I just sort of assumed . . ."

"We were not taking precautions all of the time. In fact, we rarely remembered them when we came out of our trips into the time corridor," he reminded her bluntly. "And we did a lot of practice sessions with the psychic stuff this past winter."

She sighed. "I know. I think I somehow convinced myself that sex after one of those trips was different in some way. It always seems so urgent, so demanding. I think of it as being connected to the psychic stuff."

"And you convinced yourself you couldn't get pregnant as long as the sex was taking place on a higher plane? A psychic plane? Is that it?" There was laughter in his voice.

"Don't you dare make fun of me!"

"I wouldn't dream of it, honey. But there is something a tad amusing about you pretending the sex we have after a mind trip is different from the kind we have the rest of the time. Talk about rationalization. This from a woman who prides herself on having more common sense than other people, specifically the male of the species?"

"I'm warning you, Jonas."

"Yes, ma'am," he said, chuckling. "I hear the warning. I seem to be inundated with threats and warnings from you lately. After a while it gets hard to take them all seriously."

"You don't sound terribly upset." Verity lifted her head, puzzled at the cheerfulness in his tone. "I thought it would be a terrible shock for you."

"Well, the news did knock me on my ass at first, as you saw, but fortunately I recover fast."

Verity started to relax, truly relax, for the first time in days. A great sense of relief began to unfurl inside her. She hadn't realized how tense she had been. "You really don't mind being a father?"

"If I minded," he told her softly, "I wouldn't have forgotten to take precautions after we made a trip into the psychic corridor, or any other time we made love. I may have my faults, sweetheart, but I'm good at details. Especially those kinds of details."

Verity smiled tremulously and swallowed tears that seemed to have welled up out of nowhere. "My whole life is undergoing a massive change. It's scary, Jonas. I never thought much about having children. I think that somewhere along the line I just came to the conclusion that I wasn't the type or something."

"I think this must be the first and only time I've ever seen you unsure of yourself," Jonas remarked.

"You've recovered from the shock a lot faster than I have. I still feel strange. I've been feeling that way for days."

"Just leave everything to me, boss. I'll take care of business for you. All you have to do is sit back and get fat."

"That's not funny, Jonas."

"I've been telling you for months you need to put on a little weight."

"This is a rather drastic way to do it," Verity muttered.

Jonas chuckled softly as he picked her up and carried her to the bed. "One of these days you're going to have to learn a few facts of life."

"Such as?"

"Such as the fact that there are some things even an independent, assertive, bossy little tyrant like you has no control over. I can't wait to watch you get nice and round with my baby."

* * *

Jonas lay quietly studying the ceiling an hour later. Verity was dozing in his arm, her soft, inviting body relaxed and warmed from his lovemaking. Intermingled with the faint, womanly fragrance that teased his nostrils was his more pungent aroma. The primitive part of him always took satisfaction in the combination of scents that hovered in the air after he had made love to Verity. It was a subtle but absolute confirmation of his recent possession of her.

He took enormous pleasure in the knowledge of what he could do to Verity. He could make her turn to fire in his arms—sweet, hot fire. He was thoroughly addicted to the way she made him feel, hooked on the satisfaction he got from satisfying her. He didn't even want to think about facing the hard, lonely world without her by his side. Verity had brought him the only peace of mind he had known in more years than he wanted to count.

And now she was pregnant with his baby.

The knowledge gave him an odd, almost euphoric rush. Soon there would be three of them—a family. He was going to have all the responsibilities and obligations of fatherhood.

It was a role he knew little about. His own father had walked out on his mother before he was born. But Jonas figured he knew what he had missed as a kid. A father's love, a firm hand when he'd needed it, someone to talk with about life. Someone to help him prepare for the world.

Thus, Jonas knew what being a father was going to entail. It meant giving his kid the things he had never gotten from his own father. No sweat, he could handle it.

But first he had to give Verity what she needed.

He had been blind, deaf, and dumb not to realize how insecure and unstable their relationship had appeared to her. He had been so content with the situation that he hadn't bothered to consider how Verity felt.

The fact that she had delayed so long in telling him about

the baby was proof enough that he had been inexcusably remiss in making her feel secure. Emerson Ames loved his daughter dearly. He'd taught her to look after herself and had given her a fine, albeit unusual, education. He had given her a lot, but the one thing Emerson had not been able to provide Verity was a stable home life.

Jonas chastised himself thoroughly for not having realized weeks ago that after the rootless upbringing she'd had, Verity would need a strong sense of security before she would feel comfortable about having a baby. No wonder she had been distant and withdrawn. She was nervous, even scared, probably.

Jonas had invaded and taken over the neat, orderly, home-bound little world Verity had created for herself. Then, before she had fully adjusted to having him in her life, he had given her a baby.

The lady who had planned to be alone and independent all her life had suddenly had her whole world turned upside down, in the span of a few short months. Jonas mentally ticked off the things Verity now needed from him.

She needed reassurance.

She needed security.

She needed to know she could count on him.

She needed a last name for the baby.

She needed a husband.

Jonas rolled onto his side and gently shook Verity awake. Her lashes fluttered and then rose lazily, revealing the beautiful depths of her aquamarine eyes.

"What is it?" she asked, yawning. She stretched languidly, her breasts gently undulating. "Something wrong?"

"Nothing's wrong. I've just decided we're going to get married," he announced. "As soon as we get back to Sequence Springs."

Verity, caught in midyawn, stared at him for a good

thirty seconds. Then her mouth closed with a snap. "*Married.* Why?"

Her dumbfounded expression wasn't quite what he had expected. Jonas narrowed his eyes. "*Why?*"

She nodded. "Why?"

"For all the obvious reasons," he exploded. "We're living together, and you're pregnant. How many more reasons do you need to get married?"

Verity sat up and reached for her robe. "It just now occurred to you that maybe we ought to get married?" she asked politely as she secured the robe.

"I was lying here thinking about the baby and the future, and how you grew up without a permanent home. I realized you'd probably be a lot more happy about the baby if you had a sense of security. So I'm going to marry you." Jonas realized he was sounding a bit pompous, perhaps even a touch patriarchal. He couldn't help it. He had expected her to leap at the idea of marriage. The fact that she wasn't absolutely thrilled left him floundering.

"Well, that's very nice of you to offer to marry me, Jonas, but I really don't think it's necessary, thank you very much."

Jonas's mind went blank for a moment. He couldn't believe what he was hearing. When his brain kicked into gear again a few seconds later, it was all he could do to keep from yelling so loud that every guest on the floor would hear.

"What the hell do you mean, you-don't-think-it's-necessary-thank-you-very-much?" he ground out between clenched teeth. "We have to get married."

She drew her knees up under the sheet and wrapped her arms around them tightly. Her hair was in wild disarray, and the expression on her face was more set and stubborn than Jonas had ever seen it.

"I don't see that anything has changed much, Jonas. If we didn't have to get married last week, we don't have to get married this week."

"You're pregnant!"

"So?"

His mind raced, searching for the correct approach. "You want this kid to be born a bastard?"

"There are no bastards in the state of California. By law every child is legitimate. Your name can go on the birth certificate."

"Thank you very much. Jesus." He quickly abandoned that tactic and tried another. "I thought you'd want marriage. I thought you'd be happier married, more secure. I thought you'd appreciate the sense of stability. Verity, this is ridiculous. You know you'd be happier married now that you're going to have a baby."

"I don't want to be married simply because I'm pregnant."

Jonas's mouth fell open as he dimly began to perceive the source of the trouble. "Oh, Christ," he said. "Don't tell me . . ."

"If you had really wanted to marry me you could have asked me anytime during the past few months. You never said a word."

"Now, Verity . . ."

"I wonder when Caitlin is going to call." Verity glanced at the phone, then at her watch. "It's only ten. She's a night person. She's probably still going through those old files."

"Verity, shut up and listen to me, dammit. You've got this all wrong," Jonas said harshly. "The only reason I didn't ask you to marry me before now was because . . . because . . ." *For Christ's sake, think, you fool.* But how could he explain that he had just never thought about the matter until now? Everything had been so comfortable. He had been content. "There was no need. No rush, I mean.

Everything was going along fine, we were getting to know each other. Establishing a relationship. Yeah, that's what we were doing—establishing a relationship."

"A relationship, Jonas?"

Jonas wished he'd read some of those pop psychology books about male-female relationships that were always being churned out. Trouble was, women were the only ones who read that sort of thing. Therefore, only women knew the right words and euphemisms; only women had a good command of the vocabulary needed to talk oneself out of a mess like this. A man was left stranded and helpless.

"I would have gotten around to marrying you eventually. The baby just speeds things up a little, that's all."

Verity smiled wryly. "Relax, Jonas. You don't have to think of any excuses. I appreciate the gesture, but I assure you it's not necessary. There really is no need for us to get married."

"This is not a gesture, dammit. I am not thinking up excuses. You want an apology? All right, I apologize for not having asked you to marry me before you got pregnant. It was just an oversight."

"Don't *apologize*. I don't want any apologies. And I don't like being an oversight." Her self-control slipped for a moment. For a split second Jonas caught a glimpse of the wariness and the very feminine anger that lay in the depths of her eyes. Then she had herself back in hand. "You've been honest with me this far, don't spoil your track record. As I said, I appreciate your offer of marriage, but there's no need for it. There's no reason things can't continue just as they have been for the past few months."

"What about your father? You think Emerson is going to like this?" He was clutching at straws and he knew it.

Verity chuckled. "You know my father well enough to realize that if he hasn't come after you with a shotgun by now, he's not likely to ever. He likes you. I'm sure he'll be pleased about the baby. But he raised me to make my own decisions. If he gives you a hard time, just tell him you did the noble thing and offered marriage. When he hears I'm the one who chose not to accept the offer, he'll back off. He knows me."

"I know you, too, Verity. Well enough to realize you're making the wrong decision here. You'll be much happier married. Trust me."

"In spite of the psychic link we share, Jonas, there are still a lot of things we don't know about each other. Don't assume you understand me perfectly, and don't assume you know what's best for me. You don't. Now, if you'll excuse me, I think I'll go down the hall to the bathroom." She reached for her cane and slid out of bed.

"Maybe you don't understand me all that well, either," he shot back, feeling frustrated. "Maybe you're making some dumb assumptions here, lady."

She didn't bother to answer. She was sliding her feet into her slippers.

Jonas's hand clenched and unclenched as he watched her with brooding eyes. A few minutes ago everything had seemed crystal clear and totally straightforward. He and Verity had been living together. They were in love. She was pregnant with his kid. It was time to get married. Nothing could be simpler or more logical.

It hadn't even occurred to him that she would refuse him. But it should have, he thought angrily as he watched her make her way to the door. He should know by now that Verity was stubborn, unpredictable, and far too independent for her own good. He'd complained to her father about those faults on several occasions.

But this was one of the few times Jonas had run up against Verity's feminine pride, and he didn't know quite how to deal with it. Apparently the little firebrand was too proud to marry him just because of the baby.

She had wanted to be asked properly, he realized. She had wanted to be married for her own sake, not simply because there were extenuating circumstances.

But he wasn't marrying her just because of the baby. He knew that, even if she didn't understand.

Why in hell hadn't he thought about marrying her last month? Jonas wondered in disgust. The answer was simple: last month he had taken everything about their relationship for granted. It hadn't occurred to him to formalize things, for the simple reason that everything was working out just fine. He had assumed that Verity was happy too, at least until she had started subtly withdrawing from him.

Jonas wondered how long she would hold his bad timing against him.

The phone rang just as Verity reached the bedroom door. Her hand on the knob, she turned around to watch him answer.

Jonas grabbed the receiver. "Quarrel here."

"Did I call at a bad time?" Caitlin Evanger asked politely. "You sound upset. I can call back."

Jonas reached for a pen and paper. His eyes stayed on Verity's face. "Now is fine. What have you got?"

"Tavi and I turned up nothing on all but one of the names you gave me," Caitlin said. "But we found a file on Preston Yarwood."

Chapter Ten

VERITY let go of the doorknob and moved back across the room. She knew who was on the other end of the line, and she could tell from Jonas's intent expression that Caitlin had found something of interest. She leaned over the bed to watch as Jonas wrote down Preston Yarwood's name.

"Yarwood?" Jonas was all business now. "How long ago? Who did the testing? Which tests? Are you sure? The whole battery, or just the initial workup? Okay, okay, I'm listening."

There was silence on Jonas's end as he stopped talking. Verity could hear the thin sound of Caitlin's voice rattling off information, but she couldn't make out the words. It was several minutes before Jonas hung up the phone with a brisk "Thanks."

As the receiver clattered into place, Verity looked at him expectantly. "Well?"

Jonas sat on the edge of the bed, adding a few final notes.

"The only name that turned up in the old department records was Yarwood. He was tested in the lab during the same time I was going through my tests, although I never ran into him."

"Yarwood has psychic talent? Real talent?" Verity was startled.

Jonas shook his head. "No. But he was totally convinced that he did, and he demanded to be run through the standard tests time after time. According to Caitlin, the lab researchers finally had to tell him they weren't going to waste any more time on him, no matter how much he contributed to the department. He claimed the tests were faulty. He believes in his own talent."

"A lot of people who are into the psychic thing believe in their own talent," Verity mused. "A few coincidences, a couple of dreams that could be interpreted in a variety of ways, and presto, they're psychics."

"Yarwood is in that category, according to the lab report Caitlin found. Some lucky guesses, a good sense of intuition, smart enough to reason through matters and leave other people wondering how he reached his conclusions. And above all the useful skill of being able to convince others he's whatever he says he is. But he couldn't fool the machines or the Vincent researchers. Yarwood has all the talents of a successful con man, but no psychic ability. That's not the problem."

"What is the problem?"

Jonas looked up from his notes, his eyes thoughtful. "Caitlin says there's an entry on one of the reports stating that Yarwood might be dangerous under certain circumstances."

"Dangerous? I don't believe it. He's not the type."

"There were a lot of psychologists involved in the testing at Vincent," Jonas said slowly. "I remember them. Always looking for an abnormal psychological pattern to parallel the paranormal development. There was a strong theory that people who tested positive for psychic talent would test weird in other ways. I was a walking testimonial to that theory."

"Nonsense. You're a perfectly normal person," Verity said instantly.

He gave her an odd smile. "I love it when you immediately jump to my defense, in spite of all the evidence."

"What evidence?" she demanded.

"I nearly killed an innocent man."

"Not because you've got a warped psychological profile," she insisted. "Only because your talent is so strong, and you hadn't learned how to control it."

"I'm not sure the shrinks would fine-tune their analysis that far, but thanks for the vote of confidence. Speaking of confidence, if you have so much of it in me, why don't you take a chance and marry me?"

For a second Verity could not think. "We're discussing Preston Yarwood," she finally pointed out. Jonas and his one-track mind! The last thing she wanted to talk any more about tonight was marriage. The business with Yarwood made a good distraction. "What made the lab people think he was dangerous?"

"Something to do with his, and I quote, 'inability to let go of his fantasy obsession.'"

"In other words, he really believed in his own talent. I don't think that makes him dangerous, Jonas."

"Maybe. Maybe not." Jonas slapped the notepad down on the table. "I wish Caitlin had turned up information on some of the others."

"Why? What is it you're looking for?"

"I'm not sure. I just have a feeling that I ought to know more about those people." He was silent for a moment. "You know, the Warwicks claimed that Yarwood got my name from the editor of that history journal. But if Yarwood was being tested at Vincent College while I was going through the program, he might have heard about me there. Why not mention it?''

''Perhaps because he didn't hear about you there.'' Verity smiled gently. ''Maybe he was there before you became notorious.''

''Yeah. Possible.''

''That's all the information Caitlin had?''

''That's it.''

''Then,'' said Verity, ''I will head off down the hall. Send out a search party if I'm not back by morning.''

''Verity?''

''Yes, Jonas?'' She turned once again at the door.

''Think about it.'' It was a soft-voiced command.

Verity didn't have to ask what it was he wanted her to think about. She opened the door and stepped out into the carpeted hall.

The hall light was out. It reminded her of the night she had returned to her cabin in Sequence Springs and found the deck light off. It was not a pleasant memory. There were no cracks of light under the other doors. Either she and Jonas had this floor all to themselves, or the other guests had already retired for the evening. Well, that should leave the bathroom free.

Verity pulled her robe more snugly around her and leaned a little on the cane. She didn't have to lean much, she realized. Her ankle was almost back to normal. She thought of Oliver Crump and his poultice and crystal. Of course, mildly twisted ankles healed quickly. There was no reason to attribute her rapid cure to Crump's abilities.

There was enough street light coming in through the window at the end of the hall to enable Verity to distinguish between the door marked LADIES and the one marked MEN. A lot of the places she had lived in during her younger years hadn't bothered with such niceties.

She still remembered one nasty encounter with a drunk who had followed her into a down-the-hall bathroom years ago. Her father had heard her screams and come running. The only thing that had saved the drunk from being beaten to death was the arrival of several other tenants. They had pulled Emerson off the man not because they felt any sympathy for the drunk, but because everyone liked Emerson and no one wanted to see him jailed for murder.

Verity decided she had no good memories of places where the bathroom was down the hall. Give her a Sheraton or a Hilton every time.

She opened the door of the ladies' room and found that the light was off in there, too. She began to get nervous, then anger set in. This had gone far enough! For the price she and Jonas were paying, they deserved decent lighting in the bathrooms. She would go wake the manager. Resolutely, Verity started to back out of the bathroom.

She sensed the man's presence behind her a split second before an arm in a heavy wool sweater wrapped around her throat. There was a faint, smoky scent on the wool. The adrenaline of fear flooded her veins, and she opened her mouth to scream. Her cry was cut off by a hot, damp palm.

Verity started to struggle desperately, throwing herself from side to side. It was useless—the man was much stronger than she was. He was overpowering her quickly, dragging her out into the hall and presumably toward the staircase. A jolt went through her sore ankle as it struck the side of the door and Verity's fingers clenched instinctively around the handle of her cane.

The cane!

Without stopping to think, she lashed out with the hardwood cane, seeking any available target. She struck her assailant's leg and heard a sharp intake of breath. The hand around her throat then tightened, choking her ruthlessly.

She rammed the cane backward, aiming for a vulnerable spot. The end of the stick struck somewhere in the man's midsection, and she heard him gasp. Before he could recover, she rammed again, hoping to hit his groin.

"Bitch!" The word was spoken violently but was almost inaudible as the man released Verity and doubled over in pain.

Verity immediately began to swing the cane again, this time going for the man's head. He dodged and charged blindly for the stairwell.

Verity was screaming the house down even as her assailant hit the stairs at full speed.

"Jonas! *Jonas!*"

A door slammed open down the hall and Jonas came running toward her. He hadn't stopped for his pants, she noticed. His lean, hard body gleamed like that of a naked warrior. All he lacked was a sword and shield.

"Verity, what happened. What the hell's wrong with the lights in this place?" He reached for her and pulled her tightly against him. "Are you all right? What's wrong?"

"The stairs," she managed. "He went down the back stairs. He tried to grab me when I went into the bathroom. Had something over his head, a stocking cap, I think. Wool sweater."

"Dammit! Are you okay?"

"I'm okay." She was shaking but she was all right. "He's getting away, whoever he is, Jonas." She wrenched free of him and hurried to the window. When she peered out into the darkness at the street below she saw no sign of anyone.

"He's probably long gone, but I'll take a look." Jonas raced back to the bedroom and reappeared a moment later in his jeans and boots. He started down the stairs, taking them in twos and threes, and nearly collided with the manager and his wife.

"What's going on up here?" the wife demanded anxiously. "So much noise. Is everything all right?"

"No, everything is not all right," Jonas shot back as he bounded past them. "Some joker just tried to grab my wife. I'm going to see if I can find him. Call the cops."

The woman stared in confusion at Verity as her husband switched on the stairwell lights. "I beg your pardon, my dear. Didn't realize you were married."

"A slight misunderstanding," Verity murmured, not bothering to explain who had misunderstood whom.

"This," said Verity in an aggrieved tone an hour later, "reminds me of what happened the other night back in Sequence Springs. At least I was armed this time." She hoisted the cane triumphantly. "And I didn't sprain my ankle this time, either. For these small mercies, I am grateful. Boy, do I hate places where the bathroom is down the hall. You can have cute and quaint anytime. I'll take luxury and convenience."

"I just wish to hell I could have gotten my hands on that creep." Jonas was prowling the small room, pacing up and down in front of the window as he ran his fingers through his hair in frustration. He had not found the assailant in the wool sweater. Whoever it was had vanished into the cold, wet night.

The police had been polite and efficient. They assured Verity and Jonas that they would check passengers on the ferries and keep their eyes open as they patrolled the island. They stood a good chance of finding the culprit, they said. It was a small community with limited access. Unless the guy had his own boat, he would have to use the ferry. Of course, there was always the possibility that the assailant was local. The police reluctantly admitted that there had been a similar situation just last month. A tourist had been raped at a resort on the other side of the island, and the man had not been caught.

"So you've got some guy running around this place who likes to hunt lady tourists?" Jonas had challenged angrily.

"I didn't say that, sir," the officer had replied very politely. "I just said there was an incident last month at a resort. It's possible the two incidents are related. That's all I'm saying at the moment. We'll look into it."

"You do that," Jonas had growled, with a menacing look. Verity knew he was furious with himself for not having caught the assailant.

"I should never have let you go down the hall by yourself," Jonas said now. "I should have walked you to the bathroom."

"Don't be so hard on yourself, Jonas. There was no reason on earth to think I was in any danger just going down the hall. I just happened to be in the wrong place at the wrong time."

"That's twice in a matter of days that you've been in the wrong place at the wrong time." Jonas glared at her. "How come you're so damn unlucky lately?"

Verity unconsciously patted her still-flat stomach. "Good question."

Jonas was across the room in two strides. He grabbed Verity's wrists as he crouched in front of her chair. "For Christ's sake, Verity, I wasn't talking about the baby."

She raised her eyebrows in surprise. "Neither was I." And she hadn't been. Belatedly she realized what her protective little pat had implied.

"Honey, I know it must have been a shock to discover you were pregnant, but it's going to work out. You'll see. We're both adaptable. We can handle it."

"One of us doesn't have much choice but to handle it," she observed dryly.

"We'll both handle it." His voice was flat, his words unequivocal. "Verity, we're in this together, you and me. And don't forget it."

She touched the side of his hard jaw and thought about the fact that he was the father of her child. She remembered how certain she had been of what she was doing that first time she had gone to bed with him.

Intellectually she had known back then that there were going to be problems and uncertainties, because in many ways it had seemed obvious that Jonas was not the right man for her. But paradoxically, on another level Verity had been certain he was the one she had been waiting for all her life. And she knew she would not have picked any other man to be the father of her baby.

"I won't forget, Jonas."

He tugged her into his arms and sat down on the edge of the bed, cradling her carefully. "You're sure you're all right? That bastard didn't hurt you?"

"I did more damage to him than he did to me, believe me. Me and my trusty cane."

"How could you get into so much trouble just going down the hall to the bathroom?"

"It's a knack."

It was drizzling the next morning when Jonas and Verity checked out of the Harbor Watch Inn. The slate-gray skies stretched beyond the horizon, promising rain for the foreseeable future.

"I caught the weather report on the radio while you were taking your shower," Jonas told Verity as they walked through town toward the marina. "There are a series of storms coming in from the Pacific."

"Hope the villa is waterproofed." Verity stopped in front

of a small grocery store. "I think I'll pick up a few groceries. Maggie Frampton's pantry is a bit limited."

"I don't want you volunteering to play chef for that bunch." Jonas's expression was stern. "We're supposed to be consultants, not household help."

"Yes, but we have to eat, don't we? You want to subsist on mashed potatoes for the rest of the week? I'm just going to pick up a few things. Won't be a minute."

He glanced down the street. "All right. I'll meet you back here in twenty minutes."

"Where are you going?"

"I'm going to see if I can find a newsstand," he said vaguely.

Verity eyed him curiously. She could have sworn he had made that up on the spur of the moment. "A newsstand?"

"I'll be back in a few minutes." He handed her the umbrella and loped off down the sidewalk.

Verity watched him from the shelter of the umbrella. She liked that new fleece-lined jacket on him, she decided. But then, she liked Jonas in almost anything. Or nothing at all. With a faint smile she went into the grocery store.

Twenty minutes later she was waiting for Jonas under the store awning, three large bags at her feet. Jonas came around the corner, took one look, and groaned.

"Who's going to carry all those sacks and my duffel bag back to the launch?"

"Now, Jonas, don't be difficult. I'm sure we can manage. Here, you take the duffel bag and one sack. I'll carry the rest of the groceries."

"What about your cane?"

Verity tucked it under her arm. "I don't need it anymore," she said, realizing even as she spoke that it was the truth. "The ankle's a bit tender, but that's all. I think Oliver Crump's poultices worked. Or maybe it was the effect of the crystal."

"I think your ankle got better all by itself," Jonas muttered, picking up a bag of groceries. "No need to go looking for psychic explanations. Watch your step."

"Don't you like Oliver?"

"He's all right, I guess. Just another weirdo."

Verity giggled. "You're loaded with strange psychic talent, and you've got the nerve to call him weird!"

Jonas was quiet for a moment. "The thing is, I don't think of my talent as weird. It's a part of me, just like being able to see, or hear, or touch is a part of me. It's like having a sixth sense. It's given me trouble for a good portion of my adult life, and there have been times when I thought it would drive me insane, but it's never seemed alien or strange. It's just part of me." He hesitated again, then added, "It's like you, in a way."

"Me!"

"Yeah, you." He smiled. "You give me a lot of trouble, and there are times when I think you'll drive me insane, but I'm stuck with you. You're a part of me. Here." He juggled the sacks and duffel bag until he could fish a small white package out of his jacket pocket. "This is for you."

"A present? For me?" Verity was startled. She managed to take the package from him. It carried the logo of the shop where she had seen the fire-colored earrings. She knew instantly what was in the package. "Jonas, how sweet. Thank you." She tore the package open and peered eagerly inside. Crystal flames winked at her. "They're beautiful! Absolutely beautiful."

"They weren't very expensive," Jonas said uneasily. "Are you sure those are the ones you liked?" His gaze was very intent as he watched her delighted expression.

"Definitely. I love them. Thank you, Jonas." Verity stood on tiptoe and managed to brush his cheek with her lips even though the sacks they were carrying got in the way.

"I'm touched, really touched. It was so sweet of you to remember them this morning."

"I don't know about the color of those earrings," Jonas remarked as they resumed walking toward the marina. "I still think you'd look better with something that matched your eyes."

"These are the ones I want." She stowed the package safely in her pocket. She couldn't wait to put them on. "They're just right."

"In that case," Jonas said softly, "consider them an engagement gift."

Verity snapped her head around to stare at his rock-hard profile. "You can't do that."

"Can't do what?" he asked innocently.

"You can't give a gift with... with strings like that attached."

"Verity," he said wearily, "you're old enough to know there are strings attached to everything in life. And you're smart enough to realize that I'll put strings on you any way I can. You want the earrings?"

"You know I want the earrings," she muttered, clutching the small box. She wanted them very badly, more than she had realized when she'd first spotted them in the window. The earrings were hers, they belonged to her. She was certain of it.

"Then you keep them and the strings that come with them."

"I don't have to accept them on your terms."

"You don't have any choice. And I'd appreciate it if you'd stop whining. Whining women are extremely annoying."

"I'll whine as much as I like. Pregnant women are entitled to whine." As a snappy come-back, that lacked something, but Verity was unable to think of anything else. She definitely did not intend to return the earrings. Jonas could put all the imaginary strings he liked on his gift. She didn't have to accept them along with the jewelry.

"That's one of the things I like about you, sweetheart. You always go down fighting."

"Don't push your luck, Quarrel."

"It's not luck I'm pushing. It's you."

Forty minutes after leaving the marina, Jonas docked the launch in the cove below the villa. The squall line from the approaching storm dogged their heels as he and Verity climbed the path to the old fortress. Doug Warwick met them at the door.

"Glad you made it in ahead of the storm," he said as he took the packages out of Verity's arms. "Otherwise you would have been stranded in town until tomorrow. I'd rather not lose any more time than necessary this week. Find out anything interesting from your contacts?"

Much to Verity's relief, Jonas did not take noticeable offense at Doug's comment about wasting time. "Just straightened out a few details," he replied easily, his eyes on Verity. "How are things going here?"

"I think acute boredom is setting in." Doug grimaced. "I wish to hell Elyssa hadn't invited Crump, Spencer, and Yarwood. We've all been stuck inside since yesterday because of the rain, and I think we're starting to get on each other's nerves. Spencer keeps trying to bait Yarwood, and Yarwood and Elyssa seem to be feuding. Crump just reads articles about herbal remedies or wanders around the halls. I think that guy's a little strange, if you want to know the truth. He makes me nervous. I'll be glad when this week is over. What's the next phase of the big treasure hunt?"

"The west wing, I think," Jonas said, slipping into his academic voice as he discoursed on Leonardo da Vinci's influence on Milanese architecture and described how traces of it could be seen in the west wing of the villa.

"I didn't know that Leonardo da Vinci actually built anything," Verity interrupted in surprise.

Jonas glared at her with fine academic condescension. "As far as we know, he didn't. But he did a series of theoretical drawings that influenced Bramante and others."

"Oh, I see." Chastened by his authoritative tone, Verity started toward the stairs. When she glanced back over her shoulder she saw a suspicious glint of amused satisfaction in Jonas's eyes. The man was not above using the academic put-down when he wanted to dominate a situation, Verity discovered.

The upstairs bedroom was chilly, like every other room in the drafty old villa, but at least it had an adjacent bathroom. Verity fiddled with the small heater, dried her damp hair, and changed her clothes. She was thinking about going downstairs to give Maggie Frampton a hand with dinner when someone knocked on the door.

She opened the door and found Elyssa Warwick smiling serenely. Verity forced herself to smile back. "Hello, Elyssa. What can I do for you?"

"Jonas and Doug and the others have gone off to explore the west wing. I thought it might be a good time for the two of us to have a little talk. Something very important has happened."

Verity stifled a pang of uneasiness. "What do you want to talk about, Elyssa?"

"May I come in?" Elyssa walked into the bedroom without waiting for an invitation. She was wearing a pair of white wool slacks and a white sweater. Her silvery blond hair shone in the light, and the small bells on her ankles tinkled merrily. Verity felt like a slob in her jeans and plaid shirt.

"Please sit down." Verity couldn't think of anything else to say under the circumstances. Elyssa was the client, after all. "Now then, what can I do for you?"

Elyssa sat near the window. She put her palms together and held them just below her breasts, giving Verity a look of deep understanding. "This is going to be difficult for you, Verity, but I feel you will understand. I would like to talk to you about Jonas."

Verity's sense of uneasiness grew. "What about him?"

Elyssa looked out the window, apparently gathering her thoughts. When she looked back at Verity, her eyes were very large and full of either a deep, ageless wisdom or fake confidence. The two expressions looked a lot alike.

"I have explained to you that I am becoming a channeler for an ancient temple priestess named Saranantha."

"Right." Verity tried to keep an upbeat, positive tone.

"My contact with Saranantha has grown stronger lately. Today she appeared to me in a vision and told me exactly what she wishes me to do. I am to fulfill a great destiny, Verity. I am to be the mother of a brilliant, psychically talented child."

In spite of her feelings toward the woman, Verity felt a burst of sisterly kinship. "You're pregnant?"

"Not yet."

"I see." Her sense of sisterly kinship died a quick death. Verity tried another tactic. "Just exactly what sort of work did this Saranantha do? What are the duties of a temple priestess? I've herd some pretty risqué stories about ancient temple ladies."

"Saranantha was a priestess of love."

"Somehow I had a feeling that might have been her, uh, calling."

Elyssa explained gently, "She was an exalted priestess who served a very important goddess. It was Saranantha's task to receive the love offerings of men who came to beg favors from the goddess . . ."

"In other words, she slept with every Tom, Dick, or Harry who showed up at the temple with the right amount of cash?" Verity interpreted.

"You mock me. But I am prepared for that. It is the fate of a channeler to deal with skepticism and mockery. But today Saranantha revealed the deep truth about my relationship with her. It will change my entire life, Verity."

"What is this deep truth?"

"I am her, and she is me." Elyssa's eyes brimmed with emotion. "You see, I was Saranantha in a past life. And now she has come to tell me that I must fulfill the same destiny in this lifetime that I fulfilled in my previous life in Utilan."

"She wants you to become a prostitute? I've got news for you, Elyssa. That may have been a viable career option twenty thousand years ago, but today it's considered a dead-end job. No pension plan, no sick leave, and extremely limited opportunities for advancement."

"Verity, try to understand. This is not a matter of prostitution or lust. It is a matter of boundless love; love that is not restricted by circumstance or petty twentieth-century morality. I am fated to fulfill my potential by mating with the man who is my true partner. I will be frank, Verity. I speak to you as one woman to another. Saranantha has revealed that it is Jonas Quarrel who is my true mate. It is his seed which must be planted in my womb; his seed which must be sowed and cultivated in me."

"Jonas? You want Jonas's, uh, seed?" Verity's voice sounded half-strangled. The woman's effrontery was unbelievable. "I think I ought to warn you that Jonas has already taken on all the gardening work he can handle."

Elyssa ignored that. "I am here to ask you to loan him to me."

Chapter Eleven

"ELYSSA," Verity said carefully, struggling to remember that she was a client, "I hate to break this to you, but times have changed. I'm afraid Jonas is not available for love offerings or guru-approved matings."

"I realize this has come as a shock to you," Elyssa said gently. "But I sense that you are a very wise and understanding woman. I think of you as a sister, an enlightened sister. Once you've had a chance to think about it, you'll see that a union between Jonas and myself is predestined. I am merely obeying the summons of my astral energy force. To resist would be bad for all of us."

"Jonas has told you he doesn't consider himself a psychic," Verity said quickly.

Elyssa shook her head, smiling. "I know for a fact that he is a very powerful one, although he chooses to deny it. Preston told me all about him."

Verity sat forward tensely. "Really? What exactly does Preston Yarwood know about Jonas?"

"He told me that Jonas was once tested at Vincent College, and that it was no secret in the lab that Jonas had great powers," Elyssa confided easily. "Preston hasn't said anything to Jonas or any of the others because it's obvious that Jonas prefers to keep his abilities a secret. One can hardly blame him. The public can be a nuisance to a true psychic. Preston respects his desire for anonymity."

"Wait a second," Verity said, trying to get to the bottom of Preston Yarwood's involvement. "Preston claimed he located Jonas by contacting the editor of the *Journal of Renaissance Studies*."

Elyssa nodded with slight impatience. "That's right. But when the editor mentioned several qualified men in the field, including Jonas, Preston recognized Jonas's name and picked him. He and I agreed we should ask Doug to hire the Renaissance expert who also happened to be psychic. Doug didn't care about the psychic part, as long as he got his history expert. But Preston and I wanted the help of a true psychic. Jonas is perfect for all of us. And when Saranantha saw him she recognized him instantly as my proper mate. You see how it all comes together to form a complete whole? The harmony of life is breathtaking when the natural forces are allowed to take their proper path, isn't it?"

"I find the nerve of some people just as breathtaking."

"You are offended that I have approached you in this way? I only want to be honest with you, my sister. I believe I can make you understand my situation. You have an open mind, and you seek the truth in your own way. I assure you that I am no threat to your long-term relationship with Jonas."

"You just want to borrow him for a little while, is that it?"

"Precisely." Elyssa's smile was almost beatific. "Jonas and I will create a beautiful child together, a child of enormous potential. You would not want to deny the world such a human being, would you?"

"Oh, I don't know. The world has gotten along without such a human being so far." Verity sat back and stretched out her legs. "Tell me what happened when Preston was tested at the Vincent College lab."

Elyssa's smooth brow acquired a tiny furrow. "The lab research equipment was not sophisticated enough to define his particular psychic talent."

"Then what makes you think the equipment was sophisticated enough to properly identify Jonas's abilities? Maybe the research people were wrong, just as they were wrong about Preston. Jonas claims he's not a psychic. It could be that he knows himself best."

"I'm sure Preston could not have made a mistake about Jonas. Preston has developed his intuitive talents through several lifetimes. They are very acute."

"I see." Verity put her hands on the arms of the chair and pushed herself to her feet. "Elyssa, I hate to disappoint you, but I'm afraid Jonas would not make a good stud for you. He's not what you think he is, and furthermore I can't possibly allow you to borrow him. Jonas is very old-fashioned in some ways, you know. I wouldn't dream of embarrassing him by sending him off to your bed. Furthermore . . ." She was warming to her topic. "Furthermore, in all good conscience, I feel I must warn you that if you attempt to seduce him—"

She broke off as the bedroom door opened and Jonas strolled blithely into the room. "I was wondering where you were, Verity. What did you do with the flashlight? It's not in the duffel bag, and we need it in the west wing. Oh, hello, Elyssa. You two having a nice visit?"

Elyssa rose to her feet. She gave Jonas one of her temple-priestess smiles. "Hello, Jonas. Verity and I were having a woman-to-woman chat. But we're finished now. I can see there is no more to be said. Goodbye, Verity. Please try to open your mind and allow yourself to be guided by your inner light. It is the only way to achieve lasting happiness and satisfaction." She walked out of the room with one last smile for Jonas.

"What the hell was that all about?" Jonas demanded as he closed the door behind Elyssa. "What's a woman-to-woman chat?"

"We were discussing your potential as a stud."

"The hell you were." He looked astounded.

"Elyssa would like to borrow your services for a short while. Until she gets pregnant." Verity hid her grin. She had never seen Jonas look so outraged. "She thinks you would make an ideal mate. She ought to know. Apparently she's already spent one previous lifetime fooling around with anything in pants, and intends to spend this one the same way. She wants you, but being the noble, sincere, honest little hussy that she is, she thought she would clear it with me first."

"Let me get this straight. She asked you for permission to screw me?" A dull redness was staining Jonas's high cheekbones. "I don't believe it!"

"I guess it's the New Age approach to the man shortage."

"Verity, do you mean to tell me that you sat here and calmly discussed this with that blond kook?"

Verity smiled sedately. "Of course. We women communicate very well with each other."

"Jesus, I just can't believe it." Jonas slammed his hand against the wall. He stared at Verity from beneath hooded lashes. "Well?"

"Well, what?" she asked innocently.

"What did you tell her when she asked to borrow me?"

"I told her you weren't that kind of man."

Jonas stalked over to Verity. His expression was only one step short of rage. "You think this is all very funny, don't you?"

"It had its moments." Verity could no longer repress a giggle. Her eyes were brimming with laughter when she looked up into his thunderous glare. "I thought about telling her you'd already given your procreative all to me and that I doubted if there was anything left over, but I figured you might be insulted."

"I ought to turn you over my knee. Dammit, Verity, one of these days you're going to go too far."

"Promises, promises," she said, mimicking him.

"A joke. That's all it is to you, isn't it? A stupid joke. Some other woman tells you she wants to hop into the sack with me and make a baby, and you just laugh it off. Where's the goddamned flashlight?"

It finally dawned on Verity that Jonas was not seeing the humor in the situation. He was disgruntled and aggrieved, as if her lack of jealousy hurt him.

She opened her mouth to explain to him that it wasn't other women she feared. When it came to their relationship, her fears focused on the unknown factors in Jonas himself, not anything as straightforward and simple as another female making a pass at him. The truth was, she trusted him implicitly in some matters. Jonas would never have an affair behind her back. But it was clear that he was not in the mood for another relationship discussion.

"The flashlight is under the bed," Verity said slowly, in answer to his question. "I didn't have room for it when I packed your duffel bag for the trip to town." Verity leaned down and retrieved the large flashlight.

Jonas raised beseeching eyes toward the ceiling. "Anything else of mine hidden under there?"

"Nope. That's it."

"I'm grateful."

Verity ignored his sarcasm as she slowly sat down on the bed. She didn't know how to apologize for not having shown sufficient jealousy, so she decided to move on to a safer topic.

"You know something, Jonas? Elyssa and Preston are both aware of the fact that you were tested at Vincent College. Preston has kept it quiet. He claims he respects your desire for anonymity. The only one he told was Elyssa—that's why she's convinced you're a psychic."

Jonas glanced up from checking the flashlight batteries. He frowned. "How much do they know about what happened at Vincent? Did you find out?"

Verity shook her head. "No, but I gather they don't know too much, other than that the researchers confirmed your psychic abilities. That's all that matters to Little Miss Sunshine, by the way. She wants to mate with a true psychic. Maybe she's begun to have a few doubts about Preston. Her temple-priestess mentor thinks your genes might produce more impressive offspring."

"She's crazy."

"Elyssa?" Verity gave him a wry glance. "I think Elyssa is just the overly enthusiastic type. Which is why I didn't make a scene just now. I mean, after all, she's basically harmless, and she is a client, and I . . ."

"Forget it. I've got to get back to work. Warwick is paying me to make a thorough inspection of this joint, and time is running out. I'll see you at dinner."

Verity sighed as he left the room. She sat staring at the grimy portrait on the wall, wondering why she hadn't had the sense to make a scene over the issue of another woman setting her sights on Jonas.

But how could she explain to Jonas that she didn't see other women as a threat? Compared to the real dangers their relationship faced, other women were a piece of cake. *Jonas, my love,* she thought bleakly, *you don't know what real fear and jealousy are. I've got them in spades, and they've got nothing to do with other women.*

Real fear was the kind that woke her up in the middle of the night and made her wonder if the psychic link between her and Jonas was all that held him at her side. Real jealousy was torturing herself with visions of what might happen if that link ever dissolved, or if Jonas discovered that he no longer needed her to control his talent. And there was another fear she carried deep in her heart. There was a part of Jonas that reminded her of her father. It was the part of him that had an easy acquaintance with violence and adventuring. And every time she caught a glimpse of that part of his nature she found herself wondering how long he would be content to stick around her, and the baby, and Sequence Springs.

Other women? No, Verity could laugh off that threat. There were too many other things in this relationship to panic over.

But until now it had never occurred to her that Jonas might be panicking, too. It was clear for the first time that she wasn't the only one who needed reassurance.

She had been so wrapped up in her own uncertainties and fears that she hadn't even realized that Jonas had a few of his own.

After a few minutes of pondering that revelation, Verity remembered her new earrings. She got up and went to the dresser to put them on. When they were in place, she turned her head from side to side, examining the effect.

Jonas was wrong—she didn't need earrings the color of her eyes. These red crystals were perfect for her. The fire in them danced whenever she moved her head.

"We are as one in our search for the higher levels of truth," Preston Yarwood intoned. "Our combined psychic energy is a powerful force. Together we will project it into the crystal, where it will be tuned, amplified, and fed back to us. Together we will make the journey this evening to another plane. Together we will find a state of altered consciousness in which we can leap across the limitations of normal logic, and use our intuition to arrive at new answers. Together. We must work together."

Rain beat down in the dark courtyard. Verity could hear it slapping against the windows of the salon. Her left hand was gripped firmly by Jonas and her right hand was held loosely by Oliver Crump. She narrowed her eyes and risked a quick glance around the small circle seated on the floor in front of the fireplace.

The room was dark except for the glow from the fire. Yarwood had turned off the lights, saying that it was easier to harmonize a variety of psychic energies in darkness. In the center of their circle sat a large piece of pink crystal. The idea, Yarwood had explained, was to focus their psychic energy on the crystal. Theoretically the rock would channel and enhance that energy.

Verity saw that Jonas's eyes were open and he looked bored. He had joined the circle reluctantly, at Elyssa's urging. Catching Verity peeking, he flashed her a sexy grin. She smiled back at him ruefully. *Talk about a waste of time,* she thought. But this sort of thing was part of humoring the client, as she had explained to Jonas earlier.

"We must all focus together," Yarwood said with a hint of rebuke.

Verity realized that Preston must have caught her and Jonas exchanging their silent joke. Obediently, she closed her eyes again. Yarwood resumed droning in a steady, hypnotic chant.

Jonas started to tickle Verity's palm with his middle finger. She ignored it for as long as she could, but after several moments she couldn't stand it. She tightened her hand around his, and he stopped. As soon as she loosened her warning grip, however, he started in again. Verity nudged him with her knee. Jonas turned the tickling action into a long, intimate stroking that was blatantly erotic. His finger slipped slowly from her palm to her wrist and back again in a movement that she knew was meant to simulate sex.

Verity used her nails briefly to punish him. Jonas obligingly stopped the teasing motion of his finger until she withdrew her nails from his skin, then he started it up again.

Verity tried desperately to concentrate on something else. She thought about the legendary treasure, picturing the frozen vision of the Renaissance man seated at the writing desk with the full treasure chest behind him.

Something shimmered in her mind.

Startled, she stopped playing hand games with Jonas. He stopped too, as if sensing her surprise. The shimmering feeling came again. Verity opened her eyes and stared at the crystal. The shard of pink rock sat in the middle of the circle. It wasn't glowing, or changing color, or doing anything mysterious.

But Verity's earrings suddenly felt very warm.

She frowned intently and closed her eyes again. Her imagination was working overtime. Preston Yarwood continued to talk, urging everyone to project harder. Verity wished he would shut up. She felt a sudden need to concentrate.

The shimmering image in Verity's mind began to take shape. She became very still, gripping Jonas's hand hard.

This wasn't like the times she had entered the psychic corridor with Jonas. This was different. There was a faint image appearing inside her head, but it had nothing to do with the time tunnel.

She knew that Jonas was aware that she was suddenly distracted. His fingers closed tightly around hers. On the other side of her, Oliver Crump also started to squeeze her fingers more firmly.

Verity studied the picture in her head. It was a dark stone room. Against one wall of the forbidding little room was a heavily carved chest, fashioned out of black wood.

A cold draft sliced suddenly through the salon. The fire flickered and nearly died.

"Maggie must have left a window open," Elyssa Warwick complained. "It's cold in here."

Her words broke the spell. The image in Verity's mind vanished abruptly, and her earrings no longer felt warm. On her right, Oliver Crump slowly released her hand. When she opened her eyes she found him looking at her with a strange expression. Jonas squeezed her left hand so tightly Verity thought he might cut off the circulation in her fingers.

"I think that's enough projecting for this evening," Jonas announced as he got to his feet and pulled Verity up beside him. "It's late, and Verity and I are going to bed. Good night, everyone."

"I'm with you," Doug Warwick said. "I wish there were a television in this place."

"At least we've got booze," Slade muttered, walking to the liquor cabinet. He surreptitiously uncapped his pill bottle. "Good booze at that." He downed the pills with a stiff shot of whiskey.

Verity had noticed earlier in the evening that Spencer's

bruises had worsened slightly during the past twenty-four hours. It was not uncommon for a bruise to show more color two or three days after it had been caused. She winced as she said good night to him, hoping that every time he looked in the mirror he didn't think of contacting a lawyer.

"I'll have Maggie find that open window," Elyssa murmured as she swept out of the room. "She's really not the most efficient housekeeper, is she?" Preston followed her.

Oliver peered at her intently through his wire-rimmed glasses. "Good night, Verity. Sleep well."

"Let's go." Jonas tugged Verity toward the door, using more force than was necessary. As soon as they reached their bedroom, he said sternly, "All right, what happened back there?"

Verity pulled her wrist free of his hand and sat down. "I'm not sure," she said honestly. "Did you see it, too?"

"See what?"

"An image of a room. A stone-walled room with a black chest sitting in it. I would swear it's the chest we saw in the vision. I was just sitting there in that circle, Jonas, thinking about the treasure and wondering where it might be when all of a sudden this picture of a small dark room popped into my head. I thought you might have seen it too."

Jonas paced the length of the room, rubbing the back of his neck. His expression was grim. "I didn't really feel or see anything. I just got the impression you were suddenly somewhere else." He shot her a sharp glance. "I hope you're not going to get sucked into believing in this psychic crap about crystals and astral energy and the rest of that nonsense."

"I got sucked into believing in your psychic abilities, didn't I?" Verity retorted.

He stopped pacing long enough to throw her a severe glance. "That's different."

"I see. Thank you for pointing that out."

"You didn't really see an image of a room tonight, did you?" he demanded.

"I saw it."

"It was your imagination."

"Possibly." She shrugged. "Or maybe I was picking up on someone else's thoughts," she said slowly, thinking of Oliver Crump. "Jonas, you don't suppose that someone in that group really is psychic, do you? You and I were just playing parlor games tonight for the sake of the client, but some of the others were actually trying to project through that crystal. What if one of them really did pick up on something, and I got some of the backlash, the way I do when you use your powers?"

"I can't believe that any of those idiots are genuine psychics," Jonas said coldly.

"They're not idiots, Jonas. Two of them are clients. One of them is a very nice man who's studying herbs and crystal healing techniques, and one of them believes sufficiently in his own psychic powers that he once paid to have himself tested."

"Yarwood." Jonas considered that for a moment. "I still don't believe it. If he did have some talent, why would he have the Warwicks pay me to check out this villa? He could have done it himself."

"Doug wanted someone with genuine academic credentials, remember? Besides, Preston doesn't claim any talent for psychometry, just a little precognitive ability. That wouldn't have helped in a treasure hunt, let alone in authenticating the villa. Elyssa and Preston felt they needed you."

Jonas shook his head. "I can't believe Yarwood's got any real psychic ability. The man's a con artist, pure and simple."

"One who apparently believes in his own con."

"They're the most dangerous kind."

Verity looked at Jonas. "Are we going into that hidden tunnel tonight?"

"I'm going in. But I think you ought to stay here."

"We've already been through this, Jonas. I insist on coming with you. I'm warning you, I'll follow you if I have to."

"I don't like it, Verity." But it was obvious that he had no real hope of talking her out of it.

"We'll both be very careful." She rose to her feet. "Ready when you are."

"Verity . . ."

She was already at the tapestry, moving it aside. "I'm afraid you're stuck with me, Jonas."

"For better or for worse?" he asked softly.

She saw the intensity in his golden eyes. She looked away again nervously. "We'd better hurry if we want to get any sleep tonight."

"Little coward," he muttered. He picked up the flashlight and switched it on. "You stay two paces behind me at all times, and you don't touch anything or step anywhere I haven't already touched or stepped."

"Yes, O Great Psychic Hunter of the Night."

"Give my any lip and I'll tie you to the bed and leave you there while I explore this tunnel."

Verity shut up and smiled her most dazzling smile. Jonas sighed and picked up her discarded cane. He hefted it experimentally and stepped into the stone passage.

"Is it still there?" Verity asked as she followed him into the tunnel.

"Is what still here?" His voice was a soft echo in the passageway.

"The skeleton."

"Of course it's still here. Where did you think it might go?"

She refused to glance behind the stone door. "I was just checking. What are you going to use the cane for?"

"As a probe for booby traps."

"Good idea."

"Thank you," he replied sarcastically. "I don't know how much good it will do. I think I'm better off relying on my psychic ability and these footprints that Digby or his buddy left behind. As long as we step where someone else has already stepped, we should be safe."

They prowled slowly along the hidden passage, following the old footprints in the dust. Jonas said little as he led the way.

After following the angling corridor for some distance Jonas stopped and crouched in the dust, examining a series of steps that led downward abruptly. "The tunnel continues down between the walls to the lower level." He glanced back over his shoulder. "Be careful on these steps. They're narrow."

"Don't worry, I don't intend to twist this ankle again. Do the footprints come from that direction?"

"Yeah. Digby must have come up these steps a few times. It looks like someone else might have, also. It's hard to tell with all this dust, but I'd swear there are at least two different sets of shoe prints here."

"Digby and whoever killed him." Verity shuddered.

"Probably." Jonas straightened and started down the steps. "I think these stairs bypass the first floor. Looks like we're going down farther than one level."

"Did Renaissance homes have basements?"

"This one did. It was a combination storage facility and dungeon. I was going to check it out tomorrow."

"Maggie Frampton did mention a torture chamber, didn't she?"

The stairs led down into what seemed an endless darkness. Jonas's flashlight cut a brave swath of light, but it left a great deal of darkness untouched. Verity told herself that she was not claustrophobic and was not afraid of the dark. But she had to admit that something was sending uncomfortable chills down her spine.

The stairs stopped abruptly. Jonas halted on the last step and shone the flashlight along a new passageway. "The way this corridor is designed, it could wander all over the whole villa," he complained. "We could spend weeks exploring it."

"We don't have weeks, we've only got a few days." Verity glanced ahead into the eerie shadows. "Why build a hidden corridor that just wanders around the house? There must be other exits besides the one in our room."

"Looks like Digby or his friend found one." Jonas was studying the footprints in the dust.

"What do you mean?" Verity moved closer.

"One set of prints seems to come straight out of this section of wall. Probably another hidden door. The others come from farther down the passageway."

"Let's see if we can find the mechanism that activates this tunnel door. I wouldn't mind having an alternate route out of this damn passageway."

Jonas played the flashlight over the stone walls. "With any luck the design will be the same one used on the door that opens into our room. Ah, here we go," he added with sudden satisfaction. "Another testimonial to the Renaissance love of harmonic proportion and symmetry. The mechanism for this door is in exactly the same position as the one at the other end of the corridor. Stand back."

"Be careful, Jonas."

"I will, but I don't think this exit is booby-trapped. The other one wasn't." He traced a path between stones, pausing at various spots to push carefully. He was finally rewarded by a groaning sound that was almost human. A seam appeared in the stone, and then a heavy stone door swung slowly inward.

Verity gasped in shock as Jonas shone the flashlight into a room that looked like a wax museum's chamber of horrors.

"This is the love nest Maggie shared with Digby?" Verity asked in stunned amazement.

"And you called me kinky," Jonas chided as he stepped into the room. It was full of grim machines, chains, manacles, and other assorted implements of terror. He aimed the beam of the flashlight at one wall. "Nice collection of whips."

"Jonas, how can you stand this place?" Verity followed slowly. "If these horrible things are really left over from the Renaissance, then some of them must carry some terrible vibrations."

"I'm not picking up a thing," Jonas said cheerfully. He touched a long chain dangling from a wall. The chain ended in a wrist manacle. "Not a damn thing." He turned the manacle over and studied it with the flashlight. He chuckled.

"What's so funny?" Verity demanded.

"Made in Hong Kong. More fake antiques, honey. Just like the stuff in the bed-and-breakfast place."

"Well, that's some relief, I suppose." Verity glanced around disapprovingly. "Imagine collecting this kind of fake antique, though. It's disgusting. I can't envision the twisted mind of someone who would enjoy making love in a place like this. Maggie seems like such a nice person. And as for Digby, I had pictured him as a respectable if somewhat eccentric scholar. I never dreamed..." She broke off. "Jonas, this throws a whole new light on Digby Hazelhurst."

Jonas grinned. "Can't wait to finish this consulting job

and write the definitive biography of the man.'' He found the light switch and flipped it on. ''Hazelhurst obviously considered this room important enough to have wired for electricity.'' Jonas took a whip off the wall and examined it with great interest.

''I'm not sure a reputable publisher would even print a biography of Digby. Jonas, for heaven's sake, put down that whip.''

He laughed softly, drawing the lash through his fingers. ''You can learn a lot from a respectable scholar like Hazelhurst.''

''Don't look at me like that, Jonas.''

Jonas gave the whip a gentle flick and Verity jumped in startled reaction as the lash curled itself around her waist. It didn't hurt a bit. Jonas tugged gently on the whip handle and drew her toward him.

''This is not amusing,'' Verity announced in regal tones. She caught the tip of the lash and started to unwind it from her waist. ''It's made out of velvet,'' she exclaimed in amazement. ''No wonder it didn't hurt.''

''Want to experiment with some of the other stuff?'' Jonas asked, looking far too hopeful.

''I most certainly do not.'' Verity finished unwinding the lash from her waist. ''Put that back this instant.''

''You never let me have any fun.'' He replaced the velvet whip.

Verity studied the floor. ''Maggie's kept this area clean, I see. Sentimental reasons, no doubt. I wonder what she and Digby did in here.''

''The sort of kinky things that would make a little prude like you turn fire-engine red, I'll bet.''

''Talk about weird.'' She put down a manacle she had been examining and looked at Jonas. ''Now what? Back into the corridor?''

"I don't think so. It's getting late, and you need your sleep. I think we'll go on back to our room. But no need to do it the hard way." He walked across the torture chamber and opened the door. "Might as well use the main route. No sense going back through that stone-cold passage."

"What if someone notices us wandering around?"

"We'll just say you wanted a drink of water and I came along to keep you company."

They found their way back to the second floor of the south wing without incident. But when they passed the door to Elyssa's room, the sound of angry voices caught their attention.

"That's Yarwood in there with Elyssa," Verity observed as they hurried past. "Wonder what they're fighting about."

Jonas gave the closed door a thoughtful glance. "I don't know, but it sounds serious." He stopped to listen.

Verity frowned. "Remember what Caitlin said about Yarwood being dangerous? Maybe we should interrupt."

"The last thing any sane person does is get involved in an argument between two people who are sleeping together. You did tell me that Yarwood and Elyssa are having an affair, didn't you?"

"That's what Slade said. Yarwood sounds furious, doesn't he?"

Preston Yarwood's raised voice was barely audible behind the wooden door.

"You hot-assed little bitch," Yarwood shouted. "What the hell do you mean, you want to call things off between us? I'm the one who turned you on to your psychic potential in the first place, remember?"

"Now, Preston, you know this isn't a personal thing. I admire you very much, but Sarantha says I must seek another mate."

"Fuck Sarantha! I know what you're up to. You want

to screw Quarrel, don't you? I'm not about to let you dump me like this just so you can hop into bed with some jerk you think has stronger psychic powers.''

''Preston, please, there's no need to shout. I'm only following Saranantha's advice. She is my spirit guide. You know that.''

''I'll shout if I feel like it, goddammit. And don't use Saranantha as an excuse. You've got the hots for Quarrel because you think he's got psychic power. Well, I've got news for you, I'm the only real psychic around here. Quarrel's a fraud.''

''He is not!''

''He hasn't found that treasure, has he? He's a fraud, all right. I don't care what those lab people said. I knew it all along. I had my suspicions when I was at Vincent, and I've been proven right. Quarrel hasn't found a damn thing for us. If you want to sleep with a genuine psychic, you sleep with me, you little bitch.''

Verity looked at Jonas, her gaze uneasy. ''He sounds furious. What if he hurts her? I'm going to knock on the door. I'll pretend I wanted to talk to Elyssa and didn't realize there was anyone else in the room with her.'' She raised her hand to knock.

Jonas grabbed her wrist. ''No, you are not going to knock on the door. You are going to leave the whole situation well enough alone.'' Jonas pulled her firmly along the corridor. He got her as far as their room and was thrusting her safely inside when the door down the hall opened with a crash. ''Move it, Verity.''

Verity had no choice. She moved.

Jonas got the bedroom door shut behind them and sighed in relief. He leaned back against it and arched his brows at Verity. ''I guess Yarwood found out that Little Miss Sunshine is out scouting for new sperm donors.''

Chapter Twelve

ONE storm had passed during the night, but another was on the way. Verity stood beneath dripping pine boughs and gazed out over the cold gray waters of the Sound. In the distance she could see a Washington State ferry gliding gracefully past the scattered islands.

She had felt a compelling need to get out of the chilly villa this morning. There had been obvious tension in the air. Some of it had been generated by Elyssa and Preston Yarwood, who were apparently still at odds with each other. Oliver Crump had seemed more preoccupied than usual and Slade Spencer had retired to the salon after breakfast. He had not expressed any interest in further exploration of the villa. Verity had the feeling he was bored with the game.

Doug Warwick had taken the launch over to the small town on the other island, saying he had to make a call to the broker who was handling the deal on the villa. Maggie Frampton, as usual, was involved in the endless housecleaning that the villa demanded. Maggie's whole life seemed to revolve around the villa.

Verity had thought about joining Jonas as he worked his way through the lower level of the villa but she'd changed her mind at the last minute. She wanted to be alone for a while. She wanted time to think.

When the ferry glided out of sight, Verity turned and continued her hike along the perimeter of Hazelhurst's island. Her thoughts were filled with Jonas. She couldn't get rid of the feeling that she had failed to give him something he badly needed.

That something was reassurance.

The realization that he might need that just as much as she did was hitting her hard. She had been worrying so much about her future with him that she hadn't realized he might be harboring a few fears and concerns, too.

He had apparently been well aware of her emotional withdrawal these past few weeks; he'd tried often enough to get her to tell him what was wrong. And he had been genuinely upset that she hadn't told him about the baby as soon as she suspected she was pregnant. Then, when she hadn't immediately accepted his marriage proposal, he had been hurt and angry.

Jonas had a right to harbor a few uncertainties. They had surfaced yesterday afternoon when Verity had failed to show any real jealousy over Elyssa's outrageous request.

He was a man who had lived a restless, rootless life for the past few years, a man plagued by ghosts from the past and the constant threat of being overwhelmed by a talent he couldn't control. Such a man needed as much reassurance as he could get from the woman he loved. There were too many other factors in his life that were not the least bit certain or reliable.

Verity had done a great deal of thinking during the night.

She had awakened this morning overcome with remorse, and with a new perspective on Jonas Quarrel. She scolded herself for having been so wrapped up in her own problems lately. She hadn't paid nearly enough attention to Jonas's feelings.

Verity walked around a curving bluff and paused to glance down into a tiny cove. She was about to move on when she saw a small boat that had been drawn halfway out of the water and tethered to a pine bough. It was a sleek, fast-looking little craft. She glanced around, searching for whoever had arrived in it. There was no sign of anyone. The cove's pebbly shore was impervious to footprints.

Verity made a mental note to tell Doug Warwick that there might be visitors on the island.

She turned and walked a little farther before deciding that the brisk wind was too cold to make further hiking pleasant. She swung around and started back to the villa. It was time to give Maggie a hand with lunch preparations.

But Maggie wasn't in the kitchen when Verity arrived. Doug Warwick had not yet returned from his trip to town, either. Crump and Spencer were in the salon, but Verity decided not to strike up a conversation. She headed up to her room.

Jonas was not in the bedroom and she assumed he was busy earning his consulting fee. Verity decided to see how he was doing. She was on her way down the hall when she ran into Maggie Frampton.

"Here now, you looking for Mr. Quarrel?" Maggie said, surprisingly helpful. "I believe he decided to check out the dungeons. Saw Little Miss Sunshine with him." Maggie was obviously eager to impart that last tidbit.

"Thanks, Maggie." The thought of Elyssa and Jonas checking out the torture chamber together was annoying. "Was Preston with them?"

"Nope. Mr. Yarwood is in his room. He's not in a good mood, I can tell you. He and Little Miss Sunshine appear to have had a falling out, haven't they?" Maggie observed with relish.

"Something like that," Verity agreed dryly. "Excuse me, Maggie. I think I'll see how the big treasure hunt is going."

"You do that. But I'll tell you right now, there ain't no treasure here. Just a big lonesome old house that no one but me and Digby really loved. Now Digby's gone, and I'm not gonna get a chance to stay on to take care of the old place." Maggie shook her head and moved off down the hall. She was wearing another of her seemingly endless supply of housedresses. The dull overhead light gleamed briefly on the plain metal chain she wore around her neck. "Reckon I'll see about lunch."

"I'll give you a hand in a little while," Verity called after her. Then, with a determined stride, she headed for the stone staircase.

At the top of the stairs, something made Verity glance back over her shoulder. She caught Maggie watching her with a curious expression of anticipation.

She knows something I don't know, Verity thought. But she had a feeling she would soon be let in on the secret. She found her way down into the bowels of the villa without much difficulty, using the route she and Jonas had followed to return to their room the preceding evening. When she reached the door of the torture chamber, she found it ajar. She was not particularly surprised to hear Elyssa's sweetly cajoling voice from within.

"I have received guidance in this decision, Jonas. I have opened myself fully to the positive forces that prevail within me. I have gone inside myself and consulted with the spiritual side of my nature. Saranantha has helped me understand that what I seek is right. She has assured me that I am on the proper path. I am quite certain about what I am doing.''

''Well, I'm not.'' Jonas's voice was impatient. ''If you don't mind, Elyssa, I've got a lot of work to do here. Your brother is paying good money for my report, and I'd like to get it done on time.''

''You don't understand, Jonas. I feel I've been building toward this moment for several lifetimes. All the power of my woman's body has been developing for thousands of years, growing stronger, more fertile, more perfectly adapted as it prepares itself for the perfect mate. You are my psychic mate. You'll see. When we are joined in true harmony, there will be no doubts in your mind.''

Jonas's voice cut in, sounding a trifle hoarse. ''Look, Elyssa, I'm sure you believe everything you're saying, but the fact is, I'm not what you think. I'm not your perfect psychic mate. Trust me on this, Elyssa. I know what I'm talking about. If you want a psychic stud, go back to Yarwood or one of the others.''

''No, Jonas, you are the right man for me. I know it as surely as I know the sun will rise tomorrow morning. You're just nervous, that's all. But you have no need to be. I have envisioned everything. I have seen it all on a psychic plane that transcends this level of reality. I have seen us making love, Jonas. Beautiful, free, uninhibited love. On that other plane, I've felt your hand on my breast. Our mouths have touched. I've felt your seed pouring into my body. Now it is time to unite the reality of the higher plane with the reality of this one. This afternoon is perfect. I've checked all the astrological charts and meditated with crystal. Everything is harmonically aligned.''

''You mean everyone is either out of the villa or busy

elsewhere,'' Jonas said bluntly. ''Beat it, Elyssa, I've got work to do. Verity will be wondering where I am.''

''Verity is gone too. In any event, I feel sure she would understand. I sense that she is a very psychically aware woman. She and I are sisters in the way all women are sisters. She knows in her heart that you and I must mate. She will accept it.''

''The hell she will. You don't know Verity very well, do you?''

''Actually,'' Elyssa went on in a confidential tone, ''there's no need for her even to know about it, if you would prefer to keep it a secret.''

''Elyssa, if you're not going to get out of here, then I will. Dammit, Elyssa, get out of my way. What do you think you're doing? Jesus, what's the matter with you? Are you crazy? Elyssa, no, don't do that. Hell, I'm getting out of here. You can explain to your brother why his report is late.'' The rest of Jonas's protest was abruptly cut off.

Verity could wait no longer. She shoved open the door of the torture chamber and stood glaring with narrowed eyes at the sight of Elyssa in Jonas's arms.

Jonas saw Verity in the doorway and was momentarily stunned. He had been in the process of firmly disengaging himself from Elyssa Warwick's unwanted embrace when the chamber door burst open to reveal his obviously furious lover. He had never before seen that particular expression of outrage on her face, he realized dimly.

''Verity!'' Angrily, he shook himself free of Elyssa. ''Verity, listen, it's not what you think,'' he began quickly. Then he stopped, not at all certain what she did think. After all, she hadn't seemed particularly upset yesterday when Elyssa had asked her for a loan.

The hell with it. Jonas decided against further explanations for the moment. As it turned out, he didn't need to do the talking anyway. Verity and Elyssa were handling that end of things. Sisters, huh? He had never in his life met two women who were less like sisters than Verity and Little Miss Sunshine. Jonas leaned back against the wall near the dangling manacles, crossed his arms over his chest, and watched the open warfare with great interest.

He couldn't take his eyes off Verity. She was madder than hell. A fierce, feminine fury radiated from her, which seemed about to set fire to the room. It was certainly setting fire to him, Jonas thought with an inner grin. He felt himself getting hard just watching her as she sauntered into the chamber, looking every inch the lady of the villa.

Verity was shorter than Elyssa and far more slender, but with her wide eyes shooting blue-green sparks, her regal bearing, and that mane of fiery curls, she totally dominated the situation. Elyssa looked like a poodle facing a lioness.

"I thought I made it clear to you yesterday, Elyssa, that Jonas is not available for any moonlighting work." Verity's voice was soft and husky with warning. She advanced on the other woman in such an intimidating manner that Elyssa automatically fell back a few steps.

"Verity, please, you're overreacting. How can I make you understand?" Elyssa said pleadingly. "The union between myself and Jonas is right. It's meant to be. The consummation must take place."

"Try consummating anything with Jonas and I can personally guarantee that you'll find yourself on a very high psychic plane. I will kick your butt up there myself. In fact, I will kick it so high you'll probably never get it back down."

Elyssa blinked in astonishment. "Really, Verity, there's no need to get so upset. We are talking about a matter of deep psychic spirituality here."

"Really? I got the impression we were talking about a

quick toss in the hay with my man. A one-night stand. A cheap thrill. Isn't that all you really want, Elyssa? An opportunity to screw a guy who might have genuine psychic talent? You want to see if any of it rubs off on you? See if there's anything special about making it with a real psychic? Well, take it from me, you're not going to get the chance to find out what you're missing. Come near Jonas again and I will tear you apart into little tiny pieces and then I will throw those pieces into Puget Sound. Do you understand me, *sister*?"

Elyssa's soft eyes brimmed with tears. "You don't understand anything. Your mind is closed, after all. Don't you see, Verity? Jonas and I were meant to experience a powerful sexual experience. It's my destiny. I must fulfill it."

"Says who? Get out of here, Elyssa. Now. And don't you dare come near Jonas again unless I'm personally around to chaperone him. Move it, you twenty-thousand-year-old chippy!"

Elyssa's eyes widened further, then she burst into tears and fled from the room, her necklaces and bracelets jangling. Her sobs echoed down the stone hall.

In the taut silence that descended on the room, Jonas felt a glorious rush of triumph. It was all he could do to keep from sweeping Verity up in his arms and swinging her around in an exuberant circle.

But Jonas made himself stay where he was, one shoulder against the wall, as Verity turned to him. He didn't want to spoil her show. She had a right to the fireworks, and he wouldn't throw water on them now—not for the world. He knew the grin on his face was wide enough to show most of his teeth, but he couldn't help it. He was feeling too damn good.

Verity stalked toward him, her soft mouth tight, her red-gold brows forming a fierce line above her small nose.

Her eyes were a sea of flames, and her hair was practically crackling with energy.

"Well, well, well," she murmured, her voice deceptively smooth, "the big, brave, psychic treasure hunter almost got himself raped by the client."

"Consummated," Jonas corrected. "I was in some danger of getting consummated by the client. But you saved me."

"You think this is funny?" Verity shifted her gaze, apparently intrigued by the manacle dangling on the wall beside him.

"I think this was one hell of an embarrassing scene, and it's lucky you came along when you did," Jonas murmured.

"Why?" she challenged him abruptly. "Were you tempted to get yourself harmonically aligned with Little Miss Sunshine?"

"No, I was not tempted, and you know it. But the whole thing was getting awkward."

"Awkward?" Verity picked up one of the manacles and began swinging it idly. "Awkward is an interesting description of what I just saw. I didn't notice anything awkward about the way Elyssa had her arms around your neck. She looked very well coordinated to me."

Jonas chuckled softly and unfolded his arms. He braced one hand against the stone wall, planted the other on his hip, and grinned devilishly at Verity. "I don't know about that. Personally, I thought she looked a little top-heavy. A man could suffocate amid all those boobs if he wasn't careful. But then, maybe I'm just used to a skinny little redhead who makes me think of a sleek, sexy wildcat when she makes love to me."

"You think you're going to get out of this with a few flattering words about my talent in bed?" Verity smiled menacingly. She still held the manacle in one hand.

"Not a few flattering words, lots of flattering words."

"Talk fast, Jonas." The manacle snapped shut around his wrist.

Jonas froze for a few seconds. His wicked grin faded. He blinked at the strip of metal that now chained him to the wall. "This your idea of a joke, honey?"

"No," she said, walking slowly around him to where the other manacle dangled on the opposite side. "Nor do I find the idea of you and Little Miss Sunshine hanging around together down here in the torture chamber very amusing. I guess I have a limited sense of humor." Her eyes traveled over him as if she were inspecting him for market. She picked up the other manacle.

Jonas smiled reassuringly. "Sweetheart, you know damn well nothing would have happened." Poor Verity. She really was upset, he realized. She'd never experienced raw jealousy before. Of course, she'd never been in love before, either, he reminded himself with a wave of masculine satisfaction. He was the first and only man in her life.

"How do I know nothing would have happened, Jonas?" The manacle swung in a slow, hypnotic arc from her fingers. Her eyes were very wide and troubled as she looked up at him.

Jonas took pity on her. He knew what she was going through. He touched the side of her cheek with his free hand. "Take it easy, honey. I know how you feel. I was damned upset the night I came back from Mexico and found you being carried into the cabin by Warwick, remember? And when I found Spencer climbing all over you, I really came unglued. But it turned out that nothing out of line was happening."

"Those were different matters entirely," she snapped curtly.

"The hell they were."

Verity glared ferociously. Her hand moved suddenly, and before Jonas realized her intention, the second manacle closed around his free wrist. She stepped quickly away from him, her eyes glittering with a new kind of fire.

"For Christ's sake, Verity, what the hell do you think you're doing?" He glanced at his tethered wrists. There wasn't enough play in the chains to allow him to bring his hands together. He was anchored to the wall. Jonas's mood of amused, indulgent understanding began to evaporate rapidly.

"I'm going to teach you a lesson, Jonas Quarrel." Verity turned away from him to survey the collection of leather and velvet whips arranged on the wall. "If you want to hang around in torture chambers playing with psychic groupies, then it's time you learned the risks." She selected a whip, a long-handled one with soft, delicate tassles on the end.

Jonas eyed her with a new wariness. Verity was as unpredictable as dynamite under normal circumstances. He'd never dealt with her when she was in a jealous rage before. Things promised to get interesting. "Put that back, Verity," he said. "This has gone far enough."

"I don't think so, Jonas." She walked to the chamber door and closed it. Then she slid the bolt home. The dull *ker-chunk* sounded ominous. She moved slowly back toward Jonas, watching him through narrowed eyes. The tassled whip waved in her hand. "You want to play games in torture chambers? I'll see if I can teach you a few tricks."

Jonas was torn between laughter and a hot, sizzling excitement. He'd been aroused since Verity had arrived looking like an avenging queen. He'd taken a violent satisfaction in the knowledge that she wanted him enough to fight for him. It had given him an undeniable, heady thrill to see the possessiveness in her eyes.

But he didn't know what to make of her now. He

wondered just how much of this was serious anger and how much was nothing more than a passionate game.

"Verity," Jonas said with quiet forcefulness, "the game's gone far enough. Where are the keys to these manacles?"

She took them out of her pocket and tossed them aside. They landed with a faint tinkling sound, well out of his reach. Jonas frowned. Verity moved slowly toward him, an odd smile on her lips.

"Lesson number one," she said as she stuck the handle of the whip into the back pocket of her jeans. "You don't need to wear so many clothes in a torture chamber." She began unbuttoning his shirt. "Torture chambers are hot places."

Jonas stared down at her fingers, fascinated. His throat was suddenly dry. "Verity?" The shirt parted and she ran her slender fingers through the hair on his chest. She flicked one flat nipple and Jonas sucked in his breath. His jeans began to feel far too snug.

"Lesson number two," Verity murmured as she knelt in front of him and yanked off first one scuffed boot and then the other. "You don't hang around places like this with twenty-thousand-year-old prostitutes. Is that clear?"

"Believe me," Jonas said tightly, "it won't happen again." He was getting turned on so fast that he was afraid he might become the world's first documented case of human spontaneous combustion. Verity was back on her feet now, her hands busy at the zipper of his jeans. "Honey, you're not really going to go through with this, are you?"

"I believe in teaching a very thorough lesson." The zipper hissed in her hands. She let her fingers trail inside the opening and smiled approvingly at what she found there. Jonas inhaled deeply. Then she slid her palms under the waistband and shoved the jeans down over Jonas's hips.

Jonas groaned under the touch of her soft warm hands on

his bare thighs. He looked down and saw his manhood straining against the fabric of his tight briefs. It didn't take much urging from Verity for him to kick off the jeans. Then he glanced at the door.

"Verity, I don't think this is such a good idea. Let's go upstairs to our room. Anyone might come by and wonder what's going on in here."

"Oh, lord." Jonas closed his eyes as he felt her take him into her hands. Her nails scraped exquisitely along the heavy, throbbing length of him. "Verity, this is crazy."

"Torture. Think of it as torture."

"It's torture all right. I'm not sure I'll survive." He took a few deep breaths trying to regain some self-control. She had such good hands, he thought dazedly. She knew exactly how and where to touch him. He felt her fingers teasing the full, taut globes at the base of his shaft and instinctively he arched his hips toward her.

Verity released him and Jonas swore in dismay. He tried to reach for her to drag her close so that she could finish what she had begun. But the manacle chains went tight and Jonas opened his eyes, growling in frustration. What he saw nearly did him in.

Verity was unbuttoning her shirt. It quickly became obvious that she was not wearing a bra. She worked with tantalizing, excruciating slowness, letting the garment slowly open to reveal the soft curves of her breasts. She didn't remove the shirt once she had it unbuttoned. She just let it hang free so that the fabric moved with her, alternately revealing, then concealing her rosy nipples.

Jonas stared at her hungrily, wildly intrigued by the sight of the straining nipple that flirted with him from the shadows. She was as turned on as he was, he thought. That realization almost sent him over the edge.

But he couldn't let go yet, he told himself. This was too

good to ruin with an early, unplanned climax. He wanted to see how far Verity would go. He had to find out just what she had in mind. When she reached for the soft whip in her pocket he shook his head wonderingly.

"You wouldn't dare," he whispered.

"Oh no?" She studied him closely, frowning in concentration. Then she extended the whip experimentally.

"I swear, Verity, if you try anything with that whip, I'll . . . Oh, Christ."

The velvet tassles trailed lovingly over his thigh and moved upward to tease his thrusting shaft. Jonas jerked backward in reaction. She dragged the tassles the other way, tangling his eager manhood in the little velvet strips. Jonas swelled to new heights.

"Not bad, for a psychic," she murmured with a small, teasing grin.

Jonas swallowed heavily and took another deep breath. "Verity, so help me, when I get free I'm going to make you pay for this."

"I warned you the night you tied me to the bedpost that one day I would get even."

She twirled the whip, letting it wrap him more tightly. Then she tugged gently and the tassles pulled briefly at Jonas before reluctantly uncurling.

"Verity, you don't know what you're doing." He could barely get the words out.

"Don't I?" She knelt in front of him and replaced the whip tassles with her hot, tight mouth. Jonas stared down at her head and waged a heroic battle for self-control. Every muscle in his body was strained with the effort. His whole world was filled with a flame-haired vixen who obviously considered him her private, personal property. He thought of his baby growing within her and he wanted to shout his triumph to the world. Just when he thought he would surely explode, Verity released him.

He breathed heavily, taking a step back from the edge and regaining a small measure of control. He watched Verity set down the silly little whip and unfasten her jeans. Jonas stared, hypnotized, as she shimmied out of the denims. She then stepped daintily out of her panties and Jonas gritted his teeth. He was going under fast.

When she moved away from him he gazed raptly at the sweet, sexy curves of her derriere. He could have studied the sight all day without growing bored.

But Verity had other plans. She was dragging the padded bench toward him.

"What the hell?" he demanded as she pushed the bench toward his legs.

"Open your legs," she ordered.

He did so reluctantly, uncertain what she had in mind. She maneuvered the bench between his thighs. Jonas suddenly felt very vulnerable. He looked at her through narrowed lids. "Now what, Madam Torturer?"

"Sit down."

He obeyed slowly, discovering that there was just enough play in the manacle chains to allow him to sit on the padded bench. His legs were astride the seat. "Baby, you are going to be the death of me."

"You'll survive. Maybe." Her eyes were hot and shimmering with desire as she walked over to where he sat. She bent one knee and straddled the bench. She was only inches away from him.

Jonas inhaled the spicy, feminine scent of her arousal and thought he would go into orbit. Again he instinctively reached out to embrace her and pull her down onto him, but once more the manacles restrained him. He relaxed, swearing softly in frustration.

Verity settled herself carefully on his hips. She caught his shaft between gentle fingers, then she slowly eased him inside her softness. She took her time, allowing her body to adjust to the penetration at its own speed.

Jonas sucked in his breath and willed himself to endure the sweet torture. He could feel the familiar, initial resistance, felt the soft, clinging folds clutch at him, and then he was all the way into the tight sheath. He released the breath he had been holding deep in his lungs. Verity's fingers clamped onto his shoulders and her head tipped back as she began to move astride him.

Jonas was half-dazed. She looked so beautiful in her passion, he thought. Sweet and sexy and trembling with her desire for him.

She wanted him. Jonas had never been wanted or needed in his life the way Verity wanted and needed him.

"*Verity.*" Jonas's voice was thick with need. He knew he would never last. She had him in her power and he was violently aroused, totally at her mercy. He didn't stand a chance. When her mouth came down on his, he thrust his tongue hungrily between her lips, searching out the hot darkness inside her mouth. He felt her tighten in that special way she did just before her climax. He heard the soft whimper in her throat, and his passionately tormented body gave up the battle for control.

Jonas didn't try to stifle the hoarse shout of satisfaction that accompanied his release. He gloried in the explosion that tore through him, pumping himself heavily into Verity's softness until he felt totally drained.

Verity collapsed against him, her head on his shoulder as she recovered her breath. There was a sheen of perspiration in the valley between her breasts. Jonas relaxed deeply, enjoying the scent of her hair and the way the curls tickled his nostrils.

"So you love me, hmmm?" he drawled when he regained command of his voice.

"More than anything else in the world, Jonas." She didn't move.

"Not going to let any psychic groupie with hot pants get her hands on me?"

"You'd better not let yourself get into a compromising situation like that ever again," Verity warned fervently. But her eyes were gleaming with languid satisfaction as she raised her head to look down at him. "No telling how I might retaliate next time. Do you hear me, Jonas?"

"I hear you," he whispered. Then he tightened one hand into a fist and yanked hard on the manacle. The weak aluminum catch came apart with a snapping sound and his wrist was free. He repeated the action with the other hand.

Verity stared at his freed hands. She was outraged. "You were faking it. I thought I had you really chained. You could have gotten free anytime."

Jonas laughed softly and pulled her close. "I haven't been free since the day I met you, little tyrant. And I wouldn't have missed this torture session for the world."

He kissed her deeply and thoroughly as he listened to the cheap aluminum manacles clatter against the stone wall.

They just didn't make dungeon implements the way they used to.

Chapter Thirteen

LUNCH was a somewhat strained affair. Maggie Frampton served the meatless lasagne and minestrone Verity had helped her prepare, but she didn't even bother to make barbed remarks about the lack of animal protein. She seemed distracted, Verity thought.

Elyssa was not very talkative either. Privately, Verity did not consider that a great social loss. Verity did notice, however, that Elyssa took special pains to ignore Yarwood, Jonas, and herself. When she spoke, it was to discuss crystals with Oliver Crump or to snap at Maggie for being slow. A lot of the sweetness and light had gone out of Little Miss Sunshine. Slade Spencer was his customary morose, nervous self.

Doug Warwick and Jonas, apparently oblivious to the awkward atmosphere, talked intently at the far end of the table, discussing Jonas's observations and the overall outline of the report.

"We can hardly claim that the villa is a shining example

of Renaissance purity of line,'' Jonas said. ''So we'll have to emphasize the historical significance of the place. Don't worry, it's all going to sound impressive enough, especially when you consider the fact that you haven't got much in the way of competition. If this were Italy, you'd have a tough time convincing anyone that this was an historical treasure, but genuine Renaissance villas are scarce in North America. I think I can turn out something that will wow your potential buyers.''

''Good,'' Warwick said, sounding relieved. ''I want to get this deal going.''

Spencer spoke up, his mouth twisted in derision. ''Turning out this report is a hell of a job for a guy with a Ph.D., huh, Quarrel? Sort of like getting paid to write a flashy ad for a big real estate deal. Not exactly pure and noble scholarship.''

Verity scowled, instinctively opening her mouth to leap to Jonas's defense. But Jonas forestalled her by responding first.

''Pure and noble scholarship and fifty cents won't even buy a cup of coffee these days,'' Jonas said with surprising mildness. ''I was never all that taken with purity and nobility when it comes to scholarship, anyway. What about you?''

''Me?'' Spencer shrugged. His coffee cup rattled in the saucer as he picked it up with fingers that trembled slightly. ''I agree with you. Screw pure and noble scholarship. It won't buy shit.''

''True,'' Jonas remarked with a pointed glance at Spencer's fragrant pipe. ''But then, not all of us are in the market for shit.''

Verity shot Jonas a withering glance. Spencer turned a dull red and everyone else at the table suddenly became very busy with their food. Jonas's comment had been an all too obvious reference to Spencer's drug problems.

"You think that degree after your name entitles you to make cracks like that?" Spencer asked hoarsely.

"No, I'd probably make the same kind of cracks even without the degree."

It was Doug Warwick who stepped in to save what was left of the conversation. "As I was saying, I'd like to have that report for my buyers as soon as possible. Now that we know the villa is authentic, they'll move on the deal."

Maggie Frampton overheard the remark as she emerged from the kitchen. She heaved a sad sigh. "The last thing old Digby would have wanted was to see this place turned over to a bunch of real estate developers," she muttered. "He said that only a real scholar could ever appreciate this villa. Don't rightly think he would have thought of developers as scholars."

Warwick smiled soothingly. "I know how you feel. But the fact is, Maggie, no one but a consortium of developers could ever afford this place."

"Digby and me got by."

"You wouldn't have for much longer. By the time I inherited it there was a year's worth of back taxes to be paid, and that was just the beginning. No, the only solution is to sell it."

Elyssa spoke up. "Honestly, Maggie, you'd think this was your ancestral home, the way you carry on. I can't imagine why anyone would feel such an attachment to this old pile of rocks."

Maggie glowered at her. "Maybe you can't imagine it because you ain't had much experience staying attached to anything for longer than a couple of nights."

A second shocked silence struck the table. Yarwood looked furious, and this time it was Elyssa who turned red with anger. Doug Warwick spoke up again.

"That's enough, Maggie," he said bluntly. "We're ready for dessert."

Elyssa turned on her brother as Maggie stalked out of the room. "We should never have allowed her to stay here all this time. You were far too kind to her. Her type doesn't appreciate kindness and generosity."

"What was I supposed to do, Elyssa?" Doug asked wearily. "We've needed someone here to look after the place. I can't imagine anyone else being willing to take the job, can you?"

"I'll be glad when this place is finally sold and she gets kicked out on her ear," Elyssa muttered.

Verity arched her brows at Jonas in silent comment. He gave her a fleeting grin of acknowledgment. Little Miss Sunshine did not take well to being denied mating privileges with her chosen psychic stud. The cracks were starting to show in the mask of her gracious, smiling serenity.

Elyssa seemed to realize she was ruining her image. She stood up abruptly. "If you'll excuse me, I feel the need of some fresh air. I'm going to take a walk."

"I'll come with you," Preston Yarwood said grimly.

"I'd rather you didn't," Elyssa replied stiffly.

"I want to talk to you."

"Are you both nuts?" Doug asked. "It's cold out there. And it's going to start raining again soon."

Elyssa ignored him and left the room. Yarwood followed hard on her heels. Verity was not unhappy to see them go.

The atmosphere in the room lightened as soon as Elyssa and Yarwood had gone. Verity glanced at Doug Warwick. "I almost forgot to mention that I saw a small boat in one of the little coves this morning."

"Probably a fisherman or a tourist," Doug said without much interest. "There are hundreds of islands in these waters, and a lot of boaters enjoy exploring them. Uncle

Digby never minded people putting in here for a while, as long as they didn't bother him.''

Verity nodded and looked at Jonas. ''Are you going back to work after lunch?''

''Yeah, it's what I'm being paid to do, remember?'' he said with a lazy smile. ''Spencer's right. Screw pure and noble scholarship. I'm in this for the money. Another couple of days should wrap this up.''

Spencer glared at him and got to his feet. ''I need a drink.'' He left the room.

''I'll come with you,'' Doug Warwick said to Jonas. ''I want to see how things are progressing.''

When everyone else had left the dining room, Oliver Crump looked at Verity. ''You've told him?'' he asked quietly.

Verity smiled. ''I told him.''

''He's pleased.''

''He doesn't seem to mind as much as I thought he would,'' she admitted cautiously.

''He's definitely pleased. Probably because he sees it as another link in the chain that binds you to him. He's a possessive man.''

''You seem to know a lot about Jonas.''

Crump shrugged and reached into his pocket for the large shard of yellow crystal he carried. ''Your ankle is back to normal.''

''You can tell that from looking at the crystal?''

His mouth twitched in a rare smile. ''No, I can tell that because I can see you aren't using the cane.''

Verity laughed. ''Brilliant deduction. I think your poultice might have helped, Oliver. Or maybe it was the crystal. At any rate, thanks.''

He turned the crystal in his hands, frowning down at it. ''You're welcome.''

"What are you going to do with the crystal now?"

Oliver looked up, the intent frown still lining his features. "I'm not sure," he said slowly. "But I've been doing a lot of thinking. If you don't mind, I'd like to try an experiment." He put the crystal in the center of the table where she could reach it if she stretched out her hand.

"Sure, I'm game," Verity said cheerfully. "What are we going to do?"

"Cure Maggie Frampton's headache."

"I didn't know she had one."

"She does," Oliver said. "She told me about it before lunch."

"I thought she looked a little off-color. Does she want to be the subject of a crystal experiment?"

Maggie came through the door to pick up the last of the dishes. "What's this about an experiment?" she demanded.

"Oliver says you have a headache. Want to see if he can cure it with the crystal?"

"Bunch of damned nonsense," Maggie said stoutly. But she sat down next to Oliver. "Digby would never have approved of this crazy stuff."

"It can't do any harm," Oliver said reassuringly.

"True enough, I suppose." Maggie rubbed her head. "And the aspirin I took isn't doing much good. I'm willing to give the crystal a try. What do I do?"

Oliver picked up the crystal and gave it to her to hold. "Just keep this in your hand. Close your eyes and try to relax. Try to let your mind go blank."

"Blank, eh?" Maggie sounded skeptical but she did as instructed and closed her eyes.

Oliver motioned to Verity to come around the table. Without a word she got up and did so.

"I'm going to put my hand on the crystal Maggie's

holding,'' Oliver said in his calm, soothing voice. ''I want you to put your hand on top of mine, Verity.''

''Okay.'' She waited until he was lightly touching the crystal. Then she put out her fingers and rested them briefly on his hand.

Something was just a tad off-center.

''Do whatever you think needs doing, Verity.'' Oliver's voice was very soft.

Verity frowned and closed her eyes, trying to concentrate. Her red crystal earrings felt warm in her ears. She thought for a moment and found herself unable to describe what it was that seemed slightly out of alignment. She didn't have the words. But she sensed a way to straighten it out.

''Here,'' she said, moving Oliver's fingers slightly. ''This way. Yes, that's it. Right there.''

''Yes, I've got it now. That feels right, doesn't it? Thank you, Verity. You can take your hand away now.''

Verity opened her eyes and stepped back. She watched in fascination as Oliver bent over the crystal in Maggie Frampton's hand. He began talking quietly to Maggie in a gentle, relaxing chant.

Time passed and Oliver finally stopped speaking. He took the crystal out of Maggie's hand. ''Open your eyes, Maggie.''

She blinked at him suspiciously. ''Hmmm.'' Experimentally she turned her head first to one side and then the other. ''Better,'' she announced. ''I declare. That's a lot better, all right. Maybe you're onto something with that crystal thing.''

''Or maybe the aspirin finally kicked in,'' Oliver Crump said wryly. ''We'll never know for sure.''

''Well, either way, I appreciate it,'' Maggie said as she rose to her feet. ''Just hope the cure lasts.'' She nodded at Oliver and Verity and left the room.

There was a short silence. Oliver was staring at Verity

thoughtfully. She wanted to ask him more about crystals, but something made her glance toward the doorway.

Jonas stood there watching them. His eyes were unreadable. The lazy masculine satisfaction that had shone warmly in that golden gaze all during lunch was gone. "I came back to see if you knew what happened to my notebook, Verity. I can't find it."

"I think you left it in the salon. I noticed you writing something down in it just before lunch." She smiled at him and wondered why he was lying. He knew perfectly well where he'd left the notebook. She would have bet her life on it.

Without a word Jonas vanished from the doorway.

"That," Oliver Crump observed thoughtfully, "is a man who could be driven to kill if he thought he was going to lose you."

Verity was shocked to the core. "He would kill me?" she whispered.

"No," Crump said, shaking his head with grim finality. "Never you. But any man who tried to take you away from Quarrel would soon discover that his life wasn't worth much. I think Jonas has seen more violence that most men see in a lifetime. Perhaps he caused some of it himself. Whatever the reason, it is a part of his nature, and you must be prepared to accept that."

Verity spread her fingers on the tablecloth and looked down at them. Jonas had experienced violence from several lifetimes, she knew. He had a psychic affinity for it. She wondered if that sort of thing was an inherited trait. She took one hand off the table and touched her abdomen.

Oliver Crump sat alone at the table for a long while after Verity left. He had been right. Verity Ames had answers to questions he had been asking for a long time. She could teach him things he longed to know about working with crystals. Already he had learned more than he had ever expected.

To think he very nearly hadn't allowed Elyssa to talk him into spending the week here at the villa. In the end, Crump had come out of sheer curiosity. He'd heard the rumors about Jonas Quarrel, and he'd wanted to learn the truth.

But it was Verity who had captured Crump's immediate attention.

It was odd that she seemed totally unaware of her power. Perhaps it was because she was linked so strongly to Quarrel. It wouldn't occur to her to allow herself to form a mental bond with anyone else. On some fundamental level, Verity Ames was very innocent and very virtuous.

Crump didn't understand the nature of her link with Quarrel, but he sensed the strength of it and it awed him. He knew that he had better learn what he could from Verity while she was here, because Quarrel would never allow her to get too close to any other man, not even one who sought only a psychic connection with her.

Crump smiled wryly. Quarrel would very definitely not let her get close to any male who offered that kind of connection. In Quarrel's eyes, such a bond would be more threatening than a physical seduction.

Jonas Quarrel was an intelligent man. He was also a very possessive one.

But Crump had just discovered that he, himself, was a greedy man in some ways. He would take as much as he could get from Verity, and hope he didn't step so far out of line that Quarrel felt obliged to beat him to a pulp.

Verity saw Preston Yarwood stride furiously back into the villa an hour later. She was alone in the salon at the time, curled up in an overstuffed chair, a book on her lap. But she wasn't reading. She was thinking about babies' names.

The subject of names, she had just discovered, tended to have a sobering effect. In a strange way, it brought home the reality of her situation as nothing else had. It put a label on something that until now had not been totally real.

She was pregnant, and the baby's father wanted to marry her. Given that she loved the baby's father and he claimed to love her, it seemed that a decision would have to be made soon. Verity knew she wasn't going to be able to drag things out much longer.

It would have been nice, however, if Jonas had gotten around to thinking about marriage before he learned of the baby, Verity thought with a lingering sense of resentment. But perhaps Laura Griswald had been right when she pointed out that Verity hadn't done much to plant the concept of marriage in Jonas's brain.

Male brains, apparently, had to be carefully primed for certain subjects before they switched on and ran in the right direction.

And the truth was, Verity had never given much thought to marriage. Emerson Ames had taught her a great deal as he dragged her around the world, but he had never taught her that she needed a husband. Verity had been happily becoming a successful, single career woman when Jonas Quarrel had arrived in her life.

If she was honest with herself, Verity thought, she would admit that Jonas wasn't the only one guilty of not bringing up the subject of marriage until faced with becoming a parent. She hadn't thought much about marriage either, until she had found herself pregnant.

Verity had just arrived at that distressingly honest realization when she heard Preston Yarwood's angry footsteps on the stone staircase. She looked toward the door of the salon and caught sight of him hunched deeply in his coat as he climbed the stairs. She glanced out the window and saw that a light mist was falling again. Little Miss Sunshine had apparently stayed outdoors to commune with nature.

Verity wondered uneasily if Yarwood had found out about Elyssa's attempt to seduce Jonas in the torture chamber.

She imagined how Jonas would react if he ever found himself in Yarwood's shoes. Not that she would ever be tempted to betray Jonas with another man, that wasn't the point. The point was that Jonas was possessive, aggressive, and protective. Verity knew that if she married him, she would have to accept and deal with those elements of his nature.

Verity didn't wonder about Elyssa again for several more minutes. She had gone back to her mystery and was deep in the middle of a convoluted conspiracy plot when her earrings suddenly felt warm against her skin.

Verity absently reached up to adjust them, wondering at the way the red crystal occasionally seemed to absorb and radiate back her own body heat. Crump had said something about that being a property of crystals.

A glance out the window showed that the mist had turned into a light rain. Elyssa must really be into the communing-with-nature bit.

Verity tried to go back to her book, but she found herself unable to concentrate on the intricate plot. Restless, she wandered to the window to stare into the overgrown garden.

An overpowering urge to go outside for a few minutes gripped her. Irritated, Verity turned away from the window. This was ridiculous. The last thing she wanted to do was go outside into that cold afternoon rain. She'd already had her walk this morning.

But her craving for exercise was suddenly overwhelming. She had to take a walk. She was accustomed to working hard all day. This enforced relaxation was getting to her.

Apparently she didn't have any more sense than Elyssa, Verity thought as she went upstairs to get her parka. There must be something primeval and compelling about this Northwest rain.

A few minutes later she was huddling under the hood of her jacket, wondering if this sort of irrational behavior was common among expectant mothers. She headed automatically for the cliffs. It was miserably cold, she thought, not at all like Hawaii. If she had any brains she would go back inside to sit in front of the fire.

Verity reached the bluff overlooking the cove where she had seen the small boat earlier. She glanced down. The boat was still there, but something else was down there also. A bundle of white clothing lay sprawled half in and half out of the cold water. Verity would have recognized those white wool trousers anywhere.

It was Elyssa Warwick who lay there, her head barely above the water's edge. She wasn't moving.

Shocked, Verity realized that precious time would be lost if she ran back to the villa to find Jonas and the others. She immediately began to scramble awkwardly down the side of the short cliff. The most important thing was to get Elyssa out of the water. If she wasn't already dead, the real threat was hypothermia. The cold waters could drain a person's body heat in thirty minutes.

The task of getting down to the beach wasn't as difficult as Verity had anticipated. Adrenaline could accomplish a lot, she discovered as she half-slid, half-jumped down to the pebbly beach. She landed on her feet amid a scattering of small rocks and pine needles and raced over to where Elyssa lay. Verity crouched beside her and felt for the pulse in Elyssa's throat.

Little Miss Sunshine was alive. She moaned heavily when

Verity began searching her for blood and broken bones. Elyssa's eyes fluttered.

"Saranantha?" she whispered thickly.

"It's Verity, not Saranantha. It's all right, Elyssa. I'll get you back to the house. Can you sit up? We've got to get you out of the water." No telling how long Elyssa had been lying here with her legs in the gray, frigid water.

"Feel dizzy." Elyssa's voice was slurred. "Help me, Saranantha." She made a halfhearted attempt to sit up and promptly collapsed back into Verity's arms. Her eyes closed again.

Elyssa wasn't going to be much help. Verity stripped off her parka, shuddering as the rain hit her head and shoulders. She removed the other woman's soaked jacket and stuffed Elyssa into the warm down parka. Then she hooked her hands under Elyssa's arms and started to pull her out of the water.

It was tough going. Elyssa was no lightweight, but Verity eventually got her up onto the rocky shore. She glanced at the boat, wondering where the owner was. She hurried over to peer inside. There was a small, wadded-up paper sack in one corner, a wooden paddle for emergencies, and some fishing line. Nothing useful there.

The keys were gone, but Verity discovered that a storage locker in the stern was open. Inside was a plastic tarp. It wasn't much, but it would keep the rain off Elyssa and insulate some of her body heat. Verity dragged it out of the locker and draped it over the prone figure.

Elyssa didn't look like Little Miss Sunshine at the moment. She didn't look very seductive, either. Elyssa looked as if she might die if Verity didn't get help fast.

Verity scrambled back up the short cliff and ran for the villa. There were only a few twinges from her injured ankle.

* * *

Jonas was standing in front of a narrow window on the first floor of the villa when he caught sight of the familiar red-haired figure dashing toward the house. His first thought was that Verity had no business running like that on her injured ankle. She could easily take another fall.

His second thought was that he was going to strangle her for going outside without a coat. She was wearing only a sweater over her jeans, and her hair was soaked. Obviously the little firebrand did not know the first thing about good prenatal care.

It occurred to him briefly as he turned away from the window that this pregnancy business might well change the nature of their relationship. He was rapidly developing an urge to nag. Of course it was all for her own good.

He reached the main hall at the instant that Verity came charging through the front door.

"What the hell do you think you're doing running around without a jacket? What are you doing outside in the rain anyway, for Christ's sake? Where's your common sense, woman? You're responsible for two now, you know."

Her eyes flew to where he stood glaring at her with his arms folded and his feet braced aggressively. Relief flooded her. "Jonas! Thank goodness. It's Elyssa. She's fallen. She's lying unconscious in the cove where the little boat is anchored."

Jonas rapidly reassessed the situation. "Go get Doug and anyone else you can find."

They got Elyssa up the side of the cliff without too much difficulty. When Doug carried her into the house and set her on a sofa in front of the fire, Verity and Oliver Crump bent anxiously over the unconscious woman. They began stripping off Elyssa's soggy clothing. Crump issued orders for blankets and warm water. One by one, the entire group appeared.

Jonas stood back and watched Verity's red head hovering close to Oliver's dark one. He was aware of the same uneasy sensation he'd experienced earlier when he'd watched the two of them playing with the crystal.

It disturbed him to see Verity involved with that kind of thing. He didn't like the way Crump seemed intent on drawing her into his silly psychic games. And he did not like the way Verity seemed to be growing increasingly fascinated with Crump and the damn crystals.

Preston Yarwood was the last person to walk into the salon. Jonas watched his face as he took in the sight of his lover stretched out unconscious.

"*Elyssa!* What the hell happened?" Yarwood hurried forward, looking genuinely stricken. "Is she all right? What's wrong, dammit!"

"She must have fallen," Crump said as he and Verity wrapped Elyssa in the blankets. "The rain has probably made the ground treacherous around the top of the cliffs. She's alive, but unconscious."

"But she was fine when I left her," Yarwood said helplessly. He stopped talking as everyone glanced up at him.

Doug Warwick looked at Yarwood for a long moment before he said briskly, "As soon as you've got her warmed up, Oliver, I'll take her into town. There's a small hospital on the other island."

Oliver nodded, his attention on his patient. "She probably has a concussion, but I don't see any indication of other injury. I don't think she was in the water very long. I'll go with you in the boat."

"Thanks," Doug said. He looked at Verity. "And thank you too, Verity. If you hadn't found her when you did . . ."

"That water's mighty cold," Maggie Frampton observed grimly. She had appeared a few minutes earlier and was standing stiffly in the doorway. "Person could die of exposure. Hypothermia, they call it."

"We know, Maggie," Slade Spencer said, cutting her off. His contribution to handling the crisis was to pop another pill into his mouth.

Jonas saw Oliver, Doug, and a well-wrapped Elyssa off on the launch a half-hour later.

"Oliver and I will be back in the morning with the launch," Doug said as Jonas tossed him the lines.

"Right. We'll see you tomorrow."

Doug was silent for a moment as he stood in the bobbing launch. "Elyssa and Yarwood have been arguing a lot lately," he finally said. "Yarwood was furious about something this morning. This afternoon he came back from that walk alone."

Jonas looked at him, feeling a wave of masculine empathy. He'd be looking for someone to punish too, if anything had happened to Verity. "I wouldn't read too much into it, Doug," he counseled softly. "Chances are she really did just slip and fall."

Doug's mouth twisted wryly. "I know. Guess I was out of line. Elyssa's a pain in the ass, but she is my sister."

Jonas decided privately that he'd go along with that analysis. Elyssa was indeed a pain in the ass. But he owed her. After all, if she hadn't pulled that seduction scene in Hazelhurst's torture chamber this morning, he would have missed one of the great erotic encounters of all time.

It wasn't just the manacles and Verity's technique with a velvet whip he was going to recall for the rest of his life. It was the hungry, passionate, possessive way she had made it clear that he belonged to her and her alone.

Yeah, Jonas decided. He owed Little Miss Pain in the Ass Sunshine. He stood on the floating dock until the launch was out of sight.

But as he headed back toward the ugly villa, his thoughts were on Preston Yarwood. Caitlin Evanger had said the lab report on Yarwood declared him dangerous in some vague way.

Jonas thought about his own recent experiences with jealousy. It was a powerful force. Furthermore, he knew, from the brief occasions in the psychic corridor when he'd picked up on the rage of a wronged man, that a violent reaction was not uncommon in a jealous male. He'd held rapiers that cuckolded men had once used to avenge their honor. He'd felt the shattering fury that could lead a man to commit murder.

It was possible that Yarwood had known such fury this morning.

Jonas shook off the thoughts as he walked back into the main hall. Verity was coming downstairs. She had dried her hair and changed her clothes.

"Did they get off okay?" she asked anxiously.

"They're gone." Jonas looked up at her and came to a decision. "Put on a coat, Verity," he said softly. "I want to go for a walk."

She frowned. "Now?"

He nodded. "Now. It's stopped raining."

Verity hesitated. He thought she might ask a few more questions but she didn't. She hurried back upstairs and came down with another parka.

"Where are we going?" she asked as he helped her into the jacket.

"Out to the cliff where Elyssa fell."

Verity looked up at him questioningly as they went outside. "You suspect something, don't you?"

"I just want to see if there's anything there."

"You mean any lingering vibrations of violence? Are you

thinking about the fact that she and Yarwood have been quarreling lately?''

He raised his eyebrows. ''The thought crossed Doug's mind, too. But I'm not sure what to think yet. I just want to see if I can pick up anything.''

She nodded. ''I can't see Yarwood doing anything that drastic, though, Jonas. He isn't the type.''

''Any man is the type if he's pushed far enough.''

Verity gave him a sharp glance, then looked away. He didn't have to ask her what she was thinking. She was wondering if he was the type. ''*Any* man, Verity,'' Jonas said with quiet emphasis. ''Even a nice, gentle soul like Oliver Crump.''

''You're wrong,'' she said with the same quiet forcefulness he had used. ''A man like Oliver would never kill, except perhaps in self-defense.''

''Don't bet on it.'' He gripped her arm more tightly than was necessary, annoyed with the way she had leaped to Crump's defense.

Neither one said another word until they reached the cliff above the cove. Verity peered over the edge.

''She was lucky it was a relatively short drop. All the bushes growing on the side of the cliff probably broke the fall.''

Jonas followed her gaze. ''If she'd landed wrong, she would have broken her neck.'' He felt the shudder that went through Verity and wished he'd kept his mouth shut. ''Let's see what we can turn up.''

''You'll need something to touch, Jonas. Something that she might have touched as she went over the edge.''

''We need to find exactly where she was standing when it happened.''

''You can't see any footprints in these pine needles,''

Verity said as they started walking along the edge of the bluff.

"No, but I should be able to feel something if we find the right spot. Watch your step." He tightened his grip on her arm.

They took another dozen steps before Jonas felt the atmosphere around him shiver with the familiar sensation of violence. Verity halted at once, watching his face intently.

"Here?" she whispered.

"Close to here," he confirmed. "But it's very faint. I'll have to work to get anything at all. Are you ready?"

Verity nodded quickly and clasped her hands in front of her. "Ready."

Jonas took a step closer to the edge of the cliff and the vibrations grew stronger. There was a heady exultation in being able to control what had once threatened to overwhelm him. He could handle his talent these days, thanks to Verity.

Reality curved around him, creating a corridor that had no end and no beginning. Jonas remained aware of his external surroundings as he entered the psychic tunnel in his head. He knew that Verity was experiencing the same disorienting feeling of dealing with two realities simultaneously. It could be done. A few months ago he'd fought a duel in real time using the fencing skills he'd "borrowed" from another dimension.

"Verity?"

"I'm here."

He knew she was there, he could always sense her presence. She was his anchor here. He saw her out of the corner of his eye, standing a short distance away from him in the dark corridor. She was staring straight ahead at a weak image that was slowly forming in front of them. The vision was barely discernible, probably because it was so recent in time, Jonas thought. His talent was at its strongest when the vision took place in what he considered his prime time, the Renaissance. In the past few months he'd become powerful enough to pick up more recent scenes of violence. It had something to do with Verity. She had not only helped him control his talent, she had made him stronger. All the same, he couldn't get anything this recent to come through with much clarity.

"There she is, Jonas," Verity whispered. "You were right. Look at the ribbons."

The hazy image of a woman toppling over the edge of the cliff hovered in front of them. It was Elyssa, a look of terror on her features as she clawed uselessly at the air. There was no way to tell who or what was behind her, but Jonas sensed a second presence in the image. Snaky tendrils of violent emotion were unraveling from the animated vision, flowing first toward him and then, as if caught by a magnet, toward Verity. The snakes were pale and weak compared to those that would have emerged from an older vision.

"It's too damn hazy," he muttered. "I can't tell what's happening."

"Maybe it was just an accident—a violent accident," Verity said tightly.

"No." Jonas knew better and so did Verity. She just didn't want to admit it. His talent wasn't for random violence, like deaths caused by storms or accidents. The psychic ability that had nearly driven him insane was linked to the kind of violence men and women used against each other. "There's someone else involved. I wouldn't be picking up anything at all if there wasn't." He reached out to touch one of the sickly pale ribbons that coiled around Verity's feet. The shivering tendril leaped hungrily for him, a nasty little snake that would poison him if he wasn't very careful.

Faint traces of rage, anguish, and pain washed fleetingly through Jonas as the ribbon tried to coil weakly around his wrist. He quickly released the weak ribbon of emotion and moved back out of reach. Denied its prey, the snake rejoined the looping mass hovering around Verity.

"Are you all right?" Verity asked.

He knew she hated it when he touched one of the dangerous ribbons.

"I'm fine. Let's get out of here." In real time he took a step backward, away from the spot where Elyssa had been standing when she had fallen. The hazy image and the psychic corridor vanished instantly.

Verity stood rubbing her arms briskly. "Do you really think she was pushed, Jonas?"

He shrugged. "Something happened out here. Something that involved Elyssa and another person who was feeling both rage and heavy emotional pain. The vision was vague, but you know that I wouldn't have picked up on it at all if Elyssa had fallen by accident."

Chapter Fourteen

"I suppose it must have been Yarwood," Verity said quietly as they walked back to the villa, "although I can't really picture it. He must have found out about Elyssa's hobby of fooling around with every available male psychic. We heard them arguing, remember? And if he found out what she tried to do this morning he might have really gone crazy."

"Maybe."

Verity's brows came together in a sharp line. "What do you mean, 'maybe'? What other explanation is there?"

Jonas shrugged. "I don't know. But Elyssa's been fooling around for quite some time apparently, and Yarwood hasn't tried to kill her until now."

"Maybe he hadn't realized what she's been doing all along."

"It doesn't make sense. He must know what she's like," Jonas insisted.

"Love is blind," Verity said philosophically.

"Bullshit. I'm in love with you and I'm not blind to all your faults, or all the trouble you cause me."

Verity dug an elbow into his ribs.

"Ouch! Dammit, that hurt." Jonas stopped and pulled her into his arms. His eyes held a familiar glitter.

"Oh no you don't, not out here on the cold, wet ground." But the excitement was simmering in her veins, too. It had flooded her the instant she'd looked into his eyes. "You know something, Jonas Quarrel? I've given this matter of your getting horny every time we go into that psychic corridor a lot of thought, and I've come to a few conclusions."

"I'm not the only one who gets hot after we go into the corridor," he growled as he nuzzled her throat. "And I've told you, I never experienced this particular aftereffect until I met you. Never had the problem all those months I was being tested at Vincent College. Never had the problem when I authenticated artifacts for all those museums and collectors. No, ma'am, never had any problem like this at all. Until I met you, my thoughts were always as pure as the driven snow whenever I came out of a session in the corridor."

"Don't you dare imply that I'm the cause." She felt the heat from his body and her insides began to turn to mush, as usual. Her knees got weak. In another few minutes she would barely be able to stand.

"You know you can't lie to me, little tyrant," he said with deep satisfaction. "You feel the same way I do right now."

"Maybe, but I've decided that I don't get this way because of the corridor," Verity said, trying desperately to maintain some semblance of propriety. "It isn't being your psychic anchor that does this to me."

"No? Then what does it to you?" Jonas didn't seem very

interested in her answer. He was too busy nibbling on her ear.

"It's you, dammit. Not the experience in the corridor." She planted her palms against his chest and tried in vain to push him back a step. "You do this to me. It must be the way you look at me or something. I'm not sure, but I know it isn't the corridor that does it because I don't start feeling this way until you start leering at me. It's all your fault."

Jonas chuckled, sounding pleased. "Well then, that's just as it should be," he said complacently. "Let's go upstairs and find a whip. It's my turn."

"Jonas!" She blushed hotly.

But he was already lifting her into his arms and carrying her through the villa door.

Maggie Frampton was hovering in the main hall. She peered uneasily at Jonas and Verity. "I wondered where you two had gone."

"We just took a little walk," Jonas said smoothly. "Verity is exhausted."

"I know what you mean," Maggie said wistfully. "I used to get that same exhausted look on my face when Digby invited me to go down to the torture chamber." She turned and walked heavily out of the hall.

"She really misses him," Verity said softly. "It's going to be hard on her when Doug sells this place."

"Speaking of a hard-on," Jonas murmured as he started up the stairs, "let me tell you about my little problem."

"I've seen this problem of yours before, Jonas Quarrel, and it's not little."

Maggie listened to Quarrel's bootsteps ringing on the stone as he carried Verity up the stairs. Her hands bunched into broad fists. More than anything else she wanted them all to leave. She just wanted them out of here. Digby would have felt the same way.

How he would have despised Preston Yarwood. Yarwood was nothing but a clever con man, Digby would say. And he would have kicked Oliver Crump and his silly crystals out the front door, too. Maggie didn't like the way Oliver watched everyone and everything from behind those little round glasses. Something told her he saw far too much.

And as for Slade Spencer, Digby wouldn't have tolerated him and his drugs for a minute. Maggie frowned as she thought about Spencer. There was something vaguely familiar about him. She wished she could put her finger on it. When she got the chance, she decided, she'd have a little peek at his things upstairs. It would be easy enough to do; she had a master key to all the rooms in the villa.

But the main problem around here was Doug and Elyssa. They held the fate of the villa in their hands.

Later, Verity, who was lying on her stomach, propped herself up on her elbows and leaned over Jonas to get his attention. He opened one eye and regarded her with lazy indulgence.

"You're glaring at me again. Didn't your father ever warn you about frown lines?" he asked. "Pests are at high risk for them. They need to take extra precautions."

Verity arched her brows. "Such as?"

"Such as smiling at their lovers a lot and practicing saying yes."

"I say yes to you far too often. Look where it gets me." She tilted her chin to indicate the tousled bed.

Jonas contrived to look hurt. "I do it all for you, and this is the thanks I get."

"For *me!*"

''Sure. Think of it as a beauty treatment. Keeps you toned and lubricated.''

''Some beauty treatment. It's going to turn me into a giant whale during the next few months,'' Verity complained.

To her surprise, Jonas's expression sobered. He drew a finger along the line of her jaw. ''Are you scared, honey?'' he asked gently.

Verity automatically started to deny it, but reality stopped her. ''A little,'' she admitted.

''Don't be,'' Jonas ordered softly. ''I'll be there with you. We'll handle it together the same way we handle those transitions into the time corridor. No sweat.''

Verity's mouth curved. '' 'No sweat.' I'll remember that promise.''

He touched her lips with his fingertip. His golden eyes were brilliant and very, very serious. ''You do that.''

She sighed and rested her chin on his chest. His strength was always a source of reassurance and security. It was true there was a wide streak of the primitive in Jonas, a side of him that knew and understood far too much about violence. But she would never need to fear him. ''I do love you, Jonas.''

His gaze was intent. ''Just as well, since we're going to be married.'' He went on quickly before she could argue the point, ''Now tell me why you were glaring at me a minute ago.''

''I was not glaring at you. That was an expression of thoughtful concern.''

''Excuse me. Why were you glaring at me with an expression of thoughtful concern?'' He ruffled her curls.

''I was thinking about Elyssa and Preston Yarwood.''

''What about them?''

Verity lifted her chin and hunched forward with sudden intensity. ''Jonas, when we were talking about the possibility that Yarwood was the one who pushed Elyssa off that cliff, we forgot about another possible bad guy. Someone we haven't even considered."

Jonas tilted his head to one side on the pillow and studied her serious expression. "You mean whoever owns that boat down in the cove?"

Verity groaned. "I should have known you'd already thought of it. Why didn't you say something earlier?"

"I was too involved in other matters," he said in a lofty tone.

"You mean you were in too much of a hurry to get your jeans unzipped. Honestly, Jonas, for a man with a respectable academic reputation, you have an amazingly primitive mentality when it comes to some matters. Obviously a Ph.D. is no guarantee against simpleminded lust."

Jonas widened his eyes in astonishment. "Did you think it was?"

"One has certain illusions about academia."

"Only someone who never suffered through the formal academic process could harbor any illusions about it. Be grateful your father never sent you to a real school. Come to think of it, I'm inclined to ask Emerson to supervise the education of our kid."

"We're straying from the topic here," Verity pointed out. It was oddly disturbing to have Jonas discussing the education of their baby.

"Were we straying? I hadn't noticed."

"Another example of your simplemindedness."

"My simplemindedness is all your fault," he said dismissively. He gave a huge yawn, then he flashed her a wolfish grin.

"About that boat in the cove," Verity said determinedly.

"I'll have another look at it in the morning. Did you

notice anything special when you opened the locker to get the tarp for Elyssa?''

Verity shook her head, trying to remember. ''No. I didn't see any log books or identification papers. But I wasn't looking for them, either. Jonas, that boat means there's someone else on this island.''

''Like Doug said, probably a tourist who's camping here for a couple of days.''

''In this weather?''

Jonas contemplated that silently for a few seconds. ''I've heard these Northwest types are very hardy,'' he finally said. ''It could be a devout fisherman.''

''Then where is he? Why didn't he notice Elyssa? Why didn't he appear when the rest of us went down to the cove to get her?''

''He could be camping a long way from where he left the boat. He might know nothing at all about what happened to Elyssa.''

''Or,'' Verity declared, ''he might have been the one who pushed her.''

''Which leaves us with the question of why he would want to hurt her,'' Jonas concluded. ''When you get right down to it, Preston Yarwood is still the only one around with an honest-to-God motive.''

''It looks that way, doesn't it?'' Verity agreed gloomily.

''Verity.''

''Hmm?'' She knew that tone in his voice. It was the one Jonas used when he gave a command he expected to be obeyed.

''I'll see if I can find the guy who owns that boat in the morning,'' Jonas said slowly. ''In the meantime, whatever else happens, I want you to be damn sure you aren't alone with Yarwood.''

''I still can't quite picture him as the violent type.''

Jonas wrapped his hands in her hair and pulled her face close to his for a quick, hard kiss. "For a woman who was raised in some of the seediest island towns in the Western Hemisphere, you sure don't know much about men or violence. With Emerson Ames for a father, how could you grow up with such a streak of naïveté?"

"I am not naïve!"

"Yes, you are. In some ways." Jonas gave her a strange, speculative look. "I find it kind of endearing. Underneath that prickly exterior, you're sweet and soft and gentle, inclined to see the best in everyone until you get hit over the head with evidence to the contrary. You're a soft touch, honey. And I don't want you hanging around Preston Yarwood unless I'm in the immediate vicinity. That's an order."

Verity's smile was a little too soft and a little too sweet. "Did I ever tell you how I get weak in the knees when you turn all macho?"

"That's very interesting, Verity. I don't believe you've ever mentioned it. You want me to tie you to this bedpost while we discuss this weakness of yours, or would you prefer the one on the other side? Maybe all four at once?"

She started to tickle him unmercifully. There were some distinct advantages to having lived with a man for a while—you knew exactly where he was most sensitive.

If the atmosphere at lunch had been strained, the mood at dinner was stretched almost to the breaking point. It snapped just as the meal ended.

Things started out quietly enough. There was a subdued tension hanging over the stone room, but Verity assumed that was only to be expected. She didn't know if the others had come to the same conclusion she and Jonas had about the cause of Elyssa's fall, but she knew the subject was on everyone's mind.

Maggie Frampton served the meal of leftovers in stony

silence. Verity had a hunch her headache had returned. Slade Spencer made his appearance after having apparently served himself several drinks in the salon. He handled his knife and fork with exaggerated care. Anyone who drank the way Slade did had some serious ghosts, Verity decided.

Preston Yarwood was sunk deep in a painful, angry silence that Verity noticed immediately. There was a lot of pain in the room, she realized, but she didn't know how to relieve it. She found herself eating quickly, wanting to escape. Jonas didn't seem inclined to linger over the meal either.

As soon as possible, Verity put her crumpled napkin on the table and gave Jonas a quick, questioning glance. He nodded briefly and finished the last of his sandwich.

Preston Yarwood chose to break his self-imposed silence just as Verity started to push back her chair. He raised his head and pinned Jonas with a look of dark, anguished rage.

"She thought you were for real, you know," Yarwood said in a strained voice. "She thought you were a genuine, grade A, goddamned real psychic."

Verity tensed and shot Jonas an anxious glance. He ignored her. Putting both elbows on the table, he regarded Yarwood with quiet challenge. "Is that right?" he asked softly. "I wonder where in hell she got that idea."

"Cut the crap, Quarrel. You know damn well where Elyssa got that idea. I know all about you. You were at Vincent College."

"A lot of people were at Vincent College."

"You were tested in their Department of Paranormal Research," Yarwood said belligerently.

"So what? I heard you were tested there too. But they didn't find any trace of psychic talent in you, did they, Yarwood? What makes you think they found any in me?"

"Oh, they thought they had found something, all right."

Yarwood picked up his glass and took a large swallow of the martini he'd been nursing through dinner. "I know all about those damn lab technicians and their bloody stupid research techniques. They found something. It was supposed to be a big secret. You were their prize guinea pig and no one wanted to lose you to a major-league research institution. So they kept it quiet. But there were rumors, lots of rumors. All those museums and private collectors who wanted you to check out their acquisitions believed you were for real —just like Elyssa did."

"But you know better, right, Yarwood?"

"Why are you playing these fucking games with me?" Preston demanded furiously. "I know about you. I know just how for-real you are. You're so goddamned real, you tried to kill a man in that damned lab! And maybe you tried to kill Elyssa, too." Yarwood leaped to his feet.

"Why would I want to kill Elyssa?" Jonas asked softly. His eyes held a savage gleam.

"How the hell should I know? Maybe because you didn't like the fact that she knew too much about you. Maybe you want to keep your damn talent a secret, so you can use it to rip off people like Doug Warwick. All I know is, Elyssa almost died out there on those cliffs, and I don't believe she fell accidentally. The only one around who's got a track record when it comes to attempted murder is you, you fucking psychic bastard." Yarwood stomped out of the room.

Slade Spencer had watched the small scene with bleary eyes. He said nothing. Jonas's fingers flexed as he toyed with the handle of his dinner knife.

Verity sat frozen, staring at the empty doorway. She was so furious that for an instant she couldn't even move. Then she found her tongue. "How dare he accuse you!" She leaped to her feet.

"Sit down, Verity."

"I will not sit down. That man made a terrible accusation. I'm going to set him straight." She started to move past his chair to get to the door.

Jonas reached out and snagged her wrist, yanking her to a halt. "I said, sit down." His face was set in hard, uncompromising lines.

"But, Jonas, we can't let him think . . ."

"Who knows what he thinks? All we heard was what he said. Sit." He used his grip on her wrist to force her back down into her chair.

"You're right," Slade Spencer said, finally speaking. His voice was slurred. "We heard what he said. Is it true? You kill some dude in a lab?"

"No, he did not kill anyone in any lab," Verity retorted hotly. "Yarwood was lying."

"That's enough, Verity," Jonas said.

Spencer scratched his nose and made a production out of lighting his fragrant pipe. The heavy scent filled the room. "I guess he didn't actually say you killed someone, did he, Quarrel? He said you *tried* to kill someone. I take it something interesting did happen at Vincent College?"

"Nothing that concerns you, Spencer."

"Hey, man, I gotta right to know if I'm staying in the same house as a fucking murderer."

Maggie Frampton appeared in the kitchen doorway, frowning darkly as she wiped her hands on a towel. "What's this about murder?"

"He's not a murderer," Verity shouted.

Jonas got to his feet and tugged Verity up beside him. "Come on, honey. Let's get out of here."

She dug in her heels. "But, Jonas, I want to explain. I don't want these people thinking you're a murderer."

Jonas shot her a cool glance as he pulled her toward the door. ''Leave it, Verity.''

''Just because you're too damn proud to make explanations,'' she said angrily, ''doesn't mean I can't.''

''There's nothing to explain.'' He had her through the door now, and led her down the hall to the stone staircase. ''Yarwood is right.''

''About what happened at Vincent? But Jonas, there were mitigating circumstances.'' Verity was incensed at the injustice of it all.

''I'm sure anyone who ever sank an ice pick into someone else would claim there were mitigating circumstances. If Yarwood tried to kill Elyssa, you can bet he's busy telling himself he had cause.''

''Jonas, you did not kill that lab tech.''

He shrugged. ''I tried.''

''It was an accident,'' Verity raged. ''A lab accident. People were playing with forces they didn't understand, and someone got hurt.''

Jonas stared at her for an instant. ''Verity, even if you can argue that point, you can't forget what happened a few months ago at Caitlin Evanger's. Even Yarwood doesn't know how good a case he's got when it comes to accusing me of pushing Elyssa into the water.''

''What happened at Caitlin's was pure self-defense,'' Verity declared. Her eyes were blazing with righteous indignation. ''You were attacked by a professional killer, for heaven's sake.''

A slow smile tugged at Jonas's hard mouth. He looked down into her furious face. ''You really do love me, don't you?'' he said softly.

''I don't see what that has to do with anything.''

''Never mind.''

They were walking along the hall to the bedroom. Verity

simmered down enough to think about what Yarwood had said. ''You know, Jonas, if Preston thinks you tried to kill Elyssa, that means he's probably innocent himself,'' she said slowly. ''He looked really torn up about it all.''

''Don't be an idiot,'' Jonas said fondly as he swept her through the door of their room. ''If you've just killed someone, the logical thing to do is throw suspicion on someone else. Yarwood used the information he had on me to do just that in front of witnesses.''

''Witnesses? Oh, you mean Spencer and Maggie.''

''Yeah. Spencer and Maggie. And when Warwick and Crump get back tomorrow morning Yarwood will undoubtedly make certain they hear about my unsavory reputation.''

''I wish you wouldn't talk like that,'' Verity chided him.

Jonas shrugged. ''Maybe Elyssa will remember what happened and solve the problem for all of us. In the meantime, we have to be prepared for the possibility that Doug will want to end this consulting job in a hurry tomorrow. Can't blame him. After what happened to his sister, he'll probably be anxious to end this entire thing.''

''Can you write the report he wants with the information you've got?''

''Don't look so worried, boss. Sure I can write. The report never was a problem. I could have given him something for his clients after the first day.'' Jonas was moving around the room, collecting the flashlight and a jacket. ''But tonight could be our last shot at the treasure.''

Verity groaned. ''I should have guessed. You know, you've become obsessed by this treasure business, Jonas. I'm not sure it's at all healthy. In fact, given what happened to Digby, I'd say it very definitely is not healthy.'' She broke off. ''It's strange, isn't it?''

''What's strange? Here, put on a jacket, that passage gets

cold. You've got to keep the baby warm.'' He tossed her the parka.

''What's strange,'' Verity said as she put on the parka, ''is that two people who have a direct link with this villa have gotten into serious trouble here. Digby was murdered, and Elyssa was almost killed.''

''You're right—it is strange. Ready?'' Jonas was already at the wall, moving aside the tapestry to operate the door mechanism.

Verity followed more slowly. ''What are we going to do tonight?''

''We're going to look for that room that appears in the vision of the man sitting at the desk. I've scoured every inch of this villa during the past few days, and I haven't found a single room that matches the one in that image.''

''So you figure it's hidden somewhere in this passageway?'' Verity shivered at the cold draft that swept out from the dank tunnel.

''I think it's possible this passage leads to it. Tonight we'll find out. Bring along that broken sword hilt in case we need to access the vision again.''

''I want you to know I don't really approve of this, Jonas. Something tells me we're making a mistake.'' She picked up the rusted scrap of metal.

''The only mistake I'm probably making is in taking you along.''

''I won't let you go without me,'' she insisted.

''Just be sure you follow orders. You know the drill. Stay behind me and don't touch anything.''

''Just like taking a little kid through a department store,'' she muttered. *''Don't touch anything.''*

''When little Jonas Junior comes along we'll get to find out about things like that, won't we? I can see us now—you, me, and the kid doing all kinds of stuff together.''

"What if it's a little Verity Junior?" Verity said saucily. But it warmed her heart to hear him talking about the three of them as a family.

"I'm not picky," Jonas said generously. "Are you okay? Seems colder than usual in here tonight."

"It's gotten quite cold outside. Probably another storm on the way. I hope Doug and Oliver get back before it hits tomorrow. Jonas, I'm going to be very glad to get off this island. The bloom is off the rose of consulting work, as far as I'm concerned. I'll have to think very carefully before I sign you up for another job."

"You do that, boss."

They followed the trail of old footprints and the ones they themselves had left as far as the entrance to the torture chamber. Jonas pointed the flashlight straight ahead and kept going.

"Not that I wouldn't like to stop and tarry awhile in that chamber," he told Verity. "I've got fond memories of that seduction scene you pulled in there."

"Honestly, Jonas, I'd rather you didn't remind me." Verity was embarrassed at the memory of her sexual aggression. She didn't want to admit to herself how carried away she had gotten.

"Why not?" he taunted. Then he chuckled. "I know what's bothering you. I'll bet you don't think that sort of behavior is proper for a pregnant lady. Such a little prude."

Verity chose not to respond. There wasn't much you could say to a man who had such satisfied glee in his voice.

The stone corridor wound deeper into the bowels of the villa. Verity lost all sense of direction. It was impossible to tell what wing they were in or how deep underground they were. She huddled into her parka, grateful that Jonas had made her bring it along.

"Well, hell," Jonas said a few minutes later. He sounded disgusted.

Verity nearly collided with him when he came to an abrupt halt in front of her. She peered around him and saw that the passage ended in a stone wall. "Oh no!" she cried. "You mean it just ends? After all this running around down here, the passage just comes to an end? It's not fair."

"Maybe things got screwed up when they reconstructed the villa here on the island," Jonas suggested. He pointed the flashlight downward. "Ah, here we go. The footprints disappear into the wall. What we've got here is another door. All we have to do is find the mechanism that opens it. Stand back, honey. This should be a piece of cake."

But it was not a piece of cake. It took Jonas nearly half an hour to find the hidden lock mechanism. It wasn't the same design as the others, and it had been embedded in the floor instead of the wall.

"Here we go," he said finally. He was down on his knees, his fingers probing between two stones. There was a grinding noise from the wall in front of them.

Verity caught her breath as Jonas activated the mechanism. A wave of dank, fetid air burst from the slowly opening stone doorway. Jonas stepped back out of the way and pulled Verity with him.

"Jonas, what if we're about to uncover a pile of Florentine gold coins or a basket of jewels?" Verity asked breathlessly. "We'll be able to send the kid to Harvard."

"No kid of mine is going to Harvard," Jonas vowed. "We'll worry about how to spend the goodies after we find them. You ready?" He moved toward the entrance and shone the flashlight into a small, square room.

Verity came up behind him and followed the light. She was immediately assailed by an overpowering sense of déjà vu. This was the room she had seen last night when she had worn her new earrings, during the second psychic-awareness session.

"Jonas, I know this room. I've seen it. There should be a black chest in here somewhere."

"Christ. You're right. There it is."

A massively carved stone chest squatted in the corner of the cell-like room. Jonas went toward it cautiously.

"It must be safe enough to approach it, Jonas. The footsteps go up to it and come back." Verity didn't like the look of the black chest, though. It resembled a coffin. Her earrings felt very warm against her cheeks. "It's the chest we see in the vision, isn't it? The one with the heaps of gold coins and gems in it."

Jonas reached the chest and examined it from all angles. "The lock is open. Let's see what's inside."

"Jonas, be careful." Verity lost her nerve. A rush of anxiety came over her. "Don't touch it. I don't think we should open it. Forget Harvard, there are plenty of good state universities. Let's get out of here."

She spoke too late. Jonas raised the lid of the black chest. In spite of her fear, Verity couldn't resist going closer to see what was inside.

"Empty," she said in mingled disappointment and relief. "Damn. I wonder if whoever killed Digby cleaned it out."

"Probably. Still, this chest alone will be worth a fortune to some museum. Take a look at the carving. It's magnificent. Too bad it belongs to Doug and Elyssa. All we're going to get out of this is a consulting fee." Jonas looked up, his features stark in the glow of the flashlight. "Let me have that sword hilt."

Verity's hand tightened around the broken sword handle. "Why?" she demanded suspiciously.

"I want another look at that vision of the man at the desk. I want to see if this is the room he was sitting in."

"I'm sure it is. But I'm not sure we should mess around with that particular vision. There's something very weird about it."

Impatiently he reached out and took the chunk of metal from her. So much for trying to give good advice, Verity thought as the walls of the dark cell began to curve around them. People like Jonas rarely listened to good advice.

Verity held her breath as the image shimmered and took form. Her earrings were turning hot against her skin. She started to remove them, staring at the vision of the man as she did so. Whoever he was, he had been capable of violence, she thought suddenly. She could see that much in the forbidding lines of his aristocratic features and the malevolent glare of his frozen eyes.

The small, green, egg-shaped crystal on the desk seemed to pulse gently in the reflected glow of the flashlight. But that was impossible, Verity reminded herself. The images produced in the psychic corridor never reacted to outside illumination. They existed independently in time and space.

Verity cried out softly as her earrings became so hot they seemed to burn her fingers.

And then she knew.

"Jonas," she whispered. "The crystal. The one on his desk. It's still here in the villa. It's somewhere nearby. I'm sure of it."

Chapter Fifteen

"*WHAT* makes you think the crystal is still around here?" Jonas studied the frozen image in front of them. The sharp planes of his face were illuminated by the poisonous green glow of the vision.

"I'm not sure. I get the feeling the crystal on that desk is trying to connect with itself in real time. It's as if it tried my earrings and they didn't quite work. It sounds crazy, I know." Verity shook her head. She was experiencing a disturbing sense of unreality. It was different from the feeling she usually had while in the psychic corridor.

"Nothing about this image makes much sense," Jonas said. "That's what bothers me. It's just not a normal time-corridor film clip. I've got to find out what the hell is going on here, Verity. I can't leave this place until I know what this is all about."

"It isn't even a scene of violence. You only pick up scenes of violence."

"But I tune it in by using an object associated with violence. That part is normal enough."

Verity edged backward a step. "It's almost as if the violence is about to happen, but hasn't yet taken place."

"Damn. Verity, I think you're right. That's it. That's the answer. We're looking at the scene an instant or two before the action took place. This guy was probably sitting at his desk when someone walked in and killed him."

"But why aren't we catching the actual death scene? Why would we pick up on it a few seconds before it occurs?"

"I don't know, but I've got to find out. I can feel the sense of warning emanating from this thing. It's as if that guy is just sitting there daring me to try to get at him."

"Or daring you to uncover his treasure," Verity offered, glancing around at the barren cell. "Obviously he doesn't realize someone else has already gotten to it."

Jonas walked to the chest and ran his palm along the heavily carved lid. "I'm not so sure the treasure is gone."

"Jonas, don't do that," Verity said, watching the image uneasily.

"Don't touch the chest? Why?"

"I swear his eyes are following you again."

"Just an optical illusion," he said absently.

Verity bit her lip, studying the image. The chest was still there behind the man, filled with treasure. "Why wasn't this room discovered when the villa was taken apart and shipped over here?"

"Who knows? Digby says in his diary that his relative had huge chunks of the villa left intact and transported that way. This room is small enough that it might have been shipped as a single unit. Maybe no one was even aware there was an opening behind these walls. It could look like a solid block of stone from the outside. Or it's possible Digby's crazy relative did find the room and the chest, and ordered it reconstructed exactly as it was. In which case, he's probably the one who got the treasure, although he never admitted it to anyone. *Eccentric* was a mild term for Digby's side of the family, apparently."

"But the rest of the furnishings were all sold off. I can't believe someone would have overlooked that valuable chest."

"Digby didn't know about the chest. At least not until the end of his life. Then again, maybe the chest is still here because someone wanted it left alone."

"Who?"

"The guy in the vision?" Jonas suggested softly. "Digby came to the conclusion that the treasure, whatever it was, might be protected with a curse. It was one of the last entries in his diary."

Verity closed her eyes. "Jonas, don't talk like that. We're not in the business of removing curses from haunted houses. You're a consultant, not a ghost hunter. You authenticate things. You do nifty little articles on the historical significance of old weapons and villas, and maybe an occasional treasure. That's it. End of job description."

"It's here, Verity. I know it is." Apparently Jonas was not paying much attention.

"What's here?" she demanded, scowling in the darkness.

"The treasure."

"Are you nuts? It's gone. The chest is empty. Someone has already been in here and scarfed up the lot. And then he casually knifed poor Digby on the way out the door."

"You said you knew the crystal was still around," Jonas reminded her softly.

Verity was still holding her warm red crystal earrings. She glanced at the crystal on the desk in the vision and it seemed to wink at her. "That's different," she said with great certainty.

"No, it's not. You know the crystal is still here in the

villa and I know the treasure is still here. Whatever that guy was trying to protect is still locked away, safe and sound.''

''You're a tough man to argue with,'' Verity said with a sigh. She knew he was experiencing the same sense of certainty as she felt. There was no way to contradict such a feeling with logic. ''Okay, for the sake of discussion, let's say you're right. What do we do now?''

''I've got to talk Doug Warwick into letting us stay here awhile longer,'' Jonas said, moving back across the room to stand beside her. They both gazed at the image. The menacing man at the desk gazed back implacably. ''I have a strong hunch he'll want to call a halt to everything when he returns tomorrow.''

''Can't blame him. As you said, he's got what he wants, an authentication and a professional description of the villa for his buyers. Now that Elyssa's more or less out of the picture, Doug's not going to want to spend any more time humoring her interest in psychic phenomena.''

''I've got to find out what's going on here, Verity. I need to know what that guy in the vision thought was so important he had to lock it away in time.''

Verity turned her head to stare at Jonas. ''You think he's locked it in time? That he found a way to store it here in the time corridor or something? Jonas, do you realize what you're saying? You're implying the man in the vision had psychic talent.''

Jonas nodded slowly, his eyes on the old man. ''Maybe the same kind I have. Verity, there's no reason to think I'm the only man on earth who was born with the ability to enter this time tunnel. What if that guy could access it, too? What if he found a way to leave something hidden in it?''

Verity felt chilled. She clutched her parka more tightly around her. ''Now that's a thought that could very well keep me awake nights.''

"I have to know, Verity."

"Even if it's dangerous? What if you're right about the sense of warning you get from this vision?"

"Booby traps." Jonas's half-smile was grim. "The man liked to set traps. A real Renaissance type."

"I don't think I want the father of my baby springing any of those traps," Verity said.

"I'll be careful."

"Oh yeah?" She didn't believe him for a moment. "Jonas, I think we should call it quits."

"I have to find out what this is all about. I have to know the truth."

She knew that further argument was hopeless, so she stopped wasting her energy in that direction. "Do you think you can talk Doug into letting you stay?"

"I'll find a way." Jonas spoke with absolute conviction. "Come on, let's get back to the room. We can't do any more tonight. We're going to need that crystal." Jonas handed the broken sword hilt over to Verity. The vision and the psychic corridor vanished. "Can you really sense it?"

"The crystal? Yes." Verity thought about it as she followed Jonas out of the small room. "I don't know where it is, though. I just got the strong feeling that it's here in the villa." She fingered her earrings. "There might be a way . . ."

"How?" Jonas cut in eagerly.

"Oliver knows a lot about crystals. When he and I worked them together I could feel things. Jonas, I don't know. I honestly don't know what I'm doing. But it's just barely possible that Oliver could help me tune in to that missing crystal."

"I don't want Crump involved in this," Jonas stated flatly as he led the way back down the corridor.

Verity glared at his back. "Why not?"

"Because I don't want him getting any ideas."

''Ideas about what?''

Jonas halted abruptly and swung around. He was a dark, powerful mass behind the harsh beam of the flashlight. Verity could feel the masculine aggression and possessiveness radiating from him. When he spoke, his voice was cold. ''I don't want him getting the idea that you're some kind of psychic pal for him; that he can use you to help him tune in to those damn crystals he's always playing with. Got it?''

Suddenly Verity understood. She angled her chin in angry challenge. ''You mean you don't want him using me the way you do?''

For an instant she thought she'd gone too far. In the shadows Jonas's eyes seemed to gleam like those of a predator. The stone passageway was suddenly more confining than ever, and Verity was trapped inside it. She held her breath but she never lowered her eyes from Jonas's hard face.

It was Jonas who broke the dangerous impasse. ''Right,'' he said very quietly. ''I don't want him using you the way I do. I don't want any man on the face of the earth using you the way I do. I'm glad we understand each other.'' He swung around and started back down the corridor.

Verity followed, wishing she'd kept her mouth shut. She was determined not to say another word until the storm of Jonas's anger had blown over. Sometimes a woman had to bide her time.

Jonas stopped at the door that opened onto the torture chamber. Silently he found the opening mechanism and manipulated it until the door creaked open.

There were no ribald cracks about kinky lady torturers as Verity and Jonas made their way through the room and out into the hall. In fact, neither said a word all the way back to the bedroom. Verity was feeling quite cold as she removed her parka, and the chill was not a result of the villa's lousy heating system. She shouldn't have said anything about Oliver Crump, she decided morosely. It was obviously a subject best left alone.

Jonas locked the door of the bedroom, his movements precise and careful. Then he tossed the flashlight into his duffel bag and sat on the edge of the bed. Eyes narrowed, he watched Verity as she collected her nightgown and robe.

"Do you really believe I'm just using you?" he finally asked.

Verity busied herself with the buttons of her blouse. "I shouldn't have said that. I was angry because you were making a fuss about Oliver Crump."

"You've never been absolutely sure of me, have you? You can't forget that the reason I came into your life in the first place was because I knew you could help me control my damn talent. That's why you're stalling about marrying me. A part of you is scared to death that the only real tie we have is a psychic one."

"That's not true, Jonas. We have a lot of other ties, as you've pointed out."

"We sure as hell do. Including the fact that we're both about to become parents." Jonas raked his fingers through his hair. "I guess I shouldn't have made that scene about Oliver and his crystals."

"No, you definitely should not have snapped at me the way you did," Verity said stiffly. "I like Oliver. He's sweet and genuine. I was only trying to tell you that if finding the stupid crystal really means so much to you, he might be able to help."

"I didn't want him linking with you, goddammit."

"I don't 'link' with him. Not the way I do with you."

"Well, what do you do with him when you play with those crystals?" Jonas demanded. He shot to his feet and began pacing the room. "I saw the way the two of you were touching each other when you were trying to cure Maggie's headache.''

''I'm not sure what was happening, if anything. But I got the feeling Oliver can somehow tune in to crystals and I . . . I can help him. A little.'' Verity sank down on the bed, hugging her nightgown and robe.

''The same way you help me in the time corridor?'' he demanded harshly.

''No. It's much different. It's not personal the way it is with you. There's no sense of direct contact. I'm sorry, Jonas. I can't really explain it.'' She glowered at him. ''What's the big problem here, anyway? I thought you didn't believe in the power of crystals.''

''I think I believe in the power of one particular crystal,'' he said bluntly. ''The one that man in the vision left behind here in this villa. We need it to find out what's going on in that little room at the end of the passage.''

''I don't think we should try to find out what's going on in that room, Jonas. I don't like it. I don't like any of it.''

He came across the room to stand in front of her. ''I have to know, Verity.''

She looked up at him. ''Why?''

''I don't know. I just have to find out the truth. I won't be able to rest until I solve this thing.''

''Even if it means involving me and Oliver Crump?'' she taunted.

Jonas caught her arms and hauled her to her feet. ''We don't need Crump.''

''I'm not so sure. I don't know anything about crystals. He's the one with the expertise.''

''We can do this without him, dammit.''

''How do you know? I'm the one who seems to be able to use the crystal, and I'd like some professional advice from Oliver.''

Jonas's jaw was set rigidly. "You want to work with Oliver Crump on a professional basis? All right, I'll allow you to work with him on one condition."

"Jonas, I don't think you understand the situation. I'm doing you the favor. You've got no right to set conditions on how I do it."

"The hell I don't," he snapped. "Before you try anything with Crump and his damn crystals, I want your word of honor that you'll marry me."

Verity's eyes widened in amazement. She could hardly believe what she was hearing. "Let me get this straight. You won't let me work with Oliver, not even to help you find that crystal, unless I agree to marry you?"

"I love you, you redheaded witch," he said in a thick voice. "I'm not going to risk losing you to some other man who might be able to latch on to you with a psychic connection. I'd rather call off the search for the crystal than take that chance."

Verity stood very still in his grasp, trying to marshal her thoughts into some coherent order. "You think if I agree to marry you that would keep me from getting lured away by another psychic?"

"If you agree to marry me, you'll honor your promise. I know you, Verity."

"Not well enough, apparently, if you think you have to blackmail and threaten me in order to get me to marry you." She smiled suddenly.

He stared down at her, his eyes wary. "Verity?"

"I love you, Jonas, I've told you that a hundred times. I'll marry you."

He folded her close with a low growl of relief. "Jesus, it's about time, lady."

Verity leaned her head on his shoulder and relaxed into his warmth. She wrapped her arms tightly around his waist and savored his lean strength. ''You know something, Jonas? When I first met you I would never have guessed that you'd be the marrying kind.''

''And I had the impression you'd opted for professional singlehood. We both had a lot to learn about each other.''

''I hope we're doing the right thing.''

''We are,'' he told her with grave assurance. He raised her chin with his finger and brushed his mouth across her lips. ''Believe me, the only option we have open is to get married. I couldn't stand living with any other alternative. I realized that the night you told me you were pregnant.''

He moved his lips lightly across hers again, and then he began to deepen the kiss. His arms tightened around her and Verity was pulled snugly against the taut outline of his thighs. He deliberately widened his stance and urged her closer so that she could feel his heat. His manhood, trapped beneath his jeans, pushed against the gentle curve of her stomach. Verity gave herself up to the passion that always seemed to flow so easily between them.

''It's going to be hard to think of myself as a married woman,'' she murmured against his throat.

''Don't worry, I'll remind you every chance I get.'' Jonas picked her up and settled her down on the bed.

''Jonas?''

''Yeah?'' His voice was a lazy, sleepy growl in the darkness.

''If we're going to get married, I think we should do it right.''

''Right? What do you mean? There's only one way to do it. You get some blood tests, a license and a ring, and you say a few words in front of a duly constituted authority. Then you get to go to bed. What's the big deal?''

''I want a nice wedding. A big wedding. With a cake and

a fancy dress and everyone in Sequence Springs in the church."

"I should have known."

"It'll be fun," Verity assured him, her enthusiasm rapidly growing as she envisioned the details. "It'll also be the only chance I ever get to wear a beautiful formal wedding gown."

"Verity, up until quite recently, you never even planned to get married at all. Why the sudden interest in cakes and wedding gowns?" Jonas complained.

"I've changed my mind about a lot of things lately. If I'm going to get married, I want to do it right," she stated stubbornly.

"Honey, it takes time to organize a big wedding," Jonas argued reasonably. He put a possessive palm on her belly. "And time is something we haven't got."

"Laura can help me. It won't take long at all to get things organized. And it's not like we have to keep the baby a secret. Everyone in Sequence Springs is going to know I'm pregnant as soon as I make an appointment with my doctor."

Jonas sighed heavily. "I really don't think we need to go through all this."

"It's what I want, Jonas."

"Stubborn little tyrant." He rolled onto his side and reached for her. "The things I do for you, lady." He dropped a warm, hungry kiss on the pulse point of her throat.

"You won't really mind, will you?"

"I'll survive. And I understand it's important to humor pregnant ladies." He moved his mouth slowly, teasingly down to the valley between her breasts.

"Thank you, Jonas."

"Don't thank me. Just be prepared to get out of the

wedding dress and into your black lace nightie right after we cut the cake.''

Verity giggled, feeling suddenly euphoric. ''I love you, Jonas.''

''Love you, too, tyrant. And I've just given you the ultimate proof. If I didn't love you to distraction, I sure as hell wouldn't put up with the nonsense of a big wedding.'' His tongue was suddenly hot and wet in the small depression that dimpled her stomach. His fingers slid between her thighs.

Verity shivered with pleasure and turned her head so that she could kiss the scar that marked the strong curve of his shoulder. She and the baby would be safe with this man. He would protect them and care for them. She knew that now with deep certainty.

Jonas was now bound to her as surely as she was bound to him.

It was nearly dawn when Verity awoke. Not that a person would know it by looking out the window, she thought as she turned her head on the pillow. It was pitch black outside. The storm had arrived in a flurry of rain and wild wind.

''Doug and Oliver won't be able to get back here until this lets up,'' Jonas observed as he stretched and sat up on the edge of the bed. ''Could be hours before they can return. Maybe a full day.''

Verity watched him as he moved about in the shadows. She knew what was going through his mind. ''You're going to spend every spare minute hunting for that treasure, aren't you?''

''Damn right.'' He shrugged into a denim shirt and reached for his jeans. ''But first I want to take another look at the boat in the cove.''

"Jonas, it's dark outside. You won't be able to see a thing."

He glanced at his watch. "Should be getting light by the time I get there." He disappeared into the bathroom for a few moments. When he returned he came toward the bed. He bent over and caged Verity between his arms, his eyes intense in the shadows. "You stay in here until I get back. I don't want you wandering around this place without me."

"You don't really think Yarwood would try to hurt me, do you?"

"I don't know what to think. Everything in this joint is crazy. So you're to stay put until I return." He gave her a quick, hard kiss. "Don't worry. This shouldn't take long. I'll be back in plenty of time for breakfast. Nobody will even know I'm gone." He straightened and grabbed his new jacket.

Verity sat bolt upright. "You'll ruin that coat in this rain."

"What the hell good is a jacket you can't wear in the rain?"

He reached into his duffel bag and pulled out his knife. He tried to be subtle about it, but Verity saw what was happening. She bit her lip and said nothing. In truth, she was rather glad he was not going out into that wild storm unarmed.

"You don't think whoever owns that boat will still be there, do you? Nobody in his right mind would be camping out there in this storm."

"On the whole, I'm inclined to agree with you on that last part. Which brings up some interesting possibilities."

"Such as?"

"Such as maybe whoever owns that boat is staying right here in this villa. There's plenty of room around here. A man could hide out for days in this monstrosity. Even if you knew he was there and you went looking for him, it would be hard to find him."

Verity's mouth fell open. "Good grief. I never thought of that. You're right. He could hide in one of the other wings and stay hidden for as long as he wanted. Be careful, Jonas."

"I'll be careful." He started for the door. "Get some more sleep. I'll be back soon."

"Sleep? Are you kidding? Now that you've told me you think some weirdo is running around in one of the unoccupied wings?"

"I shouldn't have mentioned that," he mumbled as he went out the door.

"No, you certainly shouldn't have mentioned it." But her words were lost, cut off by the softly closing door.

Verity fell back against the pillows, scowling. There was no way she was going to turn over and go to sleep, not now. She had always been an early riser anyway. Verity threw back the covers and climbed out of bed, wincing slightly at the slight soreness in her thighs. Jonas had been in one of his more energetic moods last night. The man had a way of leaving his mark on her, she thought wryly as she headed for the bathroom.

And now he wanted to put a ring on her finger. Talk about being marked for life. But when she looked in the bathroom mirror she was surprised at the warm and secretive smile on her face.

A vast sense of relief flooded through her.

The decision had been made—she was going to marry Jonas. Now that she'd decided to take the step, she wondered why she'd stalled for so long. She should have trusted her intuition, the same intuition that had sent her straight into his arms the very first time.

There were no guarantees in this world. It was true that

her relationship with Jonas had some bizarre twists, and there were some questions for which there would never be any real answers.

But she loved him and he loved her. For better or worse they were linked together. And now they were going to have a baby. All in all, marriage seemed reasonable, even right, under the circumstances.

A strangely familiar restlessness hit Verity as she emerged from the shower and started to dress. She had just put on the red crystal earrings and was reaching for her shoes when she felt a sudden, sinking sensation in the pit of her stomach.

''Oh, Lord. Not morning sickness,'' she begged aloud. She held her breath and the sinking feeling slowly faded.

She was starting to relax when she realized that her earrings were growing very warm. Verity tensed. She immediately associated the warmth generated by the crystals with a disturbing occurrence of some sort. She looked around the room uneasily. Everything appeared to be perfectly normal, but she could not relax.

The earrings stayed uncomfortably warm, and the restless feeling became overpowering. She had felt this way yesterday when she'd been driven out of the villa for a walk, and had found Elyssa at the bottom of the cliff.

''Oh, no, not again.'' Verity tried to ignore the growing sense of urgency, but to no avail.

Then she thought about Jonas outside by himself and she leaped to her feet, heading for the door.

Not Jonas, please don't let anything happen to Jonas!

She was out in the hall, running instinctively toward the staircase before she realized that Jonas was all right. She wasn't sure how she knew that, but she sensed that it was not Jonas who was drawing her.

But something was wrong, terribly wrong. The crystals blazed for an instant in her ears and then cooled slightly.

Verity continued down the stairs, turning down the hall to the kitchen. If Maggie was up she might be able to reassure Verity that everything was okay.

But Maggie was not in the kitchen. That in itself was unusual. Verity had learned that the housekeeper's habits were fairly predictable. By this time of day Maggie should have had a pot of coffee made.

Verity found herself visualizing Maggie Frampton as she emerged from the kitchen. Her uneasy feeling grew stronger when she pictured the woman in her faded housedress and old metal necklace. She climbed the stairs again and walked down the long corridor to the end of the south wing.

There was no answer when she knocked on Maggie's door. When she tried the handle, Verity found the door unlocked. Unable to resist, she pushed it open and called out softly, "Maggie?"

There was no response. Verity turned away, aware of the cold draft in the hall. She started down the stairs. When she reached the first floor, she kept on going.

On some half-conscious level she knew she was heading for the infamous torture chamber, but she could not explain why. She only knew she had to look for Maggie there.

A weak light burned in the basement hall. The door to the chamber of kinky delights was closed. The moment Verity touched it she knew she didn't want to see whatever was on the other side. She also knew, however, that she had no choice.

Reassuring herself that her imagination was truly out of control this morning, Verity opened the door.

She faced pitch darkness. Hardly daring to breathe, she ran her palm along the wall, searching for the old-fashioned switch. Finding it, she reluctantly flipped it on.

Two things registered at once.

Maggie Frampton lay on her back on the floor, beneath

the wall of whips. There was a pool of blood beneath her head, and she was not moving.

The second thing that hit Verity like a blow was that the stone gate opening onto the hidden passageway was ajar.

For a shocked instant, Verity could not move. A wave of nausea suddenly overtook her. With an extreme effort of will she made herself cross the room to where Maggie lay.

There was a weak pulse in Maggie's throat and Verity swallowed heavily with relief. At first glance, she had been certain that Maggie was dead. The amount of blood from her head wound was terrifying.

A faint, half-familiar odor made Verity wrinkle her nose as she bent over Maggie. She knew that acrid scent, she realized suddenly. She had smelled it briefly the night she had been attacked outside the bathroom of the bed-and-breakfast inn. It was the odor of stale smoke.

Only one person at the villa smoked.

Verity started to pull her hand away from Maggie's throat. She had to get out of here—she had to find Jonas. Her fingers brushed the chain that Maggie had always worn around her neck and her red crystal earrings suddenly burned.

Guided by pure instinct and a growing suspicion, Verity gently tugged the chain from under the collar of the faded housedress.

A green crystal glittered at the end of the chain.

Verity stared at it, mesmerized by the reality of what, until now, had been only an image trapped in time. She was trying to make sense of what she'd discovered when she heard quick, heavy footsteps in the hall.

Terror surged through her. The man who had done this to Maggie was coming back to finish his grim business. Verity knew it as surely as she knew her own name—and his.

She leaped to her feet, holding the green crystal tightly.

The metal chain snapped, but Verity didn't even notice. She turned and darted toward the only possible escape—the open corridor door.

She plunged into an endless tunnel of darkness. Where was Jonas and his industrial-strength flashlight when she needed him? Trying not to make any noise, Verity inched cautiously along the tunnel wall. She had to get away from the shaft of light that poured into the passageway from the torture chamber.

She was several feet away from the opening when she heard a scraping sound, the unmistakable noise of a body being dragged. Verity had never heard such a sound before in her life, but she recognized it immediately.

Maggie Frampton's unconscious, bulky frame was thrust unceremoniously through the opening and dumped in the corridor. A dark figure stepped in behind her and shone a flashlight beam quickly in both directions.

The beam just hit the heel of Verity's shoe as she turned and fled into the impenetrable darkness of the hidden passageway.

Chapter Sixteen

HE'D seen her! She was certain the flashlight had caught her. Verity ran recklessly into the darkness, one palm scraping along the wall as a guide. How much farther to the stairs? Adrenaline was pounding through her veins as she listened for the sound of Slade Spencer's pursuing footsteps.

But a few seconds later Verity realized she heard nothing behind her. There was not even the glare of a flashlight bearing down on her. She cast an anxious glance back over her shoulder and saw the shaft of light from the corridor exit starting to narrow.

Slade wasn't going to pursue her through the passageway—he was sealing her inside!

Her momentary relief gave way to a mounting horror as the last of the light disappeared from the stone passage. The tunnel door slammed shut with a resounding thud. The silence of a tomb descended and utter darkness engulfed her.

Verity felt the cold stone under her palm. Her eyes were wide open but she might as well have been blind. There was simply no light, no light at all.

She fought a severe attack of claustrophobia as she started to slowly, cautiously retrace her steps. Maggie was trapped in here with her, and the poor woman might very well be dying. It seemed to take forever before she stumbled over Maggie's inert frame.

"I'm sorry, Maggie." Her apology went unheard. The housekeeper was still unconscious. Verity fumbled in the darkness and located her head wound. It was hard to tell but it seemed to Verity that it wasn't leaking blood at a rapid rate. Just a slow oozing.

Verity eased the woman's head back down on the cold stone and straightened in the darkness. She had to get them out of here. She could only pray that when she finally got the stone door open, Slade Spencer would not be waiting in the torture chamber.

But it seemed most likely that he would have fled after sealing his victims inside the tunnel. He probably assumed that Maggie was dead and that Verity wouldn't know how to unlock the door.

As a matter of fact, Verity realized she didn't know how to unlock the door. She struggled to control the fear that threatened to swamp her there in the darkness. Closing her eyes, she tried to envision the movements Jonas had made when he'd opened this door.

The joyous relief Verity experienced when her searching fingers found the mechanism was instantly shattered when she tried to operate it. Nothing happened, nothing at all.

After several minutes of futile effort, Verity had to face the fact that she was either doing something wrong with the ancient mechanism, or Slade had jammed the lock from the other side.

Verity's palms were damp and she began to shiver. The passageway had never felt so cold. She forced herself to think logically.

If she couldn't escape through this entrance, she would have to try the one that opened onto the bedroom.

Verity knelt beside Maggie. "Maggie? Can you hear me?" There was no response. Verity kept talking in a reassuring voice. "I know of another way out. It will take me a while, but I'll find it. When I do I'll get help. Hold on, Maggie. Just hang in there until I get back, okay?"

Verity got to her feet again and started resolutely down the passageway. It was going to be a very long walk. When she stumbled across Digby Hazelhurst's bones, she would know she was in the right vicinity.

Verity wished that the mental link she shared with Jonas was useful, like telepathy, instead of the more esoteric connection they shared. She would do anything to be able to contact him right this minute to warn him about Spencer.

She would also have taken the opportunity to inform him that he'd been right in the beginning—the psychic-consulting business definitely sucked.

The boat was gone. Jonas stood on the edge of the cliff looking down into the cove where Verity had found Elyssa. He had his hands thrust deep in his pockets as a defense against the cold, driving wind. There were serious whitecaps on the water and the rain came in whiplike gusts. There was just enough gray light to see the rough beach.

There was no way that any sane boater would have risked taking a small craft into the teeth of this storm. Not unless it was a matter of life and death. And even then, Jonas thought grimly, if he were the guy with the boat, he would have looked for other alternatives.

He was willing to bet that the boat and its owner were still somewhere on the island.

Jonas raised his head and studied the cliffs. There were plenty of nooks and crannies around the island shoreline where a small craft could be hidden. If someone had simply wanted to get the boat out of sight, the obvious thing would be to move the craft to another location.

Given the ferocious weather, a man wouldn't have wanted to spend too long at the task of moving the boat. He would have made the move quickly and then gotten back to the shelter of the villa.

Which meant that, logically, the boat had to be nearby.

Jonas started pacing along the top of the cliffs, studying the shoreline carefully. In this pale dawn light it would be easy to miss a small gray boat.

Fifteen minutes later he found it in a tiny cove that was even smaller than the first. The boat had been hurriedly tied to an overhanging fir branch. It was tossing wildly about on the angry, choppy waves that lapped the rocky shore.

It didn't take long to scramble down the short cliff to the beach. Jonas climbed over a pile of rocks to grab the line that held the boat, a moment later stepping into the violently bobbing craft. A spray of cold water caught him as he leaned down to open a locker.

As Verity had said, there was nothing useful in the way of identification in the first locker. Hunched into his fleece-lined jacket, Jonas quickly opened another.

He found a life vest stamped PROPERTY OF DREAM HARBOR MARINA. A set of boating instructions was crumpled up next to the life vest.

So much for easy identification. The boat had been rented. There was no way to trace it until the storm cleared and he could get off the island. Even if he tracked down the owner of Dream Harbor Marina, it might lead nowhere. It was easy enough to lie on a rental application.

Jonas closed the lid of the locker and studied the bottom of the boat. There was a fair amount of rainwater slopping back and forth around his feet. He spotted a small, crumpled bag floating in one corner. On a hunch he picked it up and glanced inside. A wet piece of paper lay on the bottom of the sack, a receipt from a California pharmacy.

Jonas suddenly remembered Slade Spencer popping pills from a small bottle with a prescription label on it.

"Jesus H. Christ, talk about stupid." Jonas leaped out of the boat. He balanced on the slippery rocks with unconscious ease, jumping from one to another until he was on the beach. Then he loped up the short cliff and headed back toward the villa at a run.

He had not used the flashlight except to explore the interior of the boat locker. No need to take a chance that someone looking out a window might spot him leaving or returning to the villa.

But someone else leaving the villa was not being nearly as cautious.

A narrow beam of light bounced through the trees, moving in Jonas's direction. The erratic movement of the light indicated that whoever was holding the flashlight was running at a breakneck pace.

Jonas stopped and moved out of the way. The weak dawn light had not yet penetrated the heavy branches overhead. It would be easy to stay hidden in the shelter of the trees until he caught a glimpse of whoever was running toward the cliffs.

It had to be Spencer, Jonas thought. No one else would know where the boat was now except the man who had moved it last night. But why the sudden rush? Spencer had been lolling around in what had appeared to be an alcoholic haze for days.

Jonas didn't like the question, and he liked the possible answers even less. His stomach clenched as he thought of Verity. As long as she stayed in the bedroom she would be all right, he told himself. There was no reason why she and Spencer should have encountered each other this morning.

The flashlight darted past, accompanied by a lot of heavy breathing. Spencer was in a state of panic—Jonas could literally smell the fear on the man.

Jonas stepped out from behind a fir and threw himself forward.

"No!" Spencer shrieked as he was toppled to the ground. "No, goddammit, *no*. Let me go, you frigging bastard. Take your damned hands off me. *Let me go!*" He lurched beneath Jonas's weight, swinging wildly with the flashlight and something else—a gun.

Jonas slashed at the flailing arm holding the pistol. Spencer fought back with an unnatural strength. The man was clearly hysterical and he struggled with frantic energy.

The flashlight caught Jonas on his jaw. He reeled backward, seeing a few bright lights in his head. But he had a grip on Spencer's gun arm and he hung on with grim determination, squeezing until he was sure the small bones in Spencer's wrist had to crack.

Spencer screamed, a high, thin wail of despair and fury, and then the gun tumbled to the soggy ground.

Jonas drew back his arm for a solid blow, then abandoned the effort in disgust. There was no point in hitting his victim again. Spencer was racked with heavy sobs, totally incapacitated by his emotions.

"It was an accident," Slade gasped between gulping sobs. He lay in the mud, one arm over his face. "A damned accident. I didn't plan it. She just showed up at the wrong time. Started yelling at me, saying she knew all about me. I had to do something, don't you see? I had to shut her up."

Cold terror swept over Jonas. He grabbed a fistful of Slade's shirt and jerked him to a sitting position. "Who did you shut up, Spencer? *Who?*"

Spencer blinked, his gaze oddly vague. "That old bag Frampton. What else could I do? She knew, I tell you. Somehow she figured out who I was." Spencer swallowed more sobs. "Shit, I didn't think she'd recognize me. I lost a lot of weight in the clinic—got contacts—shaved my beard. I was so damn sure. But she knew me, the old bitch. She knew me. So I hit her and she fell, like a sack of laundry. She just fell, I tell you. I didn't mean to kill her."

In spite of what he was hearing, a sickening sense of relief swept through Jonas. His first thought had been that it was Verity whom Spencer had killed.

"You killed Maggie? This morning?" He shook Spencer. "Answer me, dammit!"

"Have to get away. Everything's gone wrong." Spencer gazed wildly about, his eyes glazed. "Hazelhurst said it would. He always claimed the treasure was protected with a curse or something. Stupid old man—crazy. He was crazy, you know. I mean, those assholes in the clinic said I had a few screws loose, but Hazelhurst was downright insane."

Jonas had his doubts about who was crazy and who wasn't, but this wasn't the time to explore them. It sounded as if Verity was all right, but he had to get back to the villa and make certain. Then he had to find poor Maggie Frampton.

"You crazy son of a bitch," Jonas said. "You killed Hazelhurst, didn't you?" He unbuckled Spencer's belt as he spoke. "You were the student who showed up two years ago to help him look for the treasure. Maggie finally recognized you this morning, didn't she? Is that what happened? She said she knew who you were?"

''I had to kill Hazelhurst,'' Spencer explained, his expression suddenly, chillingly sane. ''He was afraid, you see. Lost his nerve. Wouldn't tell me what he'd done with the treasure, said no one must ever touch it. All that was left in the chest was a ring, a scrap of metal, and a stiletto. I knew Hazelhurst had gotten there first and found the rest. I tried to make him tell me, but he wouldn't. The old bastard just kept saying the chest was empty when he found it. But I knew better.''

''So you killed him with the stiletto you found in the chest, right?'' Jonas dragged Spencer to his feet and secured his wrists behind his back with the belt.

''I had to kill him. He was so freakin' scared. The old fool wouldn't tell me a thing, but I knew I could find it on my own. It had to be there in the villa. I didn't need him to tell me where it was.''

''But you never found the treasure, did you?'' Jonas asked as he jerked Spencer back toward the villa. ''You've killed two people but all you ever got was a ring, a drug and alcohol problem, and a few loose screws. Maybe Hazelhurst was right. Maybe the treasure is cursed. You should have left well enough alone. Tell me something, how did you get that rental boat over here? Doug brought you here in his launch, didn't he?''

''That was easy. As soon as I knew about the plans to spend a week at the villa, I rented the boat. Then I hired a kid who had his own boat to follow me here. I hid the boat in that first cove and the kid gave me a lift back to the other island. I told him I planned to use the skiff for a fishing party this week.''

''Why did you think you'd need a boat?''

Spencer looked at Jonas as if he were the crazy one. ''To get off this damned island in case things went wrong.''

''The way they did this morning?'' Jonas asked harshly.

"I got scared after I had to hit that old busybody. But you know, now that I think about it, there's no need to be afraid, is there? Nobody can prove I killed Hazelhurst, even if someone does find his body. Except the old bag. When she recognized me, she started getting suspicious. Told me she'd been watching me, even went through my things one night. She found me in that torture chamber this morning."

"What were you doing in the torture chamber at this hour?"

Slade wiped the back of his hand across his mouth, his eyes haunted. "I finally decided I had to have another look at that goddamned treasure room. I didn't want to go back into that horrible tunnel but I had to. The secret's in there somewhere, I'm sure of it. I was awake all night thinking about it. I've been afraid you might stumble onto the tunnel somehow, even though I tore the last pages out of Hazelhurst's diary. I finally figured out that I had no choice but to go back inside. Jesus, I hate that tunnel. So much darkness."

"And Maggie found you there?"

"She must have been watching me all night, waiting for me, the bitch. Accused me of having done something to Hazelhurst a couple of years ago. Started screaming like a madwoman, wouldn't shut up. The damn bitch would not shut her goddamned mouth."

"So you hit her."

"Had to." A twisted craftiness appeared in Slade's eyes. "I got scared. There was so much blood. Knew I had to get out of there, so I ran back to my room to pack my things and get out. Then I realized I could just hide the body in the tunnel—no one would ever know. I went back down to the torture chamber but I was too late. The light was on and I knew someone had found her. Verity was in there. I saw her when I dumped Maggie's body in the tunnel. She must have run in there to hide when she heard me coming."

Jonas froze. He swung around, his eyes threatening violence. *"What have you done with Verity?"*

Spencer peered at him, blinking rain out of his eyes. An insane intelligence blazed in his eyes. He grinned slowly. "I left her in the tunnel with the old bitch, naturally. You don't know about the tunnel, do you? That was Hazelhurst's big secret. Verity's in there now and you'll never find her. No one will ever find any of them. But that's the best way, you see. There's no proof. As long as all of them are buried in that tunnel, there's no proof."

"Did you hurt Verity or just leave her in the tunnel?" Jonas's hands tightened around Spencer's neck. His fury and despair made him oblivious to everything except finding the truth in Spencer's mad eyes. "Answer me, you crazy bastard. What did you do to Verity?"

"You'll never find her or Frampton's body. Just like no one ever found Hazelhurst. I'll bet Verity thought she was hiding from me when she ran in there. She thought she'd be safe in that tunnel. But now she's locked in there forever. No proof. No proof." Spencer started to giggle. Then he looked frightened. "My pills. It's time for my pills."

"You don't get your pills until you tell me if you hurt Verity." Jonas tried to keep his voice calm; tried to remind himself that he was dealing with a certifiable lunatic.

Spencer looked mildly surprised. "I didn't hurt her. I didn't have to. I told you, she can't get out. Stupid woman ran right into the tunnel. She'll never find her way out. It took Hazelhurst months to learn how to operate the tunnel doors. Even if she finds the lock, it won't work. I jammed the mechanism on the outside. The only witness, you see. She's the only witness, the only one who saw me put Maggie's body into the tunnel."

Jonas thought of Verity lost in the endless darkness of the hidden corridor. If she couldn't get out through the torture-chamber door, she would have to find her way back to the bedroom entrance. And he'd never explained to her how to operate the door mechanism. She would be shivering in abject terror there in the endless blackness of the tunnel, searching for the secret to unlocking the door.

Jonas looked deep into Slade Spencer's insane eyes. He wasn't going to learn anything else from this bastard. He slammed his fist into Spencer's jaw, and the man dropped to the ground without so much as a gasp. Blood trickled from the corner of his mouth.

Jonas left Spencer lying in the mud and ran for the villa. The wind howled through the trees. Branches snapped at him and the rain was a sheet of ice.

He burst through the front door of the silent villa and took the stairs to the second floor in great, hungry strides. Then he was racing down the hall to the bedroom.

Jonas pounded into the bedroom. The tunnel door was closed. He struggled furiously with the mechanism behind the tapestry and watched the stone door swing ponderously inward. It seemed to take forever.

A quick glance through the widening crack showed no sign of Verity. Either she had not been able to find her way back to the bedroom, or she was still trying desperately to open the door at the other end of the tunnel.

Jonas stepped through the opening as soon as there was room. He shone the flashlight quickly to the right. Verity wasn't anywhere in sight.

A rattle of bones and a scraping sound from behind the tunnel door made him whip around in a dangerous crouch. The flashlight beam illuminated the face of his beloved.

Verity emerged from behind the door with a stark, savagely determined expression. Her eyes were strangely unfocused. Her arms were raised above her head, her hands clutched around the hilt of the stiletto that had been buried in Digby Hazelhurst. Digby's bones rattled at her feet.

Jonas stepped hastily out of reach and held up both hands. "Easy, honey. I'm a reasonable man. You want to delay the wedding a couple of weeks while you buy a fancy dress? We'll delay the wedding, no problem."

"*Jonas!*" Verity dropped the stiletto. It clattered on the stones as she flung herself against his chest. "It's about time you got here."

"Always nice to feel appreciated." Jonas wrapped his arms around her and held her so tightly he was afraid she would break. But all she did was give a small squeak. "Jesus, honey, I was scared. But I should have known I wouldn't find you huddled shivering in terror. Did anyone ever tell you that you do a nice impression of Lady Macbeth?"

"You were scared! You want to compare notes? I've never been so frightened in my life. And I couldn't see who was coming into the tunnel a minute ago. It's so dark in here that I was blinded when you opened the door. I thought it might be Slade." Verity lifted her head, her eyes wide. She was blinking rapidly. "Jonas, Spencer's nearly killed Maggie. She's at the other end of the tunnel, unconscious and bleeding. We've got to get her out. Then we've got to do something about Slade."

"I've already taken care of Spencer. I found him making a try for the boat. He panicked, thinking he'd killed Maggie and sealed both of you in the tunnel. I gather he lost what was left of his nerve at that point and decided it was time to vacate the premises. I don't know how far he thought he was going to get in this storm."

"But where is he? What did you do with him?"

"He's tied up outside. Come on, let's get out of here. I'm sure you've had enough of this tunnel to last you a lifetime."

"We'll have to get Maggie out. We can't just leave her there."

"I'll take care of it," Jonas said gently. He urged Verity out into the bedroom. She was shaky but in control of herself. That was the thing about tyrants, he told himself with pride. They were tough. Then he saw her looking down at something she had just pulled out of her pocket. "What have you got there?"

Wordlessly she opened her palm and displayed an egg-shaped piece of green crystal.

Jonas took a step closer, awed by the realization of what she had found. "Where the hell did you get that?" he asked softly.

"It's Maggie's. She had it on that chain she always wore around her neck. Digby must have given it to her. I found it when I checked her throat for a pulse. I must have grabbed it when I heard Spencer returning. Funny, I didn't even realize . . ." She looked up at him, her aquamarine eyes questioning. "It's the right one, Jonas. It's the crystal you've been looking for, the one you think will unlock the vision."

Jonas's gaze went from the ugly green crystal to her serious face. "Spencer says that all he or Hazelhurst ever found were the stiletto, that chunk of sword hilt, and a ruby ring. But he's convinced the rest of the treasure is still buried here somewhere."

"And so are you," Verity concluded quietly. She looked down at the crystal. "Do you believe in curses, Jonas?"

"No, but I have great respect for the intricate workings of the Renaissance mind. And a psychic Renaissance mind boggles the imagination. I don't think there's a curse on the treasure but I do believe that someone has locked it up very carefully. Hazelhurst believed that crystal was the key, and I think he might have been right."

Verity looked at him, her expression unreadable. "You're going to try it, aren't you? Sooner or later, you're going to try to unlock that frozen vision."

"If I don't, I'll probably wind up as nutty as Hazelhurst or as insane as Spencer," Jonas said harshly. "I have to know the truth about it, Verity."

She nodded. "Yes. I can see that." She carefully repocketed the crystal. "When the time comes you'll need my help."

Jonas was startled. "What makes you say that?" he demanded as she started to turn away.

She glanced back, her mouth softening slightly. "I can tune this crystal to the one on the desk in the vision."

He took a long stride forward and caught her by the arms. "Verity? What are you saying? Are you sure?"

"Unfortunately, yes. I'm fairly certain I can do it. Don't ask me how, Jonas. I really don't understand it myself. And if you want my professional opinion as your business manager, I suggest we forget the whole project. But I know you don't want my professional opinion." She turned away again and went into the bathroom to wash the dirt and blood off her hands.

After a little fiddling with a screwdriver he'd located in the kitchen, Jonas managed to open the torture-chamber entrance. Spencer had been too panicked to do a thorough job of jamming the mechanism.

Inside the passageway Maggie was still unconscious. Jonas managed to get her upstairs to the salon, where he put her on the couch. She didn't awaken but her breathing seemed steady and the bleeding had stopped. Verity left her tucked under a quilt and went outside with Jonas to retrieve Slade Spencer. They locked him in a spare storage room.

"What are we going to do with him?" Verity asked as she followed Jonas upstairs.

"There's nothing we can do until Warwick and Crump get back with the launch. We're sure as hell not going to try to get off this island in that little skiff Spencer rented. In the meantime, I want to see if we can find those missing diary pages in Spencer's things. He may have kept them."

"Doug and Oliver might not be able to get back here for hours," Verity remarked as they walked down the hall toward the room Spencer had used.

"True."

"We'd better wake Yarwood and tell him what's going on. To think that all this time we wrongly suspected him of being up to no good," Verity said, chagrined. "I suppose it must have been Spencer who pushed Elyssa off the cliff. Maybe he thought she was getting suspicious about the boat."

"I don't know about that," Jonas said thoughtfully. "You mentioned finding the boat earlier and he never made an attempt on your life."

"He didn't make an attempt on my life then, but he tried to do something nasty to me before that," Verity stated quietly.

Jonas's head snapped around abruptly, his eyes fierce. "What? He tried to hurt you? When?"

"That night we stayed in the bed-and-breakfast inn."

"The joker who tried to grab you outside the bathroom?" Jonas asked in amazement. "It was him? You're sure?"

"I recognized the tobacco he uses. I just caught a whiff of it on his sweater that night, not enough to make a real impression. I didn't recognize it when he was smoking his pipe around here because the odor was so much stronger then—it overpowers you. But when I caught a trace of it again in the torture chamber, I knew it was the same tobacco. No one else smokes around here except Spencer."

Jonas started back down the hall, his fury reignited. "I'll kill him."

Verity grabbed his arm. "No, wait, Jonas. There's no need for that. He's already under lock and key."

"I should have strangled him the night he made a pass at you." He shook off her hand.

Verity made another grab for him and caught hold of his sleeve. "Jonas, stop it. Listen to me. Everything is under control, there's no need for any more violence. Lord knows there's been enough in this place. Let's go wake Yarwood and tell him what's going on. He's got a right to know."

A door creaked. Verity and Jonas both turned.

"I'm glad you feel that way, Verity." Preston Yarwood stood in the doorway of his bedroom. "I would very much like to know exactly what is going on. And when you've finished telling me, we'll all go searching for Hazelhurst's missing treasure. But when we find it, I'm afraid there will be a slight change of plans. You see, too many psychic treasure hunters spoil the image."

"What the hell do you think you're doing, Yarwood?" Jonas asked softly.

"I've decided we don't need your name attached to this particular find, my friend. You're a fraud, you see. I'm the one with real psychic talent around here, and finding the treasure is going to prove that once and for all. This is my project, and I'm the one who's going to get the credit. When this is all over, people will be forced to admit that I've got psychic power. And with you and Verity mysteriously gone, there won't be anyone left alive to tell them differently."

Verity stared in shock at Preston Yarwood's face for a long time before her eyes dropped to the gun in his hand.

Chapter Seventeen

JONAS contemplated the gun in Preston Yarwood's hand. The man looked as though he knew exactly what he was doing with it. *The report says he's dangerous*, Caitlin Evanger had said.

"There's no treasure, Yarwood." Jonas edged a few steps away from Verity, making it more difficult for Yarwood to keep both of them covered with the weapon.

"Don't try to bullshit me, Quarrel," Yarwood said genially. "The treasure is here, I know it. I've had a psychic premonition of it all along."

"Talk about bullshit," Jonas muttered. "You've just got treasure fever."

"I know it's here," Preston snapped. "I had sections of Hazelhurst's diary translated, you see. Not all of it, but enough to know he was onto something. It's here, I tell you. And I've heard enough this morning to convince me you're close to the answer. So you're going to take me with you when you unlock the secret."

"I'm telling you, there is no treasure, Yarwood."

Yarwood's eyes flared angrily. "Don't give me that. I know you've found something important. I heard enough in the lab at Vincent College to know you're capable of it. That's why I had you hired. You're going to show me where the treasure is, goddammit. And you're going to hurry up about it, too. Crump and Warwick will be back as soon as this storm passes. Come here, Verity."

Jonas tensed, knowing what was going to happen next. "Leave her alone, Yarwood. I'll cooperate. But I'm warning you, there's nothing to find."

"There's something here. And you know where it is. You're going to show me. *Come here, Verity*. Get over here now or I'll start putting large holes in your bedmate."

Verity took a reluctant step forward.

"Don't get near him, Verity." Jonas spoke quietly. "He wants to use you as a hostage."

Yarwood smiled faintly. "You're so right, Quarrel. And if she doesn't get over here this instant, I'm going to put the first bullet through your arm. You'll still be capable of leading me to the treasure without the use of one arm. You could do it without the use of either arm, in fact." He raised the pistol.

"Stop it," Verity snapped. She walked stiffly to stand in front of Yarwood.

"Dammit, Verity." But it was too late and Jonas knew it. He watched in impotent fury as Yarwood grabbed Verity's arm and pulled her close against his side. "Let her go, Yarwood. I told you, I'll cooperate. I'll show you what we've found, but I'm warning you, it isn't much. Just an empty chest in a hidden room. Spencer was here ahead of us, Yarwood. Hell, there was probably someone else ahead of him. Maybe someone a century or two ago back in Italy. The treasure's gone."

"I don't believe you. There's the crystal," Yarwood snapped, his gaze going hungrily to Verity's hand. "It's still here. I read enough of Hazelhurst's diary to know that no one gets anything without the crystal. And you've got it, don't you? Open your hand, Verity. Show it to me."

Verity opened her palm and displayed the green crystal. "It won't do you any good, Preston. You don't know how to use it. None of us do."

"We'll find out, won't we? Show me this hidden room you've found, Quarrel."

"I've told you, there's nothing in it, you stupid bastard."

"Show me, or I'll start putting bullets in the little lady." Yarwood pushed the barrel of the gun against Verity's throat.

"*No*. Don't hurt her, damn you. If you want to see the room, I'll show it to you. But it won't do you any good, there's nothing in it." Jonas wanted to kill Yarwood more than he'd wanted anything in his life. Verity said nothing. She just looked at Jonas with a calm trust that was shattering.

"Let's go see this hidden room." Yarwood yanked Verity a little closer.

Jonas thought about the stiletto lying amid the tangle of bones just inside the bedroom entrance. "This way," he said quietly, leading the way toward the bedroom he had shared with Verity.

Yarwood followed, hustling Verity ahead of him. The end of the gun never wavered from her throat.

When Jonas pushed open the bedroom door, the gaping hole that marked the entrance to the hidden corridor was immediately evident. Yarwood stared at it in fascination.

"A hidden passage," Yarwood whispered. "Where does it lead?"

"To the empty treasure room." Jonas hooked a thumb in his belt. "Got any problems with claustrophobia, Yarwood?

Because the passage is as narrow as virtue and darker than sin. It's a long walk to the treasure room."

"Don't try to scare me, Quarrel." There was a feverish excitement in Yarwood's gaze now. "Just be sure you don't try anything clever once we're inside. I can kill Verity before you can do anything to me."

Verity spoke up, her voice soft. "There's a body inside, Preston."

That jolted him slightly. "Whose?" he demanded.

"Hazelhurst's, we think," she said. "In the end he decided the treasure was cursed. Slade Spencer came to agree with him, I think. Maybe they were right. Neither one of them ever got to enjoy any of it."

"Show me the room," Yarwood ordered as he pushed her roughly toward the hole in the wall. "You first, Quarrel."

Jonas obediently moved toward the entrance. He picked up the flashlight and his new jacket en route. He wasn't going to have much time to scoop up the stiletto and hide it in his deep jacket pocket. He needed a distraction. "Let me kick Hazelhurst's body out of the way, first. It makes Verity queasy." He could only hope the prospect of having to step over a pile of old bones was making Yarwood queasy, too.

"Go ahead," Yarwood said quickly. "Get it out of the way. Jesus. Did the old bastard really die in there?"

"Yeah. Hell of a place to croak, huh?" Jonas stepped into the entrance. He kept the flashlight aimed at the opposite corridor wall. The floor was in darkness except for the wedge of light that filtered in from the bedroom. He could just barely make out the tip of the stiletto among the scattered bones. Behind him Verity started talking rapidly, her voice tremulous. She had guessed what he was trying to do and was doing her part to distract Yarwood.

"It's awful in there, Preston," she said. "Hazelhurst's bones are lying all over the floor. You can see the skull and everything. It's easy to imagine how he must have been struggling to find the exit mechanism when he died. It's enough to give you nightmares. I think he was right. I think he found the treasure and died from the curse that was put on it."

"Shut up, you silly woman," Yarwood said impatiently. But he stayed back with Verity while Jonas crouched down on the floor of the corridor. "Hurry up, Quarrel."

"I'm hurrying, but it's a mess in here." Jonas silently thanked Verity for being willing to play the frightened, weak-kneed female. She was giving Yarwood a few second thoughts about rushing into the endless darkness of the corridor. Jonas decided he might as well add a few subtle suggestions of his own. "Got to be careful this door doesn't close on us while we're inside. Wouldn't want to end up the same way Digby did. You want to grab that chair to prop it open, Yarwood?"

"Get the chair," Yarwood said to Verity. "Go on, get it. Hurry."

Verity made a production out of dragging the heaviest chair in the room across the floor. That was all the distraction Jonas needed. He reached down and rattled a few bones in the darkness. "Sorry, Digby, old pal," he muttered. "You never did get much respect from the academic community, did you?" He palmed the stiletto and slipped it up under his sleeve.

Reality started to shimmer in a familiar way. Jonas fought the transition and quickly slid the lethally thin stiletto into his jacket pocket. Reality returned to normal as soon as he was no longer touching the stiletto. He would have to be careful not to touch it again until he was ready to use it. He didn't need the added distraction of watching Hazelhurst's murder over and over during the trek to the hidden room.

"Okay, looks like this is as good as it's going to get."

Jonas stood up and kicked one of Hazelhurst's loafers out of the way.

"You finished?" Yarwood called, peering into the gloom.

"Best I can do. If you've got a weak stomach, don't look to the left as you come through the door."

"Let me worry about my stomach," Yarwood snapped. He prodded Verity through the entrance. The blackness of the corridor loomed ahead of him. It was then that Yarwood realized that the one who held the flashlight in this situation was as powerful as the one who held the gun. "Give Verity the light, Quarrel."

Jonas swallowed an oath and put the flashlight in Verity's hand. She looked up at him, her eyes wide. He saw far too much understanding in her gaze. She would try something reckless if he didn't squelch the idea immediately. He knew it as surely as he knew that she had red hair.

But she wouldn't be able to pull it off without getting hurt. Jonas was equally sure of that. Silently he shook his head, the movement barely perceptible. But he knew she got the message, because he saw the disappointment flare in her eyes. Jonas turned and started into the darkness.

"Not so fast, Quarrel." Yarwood urged Verity ahead of him as he started down the corridor. "Stay within the light beam. I want to be able to see you at all times."

"Don't worry. I've got no particular desire to fall down the stairs."

"What stairs?"

"The ones up ahead. This corridor goes straight down to the bottom of the villa. It ends up on the same level as the torture chamber. Relax, Yarwood. We've got a long walk ahead of us."

Verity gripped the flashlight tightly and wondered frantically what Jonas was planning. She'd felt him retrieve the stiletto, and she knew he was up to something. She could sense it.

But he made no move, gave no signal as the three of them trooped down the narrow staircase and into the bottom level of the corridor. She finally realized that he was actually going to lead Yarwood to the room. Well, why not? There was nothing there to find.

But the warmth of her earrings against her skin and the chill of the green crystal in her pocket whispered another message. The closer they got to the hidden room, the stronger that message became. Verity was constantly aware of the gun pointed at her neck, but she was beginning to worry about other matters. The secrets in the vision were every bit as dangerous as the bullets in Yarwood's gun. Verity had a feeling that Jonas had decided to try something risky in the hidden room.

They reached the end of the corridor. Jonas came to a halt in front of the stone wall that concealed the entrance to the hidden room.

"This is it, Yarwood."

"Where? Show me, dammit. All I see is a blank wall."

"Watch." Jonas went to work on the mechanism.

Yarwood stared in fascination as the wall began to creak and move. He was breathing heavily. Verity could feel the tension in him.

"Fucking hell," Yarwood said in a tone of burning excitement.

The door swung open slowly, revealing the small, cold room behind it. Jonas walked through the entrance. Yarwood pushed Verity inside. Instinctively, Verity pointed the flashlight beam at the heavy black chest.

"I'll be damned," Yarwood said. "What's inside?"

"I told you, Yarwood. There's nothing inside."

''There's got to be something inside. It's a chest. A treasure chest.''

''Take a look for yourself.'' Jonas walked over to where the rusted sword hilt lay on the stone floor. He picked it up.

Verity sucked in her breath, realizing too late what Jonas had just done. He was going to access the vision. But why now?

The room was already twisting around her. Verity struggled to hang on to her awareness of what was happening in real time even as she was pulled into the psychic corridor.

The vision leaped into focus, sharper, stronger, and glowing more malevolently than it ever had before. The crystal in her pocket was radiating a fierce chill, and her earrings burned.

''Jonas?'' she whispered, searching for him in the time tunnel. She knew where he was in real time. He was standing quietly, gazing at the chest. But in the psychic corridor she could speak to him and Yarwood wouldn't hear a thing.

''The crystal may be the key,'' Jonas said aloud to Yarwood. ''But we haven't figured out how to use it.'' Inside the psychic corridor he moved up behind Verity. ''We need to be able to talk. If I had used the stiletto to get into the corridor, Yarwood would have noticed. He's not paying any attention to this old scrap of metal.''

''Look at the way the image is starting to pulse. Jonas, I don't like this.''

''You think I do? It's our one chance. Yarwood isn't going to let either of us walk out of here alive.''

Verity reached into her pocket and closed her hand around the crystal. Cold shot through her. The crystal sitting on the desk in the vision suddenly flared a brilliant, pulsating green. ''Jonas, something's going to happen.''

''Damn right. Just as soon as I get an opening. We need

another distraction. In a few more seconds Yarwood is going to start to wonder why we're all just standing around here staring at an empty treasure chest."

"The two crystals are tuning to each other," Verity said, as realization dawned. "I can feel it. Oh my God, Jonas, this isn't what we want. It won't do us any good. Everything's going to come apart. This is dangerous."

"Just hang on a second."

Verity set her teeth against the cold. She could feel the vibrations of the two green crystals adjusting to each other, tuning in to each other through the peculiar form of time and space that existed in the psychic corridor.

In real time Yarwood stepped closer to the treasure chest, dragging Verity with him.

The vision glowed.

"I'll be damned," Jonas exclaimed softly, his attention caught by the green glow of the pulsing vision. "We're going to unlock this sucker." His voice was laced with sudden excitement. "We're finally going to unlock it and find out what the hell is going on in this place."

Inside the corridor, Verity stared at him furiously. "*Jonas*. Have you forgotten about Yarwood and his gun? I'd appreciate it if you would pay attention to our main problem here."

"Under control, boss," Jonas assured her a little too nonchalantly. In real time he said to Yarwood, "Go ahead, Yarwood, take a good look. See? Nothing in there, although the chest itself is valuable. You'd have to figure out a way to get it out of here before Warwick gets back, though. He might not take too kindly to arriving home to see the family furniture being carted off by a fake psychic."

"I'm not a fake, you bastard." Yarwood stepped forward impatiently. "Hold the lid open, Verity. Give me the flashlight."

Inside the psychic corridor, where they could communicate unheard, Verity looked at Jonas. "Should I give it to him?"

"Hand it over slowly. He's mesmerized now. He's not thinking about you or me. His mind's on treasure, and fame and fortune as a proven psychic. He's all mine."

In real time Verity started to hand the flashlight to Yarwood, who made a grab for it. She let it go, aware that the gun was no longer centered on her neck. Yarwood was leaning over the chest, playing the beam of light around the interior.

Jonas moved in real time, gliding toward Yarwood with the swiftness of an uncoiling whip. Verity could not see exactly what happened because the only light in the room was aimed down into the chest. But she sensed a second image appearing briefly in the psychic corridor. This was the familiar one of poor Digby Hazelhurst being stabbed in the back. The scene vanished instantly as Jonas released the stiletto.

The next sound she heard was a strangled scream from Yarwood as he crumpled forward into the chest. The flashlight dropped to the floor, as did the gun Yarwood had been holding.

It was difficult even under ideal circumstances to keep track of two parallel realities simultaneously. Before Verity could fully register the fact that Jonas had driven the stiletto into Yarwood, the green crystal in the corridor vision suddenly blazed violently. The two crystals had completed the tuning process—the vision had been unlocked.

"Jonas, the man in the image. He's alive!"

In real time, Jonas froze just as he was about to pick up the gun and the flashlight. "He can't be alive. Nobody survives four hundred years in this corridor. It's a trick, part of the trap that was set to protect the treasure."

"The man in the vision is moving. He's never moved

before,'' Verity said hoarsely. It was true. The man behind the desk was rising to his feet. He lifted a large sheet of paper off his desk and held it up as if inviting his guests to read what he had written. The page was filled with an ancient scrawl that looked clear and fresh.

As if drawn by an invisible chain, Jonas stepped forward to stare at the page. A sudden snarl of rage crossed the apparition's features. He dropped the paper and seized the hilt of his sword.

''Jonas, what's happening?''

''I don't know,'' Jonas muttered. ''But this is getting too damned real.''

''Get back,'' Verity shouted. ''Let go of the sword hilt.''

''I can't,'' Jonas said grimly. ''My fingers are frozen around it.''

''Oh my God. Now what?''

''I don't know. Stay out of my way.''

''Jonas, something terrible is going to happen. I can feel it.''

''I know,'' Jonas said softly. ''I can feel it too.''

Verity clutched the green crystal and wondered what his words meant. She was terribly afraid she would soon learn the truth. Then she saw the poisonous green, squirming ribbons of emotion that were unfurling from the heart of the image. ''There they are, Jonas. We always wondered why there were no tendrils of emotion in this image, but there they are. They've been locked inside the vision all along.''

''They'll head for you,'' Jonas said as he moved closer to the image. ''Chain them, Verity. You have to chain them or we're both dead.''

''I don't know if I can hold them,'' Verity whispered as the dark green ribbons struggled in vain to curl themselves around Jonas, then headed reluctantly toward her. The cold radiating from the green crystal grew painful in her hand. The only warmth she could feel came from her earrings.

She needed fire, not the cold green vibrations of the old crystal.

Verity acted on impulse. In real time she reached up and quickly removed her fire-colored crystal earrings. They nestled in her palm, emitting a reassuring heat that seemed to counter the cold in her other hand.

Then she saw that the man in the vision had his sword clear of its scabbard. He held it aloft, preparing for a powerful swing. His eyes seemed to focus directly on Jonas.

''Are you sure he can't see you?'' Verity asked desperately. The green ribbons whirled and spun around her feet.

''I think he designed the image to make it look as real as possible,'' Jonas said. He was standing directly in front of the vision, the broken sword hilt still locked in his hand. ''He found a way to lock this scene here in time. He did it deliberately. This is no accidental image caught in the time corridor.''

''It's so real,'' she said. ''More real than anything we've ever seen in here.''

''Optical illusion. It's got to be.''

''You've said that before. But this time you can't convince me.'' The green crystal suddenly vibrated violently in her hand. The green glow of the vision began to expand outward, making the image appear larger. The man in the vision raised the sword higher. His fierce eyes glittered with rage. The cloak fell back to reveal powerful shoulders.

The green light from the crystal was filling the entire room now. Verity opened her mouth to scream but it was too late.

''Jonas, this is real. *We're inside the vision itself.*''

She was a part of it, she realized with horror. The fury of the man in the vision was palpable now. It was real. As if he had suddenly spotted her, he swung toward her and began to bring his sword down in an arc that would take off her head. He was going to kill her.

"Jonas."

There was no response. Verity tried to drop the green crystal and discovered she couldn't release it. She tried to move and found that she was rooted to the spot. She looked up in stunned terror as the sword began its lethal descent. She was going to die! She was caught in the vision, and she was going to be killed by a man who had waited four hundred years to do the job. Verity couldn't even close her eyes.

"Touch her and you die!" Jonas suddenly shouted at the apparition. "She's mine." Without any warning, he was there beside Verity in the vision. He held a sword in his hand, a whole sword, not just a rusted hilt. Green ribbons were coiled around one of his arms. He leaped to put himself between Verity and the man who threatened her.

"Leave her alone, you son of a bitch," Jonas rasped. "I'm the one you want, I'm the one who got through your damn lock." Then he broke off and said something in Italian.

The old man didn't seem interested in the language problem. He maintained an eerie silence as he refocused on Jonas and swung the sword.

Jonas ducked and slid to one side. The blade passed a scant few inches over his head. He came up from a fighter's crouch and slashed at the figure in the vision.

The old man took a step backward, an expression of astonishment on his face. Viciously he swung once more. This time Jonas leaped recklessly forward, driving himself up under the arc of the swinging blade. His own blade led the way and buried itself in the man's chest. The victim opened his mouth in a silent shout of agony and rage as he toppled backward.

The sword snapped in Jonas's hand, leaving behind only the hilt.

Verity wanted to scream but she couldn't find the breath to do so. The vision was wavering. The green ribbons around Jonas's arm were leaping for his throat.

Verity sensed the rapacious hunger of the ribbons and knew what was happening. The raw emotional energy that had been trapped in the image four hundred years ago was now fighting to get free. Jonas was the conduit the ancient residual energy could use to get to the present.

The emotions that had governed this scene four hundred years ago could escape only through Jonas. He would be overwhelmed by them—driven insane, or turned into a killer. It was the risk he ran every time he stepped into the psychic corridor.

Only Verity could help him control the power, but she'd never tried to control energy ribbons that were this strong.

Verity tightened her grasp on the earrings. Concentrating on them, she managed to unclench her other hand. The green crystal fell to the floor. With an enormous sense of relief, she focused completely on the fiery crystals of her earrings.

She felt the fire in her hands and held them to her breast. A brilliant red glow seeped out between her fingers. The vibrations were strong and pure and powerful.

Verity took two steps forward to where Jonas was on his knees, struggling with the living green tongues that were wrapping themselves around him. His face was a mask of anguish and rage and his eyes were stark as he looked up at her.

"Get out of here," he said thickly. "Get out of here now.

Lock the door to this room behind you, and don't ever try to open it again."

"I can't leave you here."

"Do it, Verity. Do it for me, for the baby, for yourself. Do it now, damn you."

"I love you, Jonas. I can't leave you in here."

"If you love me as much as I love you, you'll do it. Hurry, Verity. For God's sake, hurry. Seal this room behind you, don't tell anyone about it. Go. Please, go. I can't hold out much longer. Once these ribbons take control, I will try to kill anyone in this room. Do you understand?"

"No," she whispered. "I don't understand."

"Don't you see? I will be the one who protects his damned treasure for him now. *I'll murder anyone who steps into this room, and that includes you.*"

"You would never hurt me," Verity said softly. She knelt in front of him.

"Verity."

"Put your hand on mine, Jonas." She held out her clasped fingers. The earrings pulsed warmly. "Do it, Jonas. Now."

His golden eyes were grim as he lifted his ravaged face. With enormous effort he slowly raised the hand that was not clutching the broken sword hilt. He touched her glowing fingers.

"Yes," she whispered as she felt the tuning process begin. "That's it. Just hold on to me. The fire is stronger than anything that bastard left behind. The fire is fresh and new and never grows old. The ribbons are from the past. They must stay there."

The earrings surged with heat. Verity felt Jonas's fingers tighten violently around her clasped hands.

Fire blossomed between her fingers.

The green ribbons that had been coiling around Jonas's

neck began to loosen. Verity willed them back to the tangled mass that swarmed around her feet, and they reluctantly obeyed.

The last of the green ribbons unwound itself from Jonas and joined the others.

In real time something clattered on the floor of the stone cell. Verity looked down and saw that it was the broken sword hilt Jonas had used to access the vision.

The psychic corridor faded abruptly and the last of the sickly green vision vanished with it. The fiery glow in Verity's hands died out and Jonas's fingers fell away from hers.

Darkness descended on the small room, broken only by the beam of the flashlight, which still shone futilely inside the empty chest.

Verity sighed in relief. She would never like the darkness that reigned inside this hidden room, but at least it seemed normal now.

"It's over, Jonas. We're free."

There was no answer. Verity heard a heavy thud. She raced for the chest, shoved Yarwood's body out of the way, and grabbed the flashlight.

She aimed the beam at Jonas and saw that he was lying on the stone floor, unconscious.

Chapter Eighteen

SOMETHING was missing. Gone. Burned away in a flash of green poison.

Jonas tried to ignore the distant voices that were clamoring for attention. He wanted to concentrate on whatever it was that was wrong, but the voices kept calling to him.

One voice was male and gruffly reassuring. The other was female—demanding and insistent. He recognized the second voice and wanted to let the speaker know he'd be along in a minute. Right now he was busy.

He stayed in the darkness awhile longer, struggling to think, trying to figure out what piece of himself was missing. But he couldn't get a handle on it. He had a sense that something was gone, something that had been a part of him—something important.

"Jonas? Can you hear me? Say something, damn you. Talk to me! Jonas, answer me this instant. Do you hear me?

You can't do this to me. I won't allow it. Open your eyes and answer me. *Answer me*, you bastard."

Deep in the bottomless darkness, Jonas smiled to himself. Verity was chewing his ass, as usual. His redheaded tyrant was on her throne, and all was right with the world.

He pushed the sense of wrongness to the back of his mind and made an effort to open his eyes. He wanted to see Verity's face. She sounded angry.

"I warned you about frown lines," Jonas said as he managed to lift his lashes. He wondered why his voice sounded so thick, as if he were drunk. Then he saw Verity's face, and he wanted to chuckle at the mix of emotions in her eyes. "You look like you don't know whether to kiss me or strangle me. What'd I do this time?"

"Oh, Jonas, I've been so scared." Joyous relief flared in her beautiful eyes.

"Hey, I'm here, sweetheart. Take it easy."

She threw herself across him, gathering him into her arms as best she could. "I was so worried. We've all been worried. You've been unconscious for hours. What's the matter with you?"

"Nothing's the matter, as far as I know." Her cheeks were wet. She had been crying over him, he realized in wonder. He felt her soft breasts pleasantly pressed against his chest and realized for the first time that he was lying on a bed. He put an arm around Verity, twisting his fingers in her fiery curls. Then he found himself staring at her hair and remembering another source of fire. His hand clenched abruptly. "Verity?" he got out in a husky voice.

She lifted her head, smiling her most dazzling smile of relief and welcome. She dashed a hand across her eyes to wipe away the tears. "You're sure you're okay?"

He stared into her anxious face. "I'm all right. But what about you?"

"I'm fine if you forget the fact that you've just given me the biggest scare of my life." She sat up on the edge of the bed. "Honestly, Jonas, how could you just pass out on me like that? Do you have any idea how hard it was to drag you down that corridor? I had to get a sheet and roll you onto it before I could even budge you. The sheet is ruined, naturally."

"Naturally." He just kept staring at her, bemused but content for the moment.

"Then, after I made sure you were alive, I had to go back to that awful room and drag Preston out on another sheet. He was unconscious too, and he weighed a ton. My arms are still sore. I feel like I've been doing pushups for days."

"Yarwood's alive?" Jonas struggled to make sense of the running commentary.

"Barely. Oliver says he thinks he'll live. Yarwood and poor Maggie are both in the hospital. Doug took them over to the main island a couple of hours ago. He should be back soon and he'll probably be bringing the police with him. It's all a huge mess."

Jonas opened his mouth to ask another question but before he could get the words out a familiar face loomed into view.

"Welcome back, Quarrel," Oliver Crump said. "We weren't sure where you'd gone. Doug thought we should send you to the hospital with the others, but Verity and I decided against that."

"We didn't think a doctor would have any more idea of how to treat you than we did," Verity said bluntly. "We couldn't even figure out how to explain the situation to a doctor. So we kept you here while Doug took the others away. Oliver has been working the crystal." She held up a shard of glittering lemon-colored crystal.

"From what Verity told me, I figured that crystals had caused the problem in the first place," Oliver explained.

"Probably some complicated side effect of the tuning process. She couldn't really explain what had happened in that room, but I figured that logically speaking, crystal could be used to undo the damage. But can you imagine trying to get that concept across to an emergency room physician?"

"Suckers would have locked you and Verity in padded cells while they stuck needles into me." Jonas groaned and tentatively massaged his temples. He had a headache, but that seemed a small price to pay, all things considered. "Thanks for making the executive decision to keep me here. I hate emergency rooms. Those places are full of germs. Take a risk every time you go in one."

Verity's brows drew together in a firm line. "Are you sure you feel all right?"

He gave her his most effective sympathy-getting smile, the one that implied he was suffering nobly. Verity usually fell for it. "Head hurts a little, but that's about it."

"Oh, poor Jonas." Verity leaned forward and began gently to massage his temples.

She smelled good as she leaned over him—a little feminine sweat mixed with the wonderfully familiar fragrance that was hers, and hers alone. Jonas inhaled deeply. "How's Maggie?"

"She was coming around as we loaded her into the launch," Crump said. "Elyssa is going to be all right, by the way. She woke up last night and remembered who had pushed her."

"You'll never believe this, Jonas, but Maggie was the one who pushed Elyssa off that cliff," Verity said.

"Maggie pushed her?" Jonas was startled. Then it started to make sense. "Because of the plans to sell the villa?"

Verity nodded. "She was very upset about Doug's decision to sell. Maggie considered this place her home, and she thought she had a right to stay here. She followed Elyssa out to the cliffs yesterday to see if she could persuade Elyssa to talk Doug out of the deal, but Elyssa was not in a conversational mood, apparently. They got into an argument, and Maggie lost her temper and struck Elyssa. Elyssa lost her balance and went over the edge. Maggie panicked and ran back to the house.''

''Did Maggie ever realize the significance of the green crystal necklace she wore all the time?'' Jonas asked.

''She knew it had been important to Hazelhurst, so from a sentimental point of view it was important to her. But she never knew it was the key to the treasure. She didn't really believe there was a treasure,'' Crump said. ''She was tolerant of Hazelhurst's search because she loved him. She considered the treasure hunt his hobby, that's all.''

''Hazelhurst probably thought the necklace would be safe with her. No one would think anything of an old necklace worn by his housekeeper,'' Verity mused.

Jonas nodded, then winced when his head began to throb. ''Spencer was the grad student who weaseled his way into Hazelhurst's life a couple of years ago. When Hazelhurst decided that Slade was nothing but a tacky treasure hunter, not a genuine scholar, he kicked him out on his ass. But Spencer was hooked on finding the treasure. He sneaked back several times. One night he discovered Hazelhurst going into the tunnel and he followed him to the treasure room. There was a fight, and Spencer must have chased Hazelhurst down the hall to the bedroom exit. He killed him with the stiletto that had been left behind in the chamber. Then he gathered up all that remained of the treasure, which consisted of a ruby ring, and fled. On the way out the door, he remembered the diary, I guess. He tore out the last few pages, the ones he figured might mention him or the hidden passageway.''

''But he'd left a body behind in that hidden passage,''

Crump said. "I talked to him a while ago. He was never mentally stable, but after Hazelhurst's murder he really started to come apart. He's been quietly going crazy during the past two years, sinking deeper into drugs and paranoia. He was terrified his crime would eventually be discovered. It was all he could think about—it obsessed him."

Verity spoke up. "Slade kept tabs on what was happening to the villa. He even got involved in Preston Yarwood's psychic-development seminars so he could watch Elyssa. When he found out the Warwicks were going to hire someone to look the place over, he decided he had to come along and make certain no one found out about poor Digby. He was the prowler I surprised that night in Sequence Springs. He was trying to find out information about you."

"He's been a mental wreck for nearly two years," Crump volunteered. "He was scared to death you'd figure out who he was. He even followed you and Verity to the other island two nights ago to see what you were up to. He was watching your room at the inn when Verity happened to go down the hall to the bathroom."

"That bastard," Jonas muttered. "What was he going to do with her?"

"I'm not sure he had a plan," Crump said slowly. "He just seized what he saw as an opportunity to frighten her. He thought that if he scared her badly enough, the two of you might decide to give up the treasure hunt and leave."

"And that, incidentally, is what Maggie Frampton had in mind the first night here when she closed the corridor door on us," Verity put in cheerfully. "She hoped to scare us off. She planned to reopen it the next day. That's why she was so surprised to see us bright and early in the kitchen the following morning. She hadn't yet reopened the door."

Jonas stared at her. "Maggie closed that door on us? She knew about the hidden passageway?"

"Oh, yes, she knew about it, but she had never gone into it. She was frightened of it."

"So she never found Digby's bones," Jonas concluded.

"The only entrance to the tunnel that Slade knew about, on the other hand, was the one in the torture chamber," Verity continued. "He didn't realize the night he killed Hazelhurst that Digby had been trying to escape through a second entrance. That's why, when he broke the lock on the torture-chamber entrance door, he thought he'd sealed Maggie and me away for good."

"What a mess," Jonas said.

"One you seem to have cleaned up," Crump observed. "If you'll excuse me, I'll get something for that headache." He vanished through the bathroom door.

Jonas wanted to lie quietly and enjoy the feel of Verity's fingers easing the tension in his head, but the questions wouldn't let him relax. "What did they do with Spencer?"

"Doug took him away with the others."

Jonas sucked in a deep breath and caught her wrist. "I almost got you killed."

"That's a debatable point," she said with a hint of mischief in her smile. "An unbiased soul might say that I almost got you killed. I was the one who nagged you into taking this job in the first place, remember?"

He ignored that. "If anything had happened to you, I wouldn't have wanted to wake up. My God, Verity, when I think of how dangerous the whole thing was for you I get cold all over." He shook his head in awe. "You shouldn't have stayed after I told you to get out of the room. You shouldn't have taken the risk."

She framed his head between her delicate hands. "You big idiot. There's no way I could have left you behind in that room. No more than you could have left me. You should know that by now."

Jonas closed his eyes briefly. She was right. Neither one of them could have abandoned the other. There was no point in yelling at her now for the risks she had taken. "Those red crystal earrings of yours worked somehow, didn't they?"

"Yes. Don't ask me how, though. I don't really understand it."

"There was fire. I followed it out of the cold." Jonas moved his head restlessly on the pillow, unable to remember exactly how he had used the fire to hang on to his sanity. "He almost got us, you know."

"Who? That awful man in the vision?" Verity shuddered.

"His name was Giovanni Marino. I learned at least that, but not much else about him when I grabbed the ribbons."

"What in the word was going on in there, Jonas? He came alive, didn't he?"

Jonas started to shake his head but discovered that it hurt more when he did. "No. We were dealing with a corridor image, not a real person. But the image had been created by a genius who happened to have the same kind of psychic ability I've got. Christ, Verity, it was spooky. That Marino bastard was light-years ahead of me. He understood so much more about that corridor than I do."

"Maybe because he was a lot older than you," Verity pointed out. "He'd had more time to study his power. You're probably going to understand your talent much better by the time you're his age."

Jonas smiled faintly. He could always count on Verity to say something bracing and reassuring when he needed it. "I'm not so sure. Marino had the key to understanding exactly how the images get caught in that tunnel. He understood the science behind it."

"We saw those books of mathematics and astrology on his desk. Maybe he had discovered the physical laws that govern the way it all works."

"I may have made a mistake majoring in Renaissance history," Jonas confessed wryly. "Should have stuck to the hard sciences. People always warned me about the dangers of getting a degree in a liberal-arts subject."

Verity waved that aside. "Okay, so this Marino creep knew something about the logistics of the thing. What's the rest of the story?"

"It's simple. I figured out most of what was going on when the vision finally started to cycle. He had found a way to freeze an image of impending violence and store it in the time corridor. He picked a vision he wanted to preserve, and deliberately anchored it."

Verity's eyes widened in awe. "That is pretty impressive when you think about it."

"Impressive is right. Apparently when Marino recorded the image we saw he also managed to leave behind a subtle sense of threat, a kind of warning. He wanted to scare off any other time tunnel adventurer who might happen along in search of his treasure."

"You told me that the first time you saw the image you felt you were being warned off."

"That was exactly what was happening. But, being the fearless, macho guy I am, I ignored the warning." Jonas grimaced with self-disgust. He had been obsessed with unlocking the image from the first moment he'd seen it.

"It wasn't your fault, Jonas. Stop blaming yourself." Verity gave his head a slight, admonishing shake.

Jonas inhaled sharply as pain stabbed through his temples.

"Oh, dear," Verity said, instantly contrite. "Did I hurt you?"

He managed a weak grin. "I deserved it."

"I'm so sorry." She went back to her gentle massage. "So Marino left the image as a warning to other psychics who might happen to have his talent. How does the rest of it fit together?''

''He planned to access the vision himself at a later date. He wanted to be able to get at his treasure, you see. The green crystal is the key. He programmed it to unfreeze the image.''

''Why leave the vision and the key behind?''

''He knew he was going to have to leave town for a while. He'd offended an important member of the local aristocracy, and the only safe course of action was to flee for a time. He planned to return later to retrieve his treasure.''

''You mean the treasure was somehow locked in the corridor along with the image?''

''It's been there all along. We saw it when the image started rolling.''

''What do you mean? We saw the heaps of gold and jewels in the chest,'' Verity reminded him, ''but the chest is empty now.''

''That wasn't the treasure Marino was protecting. The gold wasn't nearly as important to him as the secrets he had discovered about the psychic corridor. He wrote out his notes and left them locked in the image.''

''That piece of paper he picked up and showed us when the action started!'' Verity exclaimed.

''Exactly. The formulas and notations on that sheet of paper are his real treasure. He was probably afraid to leave the paper itself lying around. And he didn't know if he would be stopped and searched or robbed on the way out of town.''

''So he left behind the equivalent of a photographic image of his work.'' Verity's eyes widened in amazement. ''What a brilliant idea. He could access the image with the crystal.''

''Not quite.'' Jonas frowned, thinking of all he had

learned when he'd tangled with the ribbons. "The crystal does activate the image. It starts the film running, so to speak. But to actually access the vision itself, he had to have the usual sort of key. The same kind of key I always use."

"An object associated with violence," Verity said slowly. "Of course. He had to leave behind something that was connected with a violent scene in the image. The sword hilt?"

"That wasn't the object he'd intended to leave behind," Jonas said quietly. "The stiletto was supposed to be the key to the corridor image. Marino had planned to kill someone with the stiletto and then later use the stiletto to get at the vision where his work was hidden."

"He planned to murder someone?" Verity's eyes were wide with shock. "He deliberately set out to create an image and then commit murder in order to freeze the image in the corridor?"

"It's the only way it could be done."

"But whom did he intend to kill?"

Jonas's mouth hardened. "He'd planned to murder the one other person who knew what he was up to. That way he could be certain the secrets he had discovered were safe."

"But who else knew about his research?"

Jonas looked at her for a long moment. "Think about it, Verity. Who is the one other person who would know him intimately enough to realize he had made some significant discoveries about the corridor?"

Verity's eyes widened further. "His anchor," she whispered. "The one who controlled the ribbons for him when he went into the corridor. Oh, my God."

Jonas nodded grimly. "Exactly. But Marino made a slight miscalculation. He never got a chance to use the stiletto on her."

"His anchor was a woman?"

"Uh-huh. The pretty young wife of a member of the aristocracy. Her name was Isabella. He had seduced her when he realized what she could do for him."

"Isabella." Verity repeated the name softly.

"Marino was waiting for her in the chamber that last night. He intended to seal the image with her murder. He had sent for her and she had come to him, as usual. But this time she didn't come alone. Her husband, suspecting that she was having an affair—although the poor guy couldn't have known just how intimately involved his wife really was—had followed her. He entered the room right behind her. The guy behind the desk realized what was happening and grabbed his sword instead of the stiletto. Like most Renaissance aristocrats, Marino was good with a sword."

"But the husband killed him?"

Jonas nodded grimly. "With great pleasure. Matteo was skilled with a sword too, and he was younger and faster than Marino. In the end it was Marino's death that locked the image in the corridor. It was the broken sword handle that stayed behind to become the key to accessing the vision, although there was no one left to use it."

"Jonas, it's hard to believe it was only an illusion."

"I told you, Giovanni Marino was a genius, and he knew what he was doing. He did such a good job with his creation that when it started to cycle, you and I thought that we were actually a part of it. You became Isabella and I became her jealous husband, Matteo."

"I think it was more than that, Jonas," Verity insisted.

He smiled in understanding. "The illusion was probably all the more real for us because we were each temperamentally suited to assume their roles. You've had experience as an anchor who's been sleeping with the man she anchors, and I've had a hell of a lot of experience being jealous of you. I can't think of anyone I'd want to kill more, in fact, than a man who had the power to pull you into the corridor with him.'' Jonas realized his hand was clenched into a fist.

Verity gently unknotted his fingers. ''Relax, Jonas. It's all over.''

He forced himself to inhale slowly and let the tension seep out of him. ''I've told you about my end of the thing. Tell me what was happening with the crystals.''

''I still don't understand it all,'' Verity said honestly. ''I could feel the green crystal tuning itself to the crystal in the image.''

''I'll bet one of the secrets the guy in the vision was trying to hide was the technique for tuning the crystal so that it could be used as a key to unfreeze the image.'' Damn. What he wouldn't give to learn those secrets. Now that he knew what was going on, Jonas figured there had to be a safe way of activating the vision again. He wanted to study that manuscript.

''When you picked up the corridor ribbons, I concentrated on the red crystals instead of the green. They seemed to hold a more positive power somehow.'' Verity shook her head uncertainly. ''I felt I could use them. Tune them, make them work for me. I didn't feel that way about the green crystal. It was dangerous, Jonas.''

''You found a way to use the red crystals to pull me out of the grip of the ribbons, didn't you?'' Jonas searched her face. ''Those damn snakes really had a hold on me this time, Verity. They were stronger than anything I've come up against in that corridor. I grabbed them because for a while there I actually believed the whole thing was real; I believed you were going to be killed. I picked up on the emotions and skills that Matteo had used, and suddenly I was Matteo.''

''I believe you did save us, somehow. That battle was for

real, Jonas. I'm convinced we were actually in that image. But when it was over, you couldn't get rid of the ribbons.''

''They were too powerful, probably because the vision itself was so damn powerful. I would have become a walking ghost of Matteo. Not the whole man, just the part of him that had been left behind in the corridor. The part that was enraged, the part that could think of nothing but vengeance and killing. I was afraid I would turn on you next, the way Matteo probably turned on Isabella. Giovanni Marino would have had the ultimate revenge.''

''Matteo murdered his wife after he killed Marino?'' Verity's expression was one of outrage.

''I don't know what actually happened,'' Jonas said soothingly. ''For us the story ends with the creep's death. I just got the impression from the residual emotions Matteo left behind that he was as furious with his wife as he was with her seducer.''

Verity sat back. ''I don't think he killed her,'' she declared after a moment. ''I think that after he'd killed Marino, he came to his senses and realized his wife was just an innocent victim. I bet they both locked the door of that chamber, went back home, and lived happily ever after.''

Jonas eyed her indulgently. ''Sounds like a nice, cheerful ending.''

''But probably not the real ending, right, Quarrel?'' Crump spoke from the doorway. ''People back in the Renaissance had some nasty notions of vengeance, didn't they?''

Jonas snapped his head around, setting off the dull, throbbing ache again. ''I didn't hear you come in,'' he said, annoyed. ''How long have you been standing there?''

''Long enough.'' Oliver smiled reassuringly. ''But don't worry. I won't try to explain any of this to Warwick or anyone else. I'm not sure I understand it myself.'' He came toward the bed and extended his palm to reveal two white tablets. "Here. Take these and call me in the morning."

Jonas eyed the tablets with suspicion. "What are they? Some mumbo-jumbo herb treatment?"

"You could say that. They're aspirin." He handed Jonas a glass of water with his other hand.

Jonas sat up cautiously, took the glass, and swallowed the pills. "I'd appreciate it if you would keep your mouth shut about the psychic stuff."

"I will," Oliver promised calmly. "Who would believe me, except another psychic? And there aren't too many real ones running around. You're the only one I've ever met." Then he smiled faintly. "So Elyssa and Yarwood were right after all, hmmm? You really do have a talent for psychometry?"

"Something like that," Jonas said unencouragingly.

"It's a very unusual ability," Verity interjected with enthusiasm. "He can pick up on certain images from the past when he touches an object associated with those images. Unfortunately, he's a bit limited in some respects. He can only tune in to scenes of violence."

Jonas groaned. "Verity, I think that's enough."

"However," Verity continued, "the talent makes it possible for him to authenticate all kinds of objects from the past, even when they aren't associated with violence. He can't actually see an image of a chair or a piece of jewelry, the way he can with weapons, but he can feel the age of the object. Enough to know whether or not it's a reproduction."

"Verity, I doubt if Crump is really interested in all this."

"I've been telling Jonas that he should use his ability to set up a consulting business. That's why I had him take this job. Don't you think it's a marvelous idea, Oliver?"

"Not if it gets both of you killed," Oliver said bluntly.

Jonas exchanged a significant look with the other man. "Thank you for those words of wisdom. I agree completely."

Verity turned on him. "Now, just a minute. What happened on this job was bad luck, that's all. Think of it as an industrial accident. The odds of this sort of thing occurring again must be zillions to one."

"Something tells me that your math might be shaky," Jonas retorted.

"So we'll be a little more careful next time," Verity said briskly. "Actually, this assignment was completed quite satisfactorily. Doug will get the written evaluation of the villa that he wanted, and Elyssa will get a few answers about the legendary treasure. We can show everyone the secret passage and the room and the chest. That should satisfy all parties concerned." Then her eyes narrowed in disappointment. "I wish we'd found more than just an empty treasure chest, though. Finding a pile of Florentine coins would have been a nice professional touch. Great publicity."

"I think I'll live without the advertising," Jonas drawled as he sat up on the edge of the bed.

"In fact, you might live a lot longer without it," Crump said. He was smiling one of his rare smiles.

"Now that I'm going to be a father, I have to think twice about taking undue risks," Jonas agreed complacently.

Verity glared at both of them. "Why do I get the feeling that another career option for Jonas is going down the drain?"

"Face it, honey. I was born to wash dishes for you. Besides, in a few months I'll be learning a new profession. I'm going to be a hell of a daddy."

Verity's mouth curved at the corners and her eyes softened. "Think so?"

"I have a talent for it, just like I have a talent for being a husband. I can feel it in my bones."

"I think maybe I will invest in a wedding dress," Verity said thoughtfully. "Might as well do this right."

"We'll have to hurry up and get you to the altar," Jonas said blandly, his eyes roving her still-slender figure. "It won't be long before you'll be too round for a wedding gown."

She threw a pillow at him.

Verity lay quietly in the shadows of the canopied bed and listened to Jonas toss and turn beside her. She knew he hadn't slept at all since they had climbed into bed two hours ago. He had made love to her with a gentle urgency, as if he needed to assure himself that everything was really back to normal. But afterward he had not fallen asleep.

Verity had closed her eyes and drifted off immediately, only to be awakened by Jonas's restless movements. She finally decided she'd had enough. Something was bothering him, and it was time to get it out into the open. She pushed back the cover and sat up against the pillows.

"Quit trying to pretend you're asleep, Jonas," she said gently. "Tell me what's wrong."

He lay still for a few seconds, then turned on his back. His eyes gleamed in the darkness. "I want another look at the manuscript in that damned vision," he admitted bluntly.

Verity took a deep breath. "I thought that might be it."

There was silence for a long moment, then Jonas said, "I don't know if we can do it without getting ourselves into the same mess we did earlier."

"This time we know what to expect. I can take the red crystal earrings with me again. I know how to use them this time if things get rough. As long as you don't pick up any of the ribbons, we'll be safe."

"I can't let you take the risk."

"You can't get another look at that vision without me,"

she pointed out calmly. "The ribbons would overwhelm you for certain." Her mind made up, she shoved aside the covers. "No sense putting it off. We might as well get it over with." She pursed her lips in thought. "This time around we just have to keep in mind that we are watching a vision. We're not part of it. I'll know what I'm doing this time. I'll let go of the green crystal as soon as the image activates. I think I can use the earrings to keep things sane after that."

"It'll take time," Jonas said as he sat up. "That manuscript was in Latin, and written in sixteenth-century script. I need a close look at it. The problem with that vision is that it's so damn powerful. The risk is that it will distract us, make us think it's real again." He ran a hand through his hair. "Hell, I don't know, Verity. I shouldn't let you near that thing again. I shouldn't get near it myself."

Verity sat up on the edge of the bed. "But you won't be able to sleep at night until you try to read that manuscript. It's going to drive you nuts, Jonas. I don't think we have any choice."

Jonas shook his head. "I'm not sure I can let you take the risk."

Verity stood up and walked around to his side of the bed. "We have to, Jonas. This is your psychic talent we're talking about here. The more you learn about controlling it, the safer we'll both be and the more useful the talent will be. Who knows what you'll run up against next time in the corridor? We can do it. I know we can." She picked up the red crystal earrings. "The green crystal is still in that chamber. In all the confusion, no one remembered it." She stepped into her shoes and started toward the tapestry.

"Verity, come back here," Jonas ordered harshly. He stood up abruptly. "I said come back here."

But Verity had already found the hidden mechanism that

unlocked the entrance to the passageway. The ponderous stone door creaked and began to swing open. She picked up the flashlight and threw a challenging smile over her shoulder. "You're not going to let me go into that horrible passage alone, are you?"

"Jesus, Verity. You are one stubborn female." But Jonas was already sliding into his jeans.

She had known he wouldn't fight too hard to stop her. This had to be done and they both knew it. It would be impossible for Jonas to ignore secrets that had to do with his psychic talent. The more he understood it, the better off they both were, Verity told herself as she started down the dark passageway.

Jonas came up behind her and touched her shoulder. "I love you, you know."

"Good." She handed him the flashlight. "I love you, too."

"I figured as much. Otherwise, you wouldn't take another step in this damn passage. At least Digby's bones are gone now. Here, you hold this." He thrust a notebook and pen into her fingers. "I'll take the flashlight."

The door to the dark cell was open. Verity hadn't bothered to close it after she'd dragged Jonas and Preston out.

"There's the green crystal," Verity said as the flashlight beam swung across the stone floor. "And there's the sword hilt. Are you ready?"

"As ready as I'll ever be. Stay close beside me after we're in the corridor. Last time we both got too near the image. It was one of the reasons we seemed to get sucked into it so easily."

"You'll have to be close to the vision to read the manuscript, and we'll probably have to watch the thing recycle several times. I'll take notes while you read aloud."

"If I give the order to get out, I don't want any arguments."

''You won't get any,'' she assured him. She picked up the green crystal. ''Funny, it doesn't seem to be vibrating the way it was before. And the earrings don't feel hot, either.''

''We'll see what happens. Hang on, here we go.'' Jonas bent down and picked up the broken sword hilt.

Nothing happened.

Verity had tensed herself for the transition into the psychic corridor. It took her a few seconds to realize that the walls of the cell weren't curving around her.

''Jonas?''

There was a stunned silence from Jonas. She could see his taut features in the harsh glow of the flashlight. His golden eyes blazed at her.

''Jonas, what's wrong?'' she whispered.

''It's gone.'' His voice was hoarse with bewildered frustration.

''What's gone?''

''My talent. I'm empty inside. I can't pick up a damned thing. Not one damned vibration. Whatever happened in here this afternoon has burned out my talent.''

Chapter Nineteen

A week after their return to Sequence Springs, Verity was closer to despair than she had ever been in her life. Everything had changed between her and Jonas.

There was no more talk of marriage. No more planning for the baby. No more teasing, or squabbling, or joyous making up in bed. It wasn't that Jonas didn't touch her in bed. He did, but his lovemaking had undergone a critical change.

Verity sensed a fierce desperation in him instead of the many levels of passion she had come to expect in recent months. It seemed he was trying to prove something, but she didn't know what it was.

The loss of his talent had hit him hard, Verity knew. She had tried to ignore it, tried to pretend there was nothing wrong, that his psychic ability would return soon. But Jonas had convinced himself that it was gone for good, and Verity secretly wondered if he was right.

If his talent had been burned out of him, where did that leave her?

She began to grow more and more anxious as Jonas retreated behind a wall of deepening silence. Perhaps he needed to go through some sort of mourning period, she told herself. The psychic talent had been the bane of much of his adult life, but it had been an integral part of him. Losing it must have been like losing a hand, or an arm, or one of the five senses. Verity forced herself to be understanding and undemanding. She took great pains to be good-natured and sweet.

She didn't nag him to finish the report for the Warwicks. She didn't urge him to write any more articles for the academic journals. She temporarily shelved her big plans to have him do a piece on Renaissance weapons for *National Geographic*. And she didn't bring up the subject of another consulting assignment.

But the more understanding she became, the more Jonas withdrew. It was a frustrating spiral, and as she got more and more enmeshed in it all her old fears were revived. She was convinced that Jonas would leave again. And this time, she thought, he might go away for good.

The bottom line here, she thought grimly, was that Jonas didn't need her the way he once had. She was no longer his psychic anchor. She was merely his lover and the mother of his child—a child he had never planned to have.

It was unfortunate that in the dead of winter, business was light at the No Bull Cafe. Verity had too much time to think.

"When's the wedding?" Laura Griswald asked at the end of the week. The two women were sharing a spa pool after hours. Crystal-clear water bubbled and steamed around them.

"I'm not sure there's going to be one," Verity said quietly.

"You mean you two haven't talked marriage yet?" Laura's brows arched in disbelief. "I thought for sure that when you came back from the vacation up north it would all be settled."

"I thought it was."

Laura leaned forward, her expression one of deep concern. "Verity, are you telling me that Jonas doesn't want to marry you? He doesn't want the baby?"

"I don't know what Jonas wants," Verity said as she stood up and reached for her towel. "I'm not sure he knows, either."

"I can't believe this. I was so sure everything would work out between you two."

"Men are a little more complicated than I once gave them credit for," Verity said curtly. "At least Jonas is." She turned around quickly before Laura could see the tears in her eyes, and hurried toward the changing booth.

She dressed in her jeans and a yellow cotton shirt and headed for the resort's lounge. Jonas would be waiting. He still insisted on accompanying her when she wanted a late-night soak. He refused to let her walk back alone along the icy path to the cottage.

Verity saw him as she entered the lounge. He sat slouching with casual grace on a bar stool, his boots hooked over the brass foot railing. He was draining the last of his scotch. And he was not alone.

"Dad! You're back!" Verity ran toward her father. "When did you get in?"

Her father swung around on the bar stool and folded his daughter in a bear-sized embrace. "Got in about an hour ago. Found Jonas holding down the bar all by himself and thought I'd keep him company until you showed up."

Verity ignored Jonas, who was giving his full attention to his drink. She smiled brilliantly at her father. "Did Jonas tell you the news?"

"What news?"

Jonas froze. He shot Verity a glowering look over his shoulder. She paid him no attention.

"I'm pregnant," Verity said demurely and watched with delight as her father leaped to his feet.

Emerson Ames let out a whoop of joy, grabbed his daughter by the waist, and swung her around in a wide arc. Two people sitting at a nearby table ducked quickly.

"You're pregnant? I'm going to get a grandkid? Bless you, my darling red-haired daughter! What the devil took you so long? Yahoo and pour me another drink, Clement. A big one. Hell, pour everyone in the joint another drink." Emerson turned expansively to address the small crowd. "This round's on me, folks. Drink up. I'm gonna be a granddaddy." There was a smattering of applause and appreciative laughter. Emerson draped a burly arm around his daughter's shoulders and hugged her while he grinned widely at Jonas. "So when's the wedding? I gotta get me a new suit for this."

Jonas swiveled halfway around on the stool, one arm resting along the edge of the bar. He gazed at Verity through narrowed lids. "Who said anything about marriage?"

Emerson's euphoric expression turned thunderous in the wink of an eye. He released Verity. "What the hell are you talking about? Verity says she's pregnant. Haven't you gotten around to asking my daughter to marry you yet, you son of a bitch?"

The bar fell silent. Clement, the bartender, groaned. Verity held her breath.

Jonas stood up with insulting slowness. He hooked his thumbs into his belt and scowled at Emerson. "You're barking up the wrong tree, Ames. I did ask your daughter to marry me. Had a hell of a time talking her into it, too. But after I did, things changed. Important things. You want to know when the wedding will be? Ask Verity. I've been getting the impression she's had a few second thoughts."

Verity's mouth fell open in amazement. "*Jonas*. How could you think that?"

Jonas turned on her. "That's a damn fool question. What else was I supposed to think this past week? You've been acting damn weird again. You're harder to figure out now than you were when you were moping around wondering whether or not to tell me about the baby."

"I've been acting weird? What a nasty thing to say. You're deliberately reversing the situation. You're the one who's been acting strange. I got the distinct impression that you were no longer interested in marriage yourself."

Emerson took a threatening step forward. "What's going on around here? What is it with you two?"

"Stay out of this, Emerson." Jonas shot the big man a warning glance. "This is between Verity and me."

"Well, you picked a fine place to settle a private matter," Emerson roared back.

"Yeah, you've got a point. Come on, Verity. Let's get the hell out of here." Jonas caught her wrist and headed for the door.

"Ouch. Let go of me, dammit. I don't have to put up with your caveman tactics. I'm pregnant. I deserve a little consideration."

"I deserve a little honesty," he snarled, hauling her through the doorway. "I'm sick of all the sweetness and light I've been getting lately. If you've got something to tell me, you can tell me straight out. You don't need to pussyfoot around me just because I'm not..."

"Just because you're not what?" Verity goaded as he

yanked her through the rustic lobby and out into the cold night air.

Jonas exploded. He halted and swung around to face her. *''Just because I'm not the man I once was, damn you.''*

Verity stared at him, her eyes wide with amazement. ''Not the man you once were? Oh my, Jonas. Oh, Jonas.'' She started to giggle. She clapped a palm over her mouth, trying to restrain herself. But she knew her eyes were reflecting her mirth. ''Not the man you once were? Jonas, that's priceless. You make it sound like you've been castrated or something. Not the man you once were. Incredible. I can't believe I'm hearing this. Here I've been tiptoeing around all week thinking you were getting ready to leave me, and all along you were thinking I no longer wanted to marry you because you're not the man you once were. What a pair of fools.''

''Why the hell would I leave you?'' He searched her face and then caught hold of her shoulders and shook her gently. *''Tell me, Verity. Why would I leave?''*

''Because you don't need me anymore,'' she explained, her humor fading quickly. She met his eyes. ''Jonas, look at this from my point of view. You came to me in the first place because you needed me as a psychic anchor. Whenever I tried to pin you down about whether you loved me or just felt tied to me because of the psychic connection, you laughed off my fears. You told me there was no need to make a distinction between the two bonds. But now one of those bonds is gone, and I have no way of knowing how strong the other one is when it has to stand alone.''

''Jesus, honey, I didn't realize.'' He wrapped her close and buried his face in her hair. ''I've been going through the same thing from the other direction. I knew I'd used the psychic link to hold you and I was scared that once it was gone, you'd feel different about marrying me. When you started treating me strangely, I was convinced you'd changed your mind. I couldn't figure out what the hell was going on. You haven't nagged me once since we got back from that goddamned island."

Verity's head came up so quickly she caught his chin. There was a soft crack but she ignored his grimace of pain. Her eyes sparkled with indignation and relief. "So much for treating you with kid gloves. I was trying to be sweet and understanding. I decided you probably had some major adjustments to make. I didn't know how you were going to respond to the loss of your psychic ability. I didn't want to nag you or push you in any way. But I've been going quietly crazy, Jonas."

"Honey, the minute you stopped chewing my ass I knew I was in deep trouble." He rubbed his injured jaw.

"The minute you stopped deliberately provoking me every chance you got, I knew I was in real trouble."

He caught her face between his palms. "You're right. We've been a pair of idiots. Not for the first time, and probably not for the last. But I swear to you that I love you with all my heart. Nothing will ever change that. The way I feel about you doesn't depend on the psychic connection. If I didn't know it for certain before, I've sure as hell learned it the hard way this past week. You wanted me to be able to distinguish between the psychic bond and the bond of love. Well, I can, believe me. I don't ever want to have to go through that particular hell again."

Verity's hands rose to grasp his wrists. She smiled up at him with all the love in her heart. "Does this mean you're going to make an honest woman of me after all?"

He grinned. "It sure as hell does. Just as soon as we can get a ring and a license."

"And a dress," Verity reminded him. "Don't forget the dress."

He looked down at her gently curved stomach. The top button of her jeans was unsnapped. "Like I said, we'd better hurry."

"Hey!" Emerson's voice boomed from the lobby entrance. "You two get things settled out here? Christ, it's a little cold to be standing around outside, isn't it? Not good for a pregnant lady."

Verity groaned at the sound of her father's voice. She buried her nose against Jonas's jacket. "What in the world has gotten into him? Everybody in the resort must know what's going on by now. It's embarrassing."

Jonas chuckled. "So what else is new?" He gazed at his future father-in-law over the top of Verity's red curls. "Don't sweat it, Emerson. You won't need the shotgun."

"Glad to hear it. Figured you two had just gotten your wires crossed. All you needed was a little push to get 'em straightened out."

"Knock it off, Ames. No one's going to give you any credit for straightening this out. Verity and I took care of it all by ourselves. Go have another drink. You've had a long trip."

"Where are you going?" Emerson demanded.

"Home." Jonas caught hold of Verity's arm and led her toward the path that wound through the trees to the cottage.

Behind them Emerson grinned in satisfaction. Then he swung around and started for the bar. "Clement, my man," he called to the bartender. "The announcement is official. My daughter says she's actually going to marry him. Break out your best vodka. The Russian stuff."

"Why bother?" Clement said with a slow grin. "All vodka tastes the same."

"In a pig's eye." Emerson sat down on a stool. "Let's get the Griswalds in here, and you'd better call the rest of the resort staff. It's pay-off time."

"If Jonas ever finds out you've been running a pool to guess the day he and Verity announced they were engaged, he'll skin you alive, Ames."

Emerson looked offended. "Just a friendly little game of chance, that's all it was."

"I suppose now we'll all get suckered into a 'guess the date the baby arrives' pool," Rick Griswald said from the doorway.

Emerson smiled broadly. "Hell of an idea. Now why didn't I think of that?"

"Jonas?"

"What is it, love?" Jonas sucked one of Verity's nipples between his teeth and bit down very gently. He felt the little tremor go through her and was satisfied. He was taking his time making love to her tonight. It had been a long week. True, he'd taken her to bed often enough during the past few days, but he hadn't been able to relax and enjoy it.

For the past week he'd been driven, desperate, obsessed with the idea that he might be able to make her stay with him if he kept reinforcing the sexual bond. Tonight he wanted to indulge himself in the luxury of making love to his future bride without worrying about when she would kick him out.

"We should have talked more about it right after it happened." Verity's fingers curled in his hair as he dropped a warm kiss in the hollow between her breasts.

"After what happened?"

"After the experience you went through in the hidden chamber. Our mistake was in not discussing it. I know it bothered you a lot to find out you didn't have the talent any longer, but I didn't want to raise the issue until you were ready. I kept waiting for you to open up and tell me how you felt."

"I was afraid to bring up the subject because I couldn't tell how you would react." He slid a hand down to the curve of her thigh. "I've explained that. I was terrified of giving you an excuse to talk about our relationship."

"What's wrong with that? We should discuss our relationship more. We need to talk about it."

Jonas raised his head, his eyes glinting in the darkness. "Relationship discussions make me nervous. I'd rather go to bed with you than talk about our relationship."

"Well, you can see where that attitude has gotten us this past week," she admonished roundly. "We had plenty of sex, but our relationship was falling apart because you wouldn't open up and tell me how you really felt."

Jonas decided to see if a quick, abject assumption of all the blame would close her luscious mouth. "It was all my fault. I should have talked to you about the whole thing. I really screwed up, honey. I'm sorry." He tangled his fingers in the soft nest of hair above her thighs and inhaled the unique fragrance of her.

"Oh, Jonas, it wasn't really your fault," Verity said graciously. She smiled gently in the shadows, her eyes full of love. "I understand how traumatic it must have been. You had so much to adjust to it's a wonder you didn't sink into a deep depression or something."

"Or something," he repeated absently, his attention on how soft and warm she felt. Right now he wanted nothing more than to sink into Verity's welcoming warmth. He wanted the reassurance of her physical response and the peace of mind that always came afterward.

"But now that it's all out in the open we can really talk about it."

"Yeah. We'll have to do that sometime." He lowered his head and kissed the tight red curls that concealed her feminine secrets.

"Why don't we do it now, Jonas?"

"Now? I don't think that's such a good idea, honey." He slipped his fingers between her thighs and drew in his breath as his already aroused manhood grew harder and heavier.

"But this is the perfect time, Jonas."

"No, sweetheart, it's not the perfect time. I've got other things on my mind."

"What other things?" she asked with wonderful innocence.

Jonas stifled a groan as he let the pad of his thumb glide across the sensitive nub hidden in the curls. "Guess."

Verity flinched in reaction to the provocative caress. Her brows snapped together. "You mean sex."

"Now you're catching on." He parted the soft petals between her legs and circled her gently with one finger. She was already damp. The spicy scent of her grew stronger in his nostrils, inflaming him.

"Jonas, sex is not a substitute for good communication." She gasped softly as his caress became more intimate.

"Think of it as another form of communication—nonverbal communication." He lowered his head and touched his tongue to her moist flesh. Then he eased a finger inside the softening sheath.

"I think we've already mastered this form of communication," Verity whispered. "We really should talk. I'm serious, Jonas. Stop that. We need to get in the habit of talking things out when we run into problems."

"Verity," he began, trying to warn her gently that his patience was dissolving rapidly. "There's a time for talk and a time for screwing. Trust me. This is not the time for talk."

"Dammit, Jonas, if we're going to get married, I insist we practice verbal communication." Her fingers clenched on his shoulder.

Jonas sat up slowly and regarded the woman he was

going to marry. "You want to use your mouth to communicate?"

"I think it's for the best, Jonas," she said very seriously. "At least at the moment. It's not that I don't want to make love with you, but I just feel we need to learn to relate better on a verbal level."

Jonas nodded with sudden decision. "Right. You want to use your mouth, so go ahead and use your mouth." He leaned back against the pillows and reached out to cup the nape of her neck in his palm. He pushed her head gently but firmly down to where his manhood throbbed heavily.

"Jonas, this is not what I meant, and you know it!"

"Open your mouth, honey, and show me how well you can communicate that way."

"You rat! I'm trying to carry on an important, meaningful discussion here, in case you didn't notice." Her breath fanned the full, rounded tip of his shaft, and Jonas thought he would explode then and there.

"I can't wait to receive the pearls of feminine wisdom that roll off your sweet tongue, my love." He thrust upward just as she parted her lips to tell him again about the importance of verbal discussion. "Ah, that's better." He sighed blissfully as her warm mouth closed around him. "Much better. You communicate beautifully with your mouth, honey."

His last coherent thought was that he could live without the part of him that tuned him in to the past. But he would go out of his mind if he ever lost Verity.

She was his future.

"Verity?"

She stirred, drowsy and sated. "Yes, Jonas?"

"I was scared for a while. Really scared. It was like a part of me had vanished. Like I'd lost a leg or an arm."

Verity came fully awake, listening to his stark confession of fear. "I know, Jonas. I knew it must be like that for you, but you didn't say anything. I didn't know how to get you to talk about it."

"I couldn't talk about it. In my mind I linked losing my talent with the possibility of losing you. I couldn't deal with both losses. But everything is okay now."

She smiled with quiet relief and leaned over to kiss him gently. "Everything's going to be fine now. Jonas, I would love you no matter what you were missing."

"You know what my biggest fear was? Losing you to someone like Oliver Crump."

"There was never any need to be afraid I'd run off with Oliver. I like him very much, but I don't love him."

He turned his head on the pillow and looked at her, his golden eyes sober and intent. "You found something with him. Something similar to what you found with me."

"No," she said firmly. "What I found with Oliver was nothing at all like what I've found with you. Oliver and I became friends. Nothing more."

"What about your ability with the crystals?"

Verity smiled. "Whatever ability I had with the crystals didn't lead me to feel anything more than friendship for Oliver. The link, or whatever it was we shared, wasn't . . . *seductive* the way it is with you. It wasn't personal. There was no sense of being emotionally linked to him. It's hard to explain, Jonas. But it was different, trust me. Besides, that's all gone now."

"Gone?" Jonas repeated quizzically.

"Whatever ability I had with crystals seems to have been directly related to what I shared with you, not Oliver. I've felt nothing around crystals since you woke up without your psychic talent."

"You and Oliver worked the crystal to bring me out of

the unconscious state I was in after that scene in the chamber.''

Verity shook her head. ''Oliver worked it. I concentrated on yelling at you until you finally woke up and paid attention.''

He smiled faintly. ''I could hear you chewing me out and I knew it was time to come back. You've got a hell of a mouth on you, my love.''

''I'm glad you appreciate it,'' she murmured sweetly.

''I appreciate it all right.'' His grin turned wicked with remembered satisfaction. He touched her lips with his fingertips. ''I consider your mouth a very valuable portion of your anatomy. I'm thinking of having it insured.''

Chapter Twenty

"*THEY'RE* going to call him Nicholas *Emerson* Quarrel!" The halls of the small maternity ward of Sequence Springs Community Hospital rang with Emerson's announcement. If there was anyone left in the waiting room who did not yet know that Nicholas Emerson had arrived, he was now aware of it.

Inside her room Verity held the tiny bundle to her breast and smiled. She knew her father had been pacing the waiting room floor since she had gone into labor last night. When Jonas had finally gone out to tell him that he had a grandson, Emerson's roar of approval had shaken the building.

Verity raised her head and looked up at her husband. Jonas was watching his son nurse. There was deep pride in those eyes of Florentine gold. There was also a fascination in them as Jonas studied little Nicholas.

"Look at those tiny little hands," Jonas marveled.

"I think he's going to have your eyes," said Verity.

Jonas grinned. "You think so? The nurse said it was too soon to tell."

"Trust me," Verity said with smug certainty. "I'd know those eyes anywhere."

Jonas's grin widened. He had been grinning a lot for the past couple of hours. He had not been grinning last night, however, when, in the middle of serving dinner to a light crowd at the cafe, Verity had announced that her time had come.

Jonas had taken over instantly. He had chased out the last of the diners and ordered Emerson to get the Jeep. At the hospital he had issued a steady stream of instructions to Verity and her nurses, consulted with Verity's doctor, and generally assumed command of a situation that was entirely outside his field of expertise. That had not stopped him for a moment. Jonas had prepared well for the big event.

He had studied every book on pregnancy and childbirth he had been able to find during the past few months. He had supervised Verity's vitamin supplements and exercises. He had gone shopping for diapers and baby supplies. Together with Emerson he had planned an educational curriculum for the child that would have stunned the average public-school teacher. It was a lot like the one Emerson had once devised for his daughter.

Jonas had considered himself an expert on childbirth right up to the moment when Verity had gone into the delivery room and started swearing. She had gritted her teeth and shouted words Jonas had never heard her use before. At that point he had realized he was a little out of his depth. Jonas had compensated by giving more orders and holding Verity's hand so tightly that he was afraid he might crack a few of the delicate bones.

But she had clung to him even more tightly. Her nails had left marks in his palm.

Somehow they had all come through the ordeal with flying colors. Nicholas Emerson Quarrel had arrived with an ear-splitting squall, prompting Jonas to remark proudly that his son obviously had inherited his mother's verbal skills.

"Is Dad still causing a scene out there in the waiting room?" Verity inquired.

"You could say that. He bought a case of beer for the hospital staff." Jonas leaned over to get a closer look at his son. "Are you sure you feel all right, honey?"

"I'm fine. A little tired, but that's all."

"I can't believe it. We've actually made ourselves a kid. A real live baby."

Verity smiled, amused by Jonas's wonder. "Yes," she said, a little amazed herself. "We did."

The past few months had been good, she thought with satisfaction. The time she and Jonas had had together before the baby arrived had assured them both that the bonds between them were strong enough to last a lifetime. Verity's nagging, Jonas's teasing, the laughter and the loving were all back to normal. Better than normal, Verity had decided. This time she could be sure that the emotional foundation was for real, not just a byproduct of the psychic link.

The hospital room door burst open just as Jonas leaned down to place his son back in the cradle. Emerson stood on the threshold, loaded down with flowers and packages.

"Behold, I come bearing gifts and the U.S. mail. How's little Nicholas Emerson?"

"Sleepy," Jonas said. "Keep your voice down, Emerson."

"Kid might as well get used to the fact that he's got a mouthy mother, a loud grandfather, and a daddy who's good with a knife. Here you go, Jonas. A letter from some magazine. Looks like a check."

"Wonderful," Verity exclaimed. "I told you they'd love

your piece on Digby Hazelhurst's contributions to Renaissance scholarship.''

Jonas raised beseeching eyes toward the ceiling. ''Done in by success. Now I suppose I won't get any peace until I write that follow-up article for the editor who got me into that mess to begin with.'' But he was smiling with satisfaction as he ripped open the envelope and removed the check inside.

Verity knew the source of that satisfaction. During the past few months Jonas had come to the realization that his knowledge of Renaissance history and his feel for the period had not vanished along with his talent. The things he had learned in the academic world and in the time corridor were his for a lifetime.

''And more baby presents,'' Emerson continued as he placed gaily wrapped packages on the bed. ''The kid is really raking it in. A package from the Griswalds, one from that Crump fellow, and one from Sam Lehigh.''

Verity pulled off ribbons and tore paper with enthusiasm. Rick and Laura Griswald's gift was an adorable little yellow playsuit. She held it up with delight. ''Isn't it cute? It's perfect for him.''

''Looks a few sizes too big, if you ask me,'' Jonas said, examining the outfit with a critical eye.

''Don't worry,'' Emerson advised. ''Babies grow. Fast.''

''Let's see what Oliver sent,'' Verity said. She shredded more paper, lifted off the top of a white box, and revealed a beautiful chunk of amethyst crystal. ''It's lovely,'' she said, turning the glittering crystal in her hands.

''What the hell's the kid going to do with that?'' Emerson demanded.

''It's not for Nicholas,'' Verity announced, belatedly reading the small card. ''It's for me. To help me get my strength back quickly.''

"How the heck is a hunk of crystal going to do that?" Emerson growled.

"Who knows?" Jonas gave his wife a secret grin. "Look at it this way—it can't do any harm."

"Let's see what Lehigh sent," Emerson said encouragingly.

Verity obediently tore the paper off the last package. When she raised the lid on the long thin box her eyes widened in amazement. Inside lay a dagger with a jeweled handle. "Lehigh certainly has an odd notion of what to give a newborn."

Emerson chuckled and came around the side of the bed to get a closer look. "Probably expects the kid to take after his dad. Hell of a dagger though, isn't it? Look at that handle. Knowing Lehigh, those stones are real. Take a look, Jonas." Emerson stood back.

Jonas frowned as he glanced at the dagger. "Looks genuine, all right. Fifteenth- or sixteenth-century Italian."

"Probably from his collection," Emerson remarked.

Jonas reached into the box. His fingers closed around the hilt of the dagger.

Verity sucked in her breath as the walls of the hospital room began to curve around her.

"Jonas."

"Right here, honey."

She turned in the psychic corridor, searching for him. He smiled at her from the other side of the mysterious tunnel. His golden eyes were gleaming. He held the jeweled dagger in his hand.

"Your talent," she whispered. "It's back."

"Strong as ever," he said with laughing satisfaction. "Guess it just needed a little time to heal."

He tossed the jeweled dagger into the air. It spun end over end, the stones in the handle flashing brilliantly. The corridor wavered and vanished.

Jonas caught the dagger with easy grace and quickly dropped it back into its box.

''Hey, you two okay?'' Emerson demanded. ''You've both got funny expressions on your faces.''

''Everything's just fine,'' Jonas said as he leaned down to kiss his wife. ''Isn't it, my love?''

''Perfect,'' Verity agreed with a smile that was more beautiful than the crystal and the gems around her. It was a smile as brilliant as the gold in her husband's eyes.